More prais...

'Bloom has all the elegant acuity of a modern day Flannery O'Connor ... Her style is astonishingly versatile: wry and acerbic one minute; generous and passionate the next' *GQ*

'Compassionate, witty and wise' *Daily Mail*

'Ms. Bloom [has a] tremendous gift for imagining life as a series of choices, with the paths not taken as vivid as the ones that are' *New York Times*

'Bloom describes love affairs with great humanity and in tender, sensual terms ... The warmth and compassion of her fiction owe much to her gift for conveying the humour of intimate transactions without belittling them' *Times Literary Supplement*

'Her characters are never less than sympathetically rendered, making it hard to leave them behind' *Vogue*

'*Where the God of Love Hangs Out* is brilliant. The stories are shocking and lovely' Roddy Doyle, *Guardian*

'Unforgettably good. Each of these stories is like a tiny perfect novel, excitingly brilliant, full of compassion and warmth and pain. Amy Bloom is one of the greats' Charlotte Mendelson

'Some of the most sublime brief fictions currently being published ... pitch perfect' *Herald*

Rowing to Eden

Collected Stories

Amy Bloom

GRANTA

Granta Publications, 12 Addison Avenue, London W11 4QR

First published in Great Britain by Granta Books 2015

The stories in this collection were originally published in book form in: *Come to Me*, first published by Picador, an imprint of Pan Macmillan, a division of Macmillan Publishers Ltd in 1995; *A Blind Man Can See How Much I Love You*, first published by Picador, an imprint of Pan Macmillan, a division of Macmillan Publishers Ltd in 2001; and *Where the God of Love Hangs Out*, first published by Granta Books in 2010.

The credits on pp. 469-70 constitute an extension of this copyright page.

A CIP catalogue record for this book is available from the British Library.

1 3 5 7 9 10 8 6 4 2

ISBN 978 1 78378 215 4
eISBN 978 1 78378 216 1

Book design by Susan Turner
Offset by M Rules
Printed in Denmark by Nørhaven

For my family

Contents

Contents

WILLIAM AND CLARE

Love is Not a Pie

In the middle of the eulogy at my mother's boring and heart-breaking funeral, I began to think about calling off the wedding. August 21 did not seem like a good date, John Wescott did not seem like a good person to marry, and I couldn't see myself in the long white silk gown Mrs Wescott had offered me. We had gotten engaged at Christmas, while my mother was starting to die; she died in May, earlier than we had expected. When the minister said, 'She was a rare spirit, full of the kind of bravery and joy which inspires others,' I stared at the pale blue ceiling and thought, 'My mother would not have wanted me to spend my life with this man.' He had asked me if I wanted him to come to the funeral from Boston, and I said no. And so he didn't, respecting my autonomy and so forth. I think he should have known that I was just being considerate.

After the funeral, we took the little box of ashes back to the house and entertained everybody who came by to pay their respects. Lots of my father's law school colleagues, a few of his former students, my uncle Steve and his new wife, my cousins (whom my sister Lizzie and I always referred to as Thing One and Thing Two), friends from the old neighborhood, before my mother's sculpture started selling, her art world friends, her sisters, some of my friends from high school, some people I used

to baby-sit for, my best friend from college, some friends of
Lizzie's, a lot of people I didn't recognize. I'd been living away
from home for a long time, first at college, now at law school.

My sister, my father, and I worked the room. And everyone
who came in my father embraced. It didn't matter whether they
started to pat him on the back or shake his hand, he pulled
them to him and hugged them so hard I saw people's feet lift
right off the floor. Lizzie and I took the more passive route, letting people do whatever they wanted to us, patting, stroking,
embracing, cupping our faces in their hands.

My father was in the middle of squeezing Mrs Ellis, our
cleaning lady, when he saw Mr DeCuervo come in, still carrying his suitcase. He about dropped Mrs Ellis and went charging
over to Mr DeCuervo, wrapped his arms around him, and the
two of them moaned and rocked together in a passionate,
musicless waltz. My sister and I sat down on the couch, pressed
against each other, watching our father cry all over his friend,
our mother's lover.

When I was eleven and Lizzie was eight, her last naked
summer, Mr DeCuervo and his daughter, Gisela, who was just
about to turn eight, spent part of the summer with us at the
cabin in Maine. The cabin was from the Spencer side, my
father's side of the family, and he and my uncle Steve were co-
owners. We went there every July (colder water, better
weather), and they came in August. My father felt about his
brother the way we felt about our cousins, so we would only
overlap for lunch on the last day of our stay.

That July, the DeCuervos came, but without Mrs DeCuervo,
who had to go visit a sick someone in Argentina, where they
were from. That was okay with us. Mrs DeCuervo was a professional mother, a type that made my sister and me very

uncomfortable. She told us to wash the berries before we ate them, to rest after lunch, to put on more suntan lotion, to make our beds. She was a nice lady, she was just always in our way. My mother had a few very basic summer rules: don't eat food with mold or insects on it; don't swim alone; don't even think about waking your mother before 8:00 A.M. unless you are fatally injured or ill. That was about it, but Mrs DeCuervo was always amending and adding to the list, one apologetic eye on our mother, who was pleasant and friendly as usual and did things the way she always did. She made it pretty clear that if we were cowed by the likes of Mrs DeCuervo, we were on our own. They got divorced when Gisela was a sophomore at Mount Holyoke.

We liked pretty, docile Gisela, and bullied her a little bit, and liked her even more because she didn't squeal on us, on me in particular. We liked her father, too. We saw the two of them, sometimes the three of them, at occasional picnics and lesser holidays. He always complimented us, never made stupid jokes at our expense, and brought us unusual, perfect little presents. Silver barrettes for me the summer I was letting my hair grow out from my pixie cut; a leather bookmark for Lizzie, who learned to read when she was three. My mother would stand behind us as we unwrapped the gifts, smiling and shaking her head at his extravagance.

When they drove up, we were all sitting on the porch. Mr DeCuervo got out first, his curly brown hair making him look like a giant dandelion, with his yellow T-shirt and brown jeans. Gisela looked just like him, her long, curly brown hair caught up in a bun, wisps flying around her tanned little face. As they walked toward us, she took his hand and I felt a rush of warmth for her, for showing how much she loved her daddy, like I loved mine, and for showing that she was a little afraid of us, of me, probably. People weren't often frightened of Lizzie; she never left her books long enough to bother anyone.

My parents came down from the porch; my big father, in his faded blue trunks, drooping below his belly, his freckled back pink and moist in the sun, as it was every summer. The sun caught the red hair on his head and shoulders and chest, and he shone. The Spencers were half-Viking, he said. My mother was wearing her summer outfit, a black two-piece bathing suit. I don't remember her ever wearing a different suit. At night, she'd add one of my father's shirts and wrap it around her like a kimono. Some years, she looked great in her suit, waist nipped in, skin smooth and tan; other years, her skin looked burnt and crumpled, and the suit was too big in some places and too small in others. Those years, she smoked too much and went out on the porch to cough. But that summer the suit fit beautifully, and when she jumped off the porch into my father's arms, he whirled her around and let her black hair whip his face while he smiled and smiled.

They both hugged Mr DeCuervo and Gisela; my mother took her flowered suitcase and my father took his duffel bag and they led them into the cabin.

The cabin was our palace; Lizzie and I would say very grandly, 'We're going to the cabin for the summer, come visit us there, if it's okay with your parents.' And we loved it and loved to act as though it was nothing special, when we knew, really, that it was magnificent. The pines and birches came right down to the lake, with just a thin lacing of mossy rocks before you got to the smooth cold water, and little gray fish swam around the splintery dock and through our legs, or out of reach of our oars when we took out the old blue rowboat.

The cabin itself was three bedrooms and a tiny kitchen and a living room that took up half the house. The two small bedrooms had big beds with pastel chenille spreads; yellow with red roses in my parents' room, white with blue pansies in the other. The kids' room was much bigger, like a dormitory, with three sets of bunk beds, each with its own mismatched sheets and pillowcases. The pillows were always a little damp and smelled like salt and pine, and mine smelled of Ma Griffe as well, because I used to sleep with my mother's scarf tucked under it. The shower was outside, with a thin green plastic curtain around it, but there was a regular bathroom inside, next to my parents' room.

Mr DeCuervo and Gisela fit into our routine as though they'd been coming to the cabin for years, instead of just last summer. We had the kind of summer cabin routine that stays with you forever as a model of leisure, of life being enjoyed. We'd get up early, listening to the birds screaming and trilling, and make ourselves some breakfast; cereal or toast if the parents were up, cake or cold spaghetti or marshmallows if they were still asleep. My mother got up first, usually. She'd make a cup of coffee and brush and braid our hair and set us loose. If we were going exploring, she'd put three sandwiches and three pieces of fruit in a bag, with an army blanket. Otherwise, she'd just wave to us as we headed down to the lake.

We'd come back at lunchtime and eat whatever was around and then go out to the lake or the forest, or down the road to see if the townie kids were in a mood to play with us. I don't know what the grown-ups did all day; sometimes they'd come out to swim for a while, and sometimes we'd find my mother in the shed she used for a studio. But when we came back at five or six, they all seemed happy and relaxed, drinking gin and tonics on the porch, watching us run toward the house. It was the most beautiful time.

At night, after dinner, the fathers would wash up and my mother would sit on the porch, smoking a cigarette, listening to Aretha Franklin or Billie Holiday or Sam Cooke, and after a little while she'd stub out her cigarette and the four of us would dance. We'd twist and lindy and jitterbug and stomp, all of us copying my mother. And pretty soon the daddies would drift in with their dish towels and their beers, and they'd lean in the doorway and watch. My mother would turn first to my father, always to him, first.

'What about it, Danny? Care to dance?' And she'd put her hand on his shoulder and he'd smile, tossing his dish towel to Mr DeCuervo, resting his beer on the floor. My father would lumber along gamely, shuffling his feet and smiling. Sometimes he'd wave his arms around and pretend to be a fish or a bear while my mother swung her body easily and dreamily, sliding through the music. They'd always lindy together to Fats Domino. That was my father's favorite, and then he'd sit down, puffing a little.

My mother would stand there, snapping her fingers, shifting back and forth.

'Gaucho, you dance with her, before I have a coronary,' said my father.

Mr DeCuervo's real name was Bolivar, which I didn't know until Lizzie told me after the funeral. We always called him Mr DeCuervo because we felt embarrassed to call him by a nick-name.

So Mr DeCuervo would shrug gracefully and toss the two dish towels back to my father. And then he'd bop toward my mother, his face still turned toward my father.

'We'll go running tomorrow, Dan, get you back into shape so you can dance all night.'

'What do you mean, "back"? I've been exactly this same svelte shape for twenty years. Why fix it if it ain't broke?'

And they all laughed, and Mr DeCuervo and my mother rolled their eyes at each other, and my mother walked over and kissed my father where the sweat was beading up at his temples. Then she took Mr DeCuervo's hand and they walked to the center of the living room.

When she and my father danced, my sister and I giggled and interfered and treated it like a family badminton game in which they were the core players but we were welcome participants. When she danced with Mr DeCuervo, we'd sit on the porch swing or lean on the windowsill and watch, not even looking at each other.

They only danced the fast dances, and they danced as though they'd been waiting all their lives for each song. My mother's movements got deeper and smoother, and Mr DeCuervo suddenly came alive, as though a spotlight had hit him. My father danced the way he was, warm, noisy, teasing, a little overpowering; but Mr DeCuervo, who was usually quiet and thoughtful and serious, became a different man when he danced with my mother. His dancing was light and happy and soulful, edging up on my mother, turning her, matching her every step. They would smile at all of us, in turn, and then face each other, too transported to smile.

'Dance with Daddy some more,' my sister said, speaking for all three of us. They had left us too far behind.

My mother blew Lizzie a kiss. 'Okay, sweetheart.'

She turned to both men, laughing, and said, 'That message was certainly loud and clear. Let's take a little break, Gauch, and get these monkeys to bed. It's getting late, girls.'

And the three of them shepherded the three of us through the bedtime rituals, moving us in and out of the kitchen for milk, the bathroom for teeth, toilet, and calamine lotion, and finally to our big bedroom. We slept in our underwear and t-shirts, which impressed Gisela.

'No pajamas?' she had said the first night.

'Not necessary,' I said smugly.

We would lie there after they kissed us, listening to our parents talk and crack peanuts and snap cards; they played gin and poker while they listened to Dinah Washington and Odetta.

One night, I woke up around midnight and crossed the living room to get some water in the kitchen and see if there was any strawberry shortcake left. I saw my mother and Mr DeCuervo hugging, and I remember being surprised, and puzzled. I had seen movies; if you hugged someone like you'd never let them go, surely you were supposed to be kissing, too. It wasn't a Mommy-Daddy hug, partly because their hugs were defined by the fact that my father was eight inches taller and a hundred pounds heavier than my mother. These two looked all wrong to me; embraces were a big pink-and-orange man enveloping a small, lean black-and-white woman who gazed up at him. My mother and Mr DeCuervo looked like sister and brother, standing cheek-to-cheek, with their broad shoulders and long, tanned, bare legs. My mother's hands were under Mr DeCuervo's white T-shirt.

She must have felt my eyes on her, because she opened hers slowly.

'Oh, honey, you startled us. Mr DeCuervo and I were just saying good night. Do you want me to tuck you in after you go to the bathroom?' Not quite a bribe, certainly a reminder that I was more important to her than he was. They had moved apart so quickly and smoothly I couldn't even remember how they had looked together. I nodded to my mother; what I had seen was already being transformed into a standard good-night embrace, the kind my mother gave to all of her close friends.

When I came back from the bathroom, Mr DeCuervo had disappeared and my mother was waiting, looking out at the moon. She walked me to the bedroom and kissed me, first on my forehead, then on my lips.

'Sleep well, pumpkin pie. See you in the morning.'

'Will you make blueberry pancakes tomorrow?' It seemed like a good time to ask.

'We'll see. Go to sleep.'

'Please, Mommy.'

'Okay, we'll have a blueberry morning. Go to sleep now. Good night, nurse.' And she watched me for a moment from the doorway, and then she was gone.

My father got up at five to go fishing with some men at the other side of the lake. Every Saturday in July he'd go off with a big red bandanna tied over his bald spot, his Mets T-shirt, and his tackle box, and he'd fish until around three. Mr DeCuervo said that he'd clean them, cook them, and eat them but he wouldn't spend a day with a bunch of guys in baseball caps and white socks to catch them.

I woke up smelling coffee and butter. Gisela and Lizzie were already out of bed, and I was aggrieved; I was the one who had asked for the pancakes, and they were probably all eaten by now.

Mr DeCuervo and Lizzie were sitting at the table, finishing their pancakes. My mother and Gisela were sitting on the blue couch in the living room while my mother brushed Gisela's hair. She was brushing it more gently than she brushed mine, not slapping her on the shoulder to make her sit still. Gisela didn't wiggle, and she didn't scream when my mother hit a knot.

I was getting ready to be mad when my mother winked at me over Gisela's head and said, 'There's a stack of pancakes for you on top of the stove, bunny. Gauch, would you please lift them for Ellen? The plate's probably hot.'

Mr DeCuervo handed me my pancakes, which were huge brown wheels studded with smashed purpley berries; he put my fork and knife on top of a folded paper towel and patted my cheek. His hand smelled like coffee and cinnamon. He knew what I liked and pushed the butter and the honey and the syrup toward me.

'Juice?' he said.

I nodded, trying to watch him when he wasn't looking; he didn't seem like the man I thought I saw in the moonlight, giving my mother a funny hug.

'Great pancakes, Lila,' he said.

'Great, Mom.' I didn't want to be outclassed by the DeCuervos' habitual good manners. Gisela remembered her 'please' and 'thank you' for every little thing.

My mother smiled and put a barrette in Gisela's hair. It was starting to get warm, so I swallowed my pancakes and kicked Lizzie to get her attention.

'Let's go,' I said.

'Wash your face, then go,' my mother said.

I stuck my face under the kitchen tap, and my mother and Mr DeCuervo laughed. Triumphantly, I led the two little girls out of the house, snatching our towels off the line as we ran down to the water, suddenly filled with longing for the lake.

'Last one in's a fart,' I screamed, cannonballing off the end of the dock. I hit the cold blue water, shattering its surface. Lizzie and Gisela jumped in beside me, and we played water games until my father drove up in the pickup with a bucket of fish. He waved to us and told us we'd be eating fish for the next two days, and we groaned and held our noses as he went into the cabin, laughing.

There was a string of sunny days like that one: swimming, fishing with Daddy off the dock, eating peanut butter and jelly sandwiches in the rowboat, drinking Orange Crush on the porch swing.

And then it rained for a week. We woke up the first rainy morning, listening to it tap and dance on the roof. My mother stuck her head into our bedroom.

'It's monsoon weather, honeys. How about cocoa and cinnamon toast?'

We pulled on our overalls and sweaters and went into the kitchen, where my mother had already laid our mugs and plates. She was engaged in her rainy day ritual: making Sangria. First she poured the orange juice out of the big white plastic pitcher into three empty peanut butter jars. Then she started chopping up all the oranges, lemons, and limes we had in the house. She let me pour the brandy over the fruit, Gisela threw in the sugar, and Lizzie came up for air long enough to pour the big bottle of red wine over everything. I cannot imagine drinking anything else on rainy days.

My mother went out onto the porch for her morning cigarette, and when my father came down he joined her while we played Go Fish; I could see them snuggling on the wicker settee. A few minutes later Mr DeCuervo came down, looked out to the porch, and picked up an old magazine and started reading.

We decided to go play Monopoly in our room since the

grown-ups didn't want to entertain us. After two hours, in which I rotted in jail and Lizzie forgot to charge rent, little Gisela beat us and the three of us went back to the kitchen for a snack. Rainy days were basically a series of snacks, more and less elaborate, punctuated by board games, card games, and whining. We drank soda and juice all day, ate cheese, bananas, cookies, bologna, graham crackers, Jiffy popcorn, hard-boiled eggs. The grown-ups ate cheese and crackers and drank sangria.

The daddies were reading in the two big armchairs, my mother had gone off to her room to sketch, and we were getting bored. When my mother came downstairs for a cigarette, I was writing my name in the honey that had spilled on the kitchen table, and Gisela and Lizzie were pulling the stuffing out of the hole in the bottom of the blue couch.

'Jesus Christ, Ellen, get your hands out of the goddamn honey. Liz, Gisela, that's absolutely unacceptable, you know that. Leave the poor couch alone. If you're so damn stir-crazy, go outside and dance in the rain.'

The two men looked up, slowly focusing, as if from a great distance.

'Lila, really . . .' said my father.

'Lila, it's pouring. We'll keep an eye on them now,' said Mr DeCuervo.

'Right. Like you were.' My mother was grinning.

'Can we, Mommy, can we go in the rain? Can we take off our clothes and go in the rain?'

'Sure, go naked, there's no point in getting your clothes wet and no point in suits. There's not likely to be a big crowd in the yard.'

We raced to the porch before my mother could get rational, stripped and ran whooping into the rain, leaping off the porch onto the muddy lawn, shouting and feeling superior to every child in Maine who had to stay indoors.

We played Goddesses-in-the-Rain, which consisted of caressing our bodies and screaming the names of everyone we knew, and we played ring-around-the-rosy and tag and red light/green light and catch, all deliciously slippery and surreal in the sheets of gray rain. Our parents watched us from the porch.

When we finally came in, thrilled with ourselves and the extent to which we were completely, profoundly wet, in every pore, they bundled us up and told us to dry our hair and get ready for dinner.

My mother brushed our hair, and then she made spaghetti sauce while my father made a salad and Mr DeCuervo made a strawberry tart, piling the berries into a huge, red, shiny pyramid in the center of the pastry. We were in heaven. The grown-ups were laughing a lot, sipping their rosy drinks, tossing vegetables back and forth.

After dinner, my mother took us into the living room to dance, and then the power went off.

'Shit,' said my father in the kitchen.

'Double shit,' said Mr DeCuervo, and we heard them stumbling around in the dark, laughing and cursing, until they came in with two flashlights.

'The cavalry is here, ladies,' said Daddy, bowing to us all, twirling his flashlight.

'American and Argentine divisions, señora y señoritas.'

I had never heard Mr DeCuervo speak Spanish before, not even that little bit.

'Well then, I know I'm safe – from the bad guys, anyway. On the other hand ...' My mother laughed, and the daddies put their arms around each other and they laughed too.

'On the other hand, what? What, Mommy?' I tugged at her the way I did when I was afraid of losing her in a big department store.

'Nothing, honey. Mommy was just being silly. Let's get ready for bed, munchkins. Then you can all talk for a while. We're shut down for the night, I'm sure.'

The daddies accompanied us to the bathroom and whispered that we could skip everything except peeing, since there was no electricity. The two of them kissed us good night, my father's mustache tickling, Mr DeCuervo's sliding over my cheek. My mother came into the room a moment later, and her face was as smooth and warm as a velvet cushion. We didn't stay awake for long. The rain dance and the eating and the storm had worn us out.

It was still dark when I woke up, but the rain had stopped and the power had returned and the light was burning in our hallway. It made me feel very grown-up and responsible, getting out of bed and going around the house, turning out the lights that no one else knew were on; I was conserving electricity.

I went into the bathroom and was squeezed by stomach cramps, probably from all the burnt popcorn kernels I had eaten. I sat on the toilet for a long time, watching a brown spider crawl along the wall; I'd knock him down and then watch him climb back up again, toward the towels. My cramps were better but not gone, so I decided to wake my mother. My father would have been more sympathetic, but he was the heavier sleeper, and by the time he understood what I was telling him, my mother would have her bathrobe on and be massaging my stomach kindly, though without the excited concern I felt was my due as a victim of illness.

I walked down to my parents' room, turning the hall light

back on. I pushed open the creaky door and saw my mother spooned up against my father's back, as she always was, and Mr DeCuervo spooned up against her, his arm over the covers, his other hand resting on the top of her head.

I stood and looked and then backed out of the bedroom. They hadn't moved, the three of them breathing deeply, in unison. What was that, I thought, what did I see? I wanted to go back and take another look, to see it again, to make it disappear, to watch them carefully, until I understood.

My cramps were gone. I went back to my own bed, staring at Lizzie and Gisela, who looked in their sleep like little girl-versions of the two men I had just seen. Just sleeping, I thought, the grown-ups were just sleeping. Maybe Mr DeCuervo's bed had collapsed, like ours did two summers ago. Or maybe it got wet in the storm. I thought I would never be able to fall asleep, but the next thing I remember is waking up to more rain and Lizzie and Gisela begging my mother to take us to the movies in town. We went to see *The Sound of Music*, which had been playing at the Bijou for about ten years.

I don't remember much else about the summer; all of the images run together. We went on swimming and fishing and taking the rowboat out for little adventures, and when the DeCuervos left I hugged Gisela but wasn't going to hug him, until he whispered in my ear, 'Next year we'll bring up a motorboat and I'll teach you to water ski,' and then I hugged him very hard and my mother put her hand on my head lightly, giving benediction.

The next summer, I went off to camp in July and wasn't there when the DeCuervos came. Lizzie said they had a good time without me. Then they couldn't come for a couple of summers in a row, and by the time they came again, Gisela and

Lizzie were at camp with me in New Hampshire; the four grown-ups spent about a week together, and later I heard my father say that another vacation with Elvira DeCuervo would kill him, or he'd kill her. My mother said she wasn't so bad.

We saw them a little less after that. They came, Gisela and Mr DeCuervo, to my high school graduation, to my mother's opening in Boston, my father's fiftieth birthday party, and then Lizzie's graduation. When my mother went down to New York she'd have dinner with the three of them, she said, but sometimes her plans would change and they'd have to substitute lunch for dinner.

Gisela couldn't come to the funeral. She was in Argentina for the year, working with the architectural firm that Mr DeCuervo's father had started.

After all the mourners left, Mr DeCuervo gave us a sympathy note from Gisela, with a beautiful pen-and-ink of our mother inside it. The two men went into the living room and took out a bottle of Scotch and two glasses. It was like we weren't there; they put on Billie Holiday singing 'Embraceable You,' and they got down to serious drinking and grieving. Lizzie and I went into the kitchen and decided to eat everything sweet that people had brought over: brownies, strudel, pfeffernuesse, sweet potato pie, Mrs Ellis's chocolate cake with chocolate mousse in the middle. We laid out two plates and two mugs of milk and got to it.

Lizzie said, 'You know, when I was home in April, he called every day.' She jerked her head toward the living room.

I couldn't tell if she approved or disapproved, and I didn't know what I thought about it either.

'She called him Bolivar.'

'What? She always called him Gaucho, and so we didn't call him anything.'

'I know, but she called him Bolivar. I heard her talking to him every fucking day, El, she called him Bolivar.'

Tears were running down Lizzie's face, and I wished my mother was there to pat her soft fuzzy hair and keep her from choking on her tears. I held her hand across the table, still holding my fork in my other hand. I could feel my mother looking at me, smiling and narrowing her eyes a little, the way she did when I was balking. I dropped the fork onto my plate and went over and hugged Lizzie, who leaned into me as though her spine had collapsed.

'I asked her about it after the third call,' she said into my shoulder.

'What'd she say?' I straightened Lizzie up so I could hear her.

'She said, "Of course he calls at noon. He knows that's when I'm feeling strongest." And I told her that's not what I meant, that I hadn't known they were so close.'

'You said that?'

'Yeah. And she said, "Honey, nobody loves me more than Bolivar." And I didn't know what to say, so I just sat there feeling like "Do I really want to hear this?" and then she fell asleep.'

'So what do you think?'

'I don't know. I was getting ready to ask her again—'

'You're amazing, Lizzie,' I interrupted. She really is, she's so quiet, but she goes and has conversations I can't even imagine having.

'But I didn't have to ask because she brought it up herself, the next day after he called. She got off the phone, looking just so exhausted, she was sweating but she was smiling. She was staring out at the crab apple trees in the yard, and she said,

"There were apple trees in bloom when I met Bolívar, and the trees were right where the sculpture needed to be in the court-yard, and so he offered to get rid of the trees and I said that seemed arrogant and he said that they'd replant them. So I said, 'Okay,' and he said, 'What's so bad about arrogance?' And the first time he and Daddy met, the two of them drank Scotch and watched soccer while I made dinner. And then they washed up, just like at the cabin. And when the two of them are in the room together and you two girls are with us, I know that I am living in a state of grace."'

'She said that? She said "in a state of grace"? Mommy said that?'

'Yes, Ellen. Christ, what do you think, I'm making up inter-esting deathbed statements?' Lizzie hates to be interrupted, especially by me.

'Sorry. Go on.'

'Anyway, we were talking and I sort of asked what were we actually talking about. I mean, close friends or very close friends, and she just laughed. You know how she'd look at us like she knew exactly where we were going when we said we were going to a friend's house for the afternoon but we were really going to drink Boone's Farm and skinny-dip at the quarry? Well, she looked just like that and she took my hand. Her hand was so light, El. And she said that the three of them loved each other, each differently, and that they were both amazing men, each special, each deserving love and apprecia-tion. She said that she thought Daddy was the most wonderful husband a woman could have and that she was very glad we had him as a father. And I asked her how she could do it, love them both, and how they could stand it. And she said, "Love is not a pie, honey. I love you and Ellen differently because you are different people, wonderful people, but not at all the same. And so who I am with each of you is different, unique to us. I don't choose between you. And it's the same way with Daddy and Bolivar. People think that it can't be that way, but it can. You just have to find the right people." And then she shut her eyes for the afternoon. Your eyes are bugging out, El.'

'Well, Jesus, I guess so. I mean, I knew . . .'

'You knew? And you didn't tell me?'

'You were eight or something, Lizzie, what was I supposed to say? I didn't even know what I knew then.'

'So, what did you know?' Lizzie was very serious. It was a real breach of our rules not to share inside dirt about our parents, especially our mother; we were always trying to figure her out.

I didn't know how to tell her about the three of them; that was even less normal than her having an affair with Mr DeCuervo with Daddy's permission. I couldn't even think of the words to describe what I had seen, so I just said, 'I saw Mommy and Mr DeCuervo kissing one night after we were in bed.'

'Really? Where was Daddy?'

'I don't know. But wherever he was, obviously he knew what was going on. I mean, that's what Mommy was telling you, right? That Daddy knew and that it was okay with him.'

'Yeah. Jesus.'

I went back to my chair and sat down. We were halfway through the strudel when the two men came in. They were drunk but not incoherent. They just weren't their normal selves, but I guess we weren't either, with our eyes puffy and red and all this destroyed food around us.

'Beautiful girls,' Mr DeCuervo said to my father. They were hanging in the doorway, one on each side.

'They are, they really are. And smart, couldn't find smarter girls.'

My father went on and on about how smart we were. Lizzie and I just looked at each other, embarrassed but not displeased.

'Ellen has Lila's mouth,' Mr DeCuervo said. 'You have your mother's mouth, with the right side going up a little more than the left. Exquisite.'

My father was nodding his head, like this was the greatest truth ever told. And Daddy turned to Lizzie and said, 'And you have your mother's eyes. Since the day you were born and I looked right into them, I thought, "My God, she's got Lila's eyes, but blue, not green."'

And Mr DeCuervo was nodding away, of course. I wondered if they were going to do a complete autopsy, but they stopped.

My father came over to the table and put one hand on each of us, 'You girls made your mother incredibly happy. There was nothing she ever created that gave her more pride and joy than you two. And she thought that you were both so special . . .' He started crying, and Mr DeCuervo put an arm around his waist and picked up for him.

'She did, she had two big pictures of you in her studio, nothing else. And you know, she expected us all to grieve, but you know how much she wanted you to enjoy, too. To enjoy everything, every meal, every drink, every sunrise, every kiss . . .' He started crying too.

'We're gonna lie down for a while, girls. Maybe later we'll have dinner or something.' My father kissed us both, wet and rough, and the two of them went down the hall.

Lizzie and I looked at each other again.

'Wanna get drunk?' I said.

'No, I don't think so. I guess I'll go lie down for a while too, unless you want company.' She looked like she was about to sleep standing up, so I shook my head. I was planning on calling John anyway.

Lizzie came over and hugged me, hard, and I hugged her back and brushed the chocolate crumbs out of her hair.

Sitting alone in the kitchen, I thought about John, about telling him about my mother and her affair and how the two men were sacked out in my parents' bed, probably snoring. And I could hear John's silence and I knew that he would think my father must not have really loved my mother if he'd let her go with another man; or that my mother must have been a real bitch, forcing my father to tolerate an affair 'right in his own home,' John would think, maybe even say. I thought I ought to call him before I got myself completely enraged over a conversation that hadn't taken place. Lizzie would say I was projecting anyway.

I called, and John was very sweet, asking how I was feeling, how the memorial service had gone, how my father was. And I told him all that and then I knew I couldn't tell him the rest and that I couldn't marry a man I couldn't tell this story to.

'I'm so sorry, Ellen,' he said. 'You must be very upset. What a difficult day for you.'

I realize that was a perfectly normal response, it just was all wrong for me. I didn't come from a normal family, I wasn't ready to get normal.

I felt terrible, hurting John, but I couldn't marry him just because I didn't want to hurt him, so I said, 'And that's not the worst of it, John. I can't marry you, I really can't. I know this is pretty hard to listen to over the phone ...' I couldn't think what else to say.

'Ellen, let's talk about this when you get back to Boston. I know what kind of a strain you must be under. I had the feeling that you were unhappy about some of Mother's ideas. We can work something out when you get back.'

'I know you think this is because of my mother's death, and it is, but not the way you think. John, I just can't marry you. I'm not going to wear your mother's dress and I'm not going to marry you and I'm very sorry.'

He was quiet for a long time, and then he said, 'I don't understand, Ellen. We've already ordered the invitations.' And I knew that I was right. If he had said, 'Fuck this, I'm coming to see you tonight,' or even, 'I don't know what you're talking about, but I want to marry you anyway,' I'd probably have changed my mind before I got off the phone. But as it was, I said good-bye sort of quietly and hung up.

It was like two funerals in one day. I sat at the table, poking the cake into little shapes and then knocking them over. My mother would have sent me out for a walk. I'd started clearing the stuff away when my father and Mr DeCuervo appeared, looking more together.

'How about some gin rummy, El?' my father said.

'If you're up for it,' said Mr DeCuervo.

'Okay,' I said. 'I just broke up with John Wescott.'

'Oh?'

I couldn't tell which one spoke.

'I told him that I didn't think we'd make each other happy.' Which was what I had meant to say.

My father hugged me and said, 'I'm sorry that it's hard for you. You did the right thing.' Then he turned to Mr DeCuervo and said, 'Did she know how to call them, or what? Your mother knew that you weren't going to marry that guy.'

'She was almost always right, Dan.'

'Almost always, not quite,' said my father, and the two of them laughed at some private joke and shook hands like a pair of old boxers.

'So, you deal,' my father said, leaning back in his chair.

'Penny a point,' said Mr DeCuervo.

Song of Solomon

Kate stood in front of the mirror trying on dresses. She could almost get into her black suit, but that couldn't be right for the New Year and it was almost eighty outside. She put on a yellow sleeveless dress with a white linen blazer and white sandals. Too summery but not bizarre. Do they wear hats? In church, women wear hats. Do Jewish women wear hats? Kate stared into the mirror, sweating in her slip, milk starting to come through her nursing pads.

Not now, she thought. If I nurse the baby, I'll be late for the ceremony – no, the services. Be calm, you must nurse the baby, Dr Sheldon would want you to nurse the baby, you can tell him that you were almost late because you had to nurse Sarah and he'll smile. Kate relaxed, thinking of his smile, like a cool cloth on her cheek.

Okay, we're all right. Kate took off her yellow dress, laid it out, and called to Sarah, who was just starting to make her little sucking noises, 'It's okay, Mommy's coming, everything's okay.' On her way to the baby's room, she grabbed a towel and looked on the top shelf of the closet for her white cartwheel straw hat. God did love her. He knew she had to get to the temple. The hat was there, and it was unblemished and unbent.

Kate looked at Sarah and felt the milk slide under her bra,

down her rib cage. 'Here we are, little duck. Mommy's baby. Dr Sheldon's perfect girl.' She picked Sarah up and changed her, watching herself move smoothly and competently, like a Pampers commercial. Sarah didn't wiggle, just knotted her toes in Kate's long blond hair. She plunked down in the rocking chair with Sarah and nursed her, wincing for a second as that ruthless, sweet mouth clamped down on her nipple. She watched Sarah and she watched the clock.

'Okay, Sarah beans, ten on one, ten on the other, and then we're out of here. Going to temple. Going out today, Miss Sarah.' While Sarah took a short break between breasts, Kate grabbed a clean blue dress from the laundry basket and put Sarah into it.

We're almost there, Kate thought. Come on, plan ahead. Plan it so you don't screw up. Okay, she finishes nursing, I burp her, on the towel. I put her in her crib while I get dressed, my shoes are not in my closet, they're still in the hall closet. Okay, we're walking down the hall – no, the diaper bag. The diaper bag is in Sarah's room and it's already packed, with another dress. Good girl, Kate. Okay, we have a fed baby, a diaper bag, a dressed mother. The hat, the hat is still in the closet, you don't put it on until you get there and you can see what they wear.

Make-up. You put your make-up in your purse, your white purse sitting on the hall bench, ready to roll. All you need is a little lip gloss and some cover-up for your raccoon eyes. You're all right. He doesn't care for make-up. Remember, in the hospital, sitting on your bed, he said that he didn't care for make-up and that you didn't need it anyway.

Kate closed her eyes, to remember better what he said, his saying it, to feel the weight of his body at the end of the bed, her bare feet almost touching his hip.

*

The whole seventy-two hours in the hospital Kate's body was never dry. She was damp and awake for every sunrise, her wet nightgown twisted up around her waist. Blood, milk, and sweat streamed over and through her. The night nurse had told her to get up and walk, but she was terrified that when she stood up her organs would just fall out, the cut muscles and tissue crumbling away like rotted newspaper.

'I promise you, you start walking now, when all the other ladies are home taking Percoset you'll be pushing Miss Sarah around the block. I'll take that catheter out now, too.'

She saw the nurse's smooth, thick hands flick back the heavy hem of her nightgown, and she shut her eyes when she felt the slight emptying tug.

'All right, let's roll.'

Let's roll, Kate thought, and stood up, wanting her voice to match the nurse's light bounce. Let's roll on out of here. She could hear the crowds cheering in her head as she walked down the hall, the i.v. rack skittering alongside her, the nurse's hand gently pulling on her good arm. She felt the shimmery heat of his presence before she really saw him, his back to her, talking to the nurses at the coffee station. They were barricaded behind twin coffeepots, personalized mugs, wide open doughnut boxes.

Kate shook off her nurse and strolled, with great effort, toward the coffee station.

'Wonderful. You're walking already, isn't that wonderful?' Dr Sheldon turned to the nurses, who smiled politely; they didn't care if she walked or not, and Kate didn't care about them either. If she didn't say something, he'd be gone, and she was too tired to stand around waiting for the right moment.

'Could I speak to you?' The sweat slid from her underarms right down to her feet, wetting the paper slippers they'd given her.

'Of course. I'll save your nurse a trip, even if your quality of care suffers a little.'

The nurses all smiled; he was a corny old guy, but nice. He practically lived in the maternity ward. His patient, the new mother, looked like she was about to pass out, and Kate's nurse went to grab a cup of coffee before the inevitable call.

He put his hand around her bicep, and Kate could feel the blood rushing from her arm to her cheeks.

'The nurses like you,' she said, looking at the passing room numbers so he couldn't see her face.

'Yes? I like them. It's hard work, they're terribly understaffed. First there weren't enough nurses because they were paid so badly. Now there aren't enough nurses because it costs the hospitals too much to keep a full shift.'

Kate smiled. Even though her back ached, and she could picture each of her twenty stitches clearly, lighting a hot, narrow torch across her belly, she beamed. He gripped her arm a little tighter, and as her face went white and the walls around Dr Sheldon began to spin, she smiled again and he smiled back before he called the nurse.

Sarah had stopped sucking a little sooner than usual, and Kate was so grateful she sang to her all the way through burping. Everything went smoothly; little Sarah, stoned from nursing, was completely content to lie in her crib and murmur to the world. Kate dressed like a surgeon prepping, precise and careful in every movement. She checked her watch again.

Twenty-five minutes to get to the temple. She had driven there yesterday and timed it; it was only fifteen minutes away. Five minutes to find a parking space, five minutes to get Sarah out of her NASA-designed carseat and into her Snugli. Forget the Snugli, in a summer dress and a blazer you can't carry a baby in a blue corduroy Snugli. Okay, no Snugli. I carry her in my arms, wrapped in a yellow and blue blanket, to show off her eyes and her hair. Fine.

Kate moved through all of her steps, locked the front door, and got into the car, strapping Sarah in with the blanket tucked around her, supporting her soft boneless neck.

'We're rolling now. Off we go, into the wild blue yonder, flying high into the sky …' Sarah had fallen into one of her instant naps, from which she would emerge charming and alert but not yet hungry. Perfect for seeing Dr Sheldon.

Kate didn't even look pregnant until her sixth month. The other women in the library began to talk to her a little, to tell her things. They had left her alone all summer, feeling that whether her silence was due to a bad attitude, problems at home, or painful shyness, she was too much trouble. Pregnant and single and willing to take anyone's advice, Kate was not too much trouble. 'Go to Dr Sheldon,' they said over lunch in the back room. 'He's the best.' Especially for the weird, the dispossessed, the single mothers, the ones who wished they were, the ones who needed to talk at two in the morning, not just about their babies. And when Kate met Dr Sheldon and he didn't purse his lips when she said she had only met the father once and hoped she never would again, she knew that she and the baby were in the right place. When he helped her out of her chair, she felt ethereally beautiful and as delicate as baby's breath, her ankles and heartburn forgotten.

She drove up to the synagogue and was appalled to see millions of cars. It looked like an airport terminal, women and children piling out of backseats, all the women wearing hats. Kate laid her hand happily on the white hat next to her, perfect for her blond hair. He'd like it. She could tell he liked her hair from the way he commented on Sarah's duck fuzz. 'Not much now,' he said the night he sat so close to her, 'but she'll have your curls by the time she's one.' The men were pulling away from the entrance, craning their necks to find parking spaces. They weren't wearing hats, of course, just those little beanies – what were they called? She could ask Dr Sheldon. Unless he'd be offended by her ignorance, rather than charmed by her interest? Please let him find me charming, and my daughter irresistible.

She was damp and rumpled by the time she found a spot behind the A&P. She scooped up Sarah like she was going for a touchdown and trotted toward the temple, hugely domed and out of scale between a sandwich shop and a dry cleaners. A block away, Kate slowed down, licked her lips, and smoothed the front of her dress with her free hand. Please.

He was standing on the sidewalk talking to some other men, but alone. No wife. She would put one of those St Jude ads in the paper, the kind that said, 'Thank you for helping me. Now I need you more than ever.' She shifted Sarah to her left shoulder, lined up her purse and the diaper bag on her right shoulder, and smiled the way her mother had always wanted her to.

'Why, Dr Sheldon.'

'Ms Tillinghast. What a surprise, what a pleasure. I didn't know we belonged to the same shul.'

Kate thought quickly, circling the strange word. 'I've never been here before, actually, but I've wanted to come for a long time. I hope nobody will mind the baby, my regular sitter couldn't make it.' Kate smiled self-deprecatingly, showing that she knew some people didn't like babies and would consider her careless for having brought Sarah. But Dr Sheldon wouldn't think so, which was why she had told Joan not to come today.

'No, of course not. Who could object to this angel, this proof of God's goodness?'

As he bent his head toward Sarah to kiss the back of her round moist head, Kate felt so happy she thought her heart would break through her chest and fly around the temple, like a dove released.

They squinted at each other in the September light, smiling and wondering what the other person saw. Dr Sheldon thought Kate saw a pallid, overweight man sweating in an old navy blue suit, black-rimmed glasses sliding halfway down his big nose and wild gray curls floating around his bald spot. She didn't; she saw God. Kate thought he saw a slightly crazy woman, wild with exhaustion and loneliness, but he didn't see that. He saw that her dark blue eyes lit up when they rested on his face and that her hand lay tenderly, unconsciously, on his sleeve, like a lily. He saw that their house would have white flowers and bright plastic toys on the floor. He would not be alone.

'People are starting to go in,' he said.

'Oh.' She sounded wounded, which alarmed him. Had he offended her? Maybe she didn't want to sit with him.

Dr Sheldon shuffled backward, to show that he hadn't meant to intrude, and Kate's eyes filled with tears. How could he be leaving now, now that they were together?

Sarah thrust one pink foot through her blanket, and they

both looked at it, flexing in the air. Kate's face was so filled with loss and love that Dr Sheldon reached out for her, and she pressed his hand to her hip as they carried Sarah up the temple stairs.

David and Galen

Hyacinths
The Sight of You
Silver Water

Hyacinths

My father was not a careless man. He had taken measure of the world's violence and his own, and he was sometimes ashamed and sometimes frightened, but he was not careless.

He got up at four every morning, he wiped and shelved his tools every night, and every May twenty-two white hyacinths came up at the foot of the front steps. I pictured my mother planting the hyacinths, with much the same care, and a great deal more joy, than my father ever showed to me. I imagined her, with the help of the two brown portraits in the living room, as even-tempered and affectionate, with none of my father's dark turns or distance. Why a woman like that would marry a miserable soul like my father, I could not imagine. My aunts and uncles who had known her were as honest as people of that time and place could let themselves be; they did not say that she was a homely shrew (as everyone but me must have seen from the frowning photographs), but they did not tell me stories of her warmth and charm. My aunt Ida said that my mother loved me and did her best by me, and for that show of kindness to me and to my mother, I loved my aunt Ida more than the other aunts, even more than Aunt Myrtle, who sewed bear-shaped cushions for my bed, even more than Aunt Ruth, who gave me candied violets after the obligatory Sunday dinner to which she occasionally, properly, invited her sister's widower and her little nephew, me.

Each of my parents had one brother. My father had two sisters, Ida and Myrtle. My mother had Ruth. Her family was slight and dark, Jews who had come to Toronto in 1922 and made the mistake of continuing west. My mother was the county schoolteacher, an old maid by local standards and a Jewess, of whom there were very few in Manitoba at the time, believe me, but she seemed healthy and was single, and my Presbyterian father was already thirty-six and struggling to keep his farm alive. I imagine now that I can remember the orphaned look in his eye, that belligerent mistrust which barely conceals despair. I see it in many of my patients, I assume that they can see it in me, if they wish to look that closely.

Aunt Myrtle, my father's younger sister, lived in Winkler, a few miles from my parents' place in Rosebank. She and Uncle William ran the general store there and lived in the back with their two boys, Willie and Percy. She made our kitchen curtains, as well as the stuffed-bear cushions. I have no true memories of their faces, just the dusty lemon scent of the cushions and a pair of short red hands that also smelled of lemon verbena. My father and his brother, Francis, had fallen out as young men, and apparently both sisters sided with my father. Aunt Ida, older than my father by fifteen years, kept house for us, and my father treated her the way he treated his old hunting dog: obliged to be kind, after years of her willing service; resentful of being obliged, by his own rules, to give what he couldn't spare. We were both frightened of him, Ida and I, and at six and sixty, we could not conceal our infuriating uselessness. We would hide together in the henhouse, dawdling over the warm eggs and the scattering of cracked corn, until we thought we heard the stable door bang open and closed and could see him heading toward the fields, reins in one hand, canteen in the other.

Aunt Ruth, my mother's sister, had come to Rosebank to keep my mother company (or was herself desperate for companionship, I have no idea) and had married a tailor, the only other Jew for a hundred miles, I'm sure. As all the women in Rosebank did their own sewing, Uncle Morris repaired the leather and canvas goods the farmers wore out. They kept kosher as best they could, and one of my few memories of their home is watching him kill and kasher a chicken for Shab-bat dinner. For Sunday dinner, we had the roast my father contributed and bowls of potatoes.

Uncle Hi (for Hiram, changed from Hyman) was my mother's successful doctor brother. When I was six, he and Aunt Fritzi (for Frieda – the social position she upheld in Duluth did not require her to further anglicize her name) invited themselves for a visit, as they had done for each of the three years since my mother's death.

In May, a pink envelope came, with only my name neatly written in large purple letters above our address in smaller print. Aunt Fritzi took no chances. Aunt Ida held the envelope up for me to admire and read the letter aloud, ignoring all of Fritzi's indicated inflection.

> Darling David,
>
>   Your Aunt Fritzi and your Uncle Hi (who gave you the
> big blue truck last year, do you remember?) would like to
> come visit you this summer. When we come, we will
> celebrate your SIXTH birthday. What a big boy! We would

like to come June 27 and 28, when Uncle Hi can get away
from his practice. Please ask your father if this is all right. If
we don't hear otherwise, we will be there June 27, with
your birthday present and lots of birthday goodies.

   We can't wait to see you, darling. Hugs and kisses from
us to you.

At the bottom, in a curling purple scrawl, was Aunt Fritzi's
name and the imprint of two fuchsia lips. Yes, I remembered
their gift, since I had only the truck and my bear cushions to play
with. And although I had no idea what 'birthday goodies' could
possibly include, there would be lots of them. I looked at the
budding trees and longed for summer. Ida put the envelope in
her apron pocket and looked out at the trees with me. She said,
'Tell him after supper, when he's lighting his pipe.' Since Ida, I
have had no one in my life so simply decent. Perhaps people like
that all died out in the middle of this century, to be replaced by
the clever, the quick, and the entitled.

   My father was not happy that Hi and Fritzi were coming, but
he would not lower himself by saying no. Nor would he make
himself ridiculous by asking Myrtle the favor of her telephone
just to fend off visitors, visitors who were undeniably family of
some kind. They would fill the house with Hi's cigar and Fritzi's
geranium face powder, and each supper would be a tennis match
of Hi and Fritzi's long, lobbing questions and my father's one-
word answers, played so close to the net that the final sound
barely escaped before he closed his lips.

   My real birthday came and went as it probably had before: an
angelfood cake baked by Aunt Ida and a long walk down to the
barn with my father. He showed me the newest calf.

   'Son, you're six now. You name that little calf and you take care of him. Whatever we get for him, half of it's yours.' He put his hand on the back of my neck, and I could see his big brown fingers out of the corner of my eye. 'Happy birthday.'

Over the cake, for which Ida took out, and my father put back, the fancy gold-rimmed plates, they asked me for the calf's name, and I finally said Blackie, to please them. I think they were surprised, perhaps a little disappointed; they had labeled me 'fanciful' in response to my night terrors and absentmindedness, and I could come up with only the dullest and most sensible of names. I didn't care for the calf, green grass slime dripping from its mouth, manure sticking to its black and pink rear, right at eye level for me. I had loved and named all nine barn cats, whom my father alternately ignored and damned, and had connived with Ida to save at least a dozen kittens from his hand.

They came. Aunt Fritzi stepped out of a big blue Roadmaster, carrying a shiny red-handled paper sack from Warner's, the nicest department store in Duluth. I took in the magnificent car, the smiles and nice smells of my aunt and uncle, and the rest of the world faded away as Aunt Fritzi began, in defiance of my father, to hand me present upon present. I hopped madly from one foot to the other, transported by greed.

I don't know what the grown-ups did while I opened my gifts. Five boxes, all wrapped, all with ribbon. I remember Ida and Fritzi watching, smiling at me and even at each other, and the sounds of Hi and my father in the background, remarkably similar rumblings, although Hi's voice rose and fell and my father's was as flat as the pine floor. At the end of supper, for which Ida served a roast even though it was only Saturday, my father announced that he had invited Ruth and Morris and Myrtle and William and the boys to come by for a visit early Sunday afternoon.

'That's lovely of you, Walter. Really lovely.' Aunt Fritzi, born without malice or sensitivity, put her hand over my father's, and Ida and I both watched his efforts to move his hand without acknowledging her touch. Uncle Hi offered my father a cigar, Ida went in to do the dishes, and the men sat on the porch, cigar and pipe burning, while Aunt Fritzi showed me how to play Pickup Stix until bedtime.

Fritzi and Ida got ready for the party as though it were their house and my father and uncle were early-arriving guests. I was scrubbed from ear to toe and back and put into navy shorts and a navy-and-white shirt. Fritzi had also bought a sailor's white beret, but I balked and Hi backed me up. Fritzi and Ida came downstairs, both smelling of Fritzi's perfume, Ida's chest and neck blotched red with excitement, or embarrassment, or even suppressed rage, for all I know. They were smiling, and Hi said something to Ida that made her smile more, her hand covering her mouth. Fritzi straightened Hi's tie and patted him on both cheeks. No one touched my father or commented on his appearance, and I cannot remember what he wore. I heard the rattle of Uncle Mo's car (women did not have cars) and stood on the porch, watching. All the grown-ups came out too, and Fritzi waved as the rest of us stood there, pleased to see them. Hi hugged his sister and brother-in-law, and Fritzi added kisses and little squeezes to her hugs. Aunt Ruth and Uncle Mo, who had been living in Branden for several years by then, nodded to my father and Ida and went back to the car for packages. Ruth had brought two pies, and a rock candy stick for me. Just as we got settled, Aunt Myrtle and Uncle William drove up with little Willie, who was bigger than me, and Percy, who was still just a baby and was allowed to stagger around the house in his diapers, toast crumbs all over his face.

The women began supper preparation in earnest, and I still remember Fritzi's pleated yellow dress rippling above and below one of Ida's flour-sack aprons. I stood on the porch with Willie and Percy; the grown-ups would not speak to us or bother to look for us until suppertime, and we went down to the barn. I knew Willie would be impressed by the calf since he had no barn and no animals, although he did have access to jawbreakers, red-hots, and whole packages of chewing gum. Percy trailed along behind us, moaning a little with excitement and exertion.

Willie liked the calf a lot more than I did and scratched it behind its ears and laughed when its filthy tail whipped past his face.

'It's my birthday present,' I said, the calf's value increasing by the minute.

'Gee,' he said, and Percy sat down on a bale of hay, repeating 'gee' over and over.

'Let's look at this stuff,' Willie said, remembering that he was the oldest cousin. He ran his hands over my father's tools and played at cutting off my hair with a pair of secateurs.

'You're not supposed to touch the tools,' I said.

'No one's here.' Pretending not even to look at me, he reached for a harness and dropped it over his head and shoulders.

We played cowboy for a while, taking turns as the whip-wielding rider and the wild stallion, and when we got tired of the harness, Willie hung it back up, which I found reassuring. In the far corner of the barn was an old china cupboard where my father stored his guns. Willie opened it, and we all stared at the rifles, which were unlike the other tools in the barn. They gleamed, long polished snouts and shiny stocks.

Willie picked one up and I told him to put it down, and as the butt came toward me and we slipped on the mud and hay, my ears burst and Willie's chest flew out behind him, terribly dark. I couldn't hear a thing, not even Percy crying, although I could see him and see far into his wide-open mouth; I could see his tonsils as he screamed. Willie lay on the ground, and I lay down beside him. I could hear again when the men came running in, first my father, my uncles behind him in city shoes. I pretended I was dead too, as I assumed I soon would be. My father lifted me up with one hand and began to hit me with the other. William must have been holding his dead son, he never touched me. When the aunts came, there was more screaming, and while Hi and Fritzi held my father's arm, Ida grabbed me and ran into the house, her breasts lying over my face. I saw Myrtle cover Percy's eyes with her apron as she carried him to the car. I never saw either of them again, and I remember the back of her dress, crisscrossed by muslin apron strings, and Percy's fat, bare, dangling legs.

I don't remember anything else until late that night. I was in bed, in my pajamas, and I was comfortable; someone, Ida or Fritzi or both, had taken care of me. My father came into my room with a candle and sat in the corner chair, leaving the door open.

I knew better than to defend myself. Excuses and claims of persecution only made him hit me harder; he could not abide cowards. I was too surprised by the fact that he was sitting in my room to pretend to be asleep.

'Well, David,' he said, a rifle balanced on his knees. 'People can't live like this, son. Not when their hands are unclean. Our hands are not clean, are they? Answer me.'

'No, sir. Our hands are not clean.' I tried to see my hands in the dark. I thought they were probably pretty clean, that whoever had put me in pajamas seemed to have scrubbed me up pretty thoroughly.

'Good boy.' He raised his voice and looked down through the rifle sight. "'If thy right hand offend thee, cut it off." This will be over in a minute. Over,' he shouted as I pulled the covers up around my head. I heard Uncle Hi through the blankets.

'Okay, Walter. Okay.'

'Get out, Hiram. Get the hell out.'

Fritzi ran in and yanked me out of bed, taking the blankets with her. She carried me down the stairs and we sat at the bottom, listening to an argument I can no longer recall in detail. Uncle Hi came down and put his hand on my head. Ida kissed me and cried over me as they bundled me into the backseat, and I was astonished by her tears.

'Be a good boy,' she said. 'No fussing, no dwelling on the past. Be a good, good boy.'

My father stood in the front yard, his pipe making a small light. Perhaps he thought I was asleep, or perhaps they had all agreed that it would be better just to whisk me away, or perhaps if he had gotten any closer he would have tried again.

They must have driven straight through, for I awoke in a yellow bedroom filled with bright hatboxes and domestic flourishes of every kind. Having never seen much decoration, I was dazzled by the curtains, roses and ruffles, and the sateen bedspread with yards more ruffles and a slick nylon surface unlike any I'd encountered. Fritzi brought me toast with no crusts and cocoa. I did my best to indicate that I was in excellent spirits, would be a good, good boy and no trouble at all, and could be depended upon not to dwell on the past.

The days were orgies of shopping, which I found a little boring and physically disturbing; I had rarely been touched and was unnerved by the pats and probing and friendly pinches of these high-heeled women and wet-haired men. But every expedition for a suit or a cute pair of tennis shoes was matched with a trip to the soda fountain or the toy store, or even to Warner's, where we bought blue truck curtains, a blue corduroy spread, and a rug shaped like a fire engine. As a consequence of killing my cousin Willie, I lived in splendor with parents far more adoring and agreeable than those I had originally been dealt.

Sometimes, at night, I broke a toy and pressed myself hard upon the sharp pieces, or lay on top of my bedspread until my hands and feet went numb with cold. I was afraid that my father had been right and that the loving impulse that had led him to arrange for Fritzi and Hi to rescue me (which was how I now understood our flight to Duluth) was really a weak-minded avoidance of the inevitable. Sooner or later, someone was going to blow out my chest, and perhaps it would be better to get it over with than to sit up in the dark, waiting for Willie.

My bedtime, and therefore my nightmare, was regularly delayed by arguments between my aunt and uncle.

'He's a Jew, Fritz. He has to be circumcised. Only in that miserable anti-Semitic wasteland would a Jewish boy not be circumcised.'

'So he wasn't, so who cares? Let him not be a Jew. Let him be David Dunmore, our Presbyterian nephew.'

'How can you, of all people, be ashamed?'

'Ashamed? I'm not ashamed, I'm realistic. What does he need to be a Jew for? So he can become head of cardiology but never head of the hospital? What a choice. Why not let him lead a goyish life?'

'Because he's a Jew,' Hi said, gentle but relentless.

After a week of this, I knew that my aunt Fritzi couldn't have babies because of terrible things that had happened to her when she was a girl, over there, and that she loved me more than life itself. I found out that Uncle Hi was very angry that he couldn't golf with some of the other doctors, except when they invited him, but that he was proud to be a Jew and that as his adopted son, as David Silverstein, I would make him prouder still.

Fritzi kept arguing, determined to spare me the life of a Jew and the surgery, which she described in bloody, beckoning images. They fought, more pained than angry, all summer. In the middle of August, with the nights becoming familiar and cool, I received a letter from my father. It was left at my place at the breakfast table, opened but without comment, as though it had sailed right from the mailman's pouch to my plate.

Dear David,
    Be a good boy and be grateful. You can come home now. If they cannot bring you, I will come for you.
    Your father,
    Walter Dunmore

'I want to be a Jew,' I said, even before I put down the letter. I thought tenderly and briefly of Ida, her heavy arms outstretched to me, and I thought of my cats. I thought that Aunt Fritzi might get me a kitten, and I made up my mind.

'Whatever you have to cut off, I want to be a Jew. I want to be a doctor like Uncle Hi.'

Hi was determined to do it right. He called in the rabbi to explain everything to me, he told me stories of King David and Moses, and he told me how brave I was. I think I would have been less brave if I had understood what was going to happen to me. As it was, I had figured out that there would be a token mark made on my penis, which would hurt for a few days. I was ready.

Two doctors, the rabbi, who called me Dah-veed, and a full

minyan made up of my uncle's friends and colleagues, waited for me in the operating room. They stood over me, their big hands tugging at the green masks pulled taut over their big noses, smoothing the green cloth under their black-framed glasses. Beneath the huge bright light, their eyes were invisible to me. Only their green faces and their uniformly clean hands appeared, each finger outlined in white light. I heard the kind voice of Dr Riskind, who had come for dinner earlier in the week and had given me his gold cigar band. I heard his voice murmuring gently behind me, and then he strapped each of my arms down while someone else strapped my legs. I felt myself peeing, unstoppably, without wetness. They put a hard plastic mask over my face and told me to breathe in and count backward from ten. I sucked in bitter, dry air until my chest ached, and my head slowly pulled away from my body until they were miles apart. I woke up screaming with pain and then stopped. I am delivered, I thought, as tears ran down my face and blood darkened my lap.

Rose's Barbie doll tumbled between my legs, spiky feet first, and I handed it back to her, meeting her eyes in the rearview mirror. She giggled.

'Careful,' my wife warned her. 'One more toss and it's ours.'

I had planned our usual August vacation by March, but late in May I suggested we take a short trip to Canada. I wanted my children to see Rosebank; I wanted to see it again, but only with them. My wife shook her head, in what I took to be amused disbelief, and said it was all right with her if it was a trip I really wanted to make.

'Don't you ever think of going back to Kansas?'

Galen is not given to smiling, but she smiled at this. 'Never.'

'Not just for a little visit?'

'Not for thirty seconds.'

Our girls were six and eight and willing travelers, as long as they could read and color and ignore the scenery. The backseat looked like a small but modern library, and since we were not going to the beach or a fancy hotel, our destination was of no interest to Rose and Violet. Although she never said so, I know Galen was as astonished as I was that we had such delightful and unexpected children, fey, gentle, apparently happy.

They slept easily in the backseat, Rose's head on Violet's bare legs, her white-blond hair swinging in front of her blank dreaming face, trickling across Violet's thighs.

Galen was quiet beside me, as she usually was. I am quiet myself, and do not mistake silence for tranquility or goodness. I do not say what I feel, and people often take that for shyness, even kindness. I put my hand on Galen's and pressed lightly. She didn't look at me, but she didn't move her hand away. My first wife, warm and efficient, would have called Triple-A to map our vacation and arranged for comfortable motels and side trips of historic interest. Very little, beyond music and the children, interested Galen, and nothing, as far as I could tell, frightened her. The day we left, she packed a small bag for herself, a larger one for the girls, and sat down on the fender with a magazine, waiting to drive or be driven.

The girls woke up abruptly, Rose alleging that Violet had kicked her in the mouth and then righteously biting the offending foot. Violet screamed and Galen closed her eyes.

'Could you manage the girls, please?'

She didn't open her eyes. 'They're fine, David.'

They were not fine, they were moving toward hysteria, but I knew that would not prompt Galen to intervene.

'Stop it,' I said, frowning like a father while Rose and Violet watched me in the mirror and pinched each other, silently and ferociously. I pulled over and looked at the map, too tired to drive any farther, unwilling to enter Rosebank at night.

'We're coming into Canada. Gretna, Schoenwiese, Rosengart, Haskett, Blumenfeld, Osterwick, Hochfeld, Schanzenfeld, Winkler, and then up to Rosebank. Rosebank is where Daddy was born.'

'I thought you were born in Duluth, where Grampa Hi and Nana lived,' Rose said.

Violet was laughing to herself, repeating the names.

'That's quite a list,' Galen said.

Schanzenfeld, Winkler, Rosebank. I could smell manure and silage and Fels Naptha, the only cleanser Aunt Ida had ever used, carving thick slices off the white bar and rubbing them into my father's collars. I pulled into the first motel we saw, a real motel, like the ones of my Northland youth, nine shabby cabins in a horseshoe shape around a rutted gravel drive and an oval aqua pool in the center. The girls emptied out their backpacks, looking for swimsuits, leaving a familiar trail of dirty white socks, coiled panties, and stale, damp jeans. Galen pulled out her suit without disturbing any other layers, leaving me to watch the black moths gathering on the overhead light.

When I stepped outside, the pool had turned deep violet and the night air was so thick it hid the fence and the chaises. I could hear the girls better than I could see them, since most of the evening light was provided by two bug boxes electrocuting mosquitoes in short cobalt bursts.

Violet was screaming 'No, no!,' giggling and gulping water, and I could hear Rose's falsely maternal reassurances and her giddy laugh and their splashing. I came toward the fence, groping for the gate, seeing only shadowy heads and hands in the water.

I heard one of them yell, 'Daddy,' and was flattered that I had been called first, and then frightened.

'Daddy, I can't find Vi,' Rose screamed.

'Where is she?' I couldn't even see Rose.

'The end farthest from you,' she said, with extraordinary lucidity.

Without my shoes, without my glasses, I dove into the dark water looking for my daughter, thinking, 'Too late, too late,' and reached my arms in front of me, pushing the water aside. I was about to come up for air when Violet's hand hit me in the face, and I pulled us both up, one arm around her twisting waist. She suddenly stopped working against me, stretching her body out to protect me from her frantic, involuntary kicks. We sat on the hard concrete, Rose hovering over us as Violet vomited, water flowing from her mouth and nose and eyes. She sat in my lap, cold, wet, and dense under three towels, and I rocked her back and forth, telling her it was all right, Daddy was here, we'd go home tomorrow. I heard Galen's footsteps on the gravel and was furious that she had not been at the pool in the first place, and grateful and pleased to have her as my witness.

I held Violet close, wiping her nose with the towel end, enjoying the feel of Rose's arms flung over my shoulders and Galen's light hand on my back. I looked up at the night, as clear as the Rosebank sky I remembered, and I could see Willie, as I often did. Alive and chestless, he leans up against a bale of hay, one grubby, fat hand resting on the shotgun muzzle. He is smiling, not impatient. I have been spared, a small animal at the hands of a violent but distractible boy. Lucky this time.

The Sight of You

It was ninety-seven degrees and I took my kids to the club for a swim. Everybody was there, including my lover, Henry, his wife, Marie, and their two boys, whose names I forget. My husband, David, stayed home to mow the lawn and read the *Times*.

Henry and I didn't really see each other that much during the two years we were lovers. We could have, I think. I'm a musician; I could have practiced a little less. Henry ran a construction company; he was his own boss. All of our time together was shaved off something bigger, slivered into pieces so thin you could look right at them and never even see. Those two winters I would look out my window at dawn and see his crew plowing driveways. They were like angels in the snow, their little white and yellow lights turning softly in the storm, right into my bedroom.

I was watching Henry from the clubhouse deck as he showed the youngest boy how to swim, his big arms carving runnels in the water, clearing a path for the littler arms to move in. I wore huge sunglasses so I could watch him. That was all I really wanted, just to watch Henry, forever. I grew up on the Plains and didn't know how I'd longed for the ocean until my foot felt the first wave's edge. And I hadn't known the wordless, leaping power of beauty until I saw Henry.

Marie walked past my chaise looking the other way, and I tried not to blame her for her bad manners and tight red face. Grief made her ugly, and I know that she was not always ugly.

I lay back, calculating whether I had time to talk to Henry while Marie was wherever she was. I thought so and dove in from the pool's edge, surfacing next to him. Under his little boy's splashing, he put his hand on my waist, watching for Marie, who seemed to have a sixth sense about us. She worried that we were having an affair and complained, obliquely, about my presence. She never saw anything between us. I could have kissed him on the mouth that day, in front of all the neighbors, and everything would have been different.

He stood close to me and smiled. We could both look down and see his erection, even in the cold water. Marie came zipping out of the snack area, a bag of chips in one hand and a racket in the other.

'Hank, we've got a court. Go dry off and I'll get your sneakers.' Among the club set, she was a serious tennis player. She stood there, looking down on us, her hands on her hips. She didn't move until Henry headed for the wall. Then she smiled at me and walked toward the court.

I followed him to the wall, watching the small drops quiver down his back. I didn't know I was about to speak. 'Henry, I don't think this is working. What about our time together?' We were both surprised. 'If you still want me to leave him, I will.'

I swam across the pool and went back to my chaise. Henry was still standing in the water, looking dazed. He hoisted himself out, emerging smoothly like a big dark dolphin, all muscle and flex, no visible bones. He glanced at me and then headed for the court, his tennis shirt clinging to his wide wet back. I put my chin on the deck's redwood railing and watched them play.

I always felt powerful with Henry, powerful and grateful. That day, I felt like God Almighty, holding a crowd of tiny people in one huge hand. I had wanted to hold just Henry, but somehow another six had climbed aboard. David had given me the only home I'd ever had, but like the little mermaid in the fairy tale, I was prepared to cut my true self in two and walk in pain and artifice just to dance with Henry, dazzled by all that unfamiliar light.

I thought about the girls and hoped they'd be all right. The three of us had been a team, and that wouldn't have to change. David had been a good father, better than most I've seen; he played Scrabble with them, went to their concerts, picked them up from swim team when I was touring, hugged them every day, and knew how to braid their hair. I thought Henry would help out the way he did with his boys, and nothing would keep David from Rose and Violet. I used to think the girls were like my arms, I didn't need anyone's help growing them or taking care of them. When Rose was an infant, she would sleep through my practicing but wake up as soon as I started to vacuum. I stopped vacuuming. And Violet, my baby, used to help the ushers at my concerts, tripping over her Mary Janes and her lavender organdy skirt, but knowing where every seat in the hall was. I took them most everywhere I went; we all loved music and new places and hotel rooms. David usually stayed home; he's a psychiatrist and never likes to leave his patients for too long.

I didn't know what would happen when Henry finished playing tennis. We would have to talk on the phone, work out details. The girls would go to music camp for a month, and I could move then if David wanted the house. Or maybe he'd move out. The house didn't matter much to me as long as I had my piano and a bedroom for the girls. I have to force myself to sleep in a bed, even now.

When I got home, I sat down at the piano and stared at the keys, waiting for a wave of guilt or panic that would tell me to stop.

Henry loved me the way I was taught Indians loved Nature; I was everywhere for him, in the air, in the light, seeping right into his skin. It scared me a little, how much he loved me, handing over everything he had. He would kneel in front of me, big man, putting his hands around my waist as though to snap me in two, and he'd say, 'There is nothing I wouldn't do for you.' And I would rest my hands in his black curly hair.

'Nothing,' he'd say again.

And I said, 'I know,' and he'd relax and lay me on the bed.

It was like nothing else in my life, that river of love that I could dip into and leave and return to once more and find it still flowing, undisturbed by my comings and goings. And when we made love, it was the same. He would wash over me and into me and he didn't need me to smile, or cry out, or move. I lay there, like the riverbed.

I was orphaned at sixteen, by two lonely, curdled people who had hoped to divorce without too much scandal when I finished high school. Instead, their car hit a tree. I was sent off to boarding school by a committee of relatives and came home to visit Mrs Wallace (the one my father hoped to marry) and Dr Davidson (the one my mother had in the wings). I went on being their memorial tribute to thwarted love and bad planning until I turned eighteen. I escaped to Juilliard and didn't answer their letters. Being an orphan didn't bother me.

While I was at Juilliard, I met David. He was finishing his residency in psychiatry, and I was one of his guinea pigs. I was nineteen, he was twenty-nine. My faculty adviser had noticed that I never went away for holidays, never had family in the audience, never had trouble paying my tuition. I told her the highlights of my personal history, and she turned her face away and suggested that I 'talk to someone' at the Washington Square Clinic. I thought it had something to do with piano playing, so I went.

It was April, and the big waiting room was still wintry. All the chairs were gray plastic. As I put my feet up on one of them, I saw two men talking on the far side of the room. My hearing is acute, and I eavesdropped.

'I'll take her,' said the tall, chubby one.

'No,' said the other one, David. 'You're full up this week, and anyway, you couldn't handle your counter-transference.'

'My counter-transference? Please. All right, you take her. Take her.'

I was smiling when David invited me into his cubicle.

'You have a lovely smile,' he said, and then he frowned.

'Thank you. Why are you frowning?'

'I'm not . . . I'm Dr Silverstein and you're . . . Galen Nichols?'

'Yes.'

'Well.' He arched his fingertips together the way they must have taught him in Practical Psychiatry. 'What can I do for you?'

'I don't know,' I said, and I didn't say anything else.

We had three sessions like that, and at the end of the third I got up and shook his hand.

'Thanks for your time,' I said. I liked him, he acted just like me.

Two weeks later, he called and asked how I was doing. A few weeks after that, he invited me to go for coffee. I went, and we sat in the Big Apple Coffee Shoppe for two hours while he told me that he was married but just couldn't stop thinking about me. I thanked him for the coffee and went home and listened to my most recent performance tapes.

After two more coffee dates, he asked me to have dinner with him.

'I can't take a break for dinner these days, we're rehearsing. But if you want to get something for yourself and come listen, you're welcome to.'

David sat at the back of the auditorium until 1:00 A.M., and he walked me home.

'You play so beautifully. May I please come in?'

'Sure.'

By then, I had figured out that he wasn't really like me at all, but he was a gentle, sweet man, not like the cowboys at home. He touched me as if I were made of glass and gold dust. At about 3:00 A.M. he jumped out of bed and into his jeans, mumbling how sorry he was. I was too tired to walk him to the door, so I blew him a kiss and told him to take the extra key.

'I'll call you,' he said.

'All right.'

When he called, though, I couldn't see him because I'd gotten a grant to study in Paris for the rest of the summer. I gave him my address at the pension and told him to take care. Three weeks later, Madame Laverre whispered that I had a visitor waiting in the courtyard. There was David, unshaven, an enormous bouquet of flowers in his shaking hands. I was glad to see him.

He said that he'd asked his wife for a separation and that she'd agreed. I didn't want to talk about it. We found a couple of jars for the flowers and walked along the river. He took a room down the hall and stayed for ten days. I'd practice or go to class during the day, and he'd visit museums and read. At night, we'd eat in the cafe and then have sex in his room. I slept in my own room. We had a nice time, and when he was leaving I said I'd call him in September.

I remember how he smiled then. 'You've never called me.'

'I will.'

'Okay, I'll be in my own place by then, and I'll list the new number with Information right away so you can get it.' He was swinging my hand back and forth. 'Coming to Paris was the best thing I could have done. I love you, you know.'

'I'm glad you came,' I said. 'Don't miss your plane.' And he stroked my hair and cried for a minute before he left.

When I got back I did call him, and we spent most of our evenings together. For a year he asked me to marry him and I ignored him. I thought I'd be dead by the time I was twenty-five, I couldn't see getting married. One morning David started banging his fists on my kitchen table and said, 'You are killing me. All I want is to love you, and you won't let me.'

I got dressed and left him sitting in the kitchen. I bought a white silk shirt to go with my white jeans and called him from Macy's to meet me for a blood test. Ten years later, we had two girls, quiet, like me, but friendly. David is a good person, and I knew that women would be lining up six-deep, with casseroles, the minute I left him.

I walked into the kitchen, still thinking about the nice, normal woman who would become David's next wife, and watched him carry a plate of chicken to the grill, balancing tongs and a fork and a bottle of barbecue sauce. He had sent the girls to get out of their wet suits, and while I chopped red peppers and hulled strawberries I kept my head down, wondering if it'd be better to leave a note. He watched me putter, and after he had washed and dried his hands carefully, he rested them on my shoulders for just a second. Then he went into the living room and put on Vivaldi while I set the table.

After dinner, we let the girls bike around the neighborhood and we washed the dishes together. David went to work on an article, and I sat in the bedroom, in the bent willow rocking chair that we bought when I was pregnant with Rose, and waited for the phone to ring.

'Hi, it's Hank DiMartino.' We were always very careful, in case a spouse picked up simultaneously.

'Hi. David's in his study.' The study didn't have a phone, so that he wouldn't be disturbed. 'How'd the tennis game go?'

'Not bad, considering that I was out of my mind. You looked so beautiful today, and you've made me so happy. You did mean it? You'll leave?'

'Yes.'

'I can't believe that I'm going to wake up every morning for the rest of my life and look at your face on the pillow next to mine. I want to marry you, as soon as we can.'

I was picking dead leaves off the fig tree in our bedroom. 'I'll be yours until the stars fall from the sky, Henry. I don't have any thoughts about marriage.' I also had some doubts about sleeping in the same bed. David was used to my slipping onto the floor during the night.

'I want us to belong to each other.'

'That doesn't make any sense. You belonged to Marie, and you're ready to divorce her. I belonged to David, and before that, he belonged to Nina. It's really silly, the whole idea.'

'Gae, honey, I want to be with you and I want it to be forever.'

'I want to be with you too, Henry.' And I did.

David came into the bedroom. He mouthed, 'For me?' and I

shook my head. He stood in the middle of the bedroom, looking at me, before he went back to his study.

'I have to go. David's wandering around. I'll drive by the construction site tomorrow. Columbine Lane, right?'

'Right. That'll be great. I love you, you.'

'I know. See you tomorrow.'

David came to bed a little earlier than usual, and he laid his hand on my breast. After a while, he put his hand on my thigh, his sign, and I shifted my legs to let him enter me. It wasn't as nice as cooking to the Vivaldi, but it was really all right. I awoke on the floor. David had put a quilt over me and tucked his sweater under my head.

I put the sweater on and practiced for about three hours after the girls went out to play and David went downtown to see patients. This was one of my favorite times, and I didn't want to cut it short. I practiced some performance pieces I was having trouble with and threw in a little jazz at the end. My fingers were getting stiffer as I got older. I showered and went to meet Henry, wearing a shapeless blue shift that he hated. I drove over to Columbine Lane, where he was building a house.

His crew was there, taking a coffee break. Most of the guys knew me, or my car, by sight. Henry and I counted on the fact that most people, especially men, don't like to get into other people's business. I came and went freely, undisguised. Usually, I'd just pull over onto the ridge near his trailer and sit in the car waiting. Henry would come out after a few minutes and scrunch down by the window to talk to me about our schedules and try to work his plans around mine. Once in a while, if we had a chunk of time during the day, we'd go to a hotel. I would have gone to a motel, or even to the park, but Henry felt we deserved better. I didn't think it had much to do with what we deserved.

He saw me right away and hopped down from the unfinished patio. I could watch him run toward me and never tire of the sight, his right leg slightly stiff at the knee from an old baseball injury, his muscles flowing beneath his clothes. I wanted that ease, that perfect unconsciousness, to transform me so that I would never again find myself in the middle of traffic, paralyzed by the risk and complexity of the next step.

Once, the summer before, I'd been watching him from the clubhouse as he did his laps. He felt my eyes on him and he got out of the water, face turned to me, and came up the stairs to the deck, dripping water through the building. No one else was around.

'I can't not come to you,' he said. 'I just don't have any choice about it.' And he gathered up my hair into little bunches and pressed them against his wet face, like flowers. After Rose and Violet, I loved that kind of love the most.

It wasn't his wanting me that got to me. That was nice, but not so rare in my life. Men see something in me, or something missing, that they like. It's that he didn't fight the feeling; a lot of times men want you and then they get mad about wanting you, whether they have you or not. He had never been angry with me, or disappointed, or blamed me for what I couldn't do. And more than that, it was that he was so beautiful and that beauty belonged to me.

When he got to my car, I swung the door open and he knelt in front of me. I put my hand on his arm, breaking our public display rules, which now seemed irrelevant. He smiled down at my hand, a sunny, white smile that was like nothing I'd ever seen in my mirror.

'Ready to take the plunge?' he asked.

'I'm ready to tell David, after the girls go to camp. I can move out then, or he'll move out, and we can get started.'

'Started? Galen, we're a lot further along than "getting started." I really do want to marry you, and I want us to try and get custody of the boys.'

Shit, I thought. First of all, Marie does a perfectly fine job with the boys, it's not like they need to be rescued, and second of all, I could just see myself spending the next five years of my life trying to win over the older one. Making hot dogs and burgers when I've trained my girls to eat French, Thai, Indian, and whatever's put in front of them; having to wear a robe when I take a shower; going to tennis matches every weekend; stepping over GoBots and pieces of GI Joe.

'Henry, let's wait and see. Let's give ourselves a chance to enjoy ourselves, just be together and see how it goes.'

He got very dark and his brows drew down. I didn't know what else to say.

'I don't have much choice, do I? If you don't want to take what I want to give you, I can't make you. But I'm going to keep asking you, and one of these days you're going to say yes. It's meant to be, sweetheart.' He was smiling again; he believed everything he was saying.

Like hell, I thought. I was touched, of course, but I could never answer the same question over and over. And I don't believe that anything's written for us, certainly nothing good. I slept on the floor, I lost track of time, and love and death had always looked pretty much the same to me. David needed to marry someone crazy; Henry had mistaken me for someone *interesting*.

He put his big hand over mine, and I watched a little cloud of plaster dust settle on us.

'I have to go. I'll talk to you tomorrow.' I slammed the car door and drove off, watching him shrink in the rearview mirror.

My arms and legs were cold, driving home through the woods, and I thought about what I was going home to. I pulled the car off the road, picturing Henry and his boys, and his kids with my kids, and Marie bitching about money, and Henry sitting in a studio apartment with mismatched plates, waiting for me to make his divorce meaningful, valuable, decent. Waiting for me to make his life beautiful. And when I'd finally get up to leave, he'd watch me go, letting me know that I was supposed to stay with him, that I was hurting him.

I got home about ten of twelve and called David between appointments. He picked up on the first ring.

'Dr Silverstein here.'

'Ms Nichols here.'

He sounded surprised and he laughed. I didn't call him often, since he was calling home once or twice a day at this point. I used to hate that when we were first married, and he finally stopped, but that year he had started again and I didn't say anything about it. He was right to be afraid.

'I could call Mrs Stevenson for the girls and we could go to the Siam, just the two of us,' I said.

'Okay, that would be fine. That would be nice.'

I hadn't expected more than that. 'Good. See you at home.'

'Okay. I'm glad you called.'

'See you at home.'

'I love you,' he said.

'I know. See you soon.'

I practiced for another hour, and when the girls came in we took turns playing duets for a while, and then I had to go lie down. I fell asleep for about an hour, and when David woke me up I tried to focus and made the girls stir-fry vegetables and fried dumplings.

Our own dinner was pretty nice, smooth white platters of dark, peppery food, cold beer, and enough room for me to lie back against the cold vinyl seats. David kept reaching forward, touching my temples and my wrists, where my veins are big and blue.

'How do you keep so cool?' he asked. It was an old joke between us.

'No heart,' I said.

He smiled, and I thought, I cannot do this again. I smiled back at him.

I drove down to see Henry the next day, and the guys waved to me. I got out of the car and went over to Henry and kissed him on the mouth, and then on both cheeks, and then at the corner of each perfect eye. He didn't smile.

'You're not going to leave him, are you? You're going to tell me that you can't do it, and I just don't want to hear it. Please, Galen, please, baby. Don't say it.'

'I won't say I can't. That's too easy. I have to say that I'm choosing not to. I'm so sorry.'

He looked me up and down for a minute, and he put his warm face into my neck. I could feel every bone in his face pressing in, but I stood fast.

'I had an offer for the business, a pretty good offer. I could go down to North Carolina, I could go back into business with my dad. Should I take it?'

'Do you want to?' I could see him going, striding loosely down a back road, the sun shining on him, wherever he was.

'No, goddamnit, I don't want to. I want to stay here and marry you and have a child with you, that's what I want. That's all I've wanted for two years, and if I can't have that, I don't even know what to want.'

'I don't know what you should do. Does Marie want to move?'

'Of course. I haven't even told her about the offer. You know Marie, she'll have us packed before the ink's dry on the contract. Getting me away from you will make her very happy.'

We smiled; Marie had been suspicious long before there had been anything between us, and somehow that had left us feeling slightly less guilty.

'I know.' And I thought about having him near and him looking at me like he had a splinter in his heart and Marie looking at me the same way, only without the love.

'Take the offer,' I said. 'Move.'

'Okay,' he said, like a threat.

'Okay,' I said, and I kissed him, just one quick time, and I closed my eyes until he walked away.

Silver Water

My sister's voice was like mountain water in a silver pitcher; the clear blue beauty of it cools you and lifts you up beyond your heat, beyond your body. After we went to see *La Traviata*, when she was fourteen and I was twelve, she elbowed me in the parking lot and said, 'Check this out.' And she opened her mouth unnaturally wide and her voice came out, so crystalline and bright that all the departing opera-goers stood frozen by their cars, unable to take out their keys or open their doors until she had finished, and then they cheered like hell.

That's what I like to remember, and that's the story I told to all of her therapists. I wanted them to know her, to know that who they saw was not all there was to see. That before her constant tinkling of commercials and fast-food jingles there had been Puccini and Mozart and hymns so sweet and mighty you expected Jesus to come down off his cross and clap. That before there was a mountain of Thorazined fat, swaying down the halls in nylon maternity tops and sweatpants, there had been the prettiest girl in Arrandale Elementary School, the belle of Landmark Junior High. Maybe there were other pretty girls, but I didn't see them. To me, Rose, my beautiful blond defender, my guide to Tampax and my mother's moods, was perfect.

She had her first psychotic break when she was fifteen. She

had been coming home moody and tearful, then quietly beaming, then she stopped coming home. She would go out into the woods behind our house and not come in until my mother went after her at dusk, and stepped gently into the briars and saplings and pulled her out, blank-faced, her pale blue sweater covered with crumbled leaves, her white jeans smeared with dirt. After three weeks of this, my mother, who is a musician and widely regarded as eccentric, said to my father, who is a psychiatrist and a kind, sad man, 'She's going off.'

'What is that, your professional opinion?' He picked up the newspaper and put it down again, sighing. 'I'm sorry, I didn't mean to snap at you. I know something's bothering her. Have you talked to her?'

'What's there to say? David, she's going crazy. She doesn't need a heart-to-heart talk with Mom, she needs a hospital.'

They went back and forth, and my father sat down with Rose for a few hours, and she sat there licking the hairs on her forearm, first one way, then the other. My mother stood in the hallway, dry-eyed and pale, watching the two of them. She had already packed, and when three of my father's friends dropped by to offer free consultations and recommendations, my mother and Rose's suitcase were already in the car. My mother hugged me and told me that they would be back that night, but not with Rose. She also said, divining my worst fear, 'It won't happen to you, honey. Some people go crazy and some people never do. You never will.' She smiled and stroked my hair. 'Not even when you want to.'

Rose was in hospitals, great and small, for the next ten years. She had lots of terrible therapists and a few good ones. One place had no pictures on the walls, no windows, and the patients all wore slippers with the hospital crest on them. My mother didn't even bother to go to Admissions. She turned Rose around and the two of them marched out, my father walking behind them, apologizing to his colleagues. My mother ignored the psychiatrists, the social workers, and the nurses, and played Handel and Bessie Smith for the patients on whatever was available. At some places, she had a Steinway donated by a grateful, or optimistic, family; at others, she banged out 'Gimme a Pigfoot and a Bottle of Beer' on an old, scarred box that hadn't been tuned since there'd been English-speaking physicians on the grounds. My father talked in serious, appreciative tones to the administrators and unit chiefs and tried to be friendly with whoever was managing Rose's case. We all hated the family therapists.

The worst family therapist we ever had sat in a pale green room with us, visibly taking stock of my mother's ethereal beauty and her faded blue T-shirt and girl-sized jeans, my father's rumpled suit and stained tie, and my own unreadable seventeen-year-old fashion statement. Rose was beyond fashion that year, in one of her dancing teddybear smocks and extra-extra-large Celtics sweatpants. Mr Walker read Rose's file in front of us and then watched in alarm as Rose began crooning, beautifully, and slowly massaging her breasts. My mother and I laughed, and even my father started to smile. This was Rose's usual opening salvo for new therapists.

Mr Walker said, 'I wonder why it is that everyone is so entertained by Rose behaving inappropriately.'

Rose burped, and then we all laughed. This was the seventh family therapist we had seen, and none of them had lasted very long. Mr Walker, unfortunately, was determined to do right by us.

'What do you think of Rose's behavior, Violet?' They did this sometimes. In their manual it must say, If you think the parents are too weird, try talking to the sister.

'I don't know. Maybe she's trying to get you to stop talking about her in the third person.'

'Nicely put,' my mother said.

'Indeed,' my father said.

'Fuckin' A,' Rose said.

'Well, this is something that the whole family agrees upon,' Mr Walker said, trying to act as if he understood or even liked us.

'That was not a successful intervention, Ferret Face.' Rose tended to function better when she was angry. He did look like a blond ferret, and we all laughed again. Even my father, who tried to give these people a chance, out of some sense of collegiality, had given it up.

After fourteen minutes, Mr Walker decided that our time was up and walked out, leaving us grinning at each other. Rose was still nuts, but at least we'd all had a little fun.

The day we met our best family therapist started out almost as badly. We scared off a resident and then scared off her supervisor, who sent us Dr Thorne. Three hundred pounds of Texas chili, cornbread, and Lone Star beer, finished off with big black cowboy boots and a small string tie around the area of his neck.

'O frabjous day, it's Big Nut.' Rose was in heaven and stopped massaging her breasts immediately.

'Hey, Little Nut.' You have to understand how big a man would have to be to call my sister 'little.' He christened us all, right away. 'And it's the good Doctor Nut, and Madame Hickory Nut, 'cause they are the hardest damn nuts to crack, and over here in the overalls and not much else is No One's Nut' – a name that summed up both my sanity and my loneliness. We all relaxed.

Dr Thorne was good for us. Rose moved into a halfway house

whose director loved Big Nut so much that she kept Rose even when Rose went through a period of having sex with everyone who passed her door. She was in a fever for a while, trying to still the voices by fucking her brains out.

Big Nut said, 'Darlin', I can't. I cannot make love to every beautiful woman I meet, and furthermore, I can't do that and be your therapist too. It's a great shame, but I think you might be able to find a really nice guy, someone who treats you just as sweet and kind as I would if I were lucky enough to be your beau. I don't want you to settle for less.' And she stopped propositioning the crack addicts and the alcoholics and the guys at the shelter. We loved Dr Thorne.

My father went back to seeing rich neurotics and helped out one day a week at Dr Thorne's Walk-In Clinic. My mother finished a recording of Mozart concerti and played at fund-raisers for Rose's halfway house. I went back to college and found a wonderful linebacker from Texas to sleep with. In the dark, I would make him call me 'darlin'.' Rose took her meds, lost about fifty pounds, and began singing at the A.M.E. Zion Church, down the street from the halfway house.

At first they didn't know what do to with this big blond lady, dressed funny and hovering wistfully in the doorway during their rehearsals, but she gave them a few bars of 'Precious Lord' and the choir director felt God's hand and saw that with the help of His sweet child Rose, the Prospect Street Choir was going all the way to the Gospel Olympics.

Amidst a sea of beige, umber, cinnamon, and espresso faces, there was Rose, bigger, blonder, and pinker than any two white women could be. And Rose and the choir's contralto, Addie Robicheaux, laid out their gold and silver voices and wove them together in strands as fine as silk, as strong as steel. And we wept as Rose and Addie, in their billowing garnet robes, swayed together, clasping hands until the last perfect note floated up to God, and then they smiled down at us.

Rose would still go off from time to time and the voices would tell her to do bad things, but Dr Thorne or Addie or my mother could usually bring her back. After five good years, Big Nut died. Stuffing his face with a chili dog, sitting in his un-air-conditioned office in the middle of July, he had one big, Texas-sized aneurysm and died.

Rose held on tight for seven days; she took her meds, went to choir practice, and rearranged her room about a hundred times. His funeral was like a Lourdes for the mentally ill. If you were psychotic, borderline, bad-off neurotic, or just very hard to get along with, you were there. People shaking so bad from years of heavy meds that they fell out of the pews. People holding hands, crying, moaning, talking to themselves. The crazy people and the not-so-crazy people were all huddled together, like puppies at the pound.

Rose stopped taking her meds, and the halfway house wouldn't keep her after she pitched another patient down the stairs. My father called the insurance company and found out that Rose's new, improved psychiatric coverage wouldn't begin for forty-five days. I put all of her stuff in a garbage bag, and we walked out of the halfway house, Rose winking at the poor drooling boy on the couch.

'This is going to be difficult – not all bad, but difficult – for the whole family, and I thought we should discuss everybody's expectations. I know I have some concerns.' My father had convened a family meeting as soon as Rose finished putting each one of her thirty stuffed bears in its own special place.

'No meds,' Rose said, her eyes lowered, her stubby fingers,

those fingers that had braided my hair and painted tulips on my cheeks, pulling hard on the hem of her dirty smock.

My father looked in despair at my mother.

'Rosie, do you want to drive the new car?' my mother asked.

Rose's face lit up. 'I'd love to drive that car. I'd drive to California, I'd go see the bears at the San Diego Zoo. I would take you, Violet, but you always hated the zoo. Remember how she cried at the Bronx Zoo when she found out that the animals didn't get to go home at closing?' Rose put her damp hand on mine and squeezed it sympathetically. 'Poor Vi.'

'If you take your medication, after a while you'll be able to drive the car. That's the deal. Meds, car.' My mother sounded accommodating but unenthusiastic, careful not to heat up Rose's paranoia.

'You got yourself a deal, darlin'.'

I was living about an hour away then, teaching English during the day, writing poetry at night. I went home every few days for dinner. I called every night.

My father said, quietly, 'It's very hard. We're doing all right, I think. Rose has been walking in the mornings with your mother, and she watches a lot of TV. She won't go to the day hospital, and she won't go back to the choir. Her friend Mrs Robicheaux came by a couple of times. What a sweet woman. Rose wouldn't even talk to her. She just sat there, staring at the wall and humming. We're not doing all that well, actually, but I guess we're getting by. I'm sorry, sweetheart, I don't mean to depress you.'

My mother said, emphatically, 'We're doing fine. We've got our routine and we stick to it and we're fine. You don't need to come home so often, you know. Wait 'til Sunday, just come for the day. Lead your life, Vi. She's leading hers.'

I stayed away all week, afraid to pick up my phone, grateful to my mother for her harsh calm and her reticence, the qualities that had enraged me throughout my childhood.

I came on Sunday, in the early afternoon, to help my father garden, something we had always enjoyed together. We weeded and staked tomatoes and killed aphids while my mother and Rose were down at the lake. I didn't even go into the house until four, when I needed a glass of water.

Someone had broken the piano bench into five neatly stacked pieces and placed them where the piano bench usually was.

'We were having such a nice time, I couldn't bear to bring it up,' my father said, standing in the doorway, carefully keeping his gardening boots out of the kitchen.

'What did Mommy say?'

'She said, "Better the bench than the piano." And your sister lay down on the floor and just wept. Then your mother took her down to the lake. This can't go on, Vi. We have twenty-seven days left, your mother gets no sleep because Rose doesn't sleep, and if I could just pay twenty-seven thousand dollars to keep her in the hospital until the insurance takes over, I'd do it.'

'All right. Do it. Pay the money and take her back to Hartley-Rees. It was the prettiest place, and she liked the art therapy there.'

'I would if I could. The policy states that she must be symptom-free for at least forty-five days before her coverage begins. Symptom-free means no hospitalization.'

'Jesus, Daddy, how could you get that kind of policy? She hasn't been symptom-free for forty-five minutes.'

'It's the only one I could get for long-term psychiatric.' He put his hand over his mouth, to block whatever he was about to say, and went back out to the garden. I couldn't see if he was crying.

He stayed outside and I stayed inside until Rose and my mother came home from the lake. Rose's soggy sweatpants were rolled up to her knees, and she had a bucketful of shells and seaweed, which my mother persuaded her to leave on the back porch. My mother kissed me lightly and told Rose to go up to her room and change out of her wet pants.

Rose's eyes grew very wide. 'Never. I will never . . .' She knelt down and began banging her head on the kitchen floor with rhythmic intensity, throwing all her weight behind each attack. My mother put her arms around Rose's waist and tried to hold her back. Rose shook her off, not even looking around to see what was slowing her down. My mother lay up against the refrigerator.

'Violet, please . . .'

I threw myself onto the kitchen floor, becoming the spot that Rose was smacking her head against. She stopped a fraction of an inch short of my stomach.

'Oh, Vi, Mommy, I'm sorry. I'm sorry, don't hate me.' She staggered to her feet and ran wailing to her room.

My mother got up and washed her face brusquely, rubbing it dry with a dishcloth. My father heard the wailing and came running in, slipping his long bare feet out of his rubber boots.

'Galen, Galen, let me see.' He held her head and looked closely for bruises on her pale, small face. 'What happened?' My mother looked at me. 'Violet, what happened? Where's Rose?'

'Rose got upset, and when she went running upstairs she pushed Mommy out of the way.' I've only told three lies in my life, and that was my second.

'She must feel terrible, pushing you, of all people. It would have to be you, but I know she didn't want it to be.' He made my mother a cup of tea, and all the love he had for her, despite her silent rages and her vague stares, came pouring through the teapot, warming her cup, filling her small, long-fingered hands. She rested her head against his hip, and I looked away.

'Let's make dinner, then I'll call her. Or you call her, David, maybe she'd rather see your face first.'

Dinner was filled with all of our starts and stops and Rose's desperate efforts to control herself. She could barely eat and hummed the McDonald's theme song over and over again, pausing only to spill her juice down the front of her smock and begin weeping. My father looked at my mother and handed Rose his napkin. She dabbed at herself listlessly, but the tears stopped.

'I want to go to bed. I want to go to bed and be in my head. I want to go to bed and be in my bed and in my head and just wear red. For red is the color that my baby wore and once more, it's true, yes, it is, it's true. Please don't wear red tonight, oh, oh, please don't wear red tonight, for red is the color—'

'Okay, okay, Rose. It's okay. I'll go upstairs with you and you can get ready for bed. Then Mommy will come up and say good night too. It's okay, Rose.' My father reached out his hand and Rose grasped it, and they walked out of the dining room together, his long arm around her middle.

My mother sat at the table for a moment, her face in her hands, and then she began clearing the plates. We cleared without talking, my mother humming Schubert's 'Schlummerlied,' a lullaby about the woods and the river calling to the child to go to sleep. She sang it to us every night when we were small.

My father came into the kitchen and signaled to my mother. They went upstairs and came back down together a few minutes later.

'She's asleep,' they said, and we went to sit on the porch and listen to the crickets. I don't remember the rest of the evening, but I remember it as quietly sad, and I remember the rare sight of my parents holding hands, sitting on the picnic table, watching the sunset.

I woke up at three o'clock in the morning, feeling the cool night air through my sheet. I went down the hall for a blanket and looked into Rose's room, for no reason. She wasn't there. I put on my jeans and a sweater and went downstairs. I could feel her absence. I went outside and saw her wide, draggy footprints darkening the wet grass into the woods.

'Rosie,' I called, too softly, not wanting to wake my parents, not wanting to startle Rose. 'Rosie, it's me. Are you here? Are you all right?'

I almost fell over her. Huge and white in the moonlight, her flowered smock bleached in the light and shadow, her sweatpants now completely wet. Her head was flung back, her white, white neck exposed like a lost Greek column.

'Rosie, Rosie—' Her breathing was very slow, and her lips were not as pink as they usually were. Her eyelids fluttered.

'Closing time,' she whispered. I believe that's what she said.

I sat with her, uncovering the bottle of Seconal by her hand, and watched the stars fade.

When the stars were invisible and the sun was warming the air, I went back to the house. My mother was standing on the porch, wrapped in a blanket, watching me. Every step I took overwhelmed me; I could picture my mother slapping me, shooting me for letting her favorite die.

'Warrior queens,' she said, wrapping her thin strong arms around me. 'I raised warrior queens.' She kissed me fiercely and went into the woods by herself.

Later in the morning she woke my father, who could not go into the woods, and still later she called the police and the funeral parlor. She hung up the phone, lay down, and didn't get back out of bed until the day of the funeral. My father fed us both and called the people who needed to be called and picked out Rose's coffin by himself.

My mother played the piano and Addie sang her pure gold notes and I closed my eyes and saw my sister, fourteen years old, lion's mane thrown back and eyes tightly closed against the glare of the parking lot lights. That sweet sound held us tight, flowing around us, eddying through our hearts, rising, still rising.

Henry and Marie

Faultlines
Only You

Faultlines

Henry DiMartino said buying a lottery ticket gave you permission to dream of a better life. His wife, Marie, bought a lottery ticket every Friday morning on her way to work at the library. Henry never bought one. In order to dream of a new life, Henry contemplated having an affair with Mary Nordstrom, the lawyer for his construction company. Henry had had an affair five years ago, with a woman he wanted to marry, who didn't want to marry him. He had stood in his sons' bedrooms, looked at their beloved faces, and thought, 'I can do this. I can leave you.' It took two years for him to stop being ashamed that the only reason his children had a father to play ball with every night and to help them with their homework was that the woman he loved didn't love him back. When he realized he wouldn't die of heartbreak, but would live with some of it forever, he promised himself that the next time, if there was a next time, he wouldn't fall in love.

After five or six lunches, quick Chinese food across the street and pizzas in the office, Henry invited Mary and Nathan to dinner for the second Saturday in October. Marie started cooking Friday afternoon. Henry had designed their house, and the kitchen was the size of two full rooms, and the countertops were marble; it was his tribute to Marie's magnificent cooking. She made baby artichokes and gnocchi with basil and cream and veal alia marsala and a radicchio and orange salad. She made a peach tart with a hazelnut crust. Henry spent two hours choosing wines he thought Mary would like. He came upstairs, his arms full of wine bottles.

Marie waved to him silently as he put the wines in the dining room, and he waved back, excited and relieved. Marie was being so good about this, the whole evening looked different. They could all become friends, no harm would be done. He would go on flirting harmlessly with Mary, and he and Marie would go to St Kitts in November and make love in a big room overlooking the warm blue water.

Marie tried to make her voice cheerful as she called out to Henry, 'So, what's she like?' Marie knew that she was a terribly and unfashionably jealous woman, and she also knew, without admitting it, that her jealousy made Henry curl up inside himself, like a mollusk avoiding a pin. She could never decide, could never let herself know, if it was her jealousy that made her suspect he was having an affair when they lived in Connecticut, or if he really was. She didn't confront him because they moved away, and really because she could almost hear Henry admitting to the affair, could almost see him turning away from her, without apology. At night, as they got ready for bed, Marie would scowl, thinking that it was so unfair that they had both started out as attractive, athletic teenagers but Henry had matured into a startlingly handsome, broad-chested man with a permanent tan, white teeth, and black curly hair, made more beautiful by a few silver strands. Marie looked like a fairly trim, better-dressed version of her late mother. Henry didn't love her less for that, she knew. But his eyes didn't linger upon her when she undressed, and she knew that too, and he knew it and they both felt ashamed, and beyond that, obscurely resentful. Henry encouraged Marie to work out with him, but she always made it sound like a vain and childish thing for a grown-up to do. Henry did two hundred sit-ups and one hundred push-ups six days a week. Four days a week, he rode his exercycle for forty-five minutes.

Henry had no wish to tell Marie what Mary was like, but he couldn't resist talking about her, sliding his tongue over her name the way he dreamt of sliding it over the pulsing vein above her collarbone. Henry knew, having been married to Marie for twenty years, that the moment he described Mary the day would be ruined. And if he said nothing, the evening would be ruined, perhaps more dramatically, when Marie laid eyes on Mary. As Henry played with the wine bottles, he assessed his choices: ruin the day now and hope that by dinnertime Marie would have pulled herself together, or enjoy the rest of the afternoon, ignore the hot hole of his ulcer, and watch the evening collapse as Marie was helplessly rude to Mary and in a state of relentless hysteria until four in the morning. Henry poured himself a small glass of port and decided that a carefully crafted description of Mary would be better than just surprising Marie when Mary walked through the door. He went into the kitchen.

Marie braced herself for Henry's answer. Not a blonde, please.

'She's tall, kind of skinny, very short hair. She's smart, she did a great job with the contracts for that development in Laurel Springs. Her husband seems like a nice guy, he came by the office once. He's a writer, he writes about his family, Mary said, about growing up Jewish in North Carolina, which must have been a trip.' Henry leaned against the counter, willing himself to look into Marie's eyes and smile, feeling the warmth of the port and of having said her name.

He could have said, 'She is a pale, pale blonde, just like the other one. But Gae was soft and dreamy and made me want to wrap her up and carry her off to a better world. This one is cool and tough and loves baseball and runs twenty miles a week. When the light shines on that cap of blond hair and her pale blue eyes lie right on me like I am the only person in the room, I stop breathing because the tension in my chest is so great. And if I don't "run into her," I "drop by," and if that doesn't work I call and beg her to share a pizza with me, and as we sit there and drink beer from the same bottle I think about those long white legs wrapped around me, and she grins like she knows what I'm thinking and she doesn't mind. Also, something else you don't want to hear because you will feel about this exactly the way I do, Nathan isn't her husband. They've been living together for years, but you and I know that's not the same. And even though she says, other people say, it makes no difference, I hug that fact. She's not really his. And even though I don't love her, don't want to grow old together, if I don't have her I will never draw an easy breath again. That's what you really wanted to know. A blonde so pale she doesn't have to shave her legs.'

Mary was Marie's nightmare, and Marie knew it and so did Henry. And so, in a way, did Mary, although she didn't want to know it and felt both flattered and guilty. Nathan would know it after the dinner party, since he was a good observer most of the time and not unused to men being attracted to Mary. Nathan thought Mary was very good-looking, beautiful in her way, but he loved her for her brains and her humor and her easy compe- tence. Henry thought she was flawlessly beautiful and would have traded away her humor and her competence for one night beside her When Mary looked at Henry, the longing in his eyes moved her terribly, moved her away from Nathan, even though she knew that what Henry was longing for would be gone in another ten years.

Marie tried not to start screaming when she heard what Henry said, and what he didn't say. If he didn't mention hair color, the woman was obviously a blonde. She went to the stove and cooked, with skill and hatred. She would give that bitch and her castrato husband a meal they'd both remember; a peach tart that would melt on her lying tongue, gnocchi that would rest lightly in his gutless stomach, may they choke on it all and never find water.

Henry announced that he was going to take a look at the garden. Before he went outside, he slipped into the bedroom to think about what to wear for Mary. He knew he looked good in his suits, something Nathan, the writer, probably never wore. He couldn't very well wear his eight-hundred-dollar Italian suit for a casual dinner, Marie would tear it off his back. He wanted to look relaxed but not like some bricklayer, some greaseball tidied up for a special occasion. Henry wanted to lay out his clothes and fuss over them, but Marie would be listening for him to go out and garden. Mentally, he took out his black flannel slacks, a white shirt with a thin red stripe, and a red cashmere cardigan that Marie had bought for his fortieth birthday. He loved that sweater; the shape reminded him of his father and grandfather in the back of his grandfather's grocery store; the soft, monied material reminded him of how far he had come from sawdust and over-ripe vegetables.

He checked to see if his black lizard belt was in the drawer and looked for his black socks with the small gray pattern. Henry hurried out to rake leaves and to dream of Mary unbuttoning his shirt, her fingers pulling at his belt buckle. He enjoyed talking to her and admired her quick wit, but he never daydreamed of their conversations. He thought only of her square, dimpled chin, her powerful legs, her small white breasts and pointy nipples.

While she pulverized basil and sautéed pignoli, Marie also thought about what to wear. She couldn't wear white because she was bound to spatter something on it, and she wouldn't wear pants because as far as she was concerned she looked like a cow from the rear. She would not look bad in front of this woman. She would wear the heavy gold necklace Henry bought her in Florence for their twentieth anniversary, and she would add the diamond and gold earrings they picked out together in Bermuda. Let her look. She decided to wear a black and red blouse and a black pleated skirt. Marie always wore heels, even at home.

Mary was also thinking about what to wear, but she was able to talk about it with Nathan, who was bemused but willing.

'I don't know how formal they are. At work Henry's always in a suit, but I don't know.' While she was talking, Mary was fingering a pale blue silk dress with short sleeves and no back. It showed off all her best features and created the illusion of a bust. She would have preferred darker eyelashes and a smaller ass, but she had been using mascara since she was twelve, and since the men in her life had always liked her ass, she had come to like it too. It was ridiculous to wear the silk dress; Nathan would think she was crazy. She took out high-waisted gray gabardine pants and a white silk blouse, and she put on dangling silver earrings that Nathan had given her a few birthdays ago, and a wide gray suede belt to emphasize her small waist.

'You look great,' Nathan said, smiling. 'Of course, if they're both in formal evening wear, we'll be a little embarrassed.'

Mary smiled back; she loved Nathan and his fine, searching mind and his sweet humor and his endless patience. She could tell that Henry was smart enough but not brilliant, that he had a highly conventional sense of humor and an ugly, arrogant streak. She had told Nathan all those things about her new 'office friend,' but she didn't say:

'He is so hot for me he's smoking, and when he comes into my office, Alice, who wouldn't bring coffee to the Pope, falls all over herself to bring him coffee just the way he likes it. He is the sexiest thing I've ever seen, and I guess – I know – that I've just got to have him. Just once, Nathan, I swear, and then I'll be right back. You won't even notice I'm gone.'

She smiled at Nathan and buffed her nails while he put on the gray corduroy pants and the black turtleneck he wore from now until April, at which time he switched to khakis, sandals, and a white cotton shirt.

Nathan and Mary found the house easily and congratulated each other, since neither of them had a sense of direction. Mary reached into the backseat for the house gift, a pot of white mums resting prettily in a black straw basket. She wanted to please Marie, and she wanted to show Henry what a nice person she was, and beyond that, she would never dream of going to a dinner party without a gift. And if Marie wasn't pleased or wasn't smart enough to pretend to be pleased, well, that would be her mistake.

There was enough bustle over the introductions and admiring of the house and exclaiming over the mums that the first eight minutes went smoothly and they all revised their opinions about how the evening would go. It was only when they all sat down in the living room and looked at each other that the mood began to swing downward.

'What lovely earrings,' Mary said to Marie, and Marie touched her ears, proudly.

'Henry got them for me in Bermuda. I just love them.'

Everyone smiled at Henry, and the two women talked about jewelry, which they both liked, although their tastes were rather different, and they talked about Italian leathers, about which they agreed, and then the four of them talked about Italy and the air pollution in Rome and about travel in general. Nathan told a few funny, self-deprecating stories about his backpacking days in Europe, when he didn't speak any foreign languages, and Marie smiled at him. While everyone beamed messages at him, Nathan tried to keep track of Marie's emphatic enthusiasm and Mary's affectionate appreciation and Henry's watchful smile.

All through dinner, Marie talked to Nathan and to Mary, and Mary focused on Marie, and the only one who talked to Henry was Nathan.

Red wine gave Mary migraines, and Marie never drank wine if she could help it, and the two men finished a bottle and a half of St Amour, which Nathan praised, making Henry like him a little more. Henry missed having someone he could talk to about wine, someone to go in on a case with him. When Nathan said he fished, Henry found himself thinking that this was really quite a decent guy, not exactly a ball of fire, but a good guy and much more down-to-earth than he expected a writer to be. Henry thought maybe they could go out fishing together some Sunday morning.

Nathan thought Henry was a salt-of-the-earth type and certainly a very decent guy, even if he wasn't the brightest or most interesting person around. And that St Amour was superb. Nathan hadn't had wine like that since he moved back from New York ten years ago. When Henry said he also liked to fish, Nathan wondered how it would be to fish with a companion.

The dinner conversation swirled around work briefly, which bored everyone, around Nathan's writing, which embarrassed him, around the DiMartino children, at Marie's insistence, and then around great Italian red wines, at which point both women raised their eyebrows and cleared the table, bringing them all back to a safe and mildly diverting conversation about kitchen appliances.

'Henry bought me a pasta machine last Mother's Day. I like it.'

'Really? Can you use it for gnocchi?' Nathan liked talking about kitchen appliances; Mary had lived on yogurt and frozen dinners until she met Nathan.

'Yes, I just love it. It even comes with a ravioli press, and you hardly have to clean it. Everything goes into the dishwasher.'

'You're kidding. I'll help you with the coffee and you can show me, before I rush out and buy one in an impulsive fit brought on by your marvelous cooking. Really, Marie, just fabulous.'

Marie, charmed by Nathan's Southern manners and amazed to find a man who cooks, lets him lead her into the kitchen, almost forgetting that Mary and Henry will now be alone together.

As the kitchen door swings shut, Henry calls out, 'All right, you guys get dessert and I'll show Mary the garden.'

Mary smiles politely, not at all the impish, promising grin she has given Henry at their lunches; Marie is just too nice, and they have these great kids who now have names, Claude and Giulio, and even though Henry's still incredibly handsome, that doesn't mean she has to sleep with him. They can just be good friends and flirt a little bit, and since Nathan seems to like Henry and hasn't had a male friend for ages, the four of them will have dinner from time to time.

Mary follows Henry through the French doors onto the patio to look at the brilliant zinnias and amber mums and the soft, tenacious clematis, which has woven itself along the side of the house. He flicks on the patio lights and hands her a match for the squat citronella candles. As she is lighting them, Henry tells Mary how much he enjoys Nathan's storytelling. Mary praises Marie's cooking and says that it will be hard to keep up with her when Henry and Marie come to their house for dinner.

As they turn to go back to the house, one thin black heel catches on the edge of a flagstone, and Mary stumbles. He catches her and his right arm goes around her waist and the other behind her neck, and she lets her head fall back into the damp crook of his arm.

The flowers and the thick lemony air hum in their ears, drowning out the hiss of the espresso machine and the faint clinking of small cups into saucers.

A perfect kiss, like a perfect beach, or a perfect diamond, is not so common in our lives that it can be ignored. As Marie calls them for dessert, they loosen their arms but discover they cannot part, they are as inseparable as color and light.

Only You

Marie, who is not a very sexual person, who cannot forgive her body or its middle-aged alterations, gets almost all her needs met at The Cut Above, Alvin Myerson's beauty salon. When Alvin opened the shop, some friends told him to change his name to Andre or even to Alain. He couldn't be bothered and put his license, with ALVIN ROY MYERSON printed in large type, in the very front of the salon. 'I traffic in illusion,' he said, 'not in lies.' Marie, who cherishes her sons and loves and resents her husband, likes Alvin. She thinks they have something in common. All of Marie's women friends seem happy enough with their lives, those who aren't come over to Marie's house to make eyes at her handsome husband, who sometimes makes eyes back at them. Marie knows what attracts Henry, and it isn't women like her friends. They are all too maternal, too dark, too much like Marie for her to worry about.

Marie has gone in to discuss, for the third time, whether or not she should dye her gray-and-brown hair. She has been looking forward all day to feeling Alvin's strong hands on her shoulders as he pulls her head from side to side, describing the elegant, youthful woman she will become when he uses just a rinse to restore her natural color. Alvin makes it sound like she is only retrieving something that belongs to her, not doing something foolish and vain. Marie's fear of appearing vain, her conviction that she has nothing to be vain about, keeps her from making more than the slightest effort to look attractive.

'Come on,' Alvin had said last week, bending down to whisper in her ear, 'let yourself be beautiful.'

'Henry's the beautiful one,' she'd said, in a voice so hard and scared that the women sitting near her thought she must hate her husband.

When Joyce, the receptionist, tells Marie that Alvin is home today with the flu, Marie stares straight ahead at the racks of mousse and gel so that she won't cry; it's ridiculous to cry because your hairdresser isn't there, even if he is your good friend and you haven't seen him in a week. Marie drives much too fast to her father's bakery.

'Hiya, sweetheart. No work today?'

'I'm on a break, Pa. Let me have two of the baguettes, please.'

'Sure, two baguettes. The boys like the white bread, you know. Hank likes the raisin pumpernickel. Having company? On a Wednesday?' Marie's mother died two years ago, and her father is in her house more than he is in his own.

'No. I've got a sick friend, so I'm bringing some bread and soup.' Marie carefully skips pronouns. Her father wouldn't approve of her having a male friend, not even a hairdresser.

'Good girl, just like your mother, taking care of everyone. Hello, Mrs Lottman.'

Marie goes home to defrost a container of chicken and rice soup. She calls Alvin and tells him she'll be right over.

'I'm a mess, darling. Really. The place looks like shit and I look worse.'

'Five minutes, Alvin, and don't get out of bed. The super can let me in.' Marie grew up in Brooklyn and believes that all apartment dwellers are watched over by her uncle Sario or the local equivalent.

'Marie, there is no super. This is a condominium, and the manager, whom I have never, ever seen, lives on the far side of Chapel Hill. I'll let you in and then I'll crawl back into bed. God bless you.'

Marie puts a few magazines and a quilt in the car while the soup microwaves, and writes a note for Henry saying she'll meet him at Claude's softball game.

Alvin looks just as bad as he said. His sandy brown hair is plastered to his skull, exposing his receding hairline, usually hidden by his bangs. At the shop he wears loose white wool pants and looks like the captain of the cricket team; lying in his king-sized bed, he looks like a dying John Barrymore, the face ravaged, the bones magnificent. Marie slices bread, reheats the soup, and gives the kitchen counters a quick wipe-down. She bustles, parodying her maternal self so that he won't be embarrassed. She cannot bear to embarrass him, she cannot bear for him to ask her to leave. She carries in the quilt and holds it up for his approval. Marie wants to tuck it in around him, to smooth it down the length of his torso.

'Gorgeous pattern. Rose of Sharon, right? You stole it from some old lady.'

Since Alvin is trying to smile through a cold sweat, Marie pretends to be indignant. She puts the quilt over him, touching his damp cheek by accident.

Alvin takes both her hands in his and bends his head over them. 'You have nice hands, Marie. Can I say something?'

'Sure. Say anything.'

'No more of this coral shit on your nails, okay? You have small, pretty hands and pale olive skin. True reds and clear only, okay? And let's keep the nails oval, not pointed.' He kisses the back of each hand and slides down beneath the quilt, which smells slightly, pleasantly, like the soup. 'You're a doll,' he says, closing his eyes.

Marie pats the quilt down around his shoulders and washes all the dirty dishes she can find and straightens up the living room, which doesn't take long. Alvin is as neat as she is. She doesn't want to leave. She writes her home number by the kitchen phone, wraps the baguettes in foil so they can be reheated, and meets her sons and her husband at the softball game, thinking of Alvin's wet white face, and she cheers whenever Henry cheers.

After he gets over the flu, Alvin won't let Marie pay for her haircuts, or for the coloring she finally agrees to. They are friends, and he is going to make her beautiful. Marie comes home with shining mahogany hair shot with copper highlights, cut short to show off her slender neck, and the women at work say she looks completely different. Henry says he never knew she had such a pretty neck. Alvin even leaves in a few silver strands so that no one will think she dyes her hair. On Wednesdays they have lunch together in the back of the shop, and on Sundays Marie assists Alvin with the brides and the mothers of the brides. She hands him bobby pins and rattail combs and spritzes hairspray so clear and strong you could keep a full head of hair standing straight up if that was the look you were after. Alvin teaches her to do chignons and twists and french braids and to arrange white flowers in the bride's hair. All the women are happy, despite their nervousness, and very, very grateful to Alvin and Marie.

Alvin says, 'The next van is going to say "Alvin and Marie's Wedding on Wheels".'

Marie has fallen in love with beauty. Henry notices that she has stopped going to Mass, but he doesn't say anything; he doesn't mind, since helping Alvin makes her happier than church ever did. She looks better too. Marie has no occasion to go back to Alvin's apartment, and he never comes to her house.

One Sunday morning Marie is running late and Alvin rings the doorbell. Henry, in his black velour robe and bare legs, opens the door. Although Henry has never even wondered about Alvin's appearance, he knows immediately who he is. Alvin thinks Henry looks just the way he thought he would, maybe a little grayer, just as handsome.

'Come on in, she's almost ready,' Henry says. 'Coffee?'

'Coffee'd be great. I've got a bride, a mother of a bride, and two bridesmaids waiting for me in Laurel Springs. Hair *and* make-up. You don't want to get into that without coffee. Intravenous bourbon wouldn't hurt.'

Henry laughs, surprised. He didn't expect Alvin to sound like such a regular guy. 'Come into the kitchen. I was just making a cup.'

'Nice house. Marie said you designed it.'

'Yeah. When we moved down here, we saw this lot. It came out all right. My father's in construction too, we did the work ourselves. No point paying someone else to screw it up.'

'Right. I'd rather do for myself too. I worked in someone else's shop for two years, that was enough for me.'

Henry is suddenly glad to be pouring a cup of coffee for Alvin, a fellow entrepreneur and probably a tough little bastard in his own way.

Marie comes running down the stairs just as Alvin is taking his first sip of coffee.

'Hi.' Alvin doesn't stand up and kiss her cheeks, the way he always does, and Marie is so hurt she wants to slap them both, sitting there like the Goombah Brothers.

'I'm ready,' she says, jamming her hands into the pockets of the fawn suede jacket Alvin told her to buy. 'Let's go, Alvin.'

'Let the guy finish his coffee, honey. You two have a big morning ahead of you. You want another cup?'

Shut your face, she thinks. Alvin takes two more quick swallows and winks at Marie.

'Let's do it. Henry, thanks for the coffee. Good to meet you.'

'Same here.'

They shake hands while Marie finds herself rocked by feelings that make no sense to her.

''Bye, honey,' Henry says, lifting one big hand to wave to her.

''Bye,' Marie mumbles, forcing herself to wave back. 'The boys won't be home until two.'

Henry smiles and reaches for the newspaper as they leave. The house is his.

'I love that jacket on you,' Alvin says as he pulls the car into traffic.

'You do? I'm glad you made me get it, everyone loves it and it is the softest thing. Okay with these pants?'

If Marie had her way, Alvin would lay out her clothes every morning. They don't talk about Henry.

When the invitation to the International Stylists' Convention comes, Alvin hands it to Marie.

'Come on, we're going to Miami. You'll be my tax-deductible guest. Get a little sun, mambo at night. You have to come, I can't do it without you.'

'Do you really mambo?'

'Darling, you are looking at the Latin Ballroom King of Jersey City.'

'All right, tell me what to pack,' says Marie, wondering what Henry will have to say about this, seeing herself dancing with Alvin beneath the Miami moon.

The lobby is a white and silver cavern, with plexiglass stalactites spiraling down to meet the tips of silver-sprayed palm trees bearing sparkling white coconuts. Alvin begins laughing in the lobby and is still grinning when they are shown to their adjoining ice-blue rooms, both accented with raspberry flamingos etched in the mirrors and appliqued onto their queen-size bedspreads.

Alvin and Marie have a ball. Every night Alvin does her hair a little differently and lays out her clothes. The second night, as she is watching in the mirror, Alvin picks up her turquoise silk dress and begins to cha-cha around the room with it, a Latin Fred Astaire.

'Just my color, don't you think?'

Marie can tell that there is something he needs to hear. 'It does go with your eyes, I guess turquoise is your color.'

He blows her a kiss, and they go out to eat stone crabs and drink just one Mai Tai apiece. When Marie is out with Henry, there's always a big fuss over the wine list, and she has to have a glass of something bitter and flat so that he can enjoy the other three glasses. Henry makes fun of her daiquiris and Singapore Slings.

After their triumphant Botticelli bridal arrangement, Alvin orders room service champagne, and as they sit on the tiny terrace, he toasts her.

'To my darling Marie, the most beautiful woman in North Carolina.'

Marie blushes with pleasure and looks down at the hem of her ivory dressing gown.

'What would you like?' Alvin asks, his voice so soft that Marie isn't sure what he's saying.

'I have everything I want. This has been the most wonderful three days of my life, and I owe it all to you.'

Alvin smiles and kisses her hand.

'What would you like?' she asks, knowing that whatever he says, she wants to give it to him. Even if what he wants is sex, she wants to give it to him, never mind Henry, never mind her own well-known lack of interest, which is at this very moment dissolving.

Alvin tells her that what he wants is to dress in her clothes, in her lingerie, that she is so beautiful he wants to feel what it is to be her, to be even closer to her. He looks right into her eyes at first, but he ends by looking down into the courtyard. Marie has no idea what to say, she refuses even to think the hurtful words that Henry would use. Whatever Alvin wants, she wants to give him. She nods her head, hoping that that is enough.

Alvin walks over to the dresser and takes out a chemise and a half slip and a pair of pantyhose. Marie watches the waves beyond the terrace. She doesn't trust her own face.

Alvin goes into the bathroom, wanting not to frighten Marie, wanting not to embarrass either one of them. He knows what he needs to do. Slowly, he sweeps foundation up from his jawline, over his high cheekbones, all the way back to his ears, making sure there's no line on his neck. He takes out a new, sharp-edged pink lipstick, brushes on one coat, presses a Kleenex to his lips, and puts on a second coat to last. He doesn't do much with his small blue eyes, just a little dark brown mascara and the pale rose eye shadow he's taught Marie to use, to make her eyes look brighter. He passes the blush-on brush over his cheeks lightly.

Alvin pauses, looking at himself, closing his eyes a little.

There's so much he can't fix, can't fix right now, anyway. He takes out the wig he bought in Germany five years ago, six hundred dollars' worth of beautiful long blond hair, no frizzy polyester, just some young fraulein's decision to go short one summer, and there it was. He puts on the pantyhose and the half-slip and the matching chemise he had persuaded Marie to buy, hoping that he would be wearing it with her. He wraps his navy silk robe around him and finds the navy silk mules he got while picking out the ivory ones for Marie. He loves Marie's small round feet and spares himself the sight of his own well-shaped but too large feet sliding into the heels. If he wore anything larger than a ten, he would go barefoot rather than be one of those jumbo transvestites, big-knuckled hands made pathetic by pale pink nail polish, thick necks hidden by carefully tossed scarves. Alvin lets himself think only about Marie, about how much she loves him and admires him. He knows she does. You can fake a lot of things, Alvin knows, but you can't fake love. He adjusts the wig quickly, tucking up his light brown bangs, and walks out of the bathroom, away from the mirror, toward Marie.

Marie has turned down the lights and drawn the sheer white curtains closed. In the gold, shining moonlight, Alvin really looks, for one moment, like a pretty woman, strong-shouldered, with a narrow waist and long legs under her rustling silk robe.

'You look beautiful,' Marie says.

'Marie, angel, right now, I feel beautiful. I feel like you. You know I think you're a beautiful, beautiful woman. I want us to be closer. I want to be very close, okay?'

They look at each other directly, breathing uncertainty and tenderness. Alvin kneels down, carefully, hoping he won't tip over in his heels, and he removes Marie's ivory slippers. He takes her by the hand and lays her down on the bedspread. Marie relaxes a little more; when Henry wants to make love, he always pulls the covers back.

Marie cannot stand to watch Alvin's lipsticked mouth moving down her breast, but she responds to its warm shape, pressing and gently tugging. The muscles in her back ripple, and her brown hair flutters like the leaves of a small bronze tree in the wind. As the tips of his long blond hair brush lightly across her chest, Alvin looks up just in time to see Marie's slight, astonished smile, and he pulls her closer, opening her robe.

'Beautiful,' he whispers.

'Beautiful,' she says.

Light Breaks Where No Sun Shines

I didn't expect to find myself in the back of Mr Klein's store, wearing only my undershirt and panties, surrounded by sable.

'Sable is right for you, Suseleh,' Mr Klein said, draping a shawl-collared jacket over me. 'Perfect for your skin and your eyes. A million times a day the boys must tell you. Such skin.'

No one except Mr Klein had ever suggested that my appearance was pleasing. My mother, who was small and English and had decorated half the houses on Long Island with small English cachepots and porcelain dogs, bought me clothes at Lord & Taylor's Pretty Plus and looked the other way when the saleswomen dragged me out in navy blue A-line dresses and plaid jumpers. My eyes, which are almond-shaped and dark, were concealed by grimy pink-framed glasses, and my creamy, rolling flesh was too much a reminder of dead Romanian relatives and attic photographs to be appealing.

I stood on a little velvet footstool and modeled fur coats for Mr Klein. He had suggested I take off my perpetual green corduroys and hooded sweatshirt so we could see how the coats really looked. I agreed, only pretending to hesitate for a minute so I could watch his thin gray face expand and pinken. I felt the warm rushing in my chest that being with him gave me. He also gave me Belgian chocolate, because he felt Hershey's wasn't good enough for me, and he told me that if only God had blessed him and Mrs Klein with a wonderful daughter like me, he would be truly happy, *kayn ahora*. My mother never said I was wonderful. My father, who greatly admired my mother for her size and her accent, was not heard to thank God for giving him the gift of me.

'This one next, Suseleh.' Mr Klein handed me a small mink coat and set a mink beret on my unwashed hair.

'This is my size. Do kids wear mink coats?'

If you had to dress up, mink was the way to go. Much better than my scratchy navy wool, designed to turn chubby Jewish girls into pale Victorian wards. The fur brushed my chin, and without my glasses (Mr Klein and I agreed that it was a shame to hide my lovely eyes and so we put my glasses in his coat pocket during our modeling sessions), I felt glamorously Russian. I couldn't see a thing. He put the beret at a slight angle and stepped back, admiring me in my bare feet and my mink.

'Perfect. This is how a fur coat should look on a girl. Not some little stick girl in rabbit. This is an ensemble.'

I turned around to see what I could of myself from the back: a brown triangle topped by a white blur and another smudge of brown.

I modeled two more coats, a ranch mink, which displeased Mr Klein with its careless stitching, and a fox cape, which made us both smile. Even Mr Klein thought floor-length silver fox was a little much.

As always, he turned his back as I pulled on my jeans and sweatshirt. I sat down on one of the spindly pink velvet chairs, putting my sneakers on as he put away the coats.

We said nothing on the drive home. I ate my chocolate and Mr Klein turned on WQXR, the only time I have ever listened to classical music with pleasure. Mr Klein rounded my driveway, trying to look unconcerned. I think we both always expected that one Monday my parents would come rushing out of the house, appalled and avenging.

I went inside, my shoelaces flapping against the hallway's glazed, uneven brick. Could anything be less inviting than a brick foyer? It pressed into the soles of my feet, and every dropped and delicate object shattered irretrievably.

I don't remember which cleaning lady greeted me. We seemed to alternate between elderly Irish women who looked as though they'd been born to rid the world of lazy people's private filth, and middle-aged Bolivian women quietly stalking dust and fingerprints. I cannot remember the face that came out of the laundry room to acknowledge my existence, but I know someone let me in. I didn't have a house key until I was nineteen.

Every dinner was a short horror; my eating habits were remarked upon, and then my mother would talk about politics and decorating. My father's repertoire was more limited. He talked about his clients, their divorces, and their bank accounts. I would go to my room, pretend to do my homework, and read my novels. In my room, I was the Scarlet Pimpernel. Sometimes I was Sydney Carton, and once in a while I was Tarzan. I went to sleep dreaming of the nineteenth century, my oldest, largest teddy bear held tightly between my legs.

Mr Klein lived two houses down and usually drove up beside me as I was walking to the bus stop. Every time I saw the hood of his huge, unfashionable blue Cadillac slide slowly by me and pause, I would skip ahead and throw my books into the front seat, spared another day of riding the school bus. If you have been an outcast, you understand what the bus ride was like. If you have not been, you will think that I'm exaggerating, even now, and that I should have spent less time being sorry for myself and more time being friendly.

He dropped me off in front of Longview Elementary School as the buses discharged all the kids I had managed to avoid thus far. The mornings Mr Klein failed to appear, I kept a low profile and worried about him until the routine of school settled upon me, vulnerable again only during recess. The first two days of kindergarten had taught me always to carry a book, and as soon I found a place on the hardtop, I had only to set my eyes upon the clean black letters and the soft ivory page and I would be gone, spirited right out of what passed for my real life.

Our first trip to Furs by Klein was incidental, barely a foreshadowing of our afternoons together. Mr Klein had passed me on the way home from school. Having lost two notebooks since school began, I'd missed the bus while searching the halls frantically for my third, bright red canvas designed to be easily seen. I walked home, a couple of miles through the sticky, smoky leaf piles and across endless emerald lawns. No one knew I liked to walk. Mr Klein pulled up ahead of me and signaled shyly. I ran to the car, gratified to tears by a smile that I could see from the road.

'I'll give you a ride home, but I need to stop back at my shop, something I forgot. All right?'

I nodded. It was better than all right; maybe I'd never have to go home. He could have driven me to Mexico, night after night over the Great Plains, and I wouldn't have minded.

Furs by Klein stood on the corner of Shore Drive, its curved, pink-tinted windows and black lacquered French doors the height of suburban elegance. Inside stood headless bodies, six rose velvet torsos, each wearing a fur coat. There were mirrors everywhere I looked, and a few thin-legged, armless chairs. The walls were lined with coats and jackets and capes. Above them, floating on transparent necks, were the hats.

Mr Klein watched me. 'Go ahead,' he said. 'All ladies like hats.' He pulled a few down and walked discreetly into the workroom at the rear. I tried on a black cloche with a dotted veil and then a kelly green fedora with a band of arching brown feathers. Mr Klein emerged from the back, his hands in the pockets of his baggy gray trousers.

'Come, Susie, your mother will be worried about you. Leave the hats, it's all right. Mondays are the day off, the girls will put them back tomorrow.' He turned out the lights and opened the door for me.

'My mother's not home.' I'm really an orphan, adopt me.

'Tcha, I am so absentminded. Mrs Klein tells me your mother is a famous decorator. Of course, she is out – decorating.'

He smiled, just slightly, and I laughed out loud. He was on my side.

Almost every morning now, he gave me a ride to school. And without any negotiating that I could recall, I knew that on Monday afternoons I would miss my bus and he would pick me up as I walked down Baker Hill Road. I would keep him company while he did whatever he did in the back room, and I would try on hats. After a few Mondays, I eyed the coats.

'Of course,' he said. 'When you're grown up, you'll tell your husband, "Get me a sable from Klein's. It's Klein's or nothing."' He waggled a finger sternly, showing me who I would be: a pretty young woman with a rich, indulgent husband. 'Let me help you.'

Mr Klein slipped an ash blond mink jacket over my sweatshirt and admired me aloud. Soon after, he stopped going into the workroom, and soon after that, I began taking off my clothes.

The pleasure on Mr Klein's face made me forget everything I had heard in the low tones of my parents' conversation and all that I had seen in my own mirror. I chose to believe Mr Klein.

At home, to conjure up the feeling of Mr Klein's cool, round fingertips on my shoulders, touching me lightly before the satin lining descended, I listened to classical music. My father made vaguely approving noises from behind the *Wall Street Journal*.

I lay on the floor of the living room, behind the biggest couch, and saw myself playing the piano, adult and beautifully formed. I am wearing a dress I saw on Marilyn Monroe, the sheerest clinging net, with sparkling stones coming up over the tips of my breasts and down between my legs. I am moving slowly across the stage, the wide hem of my sable cape shaping a series of round, dark waves. I hand the cape to an adoring Mr Klein, slightly improved and handsomely turned out in a tuxedo cut just like my father's.

My mother stepped over me and then stopped. I was eye to toe with her tiny pink suede loafers and happy to stay that way. Her round blue eyes and her dread of wrinkles made her stare as harsh and haunting as the eyeless Greek heads she put in my father's study.

'How are you keeping busy, Susan?'

I couldn't imagine what had prompted this interest. My mother always acted as though I had been raised by a responsible and affectionate governess, and guilt and love were as foreign in my house as butter and sugar.

'School, books.' I studied the little gold bars across the tongues of her loafers.

'And that's all going well?'

'Fine. Everything's fine.'

'You wouldn't like to study an instrument, would you? Piano?

We could do a piano in the library. That could be attractive. An older piece, deep browns, a maroon paisley shawl, silver picture frames. Quite attractive.'

'I don't know. Can I think about it?' I didn't mind being part of my mother's endless redecorating; in the past, her domestic fantasies had produced a queen-size brass bed, which I loved and kept into adulthood, and a giant dollhouse, complete with working lights and a chiming doorbell.

'Of course, think it over. Let's make a decision next week, shall we?' She started to touch my dirty hair and patted me on the shoulder instead. I have no idea what she thought of me.

I didn't see Mr Klein until the following Monday. I had endured four mornings at the bus stop: leaves stuffed down my shirt, my books knocked into the trash can, my lunch bag tossed from boy to boy. Fortunately, the bus driver was a madman, and his rageful mutterings and obscene limericks captured whatever attention might have come my way once we were on the bus.

It was raining that Monday, and I wondered if I should take the bus. I had never thought about the fact that Mr Klein and I had no way to contact each other. I could only wait, in silence. I pulled up my hood and started walking down Baker Hill, waiting for a blue streak to come past my left side, waiting for the slight skid of wet leaves as Mr Klein braked to a stop. Finally, much closer to home than usual, the car came.

'You're almost home,' he said. 'Maybe I should just take you home? We can go to the store another time.' He looked rushed and unhappy.

'Sure, if you don't have time, that's okay.'

'I have the time, Susie. I have the time.' He turned the car around and drove us back to Furs by Klein.

I got out and waited in the rain while he unlocked the big black doors.

'You're soaking wet,' he said harshly. 'You should have taken the bus.'

'I missed it,' I lied. If he wasn't going to admit that he wanted me to miss the bus, I wasn't going to admit that I had missed it for him.

'Yes, you miss the bus, I pick you up. Suseleh, you are a very special girl, and standing around an old man's shop in wet clothes is not what you should be doing.'

Usually what I did was stand around with no clothes on at all, but I could tell that Mr Klein, like most adults, was now working only from his version of the script.

I sat down uneasily at the little table with the swiveling gilt-framed mirror, ready to try on hats. Without Mr Klein's encouragement, I wouldn't even look at the coats. He didn't hand me any hats.

He pressed his thin sharp face deep into the side of my neck, pushing my sweatshirt aside with one hand. I looked in the mirror and saw my own round wet face, comic in its surprise and pink glasses. I saw Mr Klein's curly gray hair and a bald spot I would never have discovered otherwise.

'Get your coat.' He rubbed his face with both hands and went to the door.

'I don't have a coat.'

'They let you go in the rain, with no coat? *Gottenyu.* Let's go, please.' He held the door open for me, and I had to walk through it.

The chocolate wasn't my usual Belgian slab. It was a deep gold foil box, tied with pink and gold wisps and crowned with a cluster of sparkling gold berries. He dropped it in my lap like it was something diseased.

I held the box in my lap, stroking the fairy ribbons, until he told me to open it.

Each of the six chocolates had a figure on top. Three milk, three bittersweet, each one carved with angel wings or a heart or a white-rimmed rose. In my parents' fat-free home, my eating habits were regarded as criminal. They would no more have bought me beautiful chocolates than gift-wrapped a gun for a killer.

'Suseleh . . .'

He looked out the window at the rain and I looked up at him quickly. I had obviously done something wrong, and although my parents' anger and chagrin never bothered me a bit, his unhappiness pulled me apart. I crushed one of the chocolates with my fingers, and Mr Klein saw me.

'Nah, nah, nah,' he said softly, wiping my fingers with his handkerchief. He cleared his throat. 'My schedule's changing, I won't be able to give you rides after school. I'm going to open the shop on Mondays.'

'How about in the morning?' I had not known that I could talk through this kind of pain.

'I don't think so. I need to get in a little earlier. It's not so bad, you should ride with other boys and girls. You'll see, you'll have a good time.'

I sat there sullenly, ostentatiously mashing the chocolates.

'Too bad, they're very nice chocolates. Teuscher's. Remember, sable from Klein's, chocolates from Teuscher's. Only the best for you. I'm telling you, only the best.'

'I'm not going to have a good time on the bus.' I didn't mash the last chocolate, I just ran a fingertip over the tiny ridges of the rosebud.

'Maybe not. I shouldn't have said you'd have a good time. I'm sorry.' He sighed and looked away,

I bit into the last chocolate. 'Here, you have some too.'

'No, they're for you. They were all for you.'

'I'm not that hungry. Here.' I held out the chocolate half and he lowered his head, startling me. I put my fingers up to his narrow lips and he took the chocolate neatly between his teeth. I could feel the very edge of his teeth against my fingers.

We pulled up in front of my house, and he put his hand over mine, for just one moment.

'I'll say it again, only the best is good enough for you. So, we'll say au revoir, Susan. Not good-bye.'

'Au revoir. Thank you for the chocolates.' My mother's instructions surfaced at odd times.

I left my dripping sneakers on the brick floor and dropped my wet clothes into the lilac straw hamper in my bathroom. I took my very first voluntary shower and dried off slowly, watching myself in the steamy mirror. When I didn't come down for dinner, my mother found me, naked and quiet, deep in my covers.

'Let's get the piano,' I said.

I took lessons from Mr Canetti for three years, and he served me wine-flavored cookies instead of chocolate. One day, he bent forward to push my sleeves back over my aching wrists, and I saw my beautiful self take shape in his eyes. I loved him, too.

Semper Fidelis

I shop at night. Thursday nights I wave good-bye to the nurse and drive off, feigning reluctance. The new mall has three department stores, a movie theater, and hundreds of little shops, and I have been in all but the Compleat Sportsman. It makes no sense to me, but I cannot sit through a movie, knowing I'm supposed to be shopping. I eat warm peanut butter cookies and wander around for almost two hours, browsing through the very slim jazz sections of the mall record stores, skimming bestsellers. At nine-thirty, when the mall is closing and it's just me and the vagrant elderly and the young security guards, I go grocery shopping.

All-night grocery stores seem to be the personal savior and favorite haunt of dazed young women of all colors, who haul their crumpled, sleeping babies like extra items in the cart; of single middle-aged men and women, too healthy and too lonely to fall asleep at ten o'clock; and of people like me, who are scared to go home. It is my belief, and sometimes my wish, that my husband will die while I am out on one of my Thursday night sprees.

Max and I have been together for almost ten years, since I was eighteen and he was fifty. We are no longer a scandal, or a tragedy. His wife's friends and the other witnesses have moved away, or fallen silent, or become friends, the limited choices of a small town. Max and I are close to ordinary, made interesting only by our past and its casualties. Women who would have, may have, spit in my soup at painfully quiet dinner parties ten years ago now bring puréed vegetables for Max and articles on the apricot-pit clinics of Mexico. I have become a wife, soon to be a widow, and I feel more helpless and unknowing after ten years of marriage than I was at eighteen, moving into Max's apartment with two T-shirts, a box of records, and no shoes. On our first outing, Max introduced me to the chairman of his department and bought me sneakers.

He has not been out of bed for three weeks, and he has not spoken since morning. I always pictured myself as an Audrey Hepburn-type widow, long-necked and pale in a narrow black linen dress. Instead, I am nearly drowning in a river of sugar and covering myself in old sweatpants and Max's flannel shirts. I only dress up on Thursday nights, to go out in an oversized sweatshirt and black tights, playing up my legs with high-heeled black ankle boots. I have never dressed like this in my life, and I am glad to put my sneakers and my jeans back on before I go into the house.

Ray, at the Deli Counter, is the one I've been looking for. He first admired my boots and then my whole outfit, and after three Thursdays in a row I felt obliged to buy another top for him to look at, and he leaned over the counter to tell me how much he liked it and winked as he went back to work. Ray can't be more than twenty-two, and I assume he is a recovering addict of some kind, since he is presently the picture of good health and says things like 'Easy does it' and 'One day at a time,' which are the kinds of things my brother, a not-recovering alcoholic, says whenever he calls to wish me well or borrow money. I think Ray is a good choice. I think we would not discuss poetry or symbolism or chemotherapy or the past, and I think I would have a beer and he would not and I would lay my hand on one thick thigh until I felt the cloth tighten under my fingers, and when we were done I would climb out of his van, or his room in his mother's house, and thank him from the bottom of my heart and go home to Max.

I come home to see the nurse leaning over Max, smoothing his covers as her big white nylon breasts swing slightly and shadow his face. He smiles, and I see that he is unaware of my presence and the nurse is not.

'The pearls,' she says, continuing their conversation, 'were extremely valuable, and irregardless of the will, my sister and I both think the pearls should have come to us. Our mother's pearls should have come to us, because they were already ours.'

I cannot even begin to understand what she's talking about, but it feels ominously metaphorical. Maybe the pearls represent Max's health, or his first marriage, or our vow to cleave unto each other: things irretrievably gone and valued more in their absence than in their presence. I want to shut her up, to keep her from tormenting us both, but Max smiles again, a quick softening of his bony gray face, and even I can see that he is not tormented. I knock against the door frame, knowing that Max, as he is now, is too innocent and the nurse too self-absorbed to appreciate the irony of my knocking. I am performing without an audience, which is how it has been for some time. If you feel sorry for yourself, can it still be a tragedy? Or are you reduced to a rather unattractive second lead, a foil for the heroes, blind and beautiful, courageously polishing the brass as the icy waters lap at their ankles? It seems to me – and I would not be sorry to find out – that I have disappeared.

'Sweetheart,' he says, and the nurse frowns.

'He's been asking for you,' she says, and I forgive her bitchiness because she seems to care about him, to feel that it matters that he misses me. The other nurses are solicitous of his health, of his illness, but his feelings are nothing more than symptoms to them. For one minute, I love her for loving him; he has made me love people I would dislike if he were going to live.

'Dawn's mother passed away recently, she was telling me.'

Shaken by love, touched by his effort to keep us together and to keep us his, I smile at Dawn. 'I'm so sorry,' I say, trying to be good. 'I lost my mother just last year. And I've got a sister too.' That's it. I cannot think of any more astonishing coincidences that will bring us together.

'My sister's my best friend,' Dawn says, sitting in the armchair near the bed as though she'd dropped in on Max for a visit.

'Mine, too.' Amazing. Dawn and I must have been separated at birth.

My sister, Irene, *is* my best friend, and while my father wept and my mother murmured congratulations from the far side of a scotch and soda, my sister took me upstairs, to what had been her room, to discuss my marrying Max.

'You can have anyone, you know. Even after all this. You can transfer to a school in California and no one will ever know. You don't have to marry him.'

'I love him, Reen. I want to marry him.'

'Okay. Okay, I'll be there. At least he won't leave you for a younger woman. Not without being arrested. Is this justice of the peace or train-and-veil?'

'Justice of the peace. Wednesday.'

'All right. How about a suit? Silk suit, roses in your hair? It won't kill you to go to a beauty parlor.'

And my sister got my legs waxed, my pores cleaned, and my

eyebrows shaped in less than forty-eight hours. In the photographs, I look radiant and only a little too young for the ivory silk suit, which Irene found, unpinned from a mannequin, and paid for in less than forty-five minutes. I have ivory roses in my upswept black hair, and Max is laughing at the camera, which is held by his oldest friend, who is astonished, amiable, and drunk for the whole afternoon. My sister looks like the mother of the bride, exhausted, vigilant, more pleased than not. My parents weren't there because I didn't invite them, despite Max's pleas.

I should have invited them. I am almost thirty now and I am coming to think that one should, when in doubt, invite them, whoever they are. The distant relatives, the cocktail party stalwarts, the friends who failed to send Christmas cards two years in a row. Invite them while you can.

Dawn rises to leave, and I can see that she doesn't love Max; he is just a better than average case, less trouble than some of the others. I am free to hate her, and I walk her to the door and open it for her, without speaking, a form of civilized rudeness I've picked up from my mother.

'Come here,' Max says, but I cannot lie in that bed.

'I'll use the cot.' When we left the hospital, a smart, angry woman in the support group told me to get a cot and didn't even pretend to listen when I said that we would continue to share a bed.

'Undress slowly, sweetheart. I can still look.'

In the books I keep hidden, the guides to grief, the how-to books of widowhood and the period that comes before, the authors mention, delicately, that the healthy spouse usually suffers hurt feelings and frustration due to the dying person's lack of sexual interest. This doesn't seem to be the case with Max.

I throw off my clothes and lie on the cot, like a Girl Scout, still in my T-shirt, panties, and socks. I hear a wet, bubbling noise, which is how he laughs now.

Max rests one cool, brittle hand on my stomach.

'How was the supermarket?'

'It was okay. I got some groceries.'

'And the mall?'

'It was fine. I got some socks.'

He strokes my stomach with just two dry fingertips, and I feel the flesh at the end of each finger, dragging slightly after the bone. I want to throw up and I want to weep.

'Do you ever meet anybody?'

'Like who?' I ask. Despite everything, I don't think of Max as a jealous man; we have simply misunderstood each other most of the time. He would remind me, as we drove home from parties, that he had made a point of not admiring the younger women so people wouldn't think that I was part of his youth fetish, that I was less than unique. He said I owed him the same consideration and should conceal my impulsive sexuality lest people think that my marriage to him was just hormonally-driven adolescent mindlessness. We agreed, many times, that he was not jealous, not insecure, not possessive, and we must have had that conversation about flirting a hundred times in our ten years together.

Max pokes me lightly. 'I don't know, like anybody. Some nice young man?'

'No. No one.' I roll over on my side, out of reach of his fingers.

'All right, don't get huffy. Dawn gave me my meds already. Good night, sweetheart.'

'Good night.' You sadistic old shit.

I lie on the cot, listening to his chalky, irregular breath until he falls asleep, and then I go downstairs to pay bills. His room, our room, fills up at night, with a thick wet mist of dark fluids and invisibly leaking sores. This is something else I don't say.

The next Thursday I smile encouragingly at Ray, who is very busy with the second-shift shopping crowd. I find myself taking a number behind a dark, dark boy, so dark the outline of his whole brown body seems drawn in charcoal. He is all roundness, high, full Island cheeks, round black eyes, rounded arms and shoulders, his pants rounded front and back. My own fullness has begun to shrink and loosen, muscle sliding down from bone a little more each year. I want to cut this boy open like a melon, and eat him, slice by slice. Cut him and taste him and have him and hurt him. I could tell Max that I understand him better now than I did ten years ago, but he would be horrified that I think this mixture of lust and resentment is anything like his love for me. I am only horrified by myself; what I want to do to this boy, Max would never do.

Ray and I exchange several devoted, affectionate glances; as aspiring lovers we are so tenderly playful and wistful it seems odd that all we really want is to fuck each other senseless and get home before we're caught. My attitude is not good.

I go home to Max and Dawn. She is in my kitchen, sipping tea out of my mermaid mug, a gift from Max after a terrible, rainy week on Block Island. The iridescent blue tail is the handle, and Dawn's smooth fingers cling to it.

After she leaves, Max questions me again.

'I don't meet anyone, for Christ's sake. I'm not a girl. I'm twenty-eight and I probably look ninety. Who would I meet?'

'You might meet anyone. Look at me. I'm sixty. I'm a dying man riddled with cancer, and I met Dawn.'

'Great. I hope you'll be very happy together.' I turn out the light so he cannot see me change, and I wonder if he gets Dawn to strip for him on Thursdays.

'Really,' he says, completely surrounded by pillows so he can't lie down and be engulfed by his own lungs. 'Tell me. Why shouldn't you meet someone?'

I try to see him in the dark as he is, everything that was broad and hard-boned now transparent at the edge, softly dimpled and concave at the center.

'Who would I meet?'

'Some good-looking young man at the mall. Not a salesman, you never like salesmen. They try too hard, don't they?'

'Yes.' I want to tell him to rest, but I don't think I would be saying it for him.

'Big and dark. Sweet-natured, not terribly bright. Not stupid, of course, but not intellectual. Not an academic. I want to spare you a long, pedantic lecture when you've only got a few hours.'

'Good idea. How long do I have?'

'Well, you know your schedule better than I. Two hours at the mall, an hour and a half at the supermarket. We can skip aerobics, I think. I cannot picture you with a man who goes to aerobics class.'

He's right. I like them big and burly or lean and lithe, but I cannot bear the compulsively athletic, the ones who measure their pulses and their biceps and their cholesterol levels.

'Tell me, sweetheart. Tell me about the man you met in the supermarket.'

'Not the mall?'

'Don't play games with me. Tell me what happened.'

'He's dark-haired but fair. Black Irish and big. Not tall but wide. Built like a wall.' I realize that I am describing the Max I have seen only in photographs, a big, wild boy with one cocky foot on his Army jeep; ramming his way through Harvard a few years later, grinning like a pirate as the wind blows both ends of his scarf behind him.

'Go on,' Max says.

'I do see him at the supermarket. I change my clothes to go there.' And I tell Max the truth about my clothes, and he says 'Ya-hoo' when I come to the black ankle boots. We are having some kind of fun, in this terrible room.

'That'll get him. Do you wear a bra?'

'Come on, Max, of course I wear a bra.'

'Just slows you down. All right, at least it's one of your pretty ones, I hope, not those Ace Bandage things. How about the purple and black one with the little cutouts?' Max likes silky peekaboo lingerie, and I buy it, but I do not wear seventy-dollar hand-finished bras and garter belts for everyday. Most of the time, I wear cheap cotton tubes, which he hates.

'I do wear the black and purple one.'

'And the panties?'

'No panties.'

'Wonderful. The first time I put my hand on your bare ass, I thought I had died and gone to heaven. And then I was afraid that it wasn't for me, that you just never wore them.'

'Max, you asked me not to wear them, remember? I always wore underpants.' I'd had some sex, more than enough, with boys and by myself when I met Max, but I had never had a lover. Everything important that I know, about literature, about people, about my own body, I have learned from this man, and he is leaving me the way we both expected I would leave him, loving, regretful, irretrievable.

'Tell me about this big guy.'

Amy Bloom

'Big guy' is what I used to call Max. Having been married to a woman who called him 'my dear,' and pursued by highly educated young women who called him Professor Boyle and thought he was God, he found terms like 'big guy' and 'butch' refreshing endearments.

'He's the night manager.' I have given Ray a promotion; I'm sure, in time, someone with his good looks and pleasant manner will be made manager, and a sexual encounter with Ray the Head Roast Beef Slicer seems to demean us all.

'Fine. Where did you do it?'

'Jesus, Max, what is wrong with you?'

'Need you ask? Come on, come on, don't get skittish now. Where did you do it?' That angry, pushing voice used to scare me to death, and I cannot bear that it doesn't scare me anymore.

'We went to Wadsworth Park.' Where Max and I used to go when I was still living with my parents and he was still living with his then-wife. Just recently, while sorting out his pills or shaving his distorted face, I find myself thinking, This is what a wife is. Now that we cannot see ourselves in the curious, excited eyes of other people, the differences that defined us are fading away. We are just a man who is dying and a woman who is not.

'A little buggy?'

'Not too bad.' I stall to avoid making a mistake, afraid that I am not telling the right story.

'You had a blanket and you didn't notice the bugs.'

'Max, what do you want from me?'

'I want you to tell me what happened when you got into the woods. You led him to those big rocks, by the stream?'

The woods are thick on both sides of the water, sheltering twin slabs of granite. When we were there, Max would press me so far backward that the ends of my hair trailed in the cold water, collecting small leaves as I lay under him.

'All right. We went to the rocks and we made love. Then I changed my clothes and came home.'

'Don't tell me like that,' he says, and begins to cough, loosely, his whole body bouncing on the plastic-covered mattress. He falls asleep, still coughing, and I go downstairs and do nothing.

For the rest of the week, he floats in and out of conversations, and Dawn turns out to be very good at injections and bed changes, which should not surprise me. On Thursday I put on my shopping costume while Max watches and smiles alertly. Dawn is reading magazines in the kitchen, waiting for me to leave.

'Tonight?' he asks, barely pushing the words through his lips.

I don't answer, just tie my boots and sit down to brush my hair.

'You know who Dawn reminds me of? Not coloring, but the build? Eren Goknar. Remember?'

I remember and I keep brushing my hair.

'I wonder where she is.'

'I don't know. Maybe she went back to Turkey.'

'Don't think so. She wrote to me from California, teaching at Berkeley. Marvelous girl,' he says, struggling with each consonant. I walk out of the room.

I put up some hot water for me and Dawn and go back to check on Max, afraid that he will die while I'm angry with him.

'Ready?'

'Yeah. I'll be back in a couple of hours.'

'I slept with Eren,' he says, and sighs.

'I know,' I say, although I hadn't known until then. And I know that he is pushing me away, furiously, as though I will miss him less because he had sex with Eren Goknar. He can no more lose me than I can lose myself, we are like those house keys that beep in response to your voice; they practically find you. I kiss the air near Max's face and return to Dawn, who has made tea. We chat for two hours, in between her runs upstairs, and she doesn't ask me why I don't go out. I send her home at eleven.

Max barely opens his eyes when I turn on the night-light to undress. He lifts one hand slightly and I go to him, still in my underwear.

'Off,' he whispers. He turns his head and coughs, the harsh, rude sound of a straw in an almost empty glass.

I take everything off and climb into the bed, trying not to press against him now that even the sheets seem to hurt him.

'Did you?'

I slide closer to him until we are face to face, and I kiss his dry lips and feel the small bumps and cracks around his mouth.

'Yes, I found him, the one I told you about. The big one. He was getting off work early, just as I got there. I didn't even have to wait.'

Max closes his eyes, and I put his hand on top of my leg.

'It was so dark we didn't go to the park. We went to a motel. There was tacky red wallpaper, and the bed was a huge heart with a red velvet bedspread."

'Route Sixty-eight,' he says.

'That one. Remember that big bed? And the headboard with the little posts, the handholds?'

I move his hand up and down my leg, very gently.

'He undressed me, Max. He knelt down and took off my shoes, and then he laid me on the bed and undressed me. He was still in his suit.'

'Suit?' Max whispered.

'His work clothes, I mean. Not a suit. He left the light on and began to kiss me all over, but every time I tried to touch him, he'd grab my hands. He wouldn't let me touch him until later.'

Max moves his head a little, to nod, and I prop his pillows up.

'He kissed the insides of my thighs and the backs of my legs, and then he kissed my back for a very long time, and when he turned me over he was undressed. And he pulled me up to him, about two feet in the air, and then he threw us both down on the bed and he came inside me and he just kept coming and coming at me until I started to cry and then we got under the covers and we both cried until we fell asleep.'

I lay my wet face next to Max's and listen for his breathing.

'It was the best, Max. Nothing in my life was ever like that. Do you hear me? Nothing in my life was ever like that.'

When the Year Grows Old

On a Wednesday afternoon, Kay Feldman came home from Italian Club, which was run by Signora Maselli and filled with other misfits, girls bright enough but too shy for the school paper, too prim or clumsy for Modern Dance, and one boy, obviously crazy, who announced that he planned to read all of Dante before the end of ninth grade. Kay called out for her mother and heard nothing. There was no note on the kitchen table, only half a cup of thickening coffee and an ashtray with stubbed-out cigarettes.

Kay's mother only drank tea, usually herbal tea, and she had never, as far as Kay knew, ever smoked a cigarette. Kay had never even seen an ashtray in their house. When her aunt Ruth came to visit, Kay's father made her go outside to smoke, even in the winter. Kay could feel cold lines of sweat sliding down her sides.

Kay called out again and walked through every room, telling herself that her mother had gone for a walk, which she sometimes did, and had just forgotten to leave a note, which was unimaginable. Kay looked through the rooms of their house, excited beneath her anxiety, wondering whether she would see something terrible. A body, not her mother's, of course, but maybe some anonymous body flung across the bed, murdered by an anonymous someone else. Even better, murdered by her father, who will rot in jail and Kay will change her name and never, ever visit him. There was no body. The beds were unmade, which was unusual, and her mother's typewriter, which sat on a small pine table in what they called the guest room, was missing. Kay heard a faint mewing sound and jumped. Her father claimed he was allergic to cats, and despite her pleas and her mother's wistful looks, there were no pets. Kay didn't think he was allergic at all; she thought, correctly, that he hated cats and didn't want to argue.

The mewing came from the basement. Kay walked down, thinking about herself in the fictional third person, as she sometimes did: 'Bravely, Portia Ives descended the creaky stairs into the dank basement . . .' The Feldman basement was not particularly dank, as basements go. Her parents would never do anything as suburban or hospitable as finishing off the basement, but it was usually dry, and the only smell was of cool concrete and minerals. At the bottom of the steps, Kay sniffed repeatedly, in disbelief: those confusing, disorienting smells were the sharp reek of cat pee and the ropy, sexy scent of cigarettes.

'Oh, hi, honey, I didn't hear you come in.'

Kay's mother was wearing clothes Kay didn't recognize. Her straight blond hair was pushed back by a wide black headband, and she had on a baggy black v-neck sweater, the sleeves pushed up to her elbows. Her pants were black too, and she was barefoot.

'Is there a cat in here?' Kay wanted to grab her mother, shouting, What kind of joke, what kind of demented game is this, cigarettes and cats and the beds not made?

Kay's mother giggled. The giggle was more frightening than the cigarettes. Kay's mother did not giggle; she smiled pleasantly at her husband's elaborate puns, and she pretended not to hear Kay's rude remarks.

'Yes, there is. He's not quite potty-trained, but we're getting there. Did you know that even very small kittens will begin using the kitty litter within twenty-four hours? And they've got this new kind of kitty litter, it's green and it's incredibly absorbent and soaks up most of the smell. He's in the corner there.'

'Whose cat is he?' And why are you sitting on a folding chair, in the middle of the afternoon, in the goddamn basement?

'Mine, ours. How about calling him Blake – you know, Tyger! Tyger! burning bright / In the forests of the night, / What immortal hand or eye / Could frame thy fearful symmetry?' Do they still teach that at school? I think Blake is still my all-time favorite. I love "Songs of Experience."'

Kay stared at her mother. Her mother, the mother she knew, taught English as a Second Language in Adult Education and was always in the kitchen at five o'clock getting dinner started so the kitchen would be clean by the time she went to teach. Kay's mother wore khaki slacks with a narrow brown belt, brown flats, and pink or white turtlenecks. Sometimes she wore navy or mint green. When she went to teach, she put on a skirt and a cardigan with one of the turtlenecks. Kay's father said, trying to be nice, that Laura dressed like a lady. More often, he said she dressed like a nun.

'Where did you get those clothes, Mom?'

Laura looked at Kay in surprise and looked down at her black pants. She shrugged. 'I found them in the trunk. I can't believe they still fit. Isn't that nice?'

At least her mother's verbal habits hadn't changed: cheerful evasion, calling everything 'nice.' Kay decided to act as though nothing else had changed.

'Are you coming upstairs? It's after five.'

'I don't think so, honey. I'm in the middle of something, and it's going to take a little longer to get Blake acclimated. Look at him, cowering over there. Do you want to pick him up?'

Kay looked at her mother, who always warned her that animals carry germs, and looked at the kitten, a tiny bundle of strawberry blond spikes. Yesterday, if they had somehow acquired a kitten, her mother would have suggested calling him Sunshine or Buttercup, and Kay would have rolled her eyes in contempt. Kay picked up the kitten and could feel him squirming, brushing the back of her hand with a tongue like a tiny thistle.

'So what am I supposed to do? Do I have to make dinner?'

'Well, no, I wouldn't think so. Didn't you stop at Swenson's? You're not hungry yet, are you?'

Kay was having trouble with the idea that this weird beatnik knew everything her mother knew and seemed to be able to make use of it, in ways her mother was never able to manage.

'No, I guess not. He's going to be really mad. Mom, you know, when dinner's not ready.'

Laura looked at her mildly. 'Well, it won't be the end of the world if dinner's a little late. How anyone can eat at six, I don't know; it always seemed to me that one had hardly finished lunch. I'll finish what I'm doing and then I'll come up. We can eat around seven. I'm not teaching tonight.'

Kay said nothing. In her head, she repeated the airy sound of 'one had hardly finished lunch' and felt a burst of joy blanketing her worries. Perhaps this would be something good, something better than anything had ever been.

Kay heard her father, Martin, come home promptly at six o'clock, as he usually did, and she heard him call out, hiding his surprise, and his immediate anger at being surprised, with a jolly impatience. 'Where the hell is everybody?'

Kay lay on her bed, stomach down, and waited for him to find her. He would only hover in her doorway; he rarely came into her bedroom.

'Hi. Where's your mother?'

'She's in the basement.'

'Come on, Kay, don't be stupid. I don't have time for it.'

Copying her mother's mild tone, Kay said, 'She's in the basement.'

'For Christ's sake.' Her father stalked off.

Kay walked quietly to the top of the basement stairs. She heard her father mumbling angrily, and she heard her mother's voice cut him off so softly no words floated up the stairs. A few minutes later, Martin came up the stairs, uneasy and looking for a fight.

'Did you do your homework?'

'Yes.' Kay knew better than to tell him that she had just gotten home.

'All right. Why don't you set the table or something? Your mother said dinner will be a little late.'

'No problem.'

'You sound like a gas station attendant when you say that. Just say, "That will be fine," like a normal, educated person.'

In her coldest voice, Kay said, 'That will be fine.' She thought, And I hate you, you fat, fat, evil pig, and I hope you die.

Kay's mother came up and made hamburgers, mashed potatoes, and a green salad. She didn't speak during dinner, and the three of them ate in silence, Kay watching them both. Laura put her own dishes in the dishwasher, and as Kay and Martin sat there, she turned to leave.

'Where are you going, Laura?' Martin couldn't move fast enough to block her way, but he wasn't going to sit by while his wife acted like some second-rate Sylvia Plath.

'Downstairs. I'm working on something, and I find that the basement is the most comfortable place. Like your office at the college is for you. Fold-out couch and all.'

Martin said nothing, and Kay watched his face turn a slow, swelling red. Her mother didn't stay to watch.

Martin went to read in their bedroom, hoping that tomorrow would find his wife in her usual clothes and her usual mildly depressed state, smelling like baby powder and not cigarettes.

At ten, Kay called downstairs, 'I'm going to bed, Mom. I did the dishes. Good night.'

'Good night, honey. That was very sweet of you, doing the dishes. I'll be up in a little bit.'

'Well, I'm going to bed now.' Kay had been ducking her mother's evening attentions for the last four years. Tonight, she wanted to be tucked in, but her mother stayed in the basement, resolute, in black.

In the morning, there was a note on the basement door.

> Give me, O indulgent fate!
> Give me yet, before I die,
> A sweet, but absolute retreat
> 'Mongst paths so lost, and trees so high,
> That the world may ne'er invade
> When the Year Grows Old
> Through such windings and such shade
> My unshaken liberty.
>
> BY ANNE FINCH, COUNTESS OF WINCHILSEA

As Kay was reading it for the third time, her father scanned it over her shoulder and then crumpled it and threw it in with the coffee grounds and melon rinds.

That night her mother did not come up to make dinner. Martin went down and made more angry noises and came back up heavily, looking defeated and a little afraid. If Kay hadn't hated his guts, she would have felt sorry for him. Stupid, scared pig.

'Why don't you ask your mother to come upstairs? If she doesn't want to make dinner, we could . . . we could bring in pizza.'

Kay didn't want to do anything that could be construed as helping her father, but she did want her mother to come upstairs; wanted her, even more, to witness her father's utter capitulation, to hear 'bring in pizza' spoken by the man who had forbidden them to eat at fast-food joints all their lives and had taken all the fun out of family vacations by insisting that Laura cook regular meals every night in whatever cabin kitchen she found herself in.

Kay wanted to shout out, with trumpets and banners, 'You can stop now, you've won. He'll bring in pizza, and he hasn't even mentioned the cat. You've won! Come back!'

Kay went downstairs and smelled the smoke and the mothballs but only a little bit of cat. The typewriter was going steadily.

'Mom?'

'I'm here.'

'Dad said why don't we bring in pizza if you don't want to cook. We could get double cheese and peppers.' Kay loved double cheese and peppers, and every time Martin went to a conference, Laura would hesitate and then yield, ordering a large for just the two of them, frowning as Kay ate three, then four slices.

When Laura failed to smile triumphantly, Kay's heart sank. It was not a contest, after all.

'If you want to,' Laura said, balancing a Dunhill cigarette in the bowl of an unfamiliar crystal ashtray. 'This ashtray belonged to my father, you never met him. He was a minor poet and a sweet man. My mother considered him a failure. I always thought so too, but now I think he was just a sweet, soft person, without ambition. Your grandmother admired ambitious men. Do you know what she said to me after she met your father for the first time? She said, "Get pregnant."' Laura pulled on her cigarette, looking younger and angrier than Kay had ever seen her.

'Yeah, Grandma was weird. So Mom, the pizza? Should we order it? Just one large? We could get some of the cheese bread-sticks too.'

'Whatever you want. I'm not hungry.'

'Mum, did you eat today?'

'I'm fine, honey. See, Blake's having his dinner.' They both looked at the kitten, lapping milk out of a small Wedgwood saucer, which Kay recognized as having come from the set her mother kept on display in their china cabinet.

'Okay, we'll order pizza. Mom, are you sleeping down here?'

'Well, yes, I am. This project is taking up so much time that it seems easier just to get everything set down here. It looks a lot like my room at college.'

Kay looked around, unhappy but curious. It looked like the room Kay herself might have when she got to college: Klimt posters taped to the cement walls, a card table covered with two purple batik scarves, a pile of notebooks and a stack of poetry books on the cement floor, curling in the almost unnoticeable damp. Laura had unrolled an old Girl Scout sleeping bag onto the cot and added a few African-looking pillows. She had stacked two boxes of Martin's only book, discounted and autographed, to make an end table, and put a small lamp on top.

'It's nice, Mom.'

Her mother beamed at her. 'Thank you. "Let the ambitious

rule the earth, / let the giddy fool have mirth, / let me still in my retreat / from all roving thoughts be freed." That's more of Anne Finch.' Her mother looked at her typewriter. 'I have to get back to work.'

'What are you working on?'

Laura's face closed abruptly. 'I'm writing some things. I wrote a lot. I have to get back to work.'

'Okay, I'm going. I'll call you when the pizza comes. Okay?'

'Fine.' Her mother, who always had ten words for every one of Kay's, pushed up her sleeves and started typing.

Kay and Martin ate pizza together silently. Laura said she was too busy to come up for dinner, and Kay's father ate six slices and threw the box in the garbage. He got his car keys and told Kay to clean up.

'Why should I clean up?'

'Just do it, Kay. I don't know what lunacy your mother is up to, but I can't correct papers, write a book, *and* clean the house.'

Kay thought of her mother, luminous in the basement, quoting that woman poet. 'I didn't say you should clean the house, did I? I just asked, why I should clean up after the two of us eat.'

Martin balled his fists and set them on the table, the picture of a man trying to keep his temper. But he wasn't, Kay knew, he was only trying to scare her.

'Kay, please, clean up the kitchen. Don't make this worse than it is. Don't make me lose my temper. Why don't you go downstairs and get your mother to stop this nonsense? And tell her she has got to stop smoking cigarettes.'

'I'll clean the kitchen if you're going to threaten me. You tell Mom to stop smoking. She's your wife.'

Her father walked out of the kitchen, and Kay could hear that he didn't go out to the car; he went right to the bedroom.

Every day, not knowing what she hoped for, Kay went downstairs to visit her mother. Sometimes Laura was charming and
recited poetry, but the next day she might turn weird and slow-
moving, hardly able to answer Kay. Martin bought milk and fruit
and dinner on his way home every night, and Kay cleaned up the
kitchen after they ate the pizza or the fried chicken or the corned
beef sandwiches. On the tenth day, Kay went downstairs, not
thinking at all about her mother; she was crying because she was
fourteen and four inches taller than the only boy who was even
a little bit nice to her.

'What's the matter, honey?'

'It was just a shitty day.' Since her mother's personality trans-
plant, swearing was now no big deal. Kay was trying to figure
out when she could ask for a cigarette.

'They happen.' Her mother lit up and leaned back in her
typing chair, turning to look at Kay. 'My God, you got so beautiful this year, every time I look at you now I think, "The
brightness of her cheek would shame those stars, / As daylight
doth a lamp; her eyes in heaven / Would through the airy region
stream so bright / That birds would sing and think it were not
night." You are really just the Juliet. Romeos are a little hard to
find in ninth grade, though.'

Kay smiled, thrilled to hear her mother, who used to tell her
she really could be cute if she smiled more, talk in this quirky,
husky voice, a voice of lovers remembered, of disappointments
survived.

'No one likes me,' Kay said, realizing that at that moment, pet-
ting tiny Blake, she didn't care.

'Then they are nearsighted fools and babies. It'll happen,
honey. Give everybody two or three more years and you'll be
beating them off with a stick, maybe two sticks.' Her mother

ground out her cigarette for emphasis. 'I have to get back to work. Come lie on the cot. You can take a nap while I type.'

Kay lay down on the green, dampish sleeping bag and put her head on one of the odd oblong pillows. Her mother pulled the folding chair closer to the cot and put one thin, colorless hand on Kay's shoulder. She sang,

> 'Oh, the summertime is coming
> and the leaves are sweetly blooming
> and the wild mountain thyme
> grows around the purple heather . . .
> Will you go, laddie, go?'

Kay didn't remember that her mother had sung to her nightly in that same breathy, bittersweet voice, rocking her in a small blue bedroom. Her mother sang until Kay fell asleep.

When she woke up, her mother was holding the kitten and staring at the air above the typewriter.

'Mom? Mom?'

The kitten jumped out of Laura's arms and tumbled over to his milk dish.

Kay put a hand on her mother's shoulder, and then both hands; she could feel thin skin shirting over ridges of bone beneath the dirty black sweater. Her mother didn't move, and Kay waited. After a while she could feel a slight heaving.

'What's going on?' Martin stood halfway down the stairs, peering at them, at their two sloping shapes rimmed by the harsh white light. When Kay was born, she could barely stop crying long enough to eat, and Martin would walk her all night, up and down the apartment stairs, while Laura put her head beneath two pillows and cried until dawn. For six months, they all slept on wet sheets. The only picture he had ever carried was of Kay, four months old.

'Nothing,' Kay said.

Every day had frightened her more as she waited for her father's move. Obviously, something was wrong with her mother; he could send her away, and she might never come back. He could get rid of Blake, too.

'All right, Kay. Go on upstairs.' He sounded the way he always did when he talked to her, as though they were strangers forced to share a seat on a terrible train ride.

Kay stood by her mother.

'Upstairs.'

'What are you going to do?' Kay asked, feelings of power, of supernatural strength, surging through her chest. She will rescue her mother the way policemen shimmy through traffic to rescue toddlers, the way acrobats catch each other at the last, impossible halfsecond. She will swing past her father, leaving him fat and clumsy on the ground, and she and her mother will whirl through light-filled air; landing softly, not even breathing hard, on their own tiny platform.

'I just want to talk to your mother privately.'

Kay stood still, squeezing her mother's shoulders, waiting for her cue.

'Martin?' Her mother's voice was softer than the kitten's.

Kay's father came down the stairs, loosening his tie. 'It's me, I'm here,' he said, and he leaned over the typewriter and took Laura's slack hands.

'Martin?'

Kay waited for her father's explosion, for him to yell at her mother for being stupid and repeating herself. She moved back, just a little, only her fingertips resting on her mother's dusty shoulders.

'Right here, Laura, I'm right here.'

'I'm very tired. I'm not sleeping at night.'

Her mother's thin whine distracted and annoyed Kay, who was trying hard to turn her into Anne Finch, into a blond, sequined acrobat effortlessly flipping from one shining trapeze to the next.

'I know, I know you can't sleep.'

How could he know? Kay thought. Thick and still under his gray, conventional blankets, how could he know what her mother was doing in the night, in the basement?

'Let's go upstairs, Laura, all right? Let's go talk to Sid Schwerner, all right? He can help you sleep.'

Laura pulled her hands back angrily, and Kay thought, Now! Leap into my arms, now!

'Martin, I have to get back to work.'

Kay's father was smarter than she thought; he didn't yell or even try to take hold of Laura's hands again.

'Of course, I didn't mean to interrupt. Let's go meet with Sid, just for a little while, and then you can get back to work. You can't work without rest, right? Even Shakespeare, even Blake, your all-time favorite, they all rested. All right?'

Laura sighed and put her head down on the typewriter keys, and Kay felt the sigh tunnel through her spine and felt the cool metal keys of the typewriter thrown hot and hard behind her eyes. She went upstairs, not wanting to see her mother's slow ascent, wrapped in her father's brown tweed arms.

Kay could hear him through her bedroom door, talking urgently on the phone, muffling his voice like a Nazi spy; rummaging in the bedroom, dragging the zipper on her mother's ancient overnight bag. She couldn't hear her mother at all.

'All right, we're going. Kay? I'll — we'll be back later. Kay? Please come out of your room and say good-bye.'

Kay pulled herself off her bed and stood in her doorway. ''Bye. Have a good time. Have fun.'

Laura looked in her direction and right past her. Martin waved his hand widely, as though from a departing plane.

'All right, Kay. Take it easy. I'll call you if I need to. Don't wait up, tomorrow's a school day.'

'Yes, I know. Thank you for telling me.'

Martin rolled his eyes and opened the door, pulling Laura through it, still gentle even when she just stood there as if she didn't know what doors were for.

He came back the next day, without Laura. He told Kay that her mother needed a complete rest and would be home in a few weeks. He was brisk and oddly cheerful, displaying her mother's upbeat stoicism as though he had stolen it.

For the next two weeks, they lived together as they had when Laura was in the basement. Martin brought home dinner, and Kay cleaned the kitchen. She ran all her father's dark and light clothes together and washed his sweaters in hot water until he stopped making her do the laundry. She met a new girl, Rachel Gevins, and on weekends she slept over at her house and they drank rum and Cokes while the Gevinses were out at the movies. Rachel told Kay that her mother got electrolysis on her stomach. Kay told Rachel that her mother had freaked out and her father had carted her off to a funny farm. Rachel laughed and looked sad and didn't say anything, and Kay knew what it was to trust someone.

When Kay came home from her second weekend at Rachel's, she went down to the basement. 'Gripping the wrought-iron banister, Dominique Beauvoir prepared to enter her past ...'

Blake, whom Kay had been surreptitiously feeding tuna fish and boned fried chicken, was gone. The litter box was gone, and so was the ten-pound bag of kitty litter. The table, the chair, the poetry books, the journals, and the cot and pillows were gone. The typewriter was gone. The air carried only faint scents of camphor and cigarettes and cat.

Kay stood in the basement, pushing out deep, uneven breaths. She will never forgive him. Beginning right now, she will never speak to him again. When Kay was little, she would walk from school to her father's office and he would lift her right onto his desk and clear a place for her among the papers so she could swing her legs over the side while she drank cocoa from the mug with the sailboats on it. He introduced her to all the pretty girls who came in and out, and they all smiled at her in a nice way and played with her hair and stood very close to her father. When she was ten, he started locking the office door, and then he said she was old enough to walk straight home by herself. Kay thought he was ashamed of her, and she was ashamed too. She wrote terrible things about him on the wall behind her dresser, but it didn't help.

If her mother does not come back now, when Kay grows up she will hire someone to murder him. Like that girl in New Jersey, she will hire some stupid guy to shoot her father in the head one night while he's reading Thomas Hardy, and she will say she doesn't know anything about it. She cries until she can barely see and locks herself in her bedroom.

When he got home, Martin rattled the doorknob a couple of times, insisting that Kay let him in. He didn't really want her to, and when she didn't, he shrugged and ate most of the fried chicken he had brought home for the two of them. He went to bed, nauseated, hating his life, still surprised by it.

Kay wouldn't leave her room the next morning, and after a few minutes Martin stopped pounding on the door. He had a breakfast meeting, and he said, feeling generous, 'It won't kill you to miss a day of school, I guess. Your mother'll be home a little later anyway.' He left, relieved that he had spared himself another splenetic fight.

When Kay hears the car grinding out of the driveway, she opens her door and goes back to the basement. She is waiting for a sign, and she wants to believe that she can sit there forever, that she is stonewalling God, not the other way around. The basement is not quite empty, and from her lookout on the stairs Kay can see the scraps that have been left behind. She examines the stubby pencil; nothing special, not even a tooth mark or a broken point. Kay puts it in her pocket and goes over to the corner where the cot had been. On the floor is an empty Dunhills packet, gold foil flowering out of the red box. Kay goes to her room and puts the box in her underwear drawer, tiny tobacco flakes drifting onto her white panties. She puts on her black jeans and an old black sweatshirt, turning it inside out to hide the bright lettering. She would wear a headband if she had one. Kay hears the car again and stands in the living room, waiting to see just who her father brings home.

She can hear them coming through the kitchen, hears her father grunting as he lugs in the suitcase, hears her mother murmuring thanks. Kay is barely breathing.

Her mother comes into the living room, unsmiling. Someone has dressed her in her khaki skirt and white turtleneck, but the brown belt is missing and her shirttail waves in and out of the waistband.

Kay wants to speak softly, to use her father's basement voice to win her mother back; they will read poetry and eat pizza, and in the end he will shrivel up and blow away, leaving nothing behind but his dorky black shoes. They will be fine then.

'Where's Blake?' is what she says, and her mother's mouth bunches in familiar, ugly ruffles.

'Here we go,' says her father, looking at his wife.

'Well? That's not an unreasonable question, is it? I mean, the cat's just gone, you know? You know that, right, Mom? Blake's gone. He had him put to sleep or something.'

Kay's mother puts her hand to her forehead, also a familiar gesture, and goes to the bedroom without looking Kay's way. Martin follows her, carrying her suitcase carefully.

In the rich late-morning light, Kay locks her bedroom door and throws the black clothes under her bed. She takes out the smooth red box and unfolds the gold foil, sniffing. Kay lies down and closes her eyes. She falls asleep, the red box clasped beneath her pillow.

Psychoanalysis Changed My Life

For three weeks, four days a week, Marianne told her dreams to Dr Zurmer. Fat, naked women handed her bouquets of tiger lilies; incomprehensible signs and directories punctuated silent gray corridors; bodiless penises spewed azalea blossoms in great pink and purple arcs. She also talked about her marriage, her divorce, and her parents. Behind her, Dr Zurmer nodded and took notes and occasionally slipped her knotted, elderly feet out of elegant black velvet flats, wiggling her toes until she could feel her blood begin to move. Marianne could hear her even and attentive breathing, could hear the occasional light scratch of her cigarlike fountain pen.

At the end of another long dream, in which Marianne's father frantically attempted to reach Marianne through steadily drifting petals, Dr Zurmer put down her pen.

'Why don't you sit up. Dr Loewe?'

Marianne didn't move, still thinking of the soft drifts and the few white petals that had clung to her father's beard as he struggled toward her. Dr Zurmer thought she had shocked her patient into immobility.

'After all, there are two of us in the room. Why should we pretend that only one of us is real, that only one of us is present?'

Marianne sat up.

'All these white flower dreams,' Dr Zurmer said, 'what are they about?'

'I'm sure they're about my mother. I don't know if you remember, my mother's name was Lily. And she was like a white flower, thin, pale, graceful. Just wafting around, not a solid person at all. Just a little bit of everything, you know, real estate, house painting, for a while she read tea leaves in some fake Gypsy restaurant. I mean, now she's a businesswoman, but then ... My father was the stable one, but she drove him away.'

Dr Zurmer said, 'He was stable, but he disappeared. You say she was "wafting around," but she never left you. And she always made a living, yes?'

'He didn't disappear. My mother was having an affair, one of many, I'm sure, she was such a fucking belle of the ball, and he couldn't stand it and he left.' Marianne was glad that she could say 'fucking.'

'It's understandable that he would choose to end the marriage. Not everyone would, but it's understandable. But why did he stop seeing you?'

'He didn't really have much choice. She got custody somehow, and then he moved to California for his work. I went to California once, for about a week, but then, I don't know, he remarried, and then he died in a car accident.' Marianne started to cry and wished she were back on the couch, invisible.

'How old were you when you went to California?'

'Nine.'

'How did you get there?'

'My mother took me by plane.'

'Your mother took you by plane to California so you could visit your father?'

'Sometimes she was overprotective. I remember he said that

when I was old enough to take the plane by myself I could come out there. I thought nine was old enough, but my mother took me.'

'Of course. Why would you send a nine-year-old three thousand miles away by herself, unless it was an emergency?'

'Lots of people do.'

'Lots of people behave selfishly and irresponsibly. It doesn't seem that your father thought nine was really old enough either. He, however, was willing to wait another year or two before you saw each other.'

'It wasn't like that.'

'I think it was. You are almost forty now. I am almost eighty-five. We are not going to have time for a long analysis, Dr Loewe, which is just as well. I will tell you what I see, when I see something, but you have to be willing to look. Your mother knew how important your father was to you, and even though your father had left her, she was willing to take the time and money to make sure that you saw him, even in the face of his indifference. You must think about why you need your father to be the hero of this story. Tomorrow, yes?'

Marianne went home, less happy than she had been the first time they met. Three weeks ago, walking into that gray-carpeted waiting room, with its two black-and-white Sierra Club photographs and the dusty mahogany coffee table offering only last week's *Paris-Match* and last year's *New Yorker*s, Marianne knew that she was in sure and authentic hands. Despite an unexpected penchant for bright, bulky sweaters, made charming and European by carefully embroidered flowers on the pockets, Dr Zurmer was just what Marianne had hoped for.

On Tuesday, Dr Zurmer interrupted Marianne's memory of her grandfather shaving with an old-fashioned straight razor to tell her that beige was not her color.

'Beige is for redheads, for certain blondes. Not for you. My hair was the same color fifty years ago. *Chatin*. Ahh, chestnut. A lovely color, even with the gray. You would look very nice in green, all different greens, like spring leaves. Maybe a ring or a bracelet, as well, to call attention to your pretty hands.'

Marianne looked at Dr Zurmer, and Dr Zurmer smiled back.

'We must stop for today. Tomorrow, Dr Loewe.'

Marianne went home and fed her cat, and as she put on her navy bathrobe and her backless slippers, she watched herself in the mirror.

During the next week's sessions, Dr Zurmer gave Marianne the name of a good masseuse, an expert hair colorist, and a store that specialized in narrow-width Swiss shoes, which turned out to be perfect for Marianne's feet and sensibilities. At the end of Thursday's session, Dr Zurmer suggested that Marianne focus less on the past and more on the present.

'Your mother invites you to her beach house every weekend, Dr Loewe. Why not go? I don't think she wants to devour you or humiliate you. I think she wants to show off her brilliant daughter to her friends and she wants you to appreciate the life she's made for herself – beach house and catering business and so on. This is no small potatoes for a woman of her background, for the delicate flower you say she is. Life is short, Dr Loewe. Go visit your mother and see what is really there. At the very worst, you will have escaped this dreadful heat and you will return to tell me that my notions are all wet.'

Charmed by Dr Zurmer's archaic Americanisms and the vision of herself and her mother walking on the beach at sunset, their identical short, strong legs and narrow feet skimming through the sand, Marianne rose to leave, not waiting for Dr Zurmer's dismissal.

Dr Zurmer began to rise and could not. Her head fell forward, and her half-moon glasses, which made her look so severe and so kind, landed on the floor.

Marianne crouched beside Dr Zurmer's chair and put just her fingertips on Dr Zurmer's shoulder. Dr Zurmer did not lift her head.

'Please take me home. I am not well.'

'Should I call your doctor? Or an ambulance? They can bring you to the hospital.'

'I am not going to a hospital. Please take me home.' Dr Zurmer raised her head, and without her glasses she looked extremely vulnerable and reptilian, an ancient turtle, arrogant in its longevity, resigned to its fate.

Terrified, Marianne drove Dr Zurmer home, regretting the Kleenex and Heath Bar wrappers in the backseat, where Dr Zurmer lay, pain dampening and distorting the matte, powdery surface of her fine old skin. When they approached a small Spanish-style house with ivy reaching up to the red tile roof and slightly weedy marigolds lining the front walk, Dr Zurmer indicated that Marianne should pull into the driveway. Marianne could not imagine carrying Dr Zurmer up the walk, although she was probably capable of lifting her, but she didn't think Dr Zurmer could make the hundred yards on her own.

'Is someone home? I can go let them know that you're here, and they can give us a hand.'

Dr Zurmer nodded twice, and her head sagged back against the seat.

A thin old man, shorter than Marianne and leaning hard on a rubber-tipped cane, opened the door. Marianne explained what had happened, even mentioning that she was Dr Zurmer's patient, which was a weird and embarrassing thing to have to say

to the man who was obviously her analyst's husband. He nodded
and followed Marianne out to the car. It was clear to Marianne
that this little old man was in no position to carry his wife to the
house, and that she, Marianne, would have to stick around for a
few more minutes and take Dr Zurmer in, probably to her bedroom, perhaps to her bathroom, which was not a pleasant
thought.

'Otto,' was all Dr Zurmer said.

They spoke softly in Russian, and Marianne gently pulled Dr
Zurmer from the backseat, handing her briefcase to the husband,
half carrying, half dragging Dr Zurmer up the walk under his
critical, anxious eye. Dr Zurmer's husband seemed not to speak
English, or not to speak to people other than his wife.

Marianne was so focused on not dropping Dr Zurmer and
following Mr or Dr Zurmer's hand signals that she barely saw her
analyst's house, although she had wondered about it, with occasional, pleasurable intensity, in the last three weeks. Dr Zurmer
slipped out of Marianne's arms onto a large bed covered with a
white lace spread and said thank you and good-bye. Marianne,
who had not wanted to come and had not wanted to stay, felt
that this was a little abrupt, even ungracious, but she was polite
and said it was no trouble and that she would find her own way
out so that they would not be disturbed. The old man had lain
down next to his wife and was wiping her damp face with his
handkerchief.

Marianne walked down the narrow, turning staircase, noticing
the scratched brass rods that anchored the faded green carpeting,
and looking into the faces in the framed photographs that dotted
the wall beside her like dark windows. Two skinny boys in baggy
dark trunks are building a huge, turreted sand castle trimmed with
sea shells, twigs, and the remains of horseshoe crabs, surrounded

by a moat that reaches up to the knees of a younger, taller Otto Zurmer. In another, the two skinny boys are now skinny teenagers sitting on a stone wall, back to back like bookends, in matching sunglasses, matching bare chests, and matching fearless and immortal grins.

Marianne was conscious of lingering, of trespassing, in fact, and she only took one quick look at the photograph that interested her the most. Dr Zurmer, whose first name, Anya, Marianne had read on the brass plaque of her office door, is sitting in a velvet armchair, legs stretched sideways and crossed at the slender white silk ankles. She cannot be more than twenty, and she looks pampered, with her lace-trimmed dress and carefully curled hair, and she looks beautiful; she peers uncertainly at the viewer, eager and afraid.

Marianne spent the next week working harder on the book she was trying to write, staking the tomato plants in her small yard, and getting her hair colored. It came out eye-catching and rich, the color of fine luggage, the color of expensive brandy, the kind drunk only by handsome old men sitting in wing armchairs by their early-evening fires. Marianne was tempted to wear a scarf until the color faded, but she could not bear to cover it up, and at night she fanned it out on her pillow and admired what she could see of the fine, gleaming strands.

She waited to hear from Dr Zurmer and decided that if she didn't get word from her by Friday, she would leave a message with the answering service. On Friday, Dr Zurmer called. She told Marianne that she was not yet well enough to return to the office but could see her for a session at home. She did not ask Marianne how she felt about meeting with her therapist, in her therapist's home, with little Dr/Mr Zurmer running in and out, she simply inquired whether Monday at nine would suit her.

That was their usual time, and Marianne said yes and hung up the phone quickly so as not to tire Dr Zurmer, who sounded terrible.

Dr Zurmer's husband let Marianne in silently, but when she was fully through the door he took her hand in both of his and thanked her, in perfectly good English.

'Please call me Otto,' he said. His smile was very kind, and Marianne said her name and was pleased with them both.

Dr Zurmer sat in bed, propped up by dozens of large and small Battenberg lace pillows, her silver hair brushed, neat and sleek as mink. She wore a remarkably businesslike grey satin bed jacket. Marianne couldn't tell if Dr Zurmer's face was slightly longer and looser than before or if she had forgotten, in a week, exactly what Dr Zurmer looked like.

'I feel much better today. A very tiny stroke, my doctor said. And no harm done, apparently. Thank you, Dr Loewe. So, I will lie down during our sessions and you will sit up.'

Marianne began by telling Dr Zurmer her latest flower dream but wrapped it up quickly in order to talk about the photograph of Dr Zurmer, not mentioning the boys; and she sat back in the little brocade chair, looking at the ceiling, in order to talk about the dislocating, fascinating oddness of being in Dr Zurmer's house. Dr Zurmer smiled, shaking her head sympathetically, and fell asleep. Marianne sat quietly, only a little insulted, and watched Dr Zurmer breathe. At her elbow was a mahogany dresser laid over with embroidered, crocheted runners, four small photographs in silver frames and three perfume bottles of striped Murano glass sitting on top. The little gold-tipped bottles were almost empty. One photograph, as Marianne expected, shows the two young men from the stone wall and the beach, a good bit older, both in suits. They are clearly at a wedding, with linen-covered tables and gladioli behind them, although there is no bride in sight. Another shows Dr Zurmer and Otto, their arms around each other, in front of the lighthouse at Gay Head, and the picture is not unlike one of Marianne and her ex-husband, at that same spot, during the brief, good time of their marriage. The other two photographs are of a dark-skinned woman in a bathrobe, holding what must be a baby wrapped in a blue and white blanket, and finally, a very little boy with black curls, jug ears, and the same slightly slant, long-lashed eyes as the woman.

As Marianne reached the front door, Otto clumped toward her.

'Tea?' he said, waving his cane toward the back of the house.

Marianne said no and went home to look up the phone numbers of other psychoanalysts.

On Thursday, Otto called. 'Please come today,' he said. 'She wants to see you.'

Marianne had already set up a consultation with another analyst, a middle-aged man with a good reputation and an office overlooking the river, but she went.

Dr Zurmer was sitting up again, her bed jacket open over a flannel nightgown and her hair tufted in downy silver puffs. She stretched out her hand for Marianne's and held on to it as Marianne sat down, much closer than planned.

'It seems that I am not well enough to be your analyst after all. But I don't think we should let that stop us from enjoying each other's company, do you? You come and visit, and we'll have tea.'

Marianne could not imagine why Dr Zurmer wanted her to visit.

'Why not? You're smart, a very kind person, you have a wonderful imagination and sense or humor – I see that in your dreams – why shouldn't I want you to visit me? Otto will bring us tea. Sit.'

Over pale green tea swarming with brown bits of leaf, Marianne and Dr Zurmer smiled at each other.

'I was very interested in the photographs on your dresser,' Marianne said.

'What about them interests you?'

'This is just a visit, remember? Tea and conversation.'

Dr Zurmer pretended to slap her own wrist and smiled broadly at Marianne, her cheeks folding up like silk ruching.

'Touché,' she said. 'Bring the photos over here, please. And there's an album in the magazine rack there.

'Oh, look at this, little Alexei. Everyone has these bathtub photographs tucked away. And this is Alexei in Cub Scouts, I think that lasted for six months. He loved the uniform, but he was not, not Scout material. And this is him with his brother, Robert. You saw some of these on the wall, I think. At Martha's Vineyard. We used to stay at a little farmhouse, two bedrooms and a tiny kitchen. Friends of Otto's lent it to us every summer. Otto designed their house, the big house in the background here, and their house, I forget, in the suburbs of Boston. We were the house pets, but it was wonderful for the children. This is Robert's college graduation. I can't remember what all the armbands represent, he protested everything. Unfortunately for him, we were liberals, so it was difficult to disturb us. He did become a banker, there was that. And here is Alexei graduating, no armbands, just the hair. But it was such beautiful hair, I wanted him to keep it long, I thought he looked like Apollo. And here are the wedding pictures, Alexei and his wife, Naria. Lebanese. They met in graduate school. And this is my only grandson, Lee. As beautiful as the day. As good as he is beautiful. Very bright child. Alexei is a wonderful father, father and mother both. This big one is Lee last year, on his fourth birthday. That's his favorite bear, I don't remember now, the train station name.'

'Paddington. He's lovely. Lee is just lovely.'

'Naria left them almost two years ago. She has a narcissistic personality disorder. She simply could not mother. People cannot do what they are not equipped to do. So, she's gone, back to Lebanon. Also, very self-destructive, to return to a place like Lebanon, divorced, a mother, clearly not a virgin. She will care for her father, in his home, for the rest of her life. Who can say? Perhaps that was her wish.'

Dr Zurmer said 'narcissistic personality disorder' the way you'd say 'terminal cancer,' and Marianne nodded, understanding that Naria was gone from this earth.

'And this is a picture Alexei took of me and Otto two years ago. Those two lovers, the gods made them into trees, or bushes? Philomena? So that they might never part. We look like that, yes? Already beginning to merge with the earth.'

Dr Zurmer lay back, and the album slid between them.

'I cannot really speak of loving him anymore. Does one love the brain, or the heart? Does one appreciate one's blood? We have kept each other from the worst loneliness, and we listen to each other. We don't say anything very interesting anymore, we talk of Lee, of Alexei, we remember Robert . . .'

Marianne waited for the terrible story.

'He died in a car accident, right after the wedding. I am still grieving and I am still angry. He was drinking too much, that was something he did. Alexei, never. My bad Russian genes. He left nothing behind, an apartment full of junk, a job he disliked, debts. I thought perhaps a pregnant girlfriend would emerge, but that didn't happen, I would have made it so, if I could have. I have to rest, my dear.'

Dr Zurmer sank back into her pillows and asked Marianne to go into the bottom drawer of the mahogany dresser. Marianne brought her the only thing in it, a bolt of green satin, thick and cool, rippling in her hands like something alive. Dr Zurmer tied it around her waist, turning Marianne's white shirt and khaki slacks into something dashing, exotic, and slightly, delightfully androgynous.

'Just so. When you leave, please say good-bye to Otto. He likes you so much. "Such a luffly girl,"' she said, mimicking Otto's accent, which was, if anything, less noticeable, less guttural, than her own. 'If he's not in the kitchen, just wait a minute. He's probably getting the newspaper, going for his constitutional. Be well, Marianne. Come again soon.'

The man sitting at the kitchen table was so clearly the slightly bigger boy from the photographs, the bearded groom, that Marianne smiled at him familiarly, filled with tenderness and receptivity, as though her pores were steaming open. He stared back at her and then, with great, courtly gestures, folded the newspaper and slid it behind the toaster.

'You must be Marianne.'

'Yes. I just wanted to say good-bye to your father, I'm on my way home,' she said.

'That will please him. I'm Alex Zurmer. I don't know where Pop is.' He looked at her again, at her deep brown eyes and long neck, his own sweet baby giraffe, and watched her blunt, bony fingers playing with the fringe of the glimmering green sash. Alex shrugged, lifting his palms heavenward, as awestruck and grateful as Noah, knowing that he had been selected for survival and the arrival of doves. He watched Marianne's restless, slightly bitten fingers twisting in and out of the thick tasseled ends, and he could feel them touching his face, lifting his hair.

'Let's have tea while we wait. Marianne,' he said, and he rose to pull out her chair, and she very deliberately laid her hand next to his on the back of the chair.

'Let's,' said Marianne. 'Let's put out a few cookies too. If you use loose tea, I'll read the leaves.'

A Blind Man Can See How
Much I Love You

Jane Spencer collects pictures of slim young men. In the bottom drawer of her desk, between swatches of silk and old business cards for Spencer Interiors, she has two photos of James Dean, one of a deeply wistful Jeremy Irons in *Brideshead*, arm in arm with the boy holding the teddy bear, a sepia print of Rudolph Valentino in 1923, without burnoose or eyeliner, B. D. Wong's glossies as Song Liling and as his own lithe, androgynous self, and Robert Mapplethorpe slipping sweetly out of his jeans in 1972. She has a pictorial history of Kevin Bacon, master of the transition from elfin boy to good-looking man without adding bulk or facial hair.

The summer Jessie Spencer turned five, she played Capture the Flag every day with the big boys, the almost-six-year-olds who'd gone to kindergarten a year late. Jane never worried, even in passing, about Jessie's IQ or her eye-hand coordination or her social skills. Jessie and Jane were a mutual admiration society of two smart, strong, blue-eyed women, one five and one thirty-five, both good skaters and good singers and good storytellers. Jane didn't mention all this to the other mothers at play group, who would have said it was the same between them and their daughters when Jane could see it was not, and she didn't mention it to her own sweet, anxious mother, who would have taken it, understandably, as a reproach. Jane didn't even mention their closeness to her pediatrician, keeper of every mother's secret fears and wishes, but it sang her to sleep at night. Jane's reputation as the play group's good listener was undeserved; the mothers talked about their knock-kneed girls and backward boys and Jane smiled and her eyes followed Jessie. She watched her and thought, That smile! Those lashes! How brave! How determined!

Jane sometimes worried that Jessie was too much of a tomboy, like Sarah and Mellie, even faster runners and more brutal partisans; it was nothing to them to make a smaller boy cry by yanking up his underpants, or to grind sand into the scalp of the girl who hogged the tire swing. These two didn't cry, not even when Mellie cut her lip on the edge of the teeter-totter, not even when Sarah got a splinter the size of a matchstick. But Sarah and Mellie, in their overalls and dirty baseball jerseys, never had the boys' heartless prankishness, the little devils dancing in the blacks of their eyes. Jessie had exactly that, and the other kids knew she wasn't a tomboy, never strained to be one of the boys. There was no teasing, no bullying line drawn in the sand. Jane knew that one day soon, in the cove behind John Lyman School, the boys would pull out their penises and demonstrate to Jessie that she could not pee standing up, and it would be terrible for Jessie. Jane was wrong. Jessie watched the boys and practiced at home, making a funnel with both hands and a baggie. When Andrew and Franklin went to pee on the far side of the rhododendron, Jessie came too, unzipping and pushing her hips forward until there was, if not a fine spray, a decent dribble. The boys thought nothing of it until first grade, and when they did and the teacher pushed Jessie firmly into the girls' bathroom, she walked home at recess, horrified by the life ahead, and Jane could not coax her back for a week.

It was worse when Jane took her to get a simple navy blue jumper for a friend's wedding. Jane held it out, pleased that she'd found something in Jessie's favorite color without a ruffle or a speck of lace, and Jessie stared at it as if her mother had gone mad, wailing in rage and embarrassment until Jane drove her to Macy's for a boy's navy blazer with grey pants and dared the salesperson to comment. They compromised on patent leather loafers and a white turtleneck. People at the wedding thought only that Jane was her fashionable self and Jessie adorable. Very Kristy McNichol, the bride's mother said. Driving home, Jane knew that she had managed not to see it, as you manage not to see that your neighbor's new baby has your husband's eyes and nose, until one day you run into them at the supermarket and you cannot help but see. Jessie slept the whole way home, smears of butter-cream on the white turtleneck, rose petals falling from her blazer pocket, and Jane cried from Storrs to Durham. She had appreciated and pitied her mother and adored her father, a short, dapper man who cartwheeled through the living room at her request and told his own Brooklyn version of Grimm's Fairy Tales at bedtime. She had liked Jessie's handsome father enough to think of marrying him until he was revealed to have a wife in Eau Claire and bad debts in five states. It did not seem possible that the great joke God would play on her was to take the love of her life, a wonderfully improved piece of Jane, and say, Oops. Looks like a girl but it's a boy! Sorry. Adjust accordingly. It took Jane all of Jessie's childhood to figure out what the adjustment might be and to save fifty thousand dollars to pay for it.

How do you get the first morning appointment with the best gender-reassignment surgeon in the world? It cannot be so different from shopping at Bergdorf's, Jane thinks. She looks twice at the pretty brown-skinned receptionist behind the big pine desk. The woman's shoulders are enormous; the fabric of her teal jacket pulls hard across her back, and when she reaches for Jess's file, the seams of her straight skirt crack and bend over her powerful thighs. Jane doesn't want to be distracted by thinking about this person's femaleness, genetic or otherwise. Jane's job is to be pleasant and patient as a gesture of respect, to be witty, if possible, and to convey, without any vulgar emphasis, that she is the kind of woman who really, really appreciates good service.

'Lovely flowers,' Jane says. 'The white alstroemeria. What do they call them? Peruvian lilies, I think.' Jane knows what most flowers are called.

Marcella Gray puts her hands together like a bishop, clicking her long red nails. She knows what Jane is thinking. Her own daughter calls her the Deltoid Queen. Her husband calls her Queen Lats. Marcella loves bodybuilding and Dr. Laurence, and when he added transsexuals to his practice she didn't love it, but she learned to live with it and the little irony that came with being their receptionist. Jane Spencer is a well-bred pain in the ass, but the boy looks like he will make it. Tall enough, small hips.

Jess hears Jane charming across the room and looks up from *Newsweek*, smiling at Marcella and running a hand through his black hair. It is a killer smile, white teeth and a dimple near his blue eyes. Marcella smiles back, which is more than she usually does. Jess doesn't think that Jane can get them a better appointment, but it's not impossible. Jane got the registrar at Reed to accept that Jess Spencer who begins there next January is a boy, even though Jessie Spencer finished her freshman year at University of Michigan as a girl. It had been Jane's thought that the anonymity of big Michigan would not be a bad idea. Substance abuse and black-market hormones and botched surgeries are the tragedies of transsexuals, but Jess suspected that pure loneliness would do him in. He had not gone out for a beer with a pal or kissed a girl since he started cross-dressing in earnest. He wouldn't go out with his transitioning self, and he didn't want the kind of person, boy or girl, who would.

Once you know there are transsexuals, you see them everywhere. Short, pear-shaped men. Tall, knobby women. When you walk out of the waiting room of the North American Gender Identity Clinic, everyone looks peculiar. You flip through magazines and think, Hmmm, Leo DiCaprio? There's something about him. And Jamie Lee Curtis? Look at those legs.

In her own mirror Jane now looks odd to herself. Maybe she's morphing; her feet look funny, her shoulders seem as wide as Marcella's, and there is a dark downy space where her hairline seems to be receding. Maybe she'll cross over before Jess does, except she'll look like Don Knotts and Jess will look like one of Calvin Klein's young men. She would like to take Jess shopping before the surgery. If Jess goes for a Western look, she could wear cowboy boots and gain a couple of inches without resorting to lifts.

Jane goes through the line in the caf, musing. Low-fat carrot-raisin muffin, girl food. Cheese Danish, boy food. Coffee, black, boy food. Tea, girl food. Bottled water, tough call. Bagel, also gender-neutral. Another mother from the support group sits down across from Jane. Jane remembers that her name is Sheila and she is an accountant from Santa Fe, but she cannot call up the child's face or name. Sheila pours three packets of Equal into her coffee. 'I had breast cancer, you know. I don't have a left breast. It must be someone's idea of a bad joke. These girls lop them off. We try to keep ours.'

Jane says, 'Well, for them, it's like their breasts are tumors. For them, I just don't think their breasts ever feel to them the way ours do to us.' She thinks, And that would be how you can tell that they're transsexual, *Sheila*.

Sheila looks at Jane sideways, pursing her lips as if to say, Well, aren't you understanding? Aren't you just Transsexual Mom of the Year? Maybe Sheila doesn't think that, maybe she just resents Jane's tone or her navy silk pantsuit and pearls, or maybe it's just Jane. She's not cuddly. The other mothers look sad and scruffy, faded sweatshirts and stretched-out pants, as if all their money has gone to the therapists and endocrinologists and surgeons, leaving not even a penny for lip gloss or new shoes or a haircut. There are two fathers in the group. One is the soft, sorry kind, the kind who sits weeping in the front row at his son's arson trial, the kind who brings doughnuts to the support group for Parents of Guys Who Microwave Cats. The other one, the General, is the kind of big, blunt man Jane likes. He's not in uniform, but there's no mistaking the posture or the brush cut or the tanned, creased neck or the feet in black lace-ups planted square on the floor. When he talks to someone in the group, he doesn't just look at them, he turns his entire head and shoulders, giving a powerful, not unpleasant RoboCop effect. Jane likes him much better than his son-turned-daughter, a shellacked glittery girl with a French manicure and pink lipstick. This man protected his slight fierce boy, steered him into karate so that he would not be teased, or if teased, could make sure it did not happen twice. Loved that boy, fed him a hot breakfast at four A.M., drove him to tae kwon do tournaments all over Minnesota and then all over

the Midwest. They flew to competitions in Los Angeles for ten
and eleven, to Boston for under thirteen, then to the National
Juniors Competitions, and there are three hundred trophies in
their house. That boy is now swinging one small-ankled foot,
dangling a pink high-heeled sandal off it and modeling himself
not on Mia Hamm or Sally Ride or even Lindsay Davenport
(whose dogged, graceless determination to make the most of
what she has, to ignore everyone who says that because she
doesn't look like a winner she won't ever be one, strikes Jane as
an ideal role model for female transsexuals) but on Malibu
Barbie. And the General has to love this girl as he loved that boy,
or be without.

Sheila picks up the other half of her sandwich and says, 'Jo' –
or perhaps Joe? – 'just walked in. I think we'll spend the rest of
the break together.'

Jane looks at Jo, an overweight young woman who must be
going into manhood; if she were going the other way, they
would already have replaced the Coke-bottle glasses with contacts and done something nicer with her short, frizzy brown
hair and treated her jawline acne. Jane thinks, No wonder
you're such a misery, Sheila. Your Jo, waddling through life, will
never be an attractive anything. Jane drinks her coffee and
thinks that it may be that in this world good-looking matters
more than anatomical anomalies – that like well-made underwear, good-looking itself smooths over the more awkward parts
of your presentation and keeps your secrets until the right
moment.

Malibu Barbie begins the next group. Dying to talk. She bats her
eyelashes at her father, which is not what Jane would do if she

wanted to win this man over, and then she looks around the room. Her make-up is better than Jane remembered; it's not Jane's taste, it's more the department store makeover look, but she's done a good job. Subtle blush, the crease of the eyelid slightly darkened, black mascara framing the big brown eyes. At the thought of this boy teaching himself the stupid, necessary girl tricks that Jess refused to learn and now doesn't need, Jane's contempt dissolves. Who does not change and hide? Maybe calf implants and tattooed eyeliner and colored contacts and ass lifts are just more trivial, even less honorable versions of gender surgery. Jane doesn't really think so, she thinks that augmentation and improvement are not the same as a complete reversal of gender, but it does occur to her that if it were as easy as getting your eyelids done, and as difficult to detect, there might be more transsexuals around and they might be considered no worse than Roseanne or Burt Reynolds.

'I'm a woman,' Barbie says. 'I'm as much a woman as any of you.'

Of course, she does not mean, As much as any of you MTF transsexuals; she means, As much as you, Jane and Sheila and Gail, as much as you, Susan, whom Jane suspects has been chosen to lead this mixed group because she manages to radiate unmistakable genetic femaleness without offering up a single enviable physical quality. Susan is the permanent PTA secretary, the assistant Brownie leader, and even the least compelling transsexual woman can feel her equal, and Barbie and the other pretty girl in the room, Pamela, can feel superior. The envy of the biologically misapprehended, of people who know that God has fucked them over in utero, is not a small thing, and the anger that plain women feel for pretty ones is a hundred times worse when it takes such drive and suffering just to get to plain.

Susan does not pick up the challenge; she doesn't even hear it as a challenge.

'Of course you are. And what does that mean to you?'

'It means this.' Pamela speaks up. She and Barbie are a tag team of newly discovered feminism and major trips to the mall. 'It means this culture looks down on women and it despises trans-sexuals, and as both, we don't plan to take it lying down.'

Take what? Jane thinks. Take fifty thousand dollars' worth of hormones and surgery and a closetful of Victoria's Secret? (It is amazing. You could stand next to naked post-op Pamela in a locker room and all you would think is, Jesus, what a great body she has.) Take the fact that because you were raised as a boy, however unhappily, there is still something there, some hidden, insistent tail of Y chromosome, that calls out when the world ignores your feelings, when it's clear that you are not the tem-plate or the bottom line of anything important, I don't have to take this shit?

'Barbie and I have invited the Transgender Avengers to come to a meeting.'

And Barbie's father looks the way military men looked when their sons grew their hair long and left the country. 'Who the hell are they? Barb, I thought the point was to just become a woman, just live your life as normally as possible.'

Barbie thrusts both slim arms out in a martial-arts jab, and her silver bracelets jingle up her tan, hairless arms. She says, 'I'm a fighter, Dad. You know that,' and Jane thinks, Oh my fucking God, and she and Jess rise at the same time to go laugh in the hall.

Jess says, 'Oh, Jesus. I don't know what to say. Transgender Avengers – is that next to Better Sportswear?'

Jane and Jess walk toward the lobby; they have twenty minutes before the meeting with Dr Laurence, and Jess knows that Jane will want a cigarette before they go choose what kind of penis Jess will have.

Jane smokes every now and then. She hates to smoke in front of Jess. She certainly doesn't want Jess to smoke, but she has thought that a small cigar, every once in a while, might help. It is all small things, Jane knows. She is now practically a professional observer of gender, and she sees that although homeliness and ungainliness won't win you any kindness from the world, they are not, in and of themselves, the markers that will get you tossed out of the restaurant, the men's room, the Michigan Womyn's Music Festival. (It is incredible to Jane that a big feminist party that has room for women who refer to themselves as leather daddies, and women wearing nothing but strap-on dildoes and Birkenstocks, and old women with sagging breasts and six labia rings, should draw the line at three women in Gap jeans and Indigo Girls T-shirts just because they were born male.) If you take hormones, if you dress in a middle-of-the-road version of whatever your size will allow (no bustiers without a bust, no big Stetsons on guys barely filling out size sixteen in the boys' department), if your fat is distributed in the usual ways and you are not more than six inches off your sex's average height, the world will leave you alone. It may not ask you for a date, but it will not kill you and it will probably not notice.

Jess would like to walk into Dr Laurence's office, go into a deep sleep, and walk out with his true body. He has known and seen this body in his dreams, behind half-closed lids, in quick glances at the mirror (with a few beers and a sock in his shorts), and he knows that it is not the body he will have. He's seen the phalloplasties on a couple of transsexual guys, both the plumped-up clitoris version and the hot-dog version with the silicone implant balls, and neither makes him happy. Inside of himself he is Magic Johnson, the world's greatest point guard. When he flips through Dr Laurence's photo album, it's clear that he'll be more like Anthony Epps of the Continental Basketball Association's Sioux Falls team. Jess lights one of his mother's Kools. In high school, when he played basketball on the girls' team, a distant cousin of Chamiqua Holdsclaw said to him, 'It's true you all can't dunk, but that doesn't mean you can't play.'

It would please Jane to know that it was Jess's smile and not her shopping good manners that got Marcella Gray at reception to fiddle with the appointment book. Right after they pick the most realistic penis, somewhere between the little and the deluxe, Dr Laurence says, 'It looks like we're good to go for the day after tomorrow.' He puts his hand on Jess's shoulder. 'You did great with your top surgery, this is going to go fine. A year from now, six months from now, you're going to be a happy young man.' Dr Laurence believes in this work. He believes in going to El Salvador to fix clubfeet, cleft palates, and botched amputations, and he believes that it's his job on this earth to give people a chance to live life as it should be lived, whole and able and knowing they have been touched by God's mercy. Dr Laurence believes that when someone like Jess is in the womb, there is a last, unaccountable blast of the opposite sex hormone and the child is born one sex on the outside and the true one on the inside.

Jess and Jane walk back to their apartment; the clinic has a row of condos, upscale and fully equipped and three blocks from the surgical center. Men and women come and go, with companions or nurses or large doses of Percocet, doubled over with pain in March and out of the chrysalis in May or June.

'A little sunbathing?' Jane says. Everyone looks better with a tan, and it will be a while before Jess can lie on their sundeck again.

Just two years ago, they lay naked in their backyard, sun block on their nipples and white asses, reading and drinking club soda. Now they turn away from each other to strip down to their underwear. Jess goes into the kitchen for two bottles of lime seltzer, and Jane sees the dark hair on his golden arms, his neat round biceps, the tight line of muscle at the back of his arms, and the two thin ridges of scar tissue on his chest. She nagged him to massage the scars four times a day with vitamin E oil and a mix from her dermatologist, and now they have almost disappeared. Jane watches this handsome boy-girl beside her put down the bottles and stretch out on the chaise.

'Don't burn,' she says.

'Oh, all right,' Jess says. 'I was going to, but now I won't.'

Jane watches her, watches him, until Jess falls asleep, a lock of black hair falling forward. Jane pushes it back and cries in the bathroom for an hour. She leaves Jess a note, suggesting that they get in some entertainment while they can and go out for Chinese and a movie. They have gone out for Chinese and a movie once a week for almost fifteen years, even when Jessie would only eat rice and chicken fingers. When Jessie was at Michigan, that was what they missed the most. Jessie sent an occasional note home, written on a stained and crumpled Chinese takeout menu. When Jane opened the envelope, the smell of General Tso's Chicken came up at her.

When she hoped that Jessie might just be a lesbian, when Jessie also thought that might be it, her hair short and spiky in front, carved into little faux sideburns, long and awkward in back, Jane took them on vacation to Northampton,

Massachusetts, the Lesbian Paradise. Jane found out that Jessie's appalling haircut had an appalling name: the mullet. Surely Nathalie Barney and Barbara Stanwyck and Greta Garbo, all lesbians of the kind Jane would be happy for Jessie to be, would not have been seen in mullet haircuts and overalls. Jessie was so happy her mouth hung open. If she took her eyes off this unexpected, extravagant gift, it might disappear. She squeezed her mother's arm and then dropped it, reluctant to show just how much this parade of everyday lesbian life meant to her, more than any other trip or present. She worried that her mother might think that all the other presents and the trips to Disney World had been wrong or unnecessary, and they had not. But it was true that this trip was the only time Jessie did not feel like a complete impostor.

Jane was just happy to see her daughter happy again. She could live with this, easily, especially with Jessie bouncing beside her, smiling right up to her thrice-pierced, beautifully shaped ears. There were unfortunate outfits, of course, and more of those haircuts on women who should have known better, and although some women were admirably, astonishingly fit in bicycle shorts and tank tops, more were too heavy for their frames, cello hips trying a John Wayne walk, big breasts swinging under washed-out T-shirts. Hopeless, Jane thought, but not bad. Jessie ate like a hungry boy, for fuel, for muscle and bone and growth, and as she worked through a double chocolate chip cone from Herrell's, her ears turned bright red. Jane started to turn around, to see what it was, but Jessie hissed, 'Don't look,' and despite Jane's hostile maternal impulse to demonstrate that it was her job to monitor public manners, not Jessie's, she sat still for another ten seconds and then strolled over to the wastebasket and dumped her half-eaten cone, pretending, if anyone cared, that she couldn't eat another bite. What had turned Jessie's ears scarlet? A man or a woman, beautiful as Apollo is beautiful, and in the cropped silver hair, loose jeans, layers of Missoni sweaters, and brown polished boots, there was no clue at all and Jane thought, Goddammit, go home, we're looking at lesbians here.

Jane liked Northampton. The Panda Garden Chinese Restaurant, elegant gold earrings shaped like ginkgo leaves, and the beautiful blunt hands of the saleswoman unfolding Italian sheets, snapping thick ivory linen down the length of a pine table, charmed her, and she still visits every couple of years on her own long after Jess has come to prefer Seattle and Vancouver.

Jane walks to the mall. They need toilet paper. Jane needs emery boards. She has to get vitamins and Tropicana Original orange juice (testosterone has not changed Jess's lifelong hatred of orange pulp and of green vegetables) and high-protein powder for shakes and maybe some books on tape until Jess has the energy to read.

Jane strolls through the entire mall, buying funny socks and aloe vera gel and Anthony Hopkins reading *The Silence of the Lambs*, and winds up at the Rite Aid, the least glamorous stop on a not very glamorous list. She recognizes the man at the end of the aisle. Not part of Dr Laurence's staff, she would have noticed those hazel eyes. Someone she knows from home? Did she decorate a house for him? An office? Cheekbones like a Cherokee and flat waves of slick dark hair like a high-style black man from the forties.

'I'm Cole Ramsey,' he says, and Jane smells bay rum aftershave. 'I think I saw you at the medical center? Down the street?' He is not really asking, he is Southern. And he keeps talking. 'Forgive me for being so forward.'

Jane has goosebumps and her chest hurts, and it has been so

long since she's had these symptoms that for a moment she thinks she's getting the flu. She introduces herself and drops the package of emery boards, which Cole Ramsey picks up and holds on to

'May I walk along with you?'

'Through the Rite Aid? Be my guest.'

By the time they've finished shopping and bought a Pooh Corners mobile from the Disney Store for Cole's brand-new nephew, Jane knows that he is an endocrinologist who sometimes consults with Dr Laurence and has his own regular-people practice on the other side of Santa Barbara. Cole likes to talk. He talks about malls and why he enjoys them ('Of course, I also like kudzu, so there you go') and Dr Laurence ('A good man and a good surgeon – a rare combination, not that I should bad-mouth the profession, but most doctors are half-people and most surgeons are not even that') and the poetry of Richard Howard ('He's so decorous but so willing to disturb'), and he tries to talk Jane into dinner.

'My son's having surgery day after tomorrow. Tonight's his last chance for Chinese food.' That's enough information, Jane thinks.

'Of course. Just a drink, then? Or a post-shopping cappuccino?'

Jane calls home, and Jess, still drowsy from the sun and anxiety, says, 'Fine. Go. Whoop it up.'

Jane says, 'I'll be home no later than seven, and we can go out for dinner and catch the nine-thirty movie.'

'Whatever, Mom,' Jess says. 'It'll be fine. I'm going back to sleep.'

*

Jane falls on her bed, after the sixteen-ounce Bloody Mary with Cole Ramsey and the beer with Jess and their all-appetizer dinner and malted milk balls at the movie, and she thinks of Cole and exhales happily. His soft, light voice. The focused, flattering attention. The self-deprecating jokes. Jane has not had a close gay male friend since Anthony died in '88, and Cole is charming and such a pleasure to look at.

In the morning Jane and Jess kick around until it's time for him to check into the hospital. They play gin and walk to the bookstore and waste time, and eventually they pack and watch an afternoon rerun of *Friends*. They act more like pilots before a big mission than like patients. At the hospital Jess is hungry and nervous and unwilling to let Jane sit with him any longer.

'Love you, Mom,' he says.

'Love you, too, honey,' Jane says, and thinks, Oh, my brave girl.

Jane sees Cole in the hospital lobby, patting the cheek of a fat blond nurse. When he sees Jane, he gives the nurse a squeeze on the shoulder and she hugs him, her wide body hiding him from view. Cole hurries to catch up with Jane.

'You must have just left your son. May I walk along with you?'

They walk through the parking lot, into the wet grass and waving palms and blooming jacarandas of the small, unexpectedly tropical city park.

'This is nice,' he says. 'A little bit of Paradise we didn't know about.' He makes it sound as if he and Jane have been exploring municipal parks together for years.

'You have a good relationship with the nurses,' Jane says.

'Patients and nurses are about everyone that counts in a hospital.'

'I bet that one's in love with you,' Jane says. She's teasing; she and Anthony used to talk about women who fell in love with him with a particularly gratifying mix of compassion and malice.

'Oh, I'm over fifty, no one falls in love with me anymore.' Cole sits down on a bench and pulls gently on Jane's hand.

'Don't be silly. Men have it easy until they're seventy. And look at Cary Grant, he looked fabulous until he died.' And he was gay too, she thinks.

'Well, I'm not Cary Grant, I'm afraid, just a skinny doc from South Carolina. Not that I wasn't a fan. Particularly *Bringing Up Baby*.'

'Well, yes,' Jane says. 'One of the best movies ever made.' They talk through the movie from beginning to end, and he applauds her imitation of Katharine Hepburn, and when they get to the scene with the crazy dog and poor Cary Grant in Hepburn's peignoir, they laugh out loud.

Cole looks at his watch and sighs. 'This has been just lovely, but I do have to run.'

Jane looks at him. 'Of course. Someone waiting at home?' It would be nice to be friends with a gay couple. She could invite them over for dinner, for pizza at least, while Jess is in the hospital, or maybe while he's recuperating and getting bored.

Cole looks down at his hands.

'I'm in mid-divorce. I promised my soon-to-be-ex-wife that we could do a last furniture divvy tonight. We've been trying to stay out of the lawyer's office as much as possible, but that does mean that we spend far too much time talking to each other. Comes under the heading of no good deed goes unpunished, I suppose.'

'What good deed?' Jane is trying to figure out whether he means 'wife' in the sense of 'woman I am married to,' or 'wife' in the sense of man in my life who played a kind of wifely role.'

'Oh, you know. I don't want to bore you. The good deed of ending twelve years of unhappy marriage with an amicable divorce. After God answered my prayers and sent her the kind of man she should have married in the first place.'

Straight? Jane thinks.

Cole holds Jane's hands in his. They are the same size.

'I am sorry to have to run, and even sorrier that this kind of dreary talk should ruin our little moment. I'll walk you home.'

'You don't have to.' Jane says. 'It's a safe couple of blocks.'

'It will be a pleasure,' he says. 'And it will be my last pleasure for a few hours.' He smiles. 'Except when I insist that my wife take back some of the horrible furniture we got from her mother, the Terror of Tallahassee. I used to hope our house would just go up in flames and we could start again.'

Actual wife, Jane thinks.

At the doorstep Cole says, 'I have to tell the truth. I saw you before our serendipitous meeting in the Rite Aid. You were day-dreaming in the cafeteria. You looked so far away and so lovely. I wanted to be wherever you were.' He brings her hand to his mouth, kisses it right above the wrist, and goes.

In bed Jane holds her wrist gently and hopes very hard that Jess will be all right. She does not believe in God, but she believes in Dr Laurence, and she believes that people who are loved and cared for have a better chance in life than people who are not.

Cole rings the doorbell at midnight.

'Forgive me. You must have been sleeping. I don't know what I was thinking. Well, I do. I was thinking about your energy, your mix of acceptance and strength, and I felt in need of it.'

He talks nonstop, flattery and Southern folk sayings, snatches of Auden and Yeats, a joke about sharks and lawyers whose punch line he mangles, and finally Jane pours him a glass of wine and wraps his hand around it.

'You must think I'm demented,' he says.

'No, just worn out. Actually, I thought you were gay.'

Cole smiles. 'Oh, my. I wouldn't mind being, except that that would require having sex with men.' He looks right at Jane. 'That is not my preference.'

'I'm embarrassed. I don't know why I thought that. Your manners are so good, I guess.'

Cole pats her hand. He doesn't look surprised or offended. 'Crazy Creole mother. Jumped-up Irish father. I was terrible at team sports. Just barely American, in fact.'

Jane pours herself a glass of wine and yawns. Cole loosens his tie.

'Spending all my time at Dr Laurence's clinic, I could have been wondering if you were, you know, genetically male.' Jane smiles.

Cole laughs. 'Mmm,' he says. 'If I were not my mother's son, if I have a few more glasses of wine, if you allow that robe to slip open another inch or two, then I might say, Oh, dear Jane, it would be my great pleasure to satisfy your curiosity.'

There is a long silence. Cole touches the side of her face with two fingers, from her brow to her chin, and Jane leans forward and kisses his temples and then his cheek.

'I'm so out of practice,' she says.

Cole kisses her neck, and the goosebumps return.

'No,' he whispers. 'There's no practicing for this.'

They kiss on Jane's couch until dawn, unbuttoned and unsure, hot, restless, and dreamy. In between, Cole says that his back is not great. Jane tells him, as she has not told anyone, that her doctor thinks she'll need a hip replacement by the time she's sixty.

'The erotic life of the middle-aged,' he says. 'Let's soldier on.'

Cole undresses Jane a little more, and at every moment of skin revealed he kisses her and thanks her. He sits behind her, biting her very gently down the spine until she cries out. Jane turns to face him, now in just her underpants, and sees that he has taken off only his shoes. She puts both hands on his belt buckle. Cole lifts them off firmly and kisses them.

'Let me go on touching you,' he says. 'For a little longer.' And he holds her hands over her head and kisses the undersides of her breasts and the untanned shadows beneath them.

His beeper goes off.

Jane puts her robe back on. 'The vibrating ones seem more discreet.'

She feels clotted and cold, and to stave off shame (really, she has known him just a couple of hours; really, is this what she does while her only child lies in a hospital bed?) she is prepared to make him feel terrible, but his hands are trembling and he cannot put his feet into the right shoes.

'I have to go. Like the Chinese sages, crawling with charity, limp with duty.' His jacket is on, his beeper is in his pocket. 'But I am prepared to grovel, for weeks on end, if necessary.' His thick hair sticks up like dreadlocks, and there are wet, lipsticky blotches on his shirt. 'I'll come look for you tomorrow in the hospital, if I may.' He stands there, slightly bent, expecting a blow, as if this is the right, inevitable moment in their relationship for Jane to backhand him.

Jane shrugs. After all his trouble, his shirttail is hanging out.

'Jane. Forgive me, please.' He says 'Forgive me. forgive me' until he is out the door.

*

Jane sits in the hospital waiting room until two P.M., and after they wheel Jess from the recovery room to his bed she sits next to him, leaning forward from the green vinyl armchair, her hand on his arm. His waist is bandaged, and tubes run from his left arm and his lower body.

The nurse, busy and kind, says, 'His vitals are good, but that's pretty heavy anesthetic, you know. He might be out for another hour or two.'

'Thank you,' Jane says. 'Thanks for your help.'

An hour later Jess opens one eye and Jane brings him the water glass. He takes a sip, gives her the thumbs-up, and falls back asleep until the nurse wakes him at six for painkiller and antibiotic. Jane is still sitting there when the shift changes and a new nurse, equally busy, equally kind, sticks her head in the door.

'Everything looks good. You know what they say about the difference between God and Dr Laurence? Sometimes God makes a mistake.'

Jane says, 'Thank you so much. That's nice to hear.' And thinks, Another group of people to be pleasant to.

Jane walks home, through the little park again, scuffing her feet through the ribbed curling leaves on the path. Cole is sitting on the steps of the condo, two bouquets of red roses beside him. He stands as she comes up the walk, and then he bends down to pick up the roses, huge and stiff in green tissue and white ribbon. Jane doesn't like roses, she especially dislikes the cliché of ardent red roses, she doesn't find short men attractive (the two she's slept with made her feel like Everest), and she doesn't want her life to contain any more irony than it already does. And standing on the little porch of the condo, barely enough room for two medium-sized people and forty-eight roses, Jane sees that she has taken her place in the long and honorable line of fools for love: Don Quixote and Hermia and Oscar Wilde and Joe E. Brown, crowing with delight, clutching his straw boater and Jack Lemmon as the speedboat carries them off to a cockeyed and irresistible future.

Cole says, '*Dum spiro, spero.* That is the South Carolina motto. While I breathe, I hope.'

'Well,' Jane says, 'I expect that will come in handy for us.

Rowing to Eden

'The Barcelona Cancer Center,' Charley says. 'Where are the tapas? Maybe there should be castanets at the nurses' station. Paella Valenciana everywhere you look.'

He says this every time they come for chemotherapy. The Barcelona family made millions in real estate and donated several to St Michael's; there is almost nothing worth curing that the Barcelonas have not given to.

Charley puts his hands up in the air and clicks his fingers. Mai ignores him; the person with cancer does not have to be amused.

Ellie smiles. She has already had breast cancer, and her job this summer is to help her best friend and her best friend's husband.

'How about the internationally renowned Sangria Treatment? Makes you forget your troubles.' Charley stamps his sneakers, flamenco style. Since Mai's mastectomy he has turned whimsical, and it does not become him. Mai knows Charley is doing the best he can, and the only kindness she can offer is not to say, 'Honey, you've been as dull as dishwater for twenty years. You don't have to change now.'

Ellie believes that all straight men should be like her father: stoic, handy, and unimaginative. They should be dryly kind, completely without whimsy or faintly fabulous qualities. As far as Ellie's concerned, gay men can be full-blown birds of paradise, with or without homemaking skills. They can just lounge around in their marabou mules, saying witty, brittle things that reveal their hearts of gold. Ellie likes them that way, that's what they're for, to toss scarves over the world's light-bulbs, and straight men are for putting up sheetrock.

Mai sits between Charley and Ellie in the waiting room as if she's alone. Charley makes three cups of coffee from the waiting-room kitchenette. The women don't drink theirs.

'This is disgusting,' Charley says.

'I'll get us some from the lobby.'

Ellie heads for the Java Joe coffee bar, a weirdly joyful pit stop at the intersection of four different Barcelona family wings, with nothing but caffeine and sugar and attractively arranged carbo-hydrates; everyone who is not confined by an IV drip or a restricted diet eats there. Mai sips herbal tea all through chemo, but Ellie goes down and back a few times, for a currant scone, for a cappuccino, for a mango smoothie. She is happy to spend three dollars on a muffin, grateful that she lives in a country where no one thinks there's anything wrong or untoward in the AMA-approved pursuit of profit at the expense of people's grief and health.

Ellie prepares a little picnic on the seat next to Charley. Coffee the way he likes it, two different kinds of biscotti, a fist-size apple fritter, two elephant ears sprinkling sugar everywhere, and enough napkins to make this all bearable to Charley, who is two steps short of compulsive. Ellie presents him with the food-covered seat.

'This is great,' says Charley. 'Treats. Honey, look how she takes care of me. Yes, folks, *that's* a wife.'

This is supposed to be funny, because Ellie is a lesbian and therefore unlikely to be anyone's wife. If Ellie lived with another woman, neither Ellie nor Charley nor Mai would think of Ellie as a wife. Ellie is pretty sure that her days of looking for a spouse are over; Mai thinks so too, and used to imagine that when Charley died, at a suitable but not horribly advanced age, of a swift-moving but not painful disease, she and Ellie would retire to her parents' house in Oslo, or buy the little yellow house on Pearl Street in Provincetown that they walked past on spring break twenty-one years ago. Now it seems possible that Ellie will sit on a porch slugging back brandy with some other old lady, and that Charley will grow old with someone who has two breasts and a full head of hair.

Ellie gives Charley a napkin, and he kisses her hand, which smells of coffee and antibacterial soap and of Ellie, for which he has no particular name. Mai has always smelled like clove; since November she smells like seaweed, and Charley, like a pregnant woman, has lost his taste for sushi, for lobster, and for salt.

They sit for two hours. Women in scarves, women in floppy denim hats, women in good wigs, even enviable wigs, and women in wigs so bad they would look better in sombreros; weary, frightened husbands; girls with tons of silky, curly, bouncing hair, whom Mai, Charley, and Ellie all take to be the daughters and friends of the patients. There are a few teenagers, the sweetest signs of their youth distorted, creamy, luminous skin swollen and ashy from chemo, nothing left of their immortal shields, so that even the women who shuffle along on their skin-less feet, even the old women whose aged ears hang off their heads like tree fungus, even they cannot bear to look at the children with cancer.

Mai's favorite nurse, Ginger, an old vaudevillian's idea of a nurse, busty and long-legged in the only tight white uniform

Mai's seen, showgirl perfect except for her snub-toed rubber-soled shoes, leads them to Corner C of Room T4, the best chemo room as far as Mai and Ellie are concerned. Charley kisses Mai at the door, as if this were the dressing room or a gynecological exam, as if everyone knows that he would stay if he could but the rules forbid it.

Ellie is disgusted, but Mai is fine. Relieved. Sitting agitates Charley, and for the same reason that she would rather do the laundry than wait for him to volunteer, and for the same reason that she does not complain when he turns on the light at five A.M. to iron his shirt by their bedside before going to his office at seven, she does not mind his leaving. He is who he is. It is what it is. She says these things to herself a hundred times a day under normal circumstances. Now she says them two hundred times a day. When Mai repeats these things to Ellie, Ellie stares at her and says, 'I hope that makes you feel better.' Ellie is an endless fixer and shaper and mender; she is as sure that life's events can be reworked and new endings attached as Mai is that they cannot and that any new ending will either mimic the first or make you long for it.

Mai prays that Ginger will stay to do the IV stick. She is the only one who can get it right, and when she walks out, without washing her hands, Mai turns her face to the wall. She can feel Ellie rise from the visitor's chair, ready to run down the hall, and the mental image of her Ellie, brown curls and horn-rims flying behind her as she chases showgirl Ginger, cheers Mai up. She puts her hand on Ellie.

'It'll be fine,' she says.

'It better be. If you get that cow again, she gets two tries and she's out of here.'

It is the cow, and she sticks Mai four times, all over her hand.

As she tries again, Mai can feel her perspiration, and she looks down to see that tiny hives have broken out along the nurse's slick hairline. Flop sweat, Mai thinks, and wonders how she knows that phrase. It must be from Ellie's theater days. Mai closes her eyes tightly, willing the stupid bitch to find a vein.

The stupid bitch leaves and returns with Ginger, who does it right, slapping and massaging the back of the left hand until a small vein lifts up, offering itself. The anonymous nurse slumps out, gratifyingly ashamed, and Ellie forgives her; at least she cares enough to feel bad. Mai forgets her as soon as the saline starts, the fat little bag hung on the curling candelabrum that holds all the drugs, each pouch attached with nursery-blue clips and clamps, clear tubing leading to the pump. Ellie has memorized everything on the machine, including the fact that it is made by the Baxter Manufacturing Company of Dearborn, Michigan. There's a column of four black buttons – Back Light, Silence, Time, Stop – and next to them the red digital letters flash on and off. Most of the time they just say Normal. When the nurses have to unplug the machine so Mai can pee, it beeps like crazy.

'Oh, Jesus, the hot packs,' Mai says. This is the only thing that eases the burning of the Taxol. Once they have been through the saline and the Benadryl and the Zoloft, it's time to get down to business, and the business of Taxol is a small well of fire at the point of entry, shooting up Mai's arm like a gasoline trail. The instant hot packs are godsends, and Ellie collects them, along with lightweight blankets from all the other patient corners, so that when Mai lies down there is a small mountain of plastic on her nightstand and a pile of thermal-weave cotton at the foot of her bed. The hot packs release their heat immediately, after one hard squeeze on their thin plastic edges. It's exactly like cracking an egg one-handed, which Ellie also likes to do for her own pleasure. Mai smiles like a junkie as soon as she hears the pop of the inner casing, and Ellie tucks three blankets up around her.

They have made a list of everything that makes Corner C in Room T4 the best bed for chemo. First, the privacy curtain pulls smoothly on its track. It's terrible to pull on the curtain, making it clear that you do not wish to watch someone else's unspeakable anguish or let them gaze upon yours, only to find yourself unable to close it fully, leaving both parties stuck with eye contact and insult. Also, all the gloves used in Barcelona seemed to be stored in T4: Chemo Plus, the Rubbermaid of latex gloves, thick-cuffed and a matte pale blue; Sensicor, sheer as muslin, ghost fingers spilling out of a dozen cardboard boxes. Mai and Ellie even like the battered plastic hospital trays filled with three kinds of tape, tongue depressors, and test tubes with lavender, red, blue, and lime-green rubber stoppers. The trays are not hospital clean; they could be holding dirty silver in the kitchen of any inner-city diner. There are pastel watercolors of lopsided seaside cottages, saccharine prints produced by Posters International of Toronto. Ellie had a lavender-and-white gingerbread cottage right in front of her the whole summer she had chemo. In Corner A, under three small rowboats permanently askew, two women lie side by side, a young woman curled up beside her bald mother. The daughter's eyes are shut, but the mother's are wide open as she stares at the ceiling, her free hand curled around her daughter's shoulder.

The Taxol drips steadily for three and a half hours, from an old-fashioned glass bottle, solid and pale blue. All the other stuff drips from Jetson-style packets, flimsy and benign. Taxol is a heavyweight in an upside-down jug, one fat bubble at a time floating up to the undersurface, entering the transparent slice of silver bubbles before it is bumped aside by the next rising bubble. Charley will be at Fishers Island by the time the Taxol is gone, making food that Mai will not eat. Ellie will eat the lamb kabobs at midnight, will eat the shepherd's pie or crab cakes for lunch, while Mai sips ginseng tea and eats barbecue potato chips.

Ellie drives them onto the ferry, and they sit in the car for the entire crossing. Mai leans her head back, and although she is always beautiful to Ellie, even Ellie can see that she looks bad. There's nothing wrong with bald babies; everything about them, even the ugly ones, is made to be revealed, and every feature is nicely in proportion to their big, satiny heads. Every time Ellie looks at Mai, she misses her silver-blond braid and is grateful that her eyebrows, narrow gold tail swipes, have held on. Mai's naked head has a pair of dents halfway up the back, and a small purplish birthmark behind the left ear, and although her skin has always been amazingly soft and poreless, the disappearance of even her fine body hair is a little jarring to both of them. They know each other's pubic hair and leg-shaving rituals and scars, completely and without comment. Ellie is furry and tan, Mai is smooth and white. But smooth is one thing, Mai says, egg is another.

When Mai and Ellie studied the wig catalogue, before going for the high-end, handmade, real-hair wigs that are brought to your house, and then to your hairdresser for final adjustment, Mai contemplated auburn pixie cuts and platinum bouffants and even a long jet-black pageboy, parted in the middle à la mid-career Cher. Charley walked in and out four times while they flipped through the catalogue, and finally he called Mai into the bedroom so he could speak to her privately.

'I don't think you need a wig,' he said.

It is love, of course, that makes Charley tell Mai that no wig is necessary, that he likes her bald and odd, and that no pretence is called for, or even tolerable, between them. It is love that he intends to convey.

'Okay. I'll see.' I'm an intelligent woman, Mai thinks, how did I marry the village idiot? After twenty years, during which you have presumably been paying some kind of dim attention to the kind of person I am, how could you imagine that I would want to parade around my own home grotesque and vulnerable? Do you think, would thinking at all lead you to believe that it would somehow please me to have you now be *kind* about my appearance?

'It might be fun to experiment. I've never been an exotic brunette – this could be your last chance,' Mai says.

Charley does not want an exotic brunette. He wants his cool, white, lanky wife back, with her normal spicy smell and her pale silky hair pulled into a smooth knot. The thought of her suddenly appearing in public with her chemically puffed face and a witch's wig makes him miserable, and so ashamed of his pettiness that he wishes Mai were completely healthy or dead.

'Whatever you want. Maybe it will liven things up around here.' They have not made love since Mai was diagnosed.

'Maybe. Don't hold your breath.' The privilege of cancer is that Mai is allowed to close her eyes, as if she is all worn out from surgery and chemo, and not look at Charley's lonely, frightened face.

Charley puts his hand on Mai's shoulder, although he thinks it may be the wrong thing to do, and she stiffens. He pulls his hand back and Mai pulls it forward, wrapping his arm around her neck. She lays her warm, inflated cheek against his skin.

'I like you very much,' she says.

'I like you very much too.'

They hear Ellie's heavy, quick step before they see her, and they are a couple again, even before she announces that she has, as always, burned the contents of whatever pan Charley has left unattended. This happens so often not even Charley thinks it's an accident. He believes that Ellie should learn how to cook. Mai can cook, of course, not that she has ever needed to, having been the most beautiful girl at college, being the only beautiful and brilliant woman Charley knows. But Ellie should learn how to cook, and if Charley followed his own thoughts, they would lead to Ellie cooking and fussing sweetly, as she does for Charley at times, and somehow, under his tutelage, revealing to herself, and then to some nice man, her hidden, heterosexual, marriageable self.

Ellie does cook. At home she cooks for friends who have never met Charley and Mai. She cooks, very well, from M. F. K. Fisher and Bobby Flay and Alice Waters, for friends who would find it hard to believe that she ever wore a mint-green sheath and three-inch dyed-to-match heels for Charley and Mai's Fishers Island wedding, the spikes digging into the lawn, a rose-covered veranda in front of her and Block Island Sound behind. Mai stood like an angel on a treetop, sleeveless white silk to her ankles, plain white ballet slippers on her narrow feet, and three luminous ropes of plain white pearls, donated with great affection and expectation by Charley's grandmother, one of the Fishers Island Cushings. Charles Cushing stood beside his new wife, beaming, sunburned, and slightly giddy at having escaped a future of dating Cushing cousins' friends, Cushing cousins' friends' sisters, and the huge net of Cushing friends of friends.

At Fishers, where they now have a small house of their own,

Charley is the chef, but when he goes back to New Haven, Ellie and Mai eat kitchen-sink omelets, microwave popcorn tossed with grated Parmesan and kosher salt, peanut butter out of the jar. They drink Red Stripe beer and smoke exactly five cigarettes apiece, burying the butts out by the Cushing family pet cemetery, home to four generations of chocolate Labs, white Persians, and Charley's own late cocker spaniel. The graves are not marked with 'Dearest Companion' headstones, too baroque and eccentric for the Cushings, the sort of thing they imagine Italians might do; nor are they unmarked, as if it doesn't matter that the little bodies are there, as if commemoration is unnecessary. Each of the twelve plots sports something both woodsy and distinct: a large chunk of mica-flecked stone, a wreath of barbed wire tamped down into the soil, and, for Charley's Pogo, a toy sailboat lashed to a two-inch dowel. It is more gushing sentiment than Ellie has seen in twenty years of Cushings, and as she stands in the cemetery, carefully placing her cigarette under the chunk of granite over Queen of Sheba, she likes Charley right then more than she sometimes does in person, and remembers the big-eared boy he was at college as if he'd been her friend and not a source of fond, irritated puzzlement and occasional drunken entertainment. It was with Charley, not Mai, that Ellie dressed the comatose football captain in drag and tied him to his bed; it was Charley and Ellie wading through Thomas Hardy and toasting marshmallows while Mai and Ellie's girlfriend skied Mount Snow until dark; and even now it is Charley and Ellie dancing for hours at endless Cushing weddings and anniversaries. Products of two very different but effective dance instructors, they move well together; Charley leads more firmly than Ellie would have thought, and she follows him neatly, as if she'd been beside him at Junior Dance

Assembly, hearing his Miss Elizabeth say, again, 'The gentleman is the frame, ladies, you are the picture.' Mai sits out with Charley's sharp-eyed father, and they talk about island real estate, politics, and indiscretions. Mr Cushing cannot talk to Charley, who cooks and dances, but he likes his clever, pretty daughter-in-law more than almost anybody.

At the Spring Dance, Charley and Ellie drank two Manhattans apiece and began with a Viennese waltz and then a fox-trot and then another break for drinks. When Ellie put an open-hip twist into their rumba, Charley laughed out loud and whispered, slurring in Ellie's ear, 'I wish I was Jewish. Then I'd only have to come to the big weddings. No one would expect me to play eighteen fucking holes of golf at the Big Club with these imbeciles tomorrow.'

Ellie said, 'I could convert and play golf with them, and you could become a lesbian.'

Charley twirled them around Mr and Mrs Fairbrother and slid his hand down Ellie's firm, damp back. 'I am a lesbian, aren't I? How am I not a lesbian? You're no help. My uncle Albert is the biggest fruit in Rhode Island, and he's teeing off with us at one. No women on the links on Saturday. Really, Jewish would be better.'

When Charley and Ellie's jitterbug slid them onto the ivy-patterned chintz couch, Mai kissed her father-in-law, gathered their coats, and put them both in the back seat. It may be true that alcohol has played a central part in every good time Ellie and Charley have had together, but even when they begin to find each other affected, possessive, and frankly a little pathetic (his lack of sperm, her lack of spouse), they remind themselves that no amount of alcohol can create affection where there is none and that they must really be very fond of each other after all.

*

'I never know what time to make dinner,' Charley says. He pours Scotch into a glass, and a quick stream over the chicken. 'Or what to make.'

If Mai's not going to join them, he might as well make something interesting. For the last three days he's cooked soft-boiled eggs, Cream of Wheat, crustless white toast. At two in the morning he made a dozen ramekins of egg custard so that Mai could try again no matter how many times she threw up.

'Coq au Scotch?' This doesn't seem like a bad idea to Ellie.

'It'll be our little secret,' Charley says.

Charley has brought hummus, pita chips, fresh mozzarella, and a case of wine from home. Ellie takes the corn onto the back porch, sorry she had a blueberry muffin and half of Mai's milkshake just an hour ago.

'Do you want to nap? I'll finish,' says Charley, sitting down to help shuck more corn than the two of them will ever eat.

'Nap? No, I'm fine. You lie down if you want to. I can set the table, make the salad.' Ellie knows there will be corn bisque tomorrow, possibly black-bean-and-corn salad. If there's too much food, they will have the Cushings senior over, and Ellie will feel like the visiting troll.

'No thanks, it's done already.'

Mai calls it the 66 Hemlock Drive Ironman Competition. When she was well, she got up first, went to bed last, and swam sixty laps in Hay Harbor, bringing crullers and the *Times* back from the bakery. Charley and Ellie were forever, contentedly, runners-up.

Charley sips his Scotch, watching the sailboats rock in their moorings. When Mai sails, she looks like Neptune's daughter, streaming gold and white across the water. One of the things Charley does like about Ellie is her ability and her willingness to do nothing, for several hours at a time. Even though Charley believes that Mai will live, her illness makes everything else, every activity and wish, smoky and false. He watches himself going to the office, making deals he has hoped for, making more money than he had expected, and thinks, This doesn't matter, and what matters I can't do a thing about.

Charley looks into his glass. 'You know, I know you've always been in love with her. I do understand.' And he does. He feels sorry for Ellie, he loves her for trailing after his beautiful Mai for twenty years, making do, admirably, with friendship, while having to contemplate Charley, every night, in the place she would like to be.

'I don't know what you understand. I've never been in love with Mai. I love her, I love her to the ends of the earth, but not *in* love.' It has puzzled Ellie sometimes. Darling Mai, all that perfect equipment and not a lick of chemistry.

'Well, it's not the kind of thing one argues about, but I see you've never been really serious with anyone. I don't blame you, you know, she's wonderful.' And Mai does seem, just now, really wonderful, irresistible, even easy to love.

'Of course, Mai's wonderful. I'm not arguing about that either. I don't seem cut out for domestic life, Charley, and it's not because I've been carrying a torch for twenty years.

Ellie chews the ice in her drink. She had come close to domestic life with a college sweetheart who moved back in with her old boyfriend three months after they all graduated; fairly close with the clothing designer who moved to Ghana, which Ellie would not even consider; and very close just five years ago, and it is clear to Ellie now, when she runs into this woman and her good-looking girlfriend and their two happy Chinese children, black smooth bangs and big white smiles, in cuddly green fleece jackets with matching hats and adorable green sneakers, that the one right door had swung open briefly and Ellie had just stood there, her lame and hesitant soul unwilling to leave her body for the magnificent uncertainty of Paradise.

When they were nineteen, she and Mai lay on Ellie's twin bed in their bikini underpants, with only the closet light on. Mai's breasts were lit in a narrow yellow strip. Mai put Ellie's left hand on her right breast.

'Is this what you do?'

Ellie patted Mai's collarbone. 'It's what I do with a girlfriend.'

Mai smiled in the dark. 'Goody for them. I'm your best friend.'

'Yup,' said Ellie, and they both rolled to the right, as they did every Sunday night, Mai in front, Ellie behind, and slept like spoons.

Ellie tucks Mai in. Mai wears Ellie's old 'If you can walk you can dance, if you can talk you can sing' T-shirt and Charley's Valentine's Day boxer shorts.

'I'm a fashion don't,' Mai says.

'Yeah,' says Ellie, 'not like me.'

'But that's okay, Elliedear, you always dress like shit.' Elliedear and Maidarling is what Mrs Cushing has called them for twenty years. 'All sociologists dress like shit. E, did your feet go numb? I don't know what it is. I thought they were cold, but they're just nothing. No feeling.'

'It's okay. Mine did too.' Ellie smooths out the top sheet and unfolds one of the beautifully faded Cushing quilts over Mai, who sweats and freezes all night.

'Did the feeling come back?'

'No.'

'You're supposed to follow that with a positive remark, like "No, but now I don't need shoes, and with the money I've saved—"'

'With the money I've saved, I'm moving to another planet.'

'That suggests that these feelings of homicidal irascibility will not be passing,' Mai says.

'Honey,' Ellie says, kissing Mai's forehead, 'how should I know? I was born bad-tempered.'

'When I'm better,' Mai says, and closes her eyes.

Ellie turns out the light and hopes that Mai will sleep until morning. When Mai has a bad night and Charley takes care of her, Ellie wakes up feeling useless and duped.

'When I'm better,' Mai says in the dark, 'we're getting you a girlfriend. Grace Paley's soul in Jennifer Lopez's body.'

Mai dreams that she is with her parents, skiing at Kvitfjell. The trees rush past her. The yellow goggles she had as a little girl cover her face, and she's wearing her favorite bright yellow parka and the black Thinsulate mittens Charley got her last Christmas. Her parents are in front, skiing without poles, shouting encouragement to her over their shoulders. Her mother's hair is still blond, still in a long braid with a blue ribbon twisting through it, and she calls out Mai's name in her sweet, breathy voice. The wind carries her father's words away, but she knows they want her to drop her poles. As Mai loosens her grip, her mother raises an arm, as if to wave, and catches something, Mai's parka. Mai is skiing in just her turtleneck now, and it whips up over her head, tangling with her bra. Her yellow goggles work themselves loose and her scarf unwinds, wiggling down the ice toward her parents. Her black overalls unsnap, flying off her legs like something possessed, tumbling a hundred feet down to her father. Her parents catch each item quickly and toss it into the trees. '*Skynde seg*, come on.' Mai has only her boots and her mittens now, and the wind drives hard and sharp, right up her crotch, pressing her skin back into her bones. Her bare chest (two breasts again, she notices, even while sleeping) aches under the stinging blue snow, her eyelids freeze shut. She is skiing blind and naked. She wakes up, fists knotted in her wet pillowcase, thinking, How obvious. It seems to Mai that even her subconscious has lost its subtlety. Mai is famous for her subtle humor, her subtle beauty, her subtle understanding of the Brontë sisters, of nineteenth-century England, of academic politics and the art of tenure, which she got at thirty. Now she feels as subtle as Oprah and not even as quick.

Mai hears Charley on the stairs and closes her eyes. If you love me, please don't come in. Don't make me look at you, don't make me act like I know you. I don't need food or attention right now. If there is anything you can give me, darling, one little thing I would ask for, it's just your absence. A bag of chips, a glass of seltzer with a slice of lemon would be okay, and if you can spare me even that quick, soft look that suggests that I am somehow connected to you, I'll be more grateful than you can imagine and I'll tell everyone how I could not have made it through this without you. Just let me live on this nice dark side of the moon a while longer.

It's not Ellie who should be alone, Mai thinks, it's me. Ellie may have missed the romantic boat a few times, may have misjudged a turn or two, but she is not incapable of love. Mai is. She cannot do, for even a minute, any of the wise, kind, self-affirming, reassuring things recommended in her stack of books. People have sent flowers and brought gifts. She would have preferred more flowers and different gifts. She now has a small library on breast cancer: *How to Think Yourself Healthy*, *How to Have More Fun with the Rest of Your Life*, *Curing Your Cancer with Fruits and Vegetables*, *Meeting the Challenge of Mastectomy*, feminist approaches and feminine approaches, and none of them telling her how to find her way back to the cheerful, steely, enviable person she has been for forty-three years. The books are story after story of breast cancer survivors – they never use the word 'victim' now, they are all warriors in the great fight, drumming their way out of the operating room, shakin' a tail feather all the way to the specialty bra shop. Mai feels like a victim. She had been walking down a sunny street, minding her own business, doing no harm, when something sank its teeth into her breast, gnawed it from her body, stripped her skin off with its great claw and dangled her, hairless head first, over a great invisible chasm while poor Charley stood on the other side, befogged but hopeful, mistaking everything he saw and heard for something that had to do with him.

Mai rolls over to face the wall, her good arm tucked under her head. She can hear Charley breathing in the doorway, and when he leaves after just a few seconds and pulls the door closed behind him, the dark in the room is the deep, delicious grey cloud she remembers from childhood; she is Thumbelina, tucked in a giant velvet pouch, comforted by the smell of pipe tobacco and leftover potatoes and by the sound of her parents' conversation.

Mai hears Charley walking away. God bless you, she thinks.

*

'That chicken's got a while to go,' Ellie says.

Charley pours another Scotch. 'Let's watch the sun set,' he says.

They twist themselves around on the porch to watch the orange sun and the brief, wavering vermilion circles on the water. The white hydrangeas turn pink, then deep rose, then their color disappears.

Charley stands up to stretch and pulls off his sweatshirt. 'I'm just rank. I'm going to take a swim, and then I'll finish dinner. You?'

'No. I'll sit. I'll cheer.'

Charley walks down to the end of the dock, shedding his jeans and briefs. He stands with his back to Ellie, dimly white against the dark. His ass is small and high around its shadowy cleft, deeply dimpled in the middle of each cheek, and his thighs bow out like a sprinter's. Ellie can see each round knot in his back, muscles bunching and moving like mice across his shoulders, unexpected slabs of muscle curving over each shoulder blade, smooth, thick lines of muscle lying on either side of his spine.

Ellie would rather that Charley was sick in bed and Mai was swimming, but looking at him now, she thinks, as she does occasionally in the face of certain art forms to which she is largely indifferent, Even I can see how beautiful this is.

Charley does a long, thrashing crawl for a quarter-mile and a breaststroke back to the dock, head lifting toward home. Ellie waves and opens a bottle of Meursault; since chemo, even the smell of red wine, even the sight of the red-tipped damp cork, makes Mai ill. Mr Cushing sends over a case of his own golden white wines every few weeks, just for Mai. Ellie and Charley drink a couple of bottles every weekend – Mai drinks a glass the day after chemo, before the nausea kicks in.

Charley climbs onto the dock, hopping from foot to foot to shake the water out of his ears, patting himself dry with his underpants.

In the living room, sitting on the wicker divan, feet up on the wicker coffee table, Charley and Ellie toast a few things: Mai, the Cushing wine cellar, the last chemotherapy session, only two weeks away, old friends.

'I have no idea ...' Charley shrugs. Water drips slowly from his hair to his sweatshirt.

'No idea what?'

'What was it like for you?' Charley and Mai spent an entire summer hiking through the dales and woodlands and lesser hamlets of the Yorkshires; they left before Ellie had even had her mammogram and came home two weeks after her last chemo.

'Pretty much like this. It sucked. You remember how pooped I was that fall.'

Charley does remember, vaguely. They brought flowers and butter crunch and a big straw hat as soon as they got back. Ellie didn't come to Fishers, but Mai was at Ellie's place half the week all that fall. By Christmas, Ellie's hair was dark brown again and wildly curly, and she and Mr Cushing were winning at Dictionary.

'What, Charley?'

'How much does it hurt?'

'Now, or then?'

'Then.' Charley hopes, of course, that it doesn't still hurt, but his concern is with Mai. Ellie is clearly fine.

Ellie sighs. 'You mean, what's it like for Mai now? How much pain is she in now?'

Charley nods.

'Lots of aching. Numb feet. Mai has that. Stiff arm. Itchy. You know, everyone's different. You could ask her.' Ellie says this to be encouraging, but it seems unlikely to her, and to Charley, that he will ask, and if he does they both expect that Mai will say, 'Not too bad,' like a true Minnesotan, or else, in the manner of her father-in-law, 'Not worth discussing.'

'But right where . . . where the breast was, how is that? How is that now? How does it look?' Charley keeps his eyes on the coffee table.

'Didn't Mai show you?' Charley and Mai are the only couple Ellie knows well. Surely not all heterosexual couples are so reticent, so determinedly unobservant. Ellie knows another straight couple who taped not only the birth of their baby but the burying of the placenta and the subsequent bris. Certainly she prefers Charley and Mai's approach, even with its obvious pitfalls. When you can share panties and Tampax and earrings with the person you have sex with, a little blurring is to be expected, a certain rapid slippage of romantic illusion, and that is not a plus as far as Ellie is concerned. On the other hand, no one except Mai and Ellie's mother has seen her scar, and Mai's mother is dead, so she and Ellie are actually even in the boldly-show-your-scar department.

Charley shakes his head.

'It hardly hurts now. And my arm is fine. Almost fine.' Ellie makes a circle with her left arm, and it is a pretty good circle if you don't know how she was able to move it before.

'Good. I'm really glad it's better.'

'What?'

'Nothing.'

'Charley, what?'

'Forget it.

Charley finishes his wine; Ellie does too.

'If you say no, I'll understand. If this makes you really angry, I apologize in advance. Could I see it?'

Ellie unbuttons her shirt, one of Charley's old shirts that she and Mai wear around the house. On Ellie, it saves the trouble of shorts. She is not wearing a bra and wishes there were some way to show only the clinically useful part of her body.

'Ah.' Charley gets on his knees in front of Ellie, his eyes almost level with hers. Ellie keeps her eyes on the fireplace.

On the left side of Ellie's narrow chest, a hand's length below her small, pretty collarbone, a few inches from the edge of her suntan, there is a smooth ivory square of skin bisected by a red-blue braid of scar tissue. In the middle of the scar is a dimple.

'That?' says Charley, pointing without touching.

'Where the nipple was.'

'Ah.' Charley wipes his eyes with the back of his hand. He cups Ellie's breast in his palm and leans forward, his other arm around her waist. He lays his cheek against the scar.

'Can you feel this?'

'I can feel pressure. That's all I feel right there.'

'Not hot or cold?' Charley can feel the water between his rough and Ellie's smooth skin, and the tiny bumps of her scar coming up lightly against his cheek.

'I don't think so. I feel your hair higher up.'

Ellie puts both hands in Charley's wet hair, the silver-blond waves coming up between her fingers. He smells of salt.

'Shut your eyes, Ellie.' Her elbows rest on his shoulders. She smells like fresh corn, of course, and underneath that, peonies.

Charley traces the tiny red rope rising from Ellie's pale marble blankness, in and out, its tight twists and shrugs crisscrossing each other under his tongue, growing bigger in his mouth. He circles the indentation in the middle, over and over, as if it will open to him, as if underneath the scar is the whole breast, not gone, but concealed.

Ellie knows it is only Charley's lips and tongue, but she feels them with the muffled longing of a woman watching rain fall.

Lionel and Julia

Sleepwalking

Night Vision

Light into Dark

Fort Useless and Fort Ridiculous

Sleepwalking

I was born smart and had been lucky my whole life, so I didn't even know that what I thought was careful planning was nothing more than being in the right place at the right time, missing an avalanche I didn't even hear.

After the funeral was over and the cold turkey and the glazed ham were demolished and some very good jazz was played and some very good musicians went home drunk on bourbon poured in my husband's honor, it was just me, my mother-in-law, Ruth, and our two boys, Lionel junior from Lionel's second marriage, and our little boy, Buster.

Ruth pushed herself up out of the couch, her black taffeta dress rustling reproachfully. I couldn't stand for her to start the dishes, sighing, praising the Lord, clucking her tongue over the state of my kitchen, in which the windows are not washed regularly and I do not scrub behind the refrigerator.

'Ruth, let them sit. I'll do them later tonight.'

'No need to put off 'til tomorrow what we can do today. I'll do them right now, and then Lionel junior can run me home.' Ruth does not believe that the good Lord intended ladies to drive; she'd drive, eyes closed, with her drunk son or her accident-prone grandson before she'd set foot in my car.

'Ruth, please,' I said. 'I'd just as soon have something to do later. Please. Let me make us a cup of tea, and then we'll take you home.'

Tea, her grandson Buster, and her son's relative sobriety were the three major contributions I'd made to Ruth's life; the tea and Buster accounted for all of our truces and the few good times we'd had together.

'I ought to be going along now, let you get on with things.'

'Earl Grey? Darjeeling? Constant Comment? I've got some rosehip tea in here, too – it's light, sort of lemony.' I don't know why I was urging her to stay; I'd never be rid of her as long as I had the boys. If Ruth no longer thought I was trash, she certainly made it clear that I hadn't lived up to her notion of the perfect daughter-in-law, a cross between Marian Anderson and Florence Nightingale.

'You have Earl Grey?' Ruth was wavering, half a smile on her sad mouth, her going-to-church lipstick faded to a blurry pink line on her upper lip.

When I really needed Ruth on my side, I'd set out an English tea: Spode teapot, linen place mats, scones, and three kinds of jam. And for half an hour, we'd sip and chew, happy to be so civilized.

'Earl Grey it is.' I got up to put on the water, stepping on Buster, who was sitting on the floor by my chair, practically on my feet.

'Jesus, Buster, are you all right?' I hugged him before he could start crying and lifted him out of my way.

'The Lord's name,' Ruth murmured, rolling her eyes up to apologize to Jesus personally. I felt like smacking her one, right in her soft dark face, and pointing out that since the Lord had not treated us especially well in the last year, during which we had both lost husbands, perhaps we didn't have to be overly concerned with His hurt feelings. Ruth made me want to be very, very bad.

'Sorry, Ruth. Buster, sit down by your grandmother, honey, and I'll make us all some tea.'

'No, really, don't trouble yourself, Julia. Lionel junior, please take me home. Gabriel, come kiss your grandma good-bye. You boys be good, now, and think of how your daddy would want you to act. I'll see you all for dinner tomorrow.'

She was determined to leave, martyred and tea-less, so I got in line to kiss her. Ruth put her hands on my shoulders, her only gesture of affection toward me, which also allowed her to pretend that she was a little taller, rather than a little shorter, than I am.

She left with Lionel junior, and Buster and I cuddled on the couch, his full face squashed against my chest, my skin resting on his soft hair. I felt almost whole.

'Sing, Mama.'

Lionel had always wanted me to record with him and I had always said no, because I don't like performing and I didn't want to be a blues-singing Marion Davies to Lionel's William Randolph Hearst. But I loved to sing and he loved to play and I'm sorry we didn't record just one song together.

I was trying to think of something that would soothe Buster but not break my heart.

I sang 'Amazing Grace,' even though I can't quite hit that note, and I sang bits and pieces of a few more songs, and then Buster was asleep and practically drowning in my tears.

I heard Lionel junior's footsteps and blotted my face on my sleeve.

'Hey, Lion, let's put this little boy to bed.'

'He's out, huh? You look tired, too. Why don't you go to bed and I'll do the dishes?'

That's my Lion. I think because I chose to love him, chose to be a mother and not just his father's wife, Lion gave me back everything he could. He was my table setter, car washer, garden weeder; in twelve years, I might've raised my voice to him twice. When my husband brought his son to meet me the first time, I looked into those wary eyes, hope pouring out of them despite himself, and I knew that I had found someone else to love.

I carried Buster to his room and laid him on the bed, slipping off his loafers. I pulled up the comforter with the long-legged basketball players running all over it and kissed his damp little face. I thought about how lucky I was to have Buster and Lion and even Ruth, who might torture me forever but would never abandon me, and I thought about how cold and lonely my poor Lionel must be, with no bourbon and no music and no audience, and I went into the bathroom to dry my face again. Lion got frantic when he saw me crying.

He was lying on the couch, his shoes off, his face turned toward the cushions.

'Want a soda or a beer? Maybe some music?' I pulled at his shoulder.

'Nope. Maybe some music, but not Pop's.'

'No, no, not your father's. How about Billie Holiday, Sarah Vaughan?'

'How about something a little more up? How about Luther Vandross?' Lion turned around to face me.

'I don't have any – as you know.' Lionel and I both hated bubblegum music, so of course Lion had the world's largest collection of whipped-cream soul; if it was insipid, he bought it.

'I'll get my tapes,' he said, and sat halfway up to see if I would let him. We used to make him play them in his room so we wouldn't have to listen, but Lionel wasn't here to grumble at the boy and I just didn't care.

'Play what you want, honey,' I said, sitting in Lionel's brown velvet recliner. Copies of *Downbeat* and packs of Trident were still stuffed between the cushion and the arm. Lion bounded off to his room and came back with an armful of tapes.

'Luther Vandross, Whitney Houston . . . what would you like to hear?'

'You pick.' Even talking felt like too much work. He put on one of the tapes and I shut my eyes.

I hadn't expected to miss Lionel so much. We'd had twelve years together, eleven of them sober; we'd had Buster and raised the Lion, and we'd gone to the Grammys together when he was nominated and he'd stayed sober when he lost, and we'd made love, with more interest some years than others; we'd been through a few other women for him, a few blondes that he couldn't pass up, and one other man for me; I'm not criticizing. We knew each other so well that when I wrote a piece on another jazz musician, he'd find the one phrase and say, 'You meant that about me,' and he'd be right. He was a better father than your average musician; he brought us with him whenever he went to Europe, and no matter how late he played on Saturday, he got up and made breakfast on Sunday.

Maybe we weren't a perfect match, in age, or temperament, or color, but we did try and we were willing to stick it out and then we didn't get a chance.

Lion came and sat by me, putting his head against my knee. Just like Buster, I thought. Lion's mother was half Italian, like me, so the two boys look alike: creamier, silkier versions of their father.

I patted his hair and ran my thumb up and down his neck,

feeling the muscles bunched up. When he was little, he couldn't fall asleep without his nightly back rub, and he only gave it up when he was fifteen and Lionel just wouldn't let me anymore.

'It's midnight, honey. It's been a long day, a long week. Go to bed.'

He pushed his head against my leg and cried, the way men do, like it's being torn out of them. His tears ran down my bare leg, and I felt the strings holding me together just snap. One, two, three, and there was no more center.

'Go to bed, Lion.'

'How about you?'

'I'm not really ready for bed yet, honey. Go ahead.' Please, go to bed.

'Okay. Good night, Ma.'

'Good night, baby.' Nineteen-year-old baby.

He pulled himself up and went off to his room. I peered into the kitchen, looked at all the dishes, and closed my eyes again. After a while, I got up and finished off the little bit of Jim Beam left in the bottle. With all Lionel's efforts at sobriety, we didn't keep the stuff around, and I choked on it. But the burning in my throat was comforting, like old times, and it was a distraction.

I walked down the hall to the bedroom – I used to call it the Lionel Sampson Celebrity Shrine. It wasn't just his framed album covers, but all of his favorite reviews, including the ones I wrote before I met him; one of Billie's gardenias mounted on velvet, pressed behind glass; photos of Lionel playing with equally famous or more famous musicians or with famous fans. In some ways, it's easier to marry a man with a big ego; you're not always fretting over him, worrying about whether or not he needs fluffing up.

I threw my black dress on the floor, my worst habit, and got into bed. I woke up at around four, waiting for something. A minute later, Buster wandered in, eyes half shut, blue blankie resurrected and hung around his neck, like a little boxer.

'Gonna stay with you, Mama.' Truculent even in his sleep, knowing that if his father had been there, he'd have been sent back to his own room.

'Come in, then, Bus. Let's try and get some sleep.'

He curled up next to me, silently, an arm flung over me, the other arm thrust into his pajama bottoms, between his legs.

I had just shut my eyes again when I felt something out of place. Lion was standing in the doorway, his briefs hanging off his high skinny hips. He needed new underwear, I thought. He looked about a year older than Buster.

'I thought I heard Buster prowling around, y'know, sleepwalking.'

The only one who ever sleepwalked in our family was Lion, but I didn't say so. 'It's okay – he just wanted company. Lonely in this house tonight.'

'Yeah. Ma?'

I was tired of thinking, and I didn't want to send him away, and I didn't want to talk anymore to anyone so I said, 'Come on, honey, it's a big bed.'

He crawled in next to his brother and fell asleep in a few minutes. I watched the digital clock flip through a lot of numbers and finally I got up and read.

The boys woke early, and I made them what Lionel called a Jersey City breakfast: eggs, sweet Italian sausage, grits, biscuits, and a quart of milk for each of them.

'Buster, soccer camp starts today. Do you feel up to going?'

I didn't see any reason for him to sit at home; he could catch up on his grieving for the rest of his life.

'I guess so. Is it okay, Mama?'

'Yes, honey, it's fine. I'm glad you're going. I'll pick you up at five, and then we'll drive straight over to Grandma's for dinner. You go get ready when you're done eating. Don't forget your cleats — they're in the hall.'

Lion swallowed his milk and stood up, like a brown flamingo, balancing on one foot while he put on his sneaker. 'Come on, Buster, I'm taking you. I have to go into town anyway. Do we need anything?'

I hadn't been to the grocery store in about a week. 'Get milk and OJ and English muffins and American cheese. I'll do a real shop tomorrow.' If I could just get to the store and the cleaners, then I could get to work, and then my life would move forward.

Finally they were ready to go, and I kissed them both and gave Lion some money for the groceries.

'I'll be back by lunchtime,' he said. It was already eight-thirty. When his father got sick in the spring, Lion gave me hourly bulletins on his whereabouts. This summer, Lion was housepainting and home constantly, leaving late, back early, stopping by for lunch.

'If you like,' I said. I didn't want him to feel that he had to keep me company. I was planning on going back to work tomorrow or the day after.

While the boys were gone, I straightened the house, went for a walk, and made curried tuna-fish sandwiches for Lion. I watched out the window for him, and when I saw my car turn up the road, I remembered all the things I hadn't done and started making a list. He came in, sweating and shirtless, drops of white paint on his hands and shoulders and sneakers.

Lion ate and I watched him and smiled. Feeding them was the easiest and clearest way of loving them, holding them.

'I'm going to shower. Then we could play a little tennis or work on the porch.' He finished both sandwiches in about a minute and got that wistful look that teenage boys get when they want you to fix them something more to eat. I made two peanut-butter-and-jelly sandwiches and put them on his plate.

'Great. I don't have to work this afternoon,' he said. 'I told Joe I might not be back – he said okay.'

'Well, I'm just going to mouse around, do laundry, answer some mail. I'm glad to have your company, you know I am, but you don't have to stay here with me. You might want to be with your friends.'

'I don't. I'm gonna shower.' Like his father, he only put his love out once, and God help you if you didn't take the hint.

I sat at the table, looking out at the morning glories climbing up the trellis Lionel had built me the summer he stopped drinking. In addition to the trellis, I had two flower boxes, a magazine rack, and a footstool so ugly even Ruth wouldn't have it.

'Ma, no towels,' Lion shouted from the bathroom. I thought that was nice, as if real life might continue.

'All right,' I called, getting one of the big, rough white ones that he liked.

I went into the bathroom and put it on the rack just as he stepped out of the shower. I hadn't seen him naked since he was fourteen and spent the year parading around the house, so that we could admire his underarm hair and the black wisps on his legs.

All I could see in the mist was a dark caramel column and two patches of dark curls, inky against his skin. I expected him to look away, embarrassed, but instead he looked right at me as he took the towel, and I was the one who turned away.

'Sorry,' we both said, and I backed out of the bathroom and

went straight down to the basement so we wouldn't bump into each other for a while.

I washed, dried, and folded everything that couldn't get away from me, listening for Lion's footsteps upstairs. I couldn't hear anything while the machines were going, so after about an hour I came up and found a note on the kitchen table.

Taking a nap. Wake me when it's time to get Buster. L.

'L.,' is how his father used to sign his notes. And their handwriting was the same, too: the awkward, careful printing of men who know that their script is illegible.

I took a shower and dried my hair and looked in the mirror for a while, noticing the gray at the temples. I wondered what Lion would have seen if he'd walked in on me, and I made up my mind not to think like that again.

I woke Lion by calling him from the hall, and I went into my room while he dressed to go to his grandmother's. I found a skirt that was somber and ill-fitting enough to meet Ruth's standard of widowhood and thought about topping it off with my EIGHT TO THE BAR VOLLEYBALL CHAMPS T-shirt, but didn't. Even pulling Ruth's chain wasn't fun. I put on a yellow shirt that made me look like one of the Neapolitan cholera victims, and Lion and I went to get Buster. He was bubbling over about the goal he had made in the last quarter, and that filled the car until we got to Ruth's house, and then she took over.

'Come in, come in. Gabriel, you are too dirty to be my grandson. You go wash up right now. Lionel junior, you're looking a little peaked. You must be working too hard or playing too hard. Does he eat, Julia? Come sit down here and have a glass of nice iced tea with mint from my garden. Julia, guess who I heard from this afternoon? Loretta, Lionel's first wife. She called to say how sorry she was. I told her she could call upon you, if she wished.'

'Fine.' I didn't have the energy to be annoyed. My muscles felt like butter, I'd had a headache for six days, and my eyes were so sore that even when I closed them, they ached. If Ruth wanted to sic Loretta McVay Sampson de Guzman de God-knows-who-else on me, I guessed I'd get through that little hell, too.

Ruth looked at me, probably disappointed; I knew from Lionel that she couldn't stand Loretta, but since she was the *only* black woman he'd married, Ruth felt obliged to find something positive about her. She was a lousy singer, a whore, and a terrible housekeeper, so Ruth really had to search. Anita, wife number two, was a rich, pretty flake with a fragile air and a serious drug problem that killed her when the Lion was five. I was the only normal, functioning person Lionel was ever involved with: I worked, I cooked, I balanced our checkbook, I did what had to be done, just like Ruth. And I irritated her no end.

'Why'd you do that, Grandma? Loretta's so nasty. She probably just wants to find out if Pop left her something in his will, which I'm sure he did not.' Loretta and Lionel had had a little thing going when Anita was in one of her rehab centers, and I think the Lion found out and of course blamed Loretta.

'It's all right, Lion,' I said, and stopped myself from patting his hand as if he were Buster.

Ruth was offended. 'Really, young man, it was very decent, just common courtesy, for Loretta to pay her respects, and I'm sure that your stepmother appreciates that.' Ruth thought it disrespectful to call me Julia when talking to Lion, but she couldn't stand the fact that he called me Ma after the four years she put in raising him while Anita killed herself and Lionel toured. So she referred to me as 'your stepmother,' which always made me feel like the coachmen and pumpkins couldn't be far behind. Lion used to look at me and smile when she said it.

We got through dinner, with Buster bragging about soccer and giving us a minute-by-minute account of the soccer training movie he had seen. Ruth criticized their table manners, asked me how long I was going to wallow at home, and then expressed horror when I told her I was going to work on Monday. Generally, she was her usual self, just a little worse, which was true of the rest of us, too. She also served the best smothered pork chops ever made and her usual first-rate trimmings. She brightened up when the boys both asked for seconds and I praised her pork chops and the sweet-potato soufflé for a solid minute.

After dinner, I cleared and the two of us washed and dried while the boys watched TV. I never knew how to talk to Ruth; my father-in-law was the easy one, and when Alfred died I lost my biggest fan. I looked over at Ruth, scrubbing neatly stacked pots with her pink rubber gloves, which matched her pink-and-white apron, which had nothing cute or whimsical about it. She hadn't raised Lionel to be a good husband; she'd raised him to be a warrior, a god, a genius surrounded by courtiers. But I married him anyway, when he was too old to be a warrior, too tired to be a god, and smart enough to know the limits of his talent.

I thought about life without my boys; and I gave Ruth a little hug as she was tugging off her gloves. She humphed and wiped her hands on her apron.

'You take care of yourself, now. Those boys need you more than ever.' She walked into the living room and announced that it was time for us to go, since she had a church meeting.

We all thanked her, and I drove home with three pink Tupperware containers beside me. The car smelled like pork chop.

I wanted to put Buster to bed, but it was only eight o'clock.

I let him watch some sitcoms and changed out of my clothes and into my bathrobe. Lion came into the hall in a fresh shirt.

'Going out?' He looked so pretty in his clean white shirt.

'Yeah, some of the guys want to go down to the Navigator. I said I'd stop by, see who's there. Don't wait up.'

I was surprised but delighted. I tossed him the keys. 'Okay, drive carefully.'

Buster got himself into pajamas and even brushed his teeth without my nagging him. He had obviously figured out that I was not operating at full speed. I tucked him in, trying to give him enough hugs and kisses to help him get settled, not so many that he'd hang on my neck for an extra fifteen minutes. I went to sit in the kitchen, staring at the moths smacking themselves against the screen door. I could relate to that.

I read a few magazines, plucked my eyebrows, thought about plucking the gray hairs at my temples, and decided not to bother. Who'd look? Who'd mind, except me?

Finally, I got into bed, and got out about twenty minutes later. I poured myself some bourbon and tried to go to sleep again, thinking that I hadn't ever really appreciated what it took Lionel to get through life sober. I woke up at around four, anticipating Buster. But there, leaning against the doorway, was Lion.

'Ma.' He sounded congested.

'Are you all right?'

'Yeah. No. Can I come in?'

'Of course, come in. What is it, honey?'

He sat on the bed and plucked at my blanket, and I could smell the beer and the sweat coming off him. I sat up so we could talk, and he threw his arms around me like a drowning man. He was crying and gasping into my neck, and then he stopped and just rested his head against my shoulder. I kept on patting his back, rubbing the long muscles under the satiny skin. My hands were cold against his warm skin.

Lion lifted his head and looked into my eyes, his own eyes like pools of coffee, shining in the moonlight. He put his hand up to my cheek, and then he kissed me and my brain stopped. I shut my eyes.

His kisses were sweet and slow; he pushed his tongue into my mouth just a little at a time, getting more confident every time. He began to rub my nipples through my nightgown, spreading the fingers on one big hand wide apart just as his father used to, and I pulled away, forcing my eyes open.

'No, Lion. You have to go back to your room now.' But I was asking him, I wasn't telling him, and I knew he wouldn't move.

'No.' And he put his soft plummy mouth on my breast, soaking the nightgown. 'Please don't send me away.' The right words.

I couldn't send my little boy away, so I wrapped my arms around him and pulled him to me, out of the darkness.

It had been a long time since I was in bed with a young man. Lionel was forty-two when I met him, and before that I'd been living with a sax player eight years older than I was. I hadn't made love to anyone this young since I was seventeen and too young myself to appreciate it.

His body was so smooth and supple, and the flesh clung to the bone; when he was above me, he looked like an athlete working out; below me, he looked like an angel spread out for the world's adoration. His shoulders had clefts so deep I could lay a finger in each one, and each of his ribs stuck out just a little. He hadn't been eating enough at school. I couldn't move forward or backward, and so I shut my eyes again, so as not to see and not to have to think the same sad, tired thoughts.

He rose and fell between my hips and it reminded me of

Buster's birth: heaving and sliding and then an explosive push. Lion apologized the way men do when they come too soon, and I hugged him and felt almost like myself, comforting him. I couldn't speak at all; I didn't know if I'd ever have a voice again.

He was whispering, 'I love you, I love you, I love you.' And I put my hand over his mouth until he became quiet. He tried to cradle me, pulling my head to his shoulder. I couldn't lie with him like that, so I wriggled away in the dark, my arms around my pillow. I heard him sigh, and then he laid his head on my back. He fell asleep in a minute.

I got up before either of them, made a few nice-neighbor phone calls, and got Buster a morning playdate, lunch included, and a ride to soccer camp. He was up, dressed, fed, and over to the Bergs' before Lion opened his eyes.

Lion's boss called and said he was so sorry for our loss but could Lionel junior please come to work this morning.

I put my hand on Lion's shoulder to wake him, and I could see the shock and the pleasure in his eyes. I told him he was late for work and laid his clothes out on his bed. He kept opening his mouth to say something, but I gave him toast and coffee and threw him my keys.

'You're late, Lion. We'll talk when you get home.'

'I'm not sorry,' he said, and I could have smiled. Good, I thought, spend the day not being sorry, because sometime after that you're gonna feel like shit. I was already sorrier than I'd ever been in my whole life, sorry enough for this life and the next. Lion looked at me and then at the keys in his hand.

'I guess I'll go. Ma ... Julia ...'

I was suddenly, ridiculously angry at being called Julia. 'Go, Lion.'

He was out the door. I started breathing again, trying to figure out how to save us both. Obviously, I couldn't be trusted to take care of him; I'd have to send him away. I thought about sending Buster away, too, but I didn't think I could. And maybe my insanity was limited to the Lion, maybe I could still act like a normal mother to Buster.

I called my friend Jeffrey in Falmouth and told him Lion needed a change of scene. He said Lion could start housepainting tomorrow and could stay with him since his kids were away. The whole time I was talking, I cradled the bottle of bourbon in my left arm, knowing that if I couldn't get through the phone call, or the afternoon, or the rest of my life, I had some help. I think I was so good at helping Lionel quit drinking because I didn't have the faintest idea why he, or anybody, drank. If I met him now, I'd be a better wife but not better for him. I packed Lion's suitcase and put it under his bed.

When I was a lifeguard at camp, they taught us how to save panicky swimmers. The swimmers don't realize that they have to let you save them, that their terror will drown you both, and so sometimes, they taught us, you have to knock the person out to bring him in to shore.

I practiced my speech in the mirror and on the porch and while making the beds. I thought if I said it clearly and quietly he would understand, and I could deliver him to Jeffrey, ready to start his summer over again. I went to the grocery store and bought weird, disconnected items: marinated artichoke hearts for Lionel, who was dead; red caviar to make into dip for his son, whose life I had just ruined; peanut butter with the grape jelly already striped into it for Buster, as a special treat that he would probably have outgrown by the time I got home; a pack of Kools for me, who stopped smoking fifteen years ago. I also bought a wood-refinishing kit, a jar of car wax, a six-pack of

Michelob Light, five TV dinners, some hamburger but no buns, and a box of Pop-Tarts. Clearly the cart of a woman at the end of her rope.

Lion came home at three, and I could see him trying to figure out how to tackle me. He sat down at the kitchen table and frowned when I didn't say anything.

I sat down across from him, poured us each a glass of bourbon, and lit a cigarette, which startled him. All the props said 'Important Moment.'

'Let me say what I have to say and then you can tell me whatever you want to. Lion, I love you very much and I have felt blessed to be your mother and I've probably ruined that for both of us. Just sit still. What happened was not your fault; you were upset, you didn't know ... Nothing would have happened if I had been my regular self. But anyway ...' This was going so badly I just wanted to finish my cigarette and take the boy to the train station, whether he understood or not. 'I think you'd feel a lot better and clearer if you had some time away, so I talked to Jeffrey—'

'No. No, goddammit, I am not leaving and I wasn't upset – it was what I wanted. You can't send me away. I'm not a kid anymore. You can leave me, but you can't make me leave.' He was charging around the kitchen, bumping into the chairs, blind.

I just sat there. All of a sudden, he was finding his voice, the one I had always tried to nurture, to find a place for between his father's roar and his brother's contented hum. I was hearing his debut as a man, and now I had to keep him down and raise him up at the same time.

'How can it be so easy for you to send me away? Don't you love me at all?'

I jumped up, glad to have a reason to move. 'Not love you? It's because I love you, because I want you to have a happy, normal life. I owe it to you and I owe it to your father.'

He folded his arms. 'You don't owe Pop anything ... He had everything he wanted, he had everything.' The words rained down like little blades.

I ignored what he said. 'It can't be, honey. You can't stay.'

'I could if you wanted me to.'

He was right. Who would know? I could take my two boys to the movies, away for weekends, play tennis with my stepson. I would be the object of a little pity and some admiration. Who would know? Who would have such monstrous thoughts, except Ruth, and she would never allow them to surface. I saw us together and saw it unfolding, leaves of shame and pity and anger, neither of us getting what we wanted. I wanted to hug him, console him for his loss.

'No, honey.'

I reached across the table but he shrugged me off, grabbing my keys and heading out the door.

I sat for a long time, sipping, watching the sunlight move around the kitchen. When it was almost five, I took the keys from Lionel's side of the dresser and drove his van to soccer camp. Buster felt like being quiet, so we just held hands and listened to the radio. I offered to take him to Burger King, hoping the automated monkeys and video games would be a good substitute for a fully present and competent mother. He was happy, and we killed an hour and a half there. Three hours to bedtime.

We watched some TV, sitting on the couch, his feet in my lap. Every few minutes, I'd look at the clock on the mantel and then promise myself I wouldn't look until the next commercial. Every time I started to move, I'd get tears in my eyes, so I concentrated on sitting very still, waiting for time to pass. Finally, I got Buster through his nightly routine and into bed, kissing his cupcake face, fluffing his Dr J pillow.

'Where's Lion? He said he'd kiss me good night.'

'Honey, he's out. He'll come in and kiss you while you're sleeping.'

'Where is he?'

I dug my nails into my palms; with Buster, this could go on for half an hour. 'He's out with some friends, Bus. I promise he'll kiss you in your sleep.'

'Okay. I'm glad he's home, Mama.'

How had I managed to do so much harm so fast? 'I know. Go to sleep, Gabriel Tyner Sampson.'

'G'night, Mama. Say my full name again.'

'Gabriel Tyner Sampson, beautiful name for a beautiful boy. 'Night.'

And I thought about the morning we named him, holding him in the delivery room, his boneless brown body covered with white goop and clots of blood, and Lionel tearing off his green mask to kiss me and then to kiss the baby, rubbing his face all over Gabriel's little body.

I got into my kimono and sat in the rocking chair, waiting for Lion. I watched the guests on the talk shows, none of whom seemed like people I'd want to know. After a while, I turned off the sound but kept the picture on for company. I watered my plants, then realized I had just done it yesterday and watched as the water cascaded out of the pots onto the wood floor, drops bouncing onto the wall, streaking the white paint. I thought about giving away the plants, or maybe moving somewhere where people didn't keep plants. Around here, it's like a law. The mopping up took me about eight minutes, and I tried to think of something else to do. I looked for a dish to break.

Stupid, inconsiderate boy. Around now, his father would have been pacing, threatening to beat him senseless when he walked in, and I would have been calming Lionel down, trying to get him to come to bed.

At about three, when I was thinking of calling the hospital, I heard my car coming up the street slowly. I looked out the kitchen window and saw him pull into the drive, minus the right front fender.

He came inside quietly, pale gray around his mouth and eyes. There was blood on his shirt, but he was walking okay. I grabbed him by the shoulders and he winced and I dug my hands into him in the dark of the hallway.

'What is wrong with you? I don't have enough to contend with? Do you know it's three o'clock in the morning? There were no phones where you were, or what? It was too inconvenient to call home, to tell me you weren't lying dead somewhere? Am I talking to myself, goddammit?'

I was shaking him hard, wanting him to talk back so I could slap his face, and he was crying, turning his face away from me. I pulled him into the light of the kitchen and saw the purple bruise, the shiny puff of skin above his right eyebrow. There was a cut in his upper lip, making it lift and twist like a harelip.

'What the hell happened to you?'

'I got into a little fight at the Navigator and then I had sort of an accident, nothing serious. I just hit a little tree and bumped my head.'

'You are an asshole.'

'I know, Ma, I'm sorry. I'll pay you back for the car so your insurance won't go up. I'm really sorry.'

I put my hands in my pockets and waited for my adrenaline to subside.

I steered him into the bathroom and sat him down on the toilet while I got some ice cubes and wrapped them in a dish towel; that year I was always making compresses for Buster's skinned knees, busted lips, black eyes. Lion sat there holding the ice to his forehead. The lip was too far gone.

I wasn't angry anymore and I said so. He smiled lopsidedly and leaned against me for a second. I moved away and told him to wash up.

'All right, I'll be out in a minute.'

'Take your time.'

I sat on the couch, thinking about his going away and whether or not Jeffrey would be good company for him. Lion came out of the bathroom without his bloody shirt, the dish towel in his hand. He stood in the middle of the room, like he didn't know where to sit, and then he eased down onto the couch, tossing the towel from hand to hand.

'Don't send me away. I don't want to go away from you and Grandma and Buster. I just can't leave home this summer. Please, Ma, it won't – what happened won't happen again. Please let me stay home.' He kept looking at his hands, smoothing the towel over his knees and then balling it up.

How could I do that to him?

'All right, let's not talk about it any more tonight.'

He put his head back on the couch and sighed, sliding over so his cheek was on my shoulder. I patted his good cheek and went to sit in the brown chair.

I started to say more, to explain to him how it was going to be, but then I thought I shouldn't. I would tell him that we were looking at wreckage and he would not want to know.

I said good night and went to my bedroom. He was still on the couch in the morning.

We tried for a few weeks, but toward the end of the summer Lion got so obnoxious I could barely speak to him. Ruth kept an uncertain peace for the first two weeks and then blew up at him. 'Where have your manners gone, young man? After all she did for you, this is the thanks she gets? And Julia, when did you get so mush-mouthed that you can't tell him to behave himself?' Lion and I looked at our plates, and Ruth stared at us, puzzled and cross. I came home from work on a Friday and found a note on the kitchen table: *Friends called with a housepainting job in Nantucket. Will call before I go to Paris. Will still do junior year abroad, if that's okay. L.* 'If that's okay' meant that he wanted me to foot the bill, and I did. I would have done more if I had known how.

It's almost summer again. Buster and I do pretty well, and we have dinner every Sunday with Ruth, and more often than not, we drive her over to bingo on Thursday evenings and play a few games ourselves. I see my husband everywhere; in the deft hands of the man handing out the bingo cards, in the black-olive eyes of the boy sitting next to me on the bench, in the thick, curved back of the man moving my new piano. I am starting to play again and I'm teaching Buster.

Most nights, after I have gone to bed, I find myself in the living room or standing on the porch in the cold night air. I tell myself that I am not waiting, it's just that I'm not yet awake.

Night Vision

For fifteen years, I saw my stepmother only in my dreams.

After my father got sick in the spring of my sophomore year, dying fast and ugly in the middle of June, I went to Paris to recover, to become someone else, *un homme du monde*, an expert in international maritime law, nothing like the college boy who slept with his stepmother the day after his father's funeral. We grieved apart after that night, and I left Julia to raise my little brother, Buster, and pay all the bills, including mine. Buster shuttled back and forth for holidays, even as a grown man, calm and affectionate with us both, bringing me Deaf Smith County peanut butter from my mother for Christmas morning, carrying home jars of Fauchon jam from me, packed in three of his sweat socks. My mother's letters came on the first of every month for fifteen years, news of home, of my soccer coach's retirement, newspaper clippings about maritime law and French shipping lines, her new address in Massachusetts, a collection of her essays on jazz. I turned the book over and learned that her hair had turned gray.

'You gotta come home, Lionel,' my brother said last time, his wife sprawled beside him on my couch, her long, pretty feet resting on his crotch.

'I don't think so.'

'She misses you. You know that. You should go see her.'

Jewelle nodded, digging her feet a little further, and Buster grinned hugely and closed his eyes.

'You guys,' I said.

My brother married someone more beautiful and wild than I would have chosen. They had terrible, flying-dishes fights and passionate reconciliations every few months, and they managed to divorce and remarry in one year, without even embarrassing themselves. Jewelle loved Buster to death and told me she only left when he needed leaving, and my brother would say in her defense that it was nothing less than the truth. He never said what he had done that would deserve leaving, and I can't think that it was anything very bad. There is no bad even in the depths of Buster's soul, and when I am sick of him, his undaunted, fat-and-sassy younger-brotherness, I think that there are no depths.

When Buster and Jewelle were together (usually Columbus Day through July Fourth weekend), happiness poured out of them. Buster showed slides of Jewelle's artwork, thickly layered slashes of dark paint, and Jewelle cooked platters of fried chicken and bragged on his triumphs as a public defender. When they were apart, they both lost weight and shine and acted like people in the final stage of terminal heartbreak. Since Jewelle's arrival in Buster's life, I have had a whole secondhand love affair and passionate marriage, and in return Buster got use of my apartment in New York and six consecutive Labor Days in Paris.

'Ma misses you,' he said again. He held Jewelle's feet in one hand. 'You know she does. She's getting old.'

'I definitely don't believe that. She's fifty, fifty-five. That's not old. We'll be there ourselves in no time.'

My mother, my stepmother, my only mother, is fifty-four and I am thirty-four and it has comforted me over the years to picture myself in what I expect to be a pretty vigorous middle age and to contemplate poor Julia tottering along, nylon knee-highs sloshing around her ankles, chin hairs and dewlaps flapping in the breeze.

'Fine. She's a spring chicken.' Buster cut four inches of Brie and chewed on it. 'She's not a real young fifty-five. What did she do so wrong, Lionel? Tell me. I know she loves you, I know she loves me. She loved Pop; she saved his life as far as I can tell. Jesus, she took care of Grammy Ruth for three years when anyone else would've put a pillow over the woman's face. Ma is really a good person, and whatever has pissed you off, you could let it go now. You know, she can't help being white.'

Jewelle, of whom we could say the same thing, pulled her feet out of his hand and curled her toes over his waistband, under his round belly.

'If she died tomorrow, how sorry would you be?' she said.

Buster and I stared at her, brothers again, because in our family you did not say things like that, not even with good intentions.

I poured wine for us all and passed around the fat green olives Jewelle liked.

'Well. Color is not the issue. You can tell her I'll come in June.'

Buster went into my bedroom. 'I'm calling Ma,' he said. 'I'm telling her June.'

Jewelle gently spat olive pits into her hand and shaped them into a neat pyramid on the coffee table.

I flew home with my new girlfriend, Claudine, and her little girl, Mirabelle. Claudine had business and a father in Boston, and a small hotel and me in Paris. She was lean as a boy and treated me with wry Parisian affection, as if all kisses were mildly amusing if one gave it any thought. Claudine's consistent, insouciant aridity was easy on me; I'd come to prefer my lack of intimacy straight up. Mirabelle was my true sweetheart. I loved her orange cartoon curls, her red glasses, and her welterweight swagger. She was Ma Poupée and I was her Bel Homme.

Claudine's father left a new black Crown Victoria for us at Logan, with chocolates and a Tintin comic on the backseat and Joan Sutherland in the CD player. Claudine folded up her black travel sweater and hung a white linen jacket on the back hook. There was five hundred dollars in the glove compartment, and I was apparently the only one who thought that if you were lucky enough to have a father, you might reasonably expect him to meet you at the airport after a two-year separation. My father would have been at that gate, drunk or sober. Mirabelle kicked the back of the driver's seat all the way from the airport, singing what the little boy from Dallas had taught her on the flight over: '*I'm* gonna kick you. I'm *gonna* kick you. I'm gonna *kick* you. I'm gonna kick *you,* right in your big old heinie.' Claudine watched out the window until I pulled onto the turnpike, and then she closed her eyes. Anything in English was my department.

I recognized the new house right away. My mother had dreamed and sketched its front porch and its swing a hundred times during my childhood, on every telephone-book cover and notepad we ever had. For years my father talked big about a glass-and-steel house on the water, recording studio overlooking the ocean, wraparound deck for major partying and jam sessions, and for years I sat next to him on the couch while he read the paper and I read the funnies and we listened to my mother tuck my brother in: 'Once upon a time, there were two handsome princes, Prince Fric, who was a little older, and Prince Frac, who was a little younger. They lived with their parents, the King and Queen, in a beautiful little cottage with a beautiful front porch looking out over the River Wilde. They lived in the little cottage because a big old castle with a wraparound deck and a million windows is simply more trouble than it's worth.'

Julia stood before us on the porch, both arms upraised, her body pale and square in front of an old willow, its branches pooling on the lawn. Claudine pulled off her sunglasses and said, 'You don't resemble her,' and I explained, as I thought I had several times between rue de Birague and the Massachusetts border, that this was my stepmother, that my real mother had died when I was five and Julia had married my father and adopted me. 'Ah,' said Claudine, 'not your real mother.'

Mirabelle said, '*Qu'est-ce que c'est, ça?*'

'Tire swing,' I said.

Claudine said, 'May I smoke?'

'I don't know. She used to smoke.'

'Did she stop?'

'I don't know. I don't know if she smokes or not, Claudine.' She reached for her jacket. 'Does your mother know I'm coming?'

'Here we are, Poupée,' I said to Mirabelle.

I stood by the car and watched my mother make a fuss over Mirabelle's red hair (speaking pretty good French, which I had never heard) and turn Claudine around to admire the crispness of her jacket. She shepherded us up the steps, thanking us for the gigantic and unimaginative bottle of toilet water. Claudine went into the bathroom; Mirabelle went out to the swing. My mother and I stood in her big white kitchen. She hadn't touched me.

'Bourbon?' she said.

'It's midnight in Paris, too late for me.'

'Right,' my mother said. 'Gin and tonic?'

We were just clinking our glasses when Claudine came out and asked for water and an ashtray.

'No smoking in the house, Claudine. I'm sorry.'

Claudine shrugged in that contemptuous way Parisians do, so wildly disdainful you have to laugh or hit them. She went outside, lighting up before she was through the door. We touched glasses again.

'Maybe you didn't know I was bringing a friend?' I said.

My mother smiled. 'Buster didn't mention it.'

'Do you mind?'

'I don't mind. You might have been bringing her to meet me. I don't think you did, but you might have. And a very cute kid. Really adorable.'

'And Claudine?'

'Very pretty. *Chien*. That's the word I remember, I don't know if they still say that.'

Chien means a bitchy, stylish appeal. They do still say that, and my own landlady has said it of Claudine.

Julia dug her hands into a bowl of tarragon and cream cheese and pushed it, one little white gob at a time, under the skin of the big chicken sitting on the counter. 'Do you cook?'

'I do. I'm a good cook. Like Pop.'

My mother put the chicken in the oven and laughed. 'Honey, what did your father ever cook?'

'He was a good cook. He made those big breakfasts on Sunday, he barbecued great short ribs – I remember those.'

'Oh, Abyssinian ribs. I remember them, too. Those were some great parties in those bad old days. Even after he stopped drinking, your father was really fun at a party.' She smiled as if he were still in the room.

My father was a madly friendly, kissy, unreliable drunk when I was a little boy, and a successful, dependable musician and father after he met Julia. Once she became my mother, I never worried about him, I never hid again from that red-eyed, wet-lipped stranger, but I did occasionally miss the old drunk.

Claudine stuck her head back into the kitchen, beautiful and squinting through her smoke, and Mirabelle ran in beneath her. My mother handed her two carrots and a large peeler with a black spongy handle for arthritic cooks, and Mirabelle flourished it at us both, our little musketeer. My mother brought out three less fancy peelers, and while we worked our way through a good-size pile of carrots and pink potatoes, she told us how she met my father at Barbara Cook's house and how they both ditched their dates, my mother leaving behind her favorite coat. Claudine told us about the lady who snuck twin Siamese blue-points into the hotel in her ventilated Vuitton trunk and bailed out on her bill, taking six towels and leaving the cats behind. Claudine laughed at my mother's story and shook her head over the lost red beaver jacket, and my mother laughed at Claudine's story and shook her head over people's foolishness. Mirabelle fished the lime out of Claudine's club soda and sucked on it.

A feeling of goodwill and confidence settled on me for no reason I can imagine.

'Hey,' I said, 'let's stay over. Here.'

My mother smiled and looked at Claudine.

'Perhaps we will just see how we feel,' Claudine said. 'I am a little *fatiguée.*'

'Why don't you take a nap before dinner,' my mother and I said simultaneously.

'Perhaps,' she said, and kept peeling.

I think now that I must have given Claudine the wrong

impression, that she'd come expecting a doddering old lady, none too sharp or tidy these days, living on dented canned goods and requiring a short, sadly empty visit before she collapsed entirely. Julia, with a silver braid hanging down her broad back, in black T-shirt, black pants, and black two-dollar flip-flops on her wide coral-tipped feet, was not that old lady at all.

My mother gave Mirabelle a bowl of cut-up vegetables to put on the table, and she carried it like treasure, the pink radishes bobbing among the ice cubes. Claudine waved her hand around, wanting another cigarette, and my mother gave her a glass of red wine. Claudine put it down a good ten inches away from her.

'I am sorry. We have reservations. Lionel, will you arrange your car? Mirabelle and me must go after dinner. Thank you, Madame Sampson, for your kindness.'

My mother lifted her glass to Claudine. 'Anytime. I hope you both come again.' She did not say anything like 'Oh no, my dear, please stay here,' or 'Lionel, you can't let Claudine drive into Boston all by herself.' I poured myself another drink. I'm still surprised I didn't offer to drive, because I was brought up properly, and because I had been sure until the moment Mirabelle pulled the lime out of Claudine's glass that I wanted to stay at the Ritz in Boston, that I had come only so that I could depart.

Mirabelle told my mother the long story of the airplane meal and the spilled soda and the nice lady and the bad little boy from Texas and Monsieur Teddy's difficult flight squashed in a suitcase with a hiking boot pressed against his nose for seven hours. My mother laughed and admired and clucked sympathetically in all the right places, passing the platter of chicken and bowls of cucumber salad and minted peas. She poured another grenadine and ginger ale for Mirabelle, who watched the bubbles rise through the fuchsia syrup. She had just reached for her glass when Claudine arranged her knife and fork on her plate and stood up.

Mirabelle sighed, tilting her head back to drain her drink, like one of my father's old buddies at closing time. We all watched her swallow. My mother made very strong coffee for Claudine, filling an old silver thermos and putting together a plastic-wrapped mound of lemon squares for the road. She doted on Mirabelle and deferred to Claudine as if they were my lovable child and my formidable wife and she my fond and familiar mother. She refused to let us clear the table and amused Mirabelle while Claudine changed into comfortable driving clothes.

Mirabelle and my mother kissed good-bye French-style, and then Claudine did the same, walking out the kitchen door without waiting to see if I followed, which, of course, I did. I didn't want to be, I wasn't, rude or uninterested; I just didn't want to leave yet. Mirabelle hugged me quickly and lay down on the backseat. I made a little sweater pillow for her, and she brushed her cheek against my hand. Claudine made a big production of adjusting the Crown Victoria's side mirror, the rearview mirror, and the seat belt.

'Do you know how to get to the city?' I asked in French.

'Yes.'

'And then you stay on—'

'I have a map,' she said. 'I can sleep by the side of the road until morning if I get lost.'

'That probably won't be necessary. You have five hundred dollars in cash and seven credit cards. There'll be a hundred motels in the next fifty miles.'

'We'll be fine. I will take care of everything,' she said. In very

fast English she added, 'Do not call me, all right? We can speak
to each other when you get back to Paris, perhaps.'

'Okay, Claudine. Take it easy. I'm sorry. I'll call you in a few
weeks. Mirabelle, *dors bien, fais de beaux rêves, mon ange.*'

I watched them drive off, and I watched the fat white moon
hanging over my mother's roof. I was scared to go back into the
house. I called out, 'Where's Buster? I thought he was coming
up.' I had threatened not to come back if my brother didn't show
up within twenty-four hours.

My mother stuck her head out the front door. 'He'll be here
tomorrow. He's jammed up in court. He said dinner at the latest.'

'With or without the Jewelle?'

'With. Very much with. It's only June, you know.'

'You don't think she gives Bus a little too much action?'

'I don't think he's looking for peace. He's peaceful enough. I
think he was looking for a wild ride and she gives it to him. And
she does love him to death.'

'I know. She's kind of a nut, Ma.'

And it didn't matter what we said then, because my lips calling her mother, her heart hearing mother after so long, blew
across the bright night sky and stirred the long branches of the
willow tree.

'Are you coming in?' she said.

'In a few.'

'In a few I'll be asleep. You can finish cleaning up.'

I heard her overhead, her heavy step on the stairs, the creak of
her bedroom floor, the double thump of the bathroom door,
which I had noticed needed fixing. I thought about changing the
hinges on that door, and I thought of my mouth around her hard
nipple, her wet nightgown over my tongue, a tiny bubble of
cotton I had to rip the nightgown to get rid of. She had reached

over me to click off the light, and the last thing I saw that night was the white underside of her arm. In the dark she smelled of honey and salt and the faint tang of wet metal.

I washed the wineglasses by hand and wiped down the counters. When my father was rehearsing and my brother was noodling around in his room, when I wasn't too busy with soccer and school, my mother and I cleaned up the kitchen and listened to music. We talked or we didn't, and she did some old Moms Mabley routines and I did Richard Pryor, and we stayed in the kitchen until about ten.

I called upstairs.

'Do you mind living alone?'

My mother stood at the top of the stairs in a man's blue terry-cloth robe and blue fuzzy slippers the size of small dogs.

'Sweet Jesus, it *is* Moms Mabley,' I said.

'No hat,' she said.

I realized, a little late, that it was not a kind thing to say to a middle-aged woman.

'And I've still got my teeth. I put towels in the room at the end of the hall. The bed's made up. I'll be up before you in the morning.'

'How do you know?'

'I don't know.' She came down three steps. 'I'm pretending I know. But it is true that I get up earlier than most people. I can make you an omelet if you want.'

'I'm not much of a breakfast man.'

She smiled, and then her smile folded up and she put her hand over her mouth.

'Ma, it's all right.'

'I hope so, honey. Not that – I'm still sorry.' She sat down on the stairs, her robe pulled tight under her thighs.

'It's all right.' I poured us both a little red wine and handed it to her, without going up the stairs. 'So, do you mind living alone?'

My mother sighed. 'Not so much. I'm a pain in the ass. I could live with a couple of other old ladies, I guess. Communal potlucks and watching who's watering down the gin. It doesn't really sound so bad. Maybe in twenty years.'

'Maybe you'll meet someone.'

'Maybe. I think I'm pretty much done meeting people.'

'You're only fifty-five. You're the same age as Tina Turner.'

'Yup. And Tina is probably tired of meeting people, too. How about you – do you mind living alone?'

'I don't exactly live alone—'

'You do. That's exactly what you do – you live alone. And have relationships with people who are very happy to let you live alone.'

'Claudine's really a lot of fun, Ma. You didn't get to know her.'

'She may be a whole house of fun, but don't tell me she inspires thoughts of a happy domestic life.'

'No.'

'That little girl could.'

I told her a few of my favorite Mirabelle stories, and she told me stories I had forgotten about me and my brother drag-racing shopping carts down Cross Street, locking our babysitter in the basement, stretching ourselves on the doorways, and praying to be tall.

'We never made you guys say your prayers, we certainly never went to church, and we kept you far away from Grammy Ruth's Never Forgive Never Forget Pentecostal Church of the Holy Fruitcakes. And there you two would be, on your knees to Jesus, praying to be six feet tall.'

'It worked,' I said.

'It did.' She stretched her legs down a few steps, and I saw that they were unchanged, still smooth and tan, with hard calves that squared when she moved.

'You ought to think about marrying again,' I said.

'You ought to think about doing it the first time.'

'Well, let's get on it. Let's find people to marry. Broomstick-jumping time in Massachusetts and Paree.'

My mother stood up. 'You do it, honey. You find someone smart and funny and kindhearted and get married so I can make a fuss over the grandbabies.'

I saluted her with the wineglass. 'Yes, ma'am.'

'Good night. Sleep tight.'

'Good night, Ma.'

I waited until I heard the toilet flush and the faucets shut, and I listened to her walk across her bedroom and heard her robe drop on the floor, and I could even hear her quilt settle down upon her. I drank in a serious way, which I rarely do, until I thought I could sleep. I made to lay my glasses on the rickety nightstand and dropped them on the floor near my clothes. Close enough, I thought, and lay down and had to sit up immediately, my eyes seeming to float out of my head, my stomach rising and falling in great waves of gin and Merlot. Stubbing my toe on the bathroom doorframe, I reached for the light switch and knocked over a water glass. I knew that broken glass lay all around me, although I couldn't see it, and I toe-danced backward toward the bed, twirling and leaping to safety. I reached for my glasses, hiding on the blue rug near my jeans, and somehow rammed my balls into the pink and brown Billie Holiday lamp.

I fell to the floor, hoping for no further damage and complete unconsciousness.

My naked mother ran into the room. I was curled up in a ball, her feet beside my ass. She knelt down, pushing back my hair to get a better look at me. Her breasts swung down, half in, half out of the hallway's dusty light.

'You do not have a scratch on you,' she said, and patted my cheek. 'Walk over toward the door – there's nothing that way. I'll get a broom.'

I could see her, both more and less clearly than I would have liked. She pushed herself up, and the view of her folded belly and still-dark pubic hair was replaced by the sharp swing of her hips, wider now, tenderly pulled down at the soft bottom edges, but still that same purposeful, kick-down-the-door walk.

She came back in her robe and slippers, with a broom and dustpan, and I wrapped a towel around my waist. I stood up straight so that even if she needed glasses as much as I did what she saw of me would look good.

'Quite the event. Is there something, some small thing in this room, you didn't run into?'

'No,' I said. 'I think I've made contact with almost everything. The armchair stayed out of my way, but otherwise, for a low-key kind of guy, I'd have to say I got the job done.'

My mother dumped the pieces of glass and the lightbulb and the lamp remains into the wastebasket.

'You smell like the whole Napa Valley,' she said, 'so I won't offer you a brandy.'

'I don't usually drink this way, Ma. I'm sorry for the mess.'

She put down the broom and the dustpan and came over to me and smiled at my towel. She put her lips to the middle of my chest, over my beating heart.

'I love you past speech.'

We stood there, my long neck bent down to her shoulder, her hands kneading my back. We breathed in and out together.

'I'll say good night, honey. Quite a day.'

She waved one hand over her shoulder and walked away.

Light into Dark

'It's six-fifteen,' Lionel says to his stepmother. 'Decent people have started drinking.'

'Maybe I should put out some food,' Julia says.

Lionel nods, looking around for the little cluster of liquor bottles Julia had thrown out when his father was alive and trying to stay sober, and which she replaced on the sideboard as soon as the man passed away. Lionel's not sorry he's dragged himself and his stepson from Paris to Massachusetts for their first trip together, but it seems possible, even probable, that this Thanksgiving weekend will be the longest four days of his life.

'It's all over with Paula?' Julia doesn't sound sorry or not sorry; she sounds as if she's simply counting places at the table.

'Yeah. Things happen.'

'Do you want to tell me more about it?'

'Nothing to tell.'

After his first wife, the terrible Claudine, Lionel had thought he would never even sleep with another woman, but Paula had been the anti-Claudine: not French, not thin, not mean. She was plump and pretty, a good-natured woman with an English-language bookstore and a three-year-old son. It did not seem possible, when they married in the garden of the Hôtel des Saints-Pères, with Paula in a short white dress and her little boy holding the rings, that after five years she would be thin and irritable and given to the same shrugs and expensive cigarettes as the terrible Claudine. After he moved out, Lionel insisted on weekly dinners and movie nights with his stepson. He wants to do right by the one child to whom he is 'Papa,' although he has begun to think, as Ari turns eight, that there is no reason not to have the boy call him by his first name instead.

'Really nothing to tell. We were in love and then not.'

'You slept with someone else?' Julia asks.

'Julia.'

'I'm just trying to see how you got to "not."'

'I bet Buster told you.'

'Your brother did not rat on you.' He had, of course. Buster, the family big-mouth, a convert to monogamy, had told his mother that Lionel slept with the ticket taker from the cinema Studio 28, and Julia was not as shocked as Buster had hoped she would be. 'A cutie, I bet,' was all she said. (The beauty of Lionel's girlfriends was legendary. Paula, dimpled, fair, and curvy in her high heels, would have been the belle of any American country club, and even so was barely on the bottom rung of Lionel's girls.)

Buster talks about everything: his wife's dissolving sense of self, Jordan's occasional bed-wetting, Corinne's thumb-sucking, all just to open the door for his own concerns and sore spots – his climbing weight, his anxiety about becoming a judge so young. Julia thinks that Buster is a good and fine-looking man, and tall enough to carry the weight well, although it breaks her heart to see her boy so encumbered. She knows that he will make a fine judge, short on oratory and long on common sense and kindness.

'Even in my day, honey, most people got divorced because they had someone else on the side and got tired of pretending they didn't.' Julia herself had been Lionel senior's someone on the side before she became his wife.

'Let's not go there. Anyway, definitely over with Paula. But I'm going to bring Ari every Thanksgiving.'

Everyone had liked Paula (even when she got so crabby, it was not with the new in-laws three thousand miles away), but no one, including Lionel, can look at the poor kid without wanting to run a thumb up his slack spine. Bringing Ari is no gift to anyone; he's a burden to Jordan, an annoyance to little Corinne. Of course, Buster doesn't mind; he's the soft touch in the family, and Jewelle, inclined to love everything even faintly Buster, tries, but her whole beautiful frowning face signals that this is an inferior sort of child, one who does not appreciate friendly jokes or good cooking or the chance to ingratiate himself with his American family. It is to Ari's credit, Lionel thinks, that instead of clinging forlornly, he has retreated into bitter, silent, superior Frenchness.

'Julia, are you listening?' Lionel asks. 'On Friday I'll fix the kitchen steps.'

Julia sets down a platter of cold chicken and sits on the floor to do Colorforms with Jordan. She puts a red square next to Jordy's little green dots.

'It's like talking to myself. It's like I'm not even in the room.' Lionel pours himself a drink, walking over to his nephew. Jordan peels a blue triangle off the bottom of Lionel's sneaker without looking up. Jordan takes after his father, and they both hate disturbances; Uncle Lionel can be a disturbance of the worst kind, the kind that might make Grandma Julia walk out of the room or put away the toys, slamming the cabinet door shut, knocking the hidden chocolates out of their boxes.

'Oh, we know you're here,' Julia says. 'We can tell because your size thirteens are splayed all over Jordy's Colorforms. Squashing them.'

'They're already flat, Julia,' Lionel says, and she laughs. Lionel makes her laugh.

Jordan moves his Colorforms board a safe distance from his uncle's feet. Uncle Lionel is sharp, is what Jordan's parents say. Sharp as a knife. Ari, not really Uncle Lionel's son, not really Jordan's cousin, is sharp, too, but he's sharp mostly in French, so Jordan doesn't even have to get into it with him. Ari has Tintin and Jordan has Spider-Man, and Jordan stretches out on the blue velvet couch and Ari gets just the blue-striped armchair, plus Jordan has his own room and Ari has to share with Uncle Lionel.

'You invite Ari to play with you,' Julia tells Jordan. 'Take your sister with you.'

'He's mean. And he only talks French, anyway. He's—'

'Jordy, invite your cousin to play with you. He's never been to America before, and you are the host.'

'I'm the host?' Jordan can see himself in his blue blazer with his feet up on the coffee table like Uncle Lionel, waving a fat cigar.

'You are.'

'All right. We're gonna play outside, then.' Ari is not an outside person.

'That's nice,' Lionel says.

'Nice enough,' Julia says. It is terrible to prefer one grandchild over another, but who would not prefer sweet Jordan or Princess Corinne to poor long-nosed Ari, slinking around the house like a marmoset.

Julia has not had both sons with her for Thanksgiving for more than twenty years. Until 1978 the Sampson family sat around a big bird with corn-bread stuffing, pralined sweet pota-toes, and three kinds of deep-dish pie, and it has been easier since her husband and in-laws died to stay in with a bourbon and a bowl of pasta when one son couldn't come home and the other didn't, and not too hard, later, to come as a pitied favorite guest to Buster's in-laws', and sweet and very easy, during the five happy, private years with Peaches Figueroa, for the two of them to wear their pajamas and eat fettuccine al barese in honor of Julia's Italian roots and in honor of Peaches, who had grown up with canned food and Thanksgiving from United Catholic Charities. With her whole extant family in the house now, sons and affectionate daughter-in-law (Jewelle must have had to promise her mother a hundred future Christmases to get away on Thanksgiving), grandson, granddaughter, and poor Ari, Lionel's little ex–step marmoset, Julia can see that she has entered Official Grandmahood. Sweet or sour, spry or arthritic, she is now a stock character, as essential and unknown as the maid in a drawing-room comedy.

'Looks good. Ari likes chicken.' Lionel walks toward the side-board.

Julia watches him sideways, his clever, darkly mournful eyes, the small blue circles of fatigue beneath them, the sparks of silver in his black curls. She does not say, How did we cripple you so? Don't some people survive a bad mother and her early death? Couldn't you have been the kind of man who overcomes terri-ble misfortune, even a truly calamitous error in judgment? It was just one night – not that that excuses anything, Julia thinks. She loves him like no one else; she remembers meeting him for the first time, wooing him for his father's sake and loving him exu-berantly, openhandedly, without any of the prickling maternal guilt or profound irritation she sometimes felt with Buster. Just one shameful, gold-rimmed night together, and it still runs through her like bad sap. She has no idea what runs through him.

There is a knot in his heart, Julia thinks, as she puts away the Colorforms, and nothing will loosen it. She sees a line of ex–daughters-in-law, short and tall, dark and fair, stretching from Paris to Massachusetts, throwing their wedding bands into the sea and waving regretfully in her direction.

Julia kisses Lionel firmly on the forehead, and he smiles. It would be nicer if his stepmother's rare kisses and pats on the cheek did not feel so much like forgiveness, like Julia's wish to convey that she does not blame him for being who he is. Lionel wonders whom exactly she does blame.

'Let's talk later,' he says. It seems safe to assume that later will not happen.

Lionel watches his niece and his sister-in-law through the kitchen door. He likes Jewelle. He always has. Likes her for loving his little brother and shaking him up, and likes her more now that she has somehow shaped Buster into a grown man, easy in his young family and smoothly armored for the outside world. He likes her for always making him feel that what she finds attractive in her husband she finds attractive, too, in the older, slightly darker brother-in-law. And Lionel likes, can't help being glad to see on his worst days, those spectacular breasts of hers, which, even as she has settled down into family life, no longer throwing plates in annoyance or driving to Mexico out of pique, she displays with the transparent pride of her youth.

'Looking good, Jewelle. Looking babe-a-licious, Miss Corinne.'

They both smile, and Jewelle shakes her head. Why do the bad ones always look so good? Buster is a handsome man, but Lionel is just the devil.

'Are you here to help or to bother us?'

'Helping. He's helping me,' Corinne says. She likes Uncle Lionel. She likes his big white smile and the gold band of his cigar, which he always, always gives to her, and the way he butters her bread, covering the slice right to the crust with twice as much butter as her mother puts on.

'I could help,' Lionel says. There is an unopened bottle of Scotch under the sink, and he finds Julia's handsome, square, heavy-bottomed glasses, the kind that make you glad you drink hard liquor.

Lionel rolls up his sleeves and chops apples and celery. After Corinne yawns twice and almost tips over into the pan of cooling corn bread, Jewelle carries her off to bed. When she comes back from arranging Floradora the Dog and Strawberry Mouse just so, and tucking the blankets tightly around Corinne's feet, Lionel is gone, as Jewelle expected.

Her mother-in-law talks tough about men. Everything about Julia, her uniform of old jeans and black T-shirt, her wild gray hair and careless independence, says nothing is easier than finding a man and training him and kicking him loose if he doesn't behave, and you would think she'd raised both her boys as feminist heroes. And Buster is good – Jewelle always says so – he picks up after himself, cooks when he can, gives the kids their baths, and is happy to sit in the Mommy row during Jordan's Saturday swim. Lionel is something else. When he clears the table or washes up, swaying to Otis Redding, snapping his dish towel like James Brown, Julia watches him with such tender admiration that you would think he'd just rescued a lost child.

Jewelle runs her hands through the corn bread, making tracks in the crust, rubbing the big crumbs between her fingers. Julia's house, even with Lionel in it, is one of Jewelle's favorite places. At home, she is the Mommy and the Wife. Here, she is the mother of gifted children, an esteemed artist temporarily on leave. At her parents' house, paralyzed by habit, she drinks milk out of the carton, trying to rub her lipstick off the spout afterward, borrows her mother's expensive mascara and then takes it home after pretending to help her mother search all three bathrooms before they leave. She eats too much and too fast, half of it standing up and the rest with great reluctance, as if there were a gun pointed at her three times a day. In Julia's house there's no trouble about food or mealtimes; Jewelle eats what she wants, and the children eat bananas and Cheerios and grilled cheese sandwiches served up without even an arching of an eyebrow. Julia is happy to have her daughter-in-law cook interesting dishes and willing to handle the basics when the children are hungry and not one adult is intrigued by the idea of cooking.

Buster will not hear of anything but the corn bread-and-bacon stuffing Grammy Ruth used to make, and Jewelle, who would eat bacon every day if she could, makes six pounds of it and leaves a dark, crisp pile on the counter, for snacking. Julia seems to claim nothing on Thanksgiving but the table setting. She's not fussy – she prides herself on her lack of fuss – but Julia is particular about her table, and it is not Jewelle or Buster who is called on to pick up the centerpiece in town, but Lionel, who has had his license suspended at least two times that Jewelle knows of. Jewelle packs the stuffing into Tupperware and leaves a long note for Julia so that her mother-in-law will not think that she has abdicated on the sweet potatoes or the creamed spinach.

In bed, spooning Buster, Jewelle runs her hand down his

warm back. Sweetness, she thinks, and kisses him between the shoulders. Buster throws one big arm behind him and pulls her close. Lucky Jewelle, lucky Buster. If Jewelle had looked out the window, she would have seen Lionel and Julia by the tire swing, talking the way they have since they resumed talking, casual and ironic, and beneath that very, very careful.

Lionel cradles the bottle of Glenlivet.

'You drink a lot these days,' Julia says in the neutral voice she began cultivating twenty years ago, when it became clear that Lionel would never come back from Paris, would improve his French, graduate from L'Institut de Droit Comparé, and make his grown-up life anywhere but near her.

Lionel smiles. 'It's not your fault. Blame the genes, Ma. Junkie mother, alcoholic dad. You did your best.'

'It doesn't interfere with your work?' It's not clear even to Julia what she wants: Lionel unemployed and cadging loans from her, or drinking discreetly, so good at what he does that no one cares what happens after office hours.

'I am *so* good at my job. I am probably the best fucking maritime lawyer in France. If you kept up with French news, you'd see me in the papers sometimes. Good and good-looking. And modest.'

'I know you must be very good at your work. You can be proud of what you do. Pop would have been very proud of you.'

Lionel takes a quick swallow and offers the bottle to Julia, and if it were not so clear to her that he is mocking himself more than her, that he wishes to spare her the trouble of worrying by showing just how bad it already is, she would knock the bottle out of his hand.

Lionel says, 'I know. And you? What are you doing lately that you take pride in?'

Julia answers as if it's a pleasant question, the kind of fond interest one hopes one's children will show.

'I finished another book of essays, the piano in jazz. It's all right. It'll probably sell dozens, like the last one. You make sure to buy a few. I'm still gardening, not that you can tell this time of year.'

'Buster says you're seeing someone.'

'You have to watch out for Buster.' Julia turns away. 'Well, "seeing." It's Peter, my neighbor down the road. We like each other. His wife died three years ago.'

'No real obstacles, then.'

'Nope.'

'How old is he? White or black?'

'He's a little older than me. White. You'll meet him tomorrow. I didn't want him to be alone. His daughter's in Baltimore this year with her husband's family.'

'That's nice of you. Your first all-family Thanksgiving in twenty years – might as well have a few strangers to grease the wheels.'

'It is nice, and he's only one person, and he is not a stranger to me or to Buster and Jewelle,' Julia says, and walks into the house, thinking that it's too late in her personal day for talking to Lionel, that if she were driving she would have pulled off the road half an hour ago.

Julia starts cooking at six A.M. Early Thanksgiving morning is the only time she will have to herself. The rest of the day will be a joy, most likely, and so tiring that when Buster and Jewelle leave on Friday, right after Corinne is wrapped up in her car seat and Jordan squirms around for one last good-bye and their new car crunches down the gravel driveway, Julia will lie down with a cup of tea and not get up until the next day, when she will say good-bye to Lionel and Ari and lie down again. She reads Jewelle's detailed note and thinks, Poor Jewelle must be thirty-one – it's probably time for her to have Thanksgiving in her own house. Julia had to wrestle the holiday out of her own mother's hands; even as the woman lay dying she whispered directions for gravy and pumpkin pie, creating a chain of panicked, resentful command from bedroom to kitchen, with her daughter and two sisters slicing and basting to beat back the inevitable. Julia managed to celebrate one whole independent Thanksgiving, with four other newly hatched adults, only to marry Lionel senior the next summer and find the holiday permanently ensconced, like a small museum's only Rodin, at her new mother-in-law's house. Julia can sit now in her own kitchen, sixty years old with a dish towel in her hand, and hear Ruth Sampson saying to her, 'My son is not cut from the same cloth as other people. You treat him right.'

After this last, unexpected hurrah, Julia will let go of Thanksgiving altogether. She'll arrive at Jewelle's house, or Jewelle's mother's house, at just the right time, and entertain the children, and bring her own excellent lemon meringue pies and extravagant flowers to match their tablecloths. If things go well, maybe she'll bring Peter, too. As Julia pictures Peter entering Buster's front hall by her side, the two of them with bags of presents and a box of butter tarts, she cuts a wide white scoop through the end of her forefinger. Blood flows so fast it pools on the cutting board and drips onto the counter before she has even realized what the pain is.

'Ma.' Lionel is behind her with paper towels. He packs her finger until it's the size of a dinner roll and holds it up over her head. 'You stay like that. Sit. And keep your hand up.'

'You're up early. The Band-Aids are in my bathroom.' Her fingertip is throbbing like a heart, and Julia keeps it aloft. It's been a long time since anyone has told her to do anything.

Her bathrobe always lies at the foot of the bed. There is always a pale-blue quilt, and both nightstands are covered with books and magazines and empty teacups. The room smells like her. Lionel takes the Band-Aids from under the sink: styling mousse, Neosporin ointment (which he also takes), aloe-vera gel, Northern Lights shampoo for silver hair, two bottles of Pepto-Bismol, a jar of vitamin C, zinc lozenges, and a small plastic box of silver bobby pins.

When he comes down, Julia is holding her finger up, still pointing to God, in the most compliant, sweetly mocking way.

'I hear and obey,' she says.

'That'll be the fucking day.'

Lionel slathers the antibiotic ointment over her finger, holding the flap of skin down, and wraps two Band-Aids around it. It must hurt like holy hell by now, but she doesn't say so. With her good hand, Julia pats his knee.

'I was going to make coffee,' she says, 'but I think you'll have to.' And even after Jewelle and Buster get up for the kids' breakfast and exclaim over the finger and Jewelle prepares to run the show, Lionel stays by Julia, changing the red bandages every few hours, mocking her every move, helping her with each dish and glass as if he were some fairy-tale combination of servant and prince.

At one o'clock, after Peter has called to say that he is too sick to come and everyone in the kitchen hears him coughing over the phone, they all go upstairs to change. They are not a dress-up family (another thing Jewelle likes, although she can hear her mother's voice suggesting that if one so disdains the holiday's traditions, why celebrate it at all), but the children are in such splendid once-a-year finery that it seems ungracious not to make an effort. Corinne wears a bronze organdy dress tied with a bronze satin sash, and ivory anklets and ivory Mary Janes. Julia knows this is nothing but nonsense and conspicuous consumption, but she loves the look of this little girl, right down to the twin bronze satin roses in her black hair, and she hopes she will remember it when Corinne comes to the dinner table ten years from now with a safety pin in her cheek or a leopard tattooed on her forehead. And Jordan is in his snappy fawn vest and white button-down shirt tucked into his navy-blue pants, and an adorable navy-blue-and-white-striped bow tie. Lionel and Buster are deeply dapper; their father appreciated Italian silks and French cotton, took his boys to Brooks Brothers in good times and Filene's Basement when necessary, and made buying a handsome tie as much a part of being a man as carrying a rubber or catching a ball, and they have both held on to that. Jewelle has the face and the figure to look good in almost everything, but Julia herself would not have chosen tight black satin pants, a turquoise silk camisole cut low, and a black satin jacket covered with bits of turquoise and silver, an unlikely mix of Santa Fe and disco fever. Julia comes downstairs in her usual holiday gray flannel pants and white silk shirt. She has turned her bathroom mirror, her hairbrushes, and her jewelry box over to Jewelle and Corinne.

'Do you mind Peter's not coming?' Buster says.

'Not really.'

Lionel looks at her. 'You must miss Pop,' he says.

'Of course, honey. I miss him all the time.' This is not entirely true. Julia misses Lionel senior when she hears an alto sax playing anything, even one weak note, and she misses him when she takes out the garbage; she misses him when she sees a couple dancing, and she misses him every time she looks at Buster, who has resembled her for most of his life, with his father apparent only in his curly hair, and now looks almost too much like the man she married.

Buster puts his arm around her waist. 'You must miss Peaches, too.' He'd met Peaches only a few times when she was well and charming, and a few more when she was dying, collapsed in his mother's bed like some great gray beast, all bones and crushed skin, barely able to squeeze her famous voice out through the cords.

Julia would like to say that missing Peaches doesn't cover it. She misses Peaches as much as she missed her stepson during his fifteen-year absence. She misses Peaches the way you miss good health when you have cancer. She misses her husband – of course she misses him and their twelve years together – but that grief has been softened, sweetened by all the time and life that came after. The wound of Peaches's death has not healed or closed up yet; at most the edges harden some as the days pass. She opens her mouth now to say nothing at all about her last love; she thinks that even if Lionel is all wrong about what kind of man Peter is, he is fundamentally right. Peter is not worth the effort.

'I do miss Peaches, too, of course.'

Lionel has all of Peaches Figueroa's albums. On the first one, dark-blond hair waves around a wide bronze face, one smooth lock half covering a round green eye heavily made up. Black velvet wraps low across her breasts, and when Lionel was nineteen it was one of the small pleasures of his life to look at the dark-amber crescent of her aureole, just visible above the velvet rim, and listen to that golden, spilling voice.

'I'm sorry I didn't meet her.' Lionel would like to ask his mother what it was like to go from a man to a woman, whether it changed Julia somehow (which he believes but cannot explain), and how she could go from his father and Peaches Figueroa, both geniuses of a kind, to Peter down the road, who sounds to Lionel like the most fatiguing, sorry-assed, ready-for-the-nursing home, limp-dick loser.

Julia raises an eyebrow and goes into the kitchen.

The men look at each other.

'We could open the wine,' Lionel says. 'You liked her, didn't you?'

'I really liked her,' Buster says. He does not say, She scared the shit out of Jewelle, but she would have liked you, boy. She liked handsome, and she knew we all have that soft spot for talent, especially musical talent, and that we don't mind, we have even been known to encourage, a certain amount of accompanying attitude. Peaches had been Buster's favorite diva.

'Open the wine up. You let those babies breathe. I'll get everyone down here.'

'It might be another half hour for the turkey,' Jewelle says. 'Sorry.'

'Don't worry, honey.' Buster eats one of Corinne's peanut-butter-stuffed celery sticks.

'Charades?' Julia says, putting out a small bowl of nuts and a larger one of black and green olives. Charades was their great family game, played in airports and hotel lobbies, played with very small gestures while flying to Denmark every summer for the Copenhagen jazz festival, played on Amtrak and in the occasional stretch limo to Newport, and played expertly by Lionel and Buster whenever the occasion has arisen since. Corinne and Jordan don't know what charades is, but Grandma Julia has already taken them back to the kitchen and distributed two salad bowls, six pencils, and a pile of scrap paper. Corinne will act out *The Cat in the Hat,* and Jordan will do his favorite song, 'Miami.' Corinne practices making the hat shape and stepping into it while Jordan pulls off his bow tie and slides on his knees across the kitchen floor, wild and shiny and fly like Will Smith. They are naturals, Julia thinks, and thinks further that it is a ridiculous thing to be pleased about – who knows what kind of people they will grow up to be? – but she cannot help believing that their mostly good genes and their ability to play charades are as reasonable an assurance of future success as anything else.

No one wants to be teamed with Jewelle. She is smart about many things, talented in a dozen ways, and an excellent mother, and both men think she looks terrific with the low cups of her turquoise lace top ducking in and out of view, but she's no good at charades. She goes blank after the first syllable and stamps her foot and blinks back tears until her time is up. She never gets the hard ones, and even with the easiest title she guesses blindly without listening to what she's said. Jewelle is famous for 'Exobus' and 'Casabroomca.'

I can't put husband and wife together, Julia thinks, feeling the tug of dinner-party rules she has ignored for twenty years. 'Girls against boys, everybody?'

Jewelle claims the couch for the three girls, and Buster and Lionel look at each other. It is one of the things they like best about their mother; she would rather be kind than win. They slap hands. Unless Corinne is very, very good in a way that is not normal for a three-year-old, they will wipe the floor with the girl team.

Jewelle is delighted. Julia is an excellent guesser and a patient performer.

Lionel says, 'Rules, everybody.' No one expects the children

Amy Bloom

to do anything except act out their charades and yell out meaningless guesses. The recitation of rules is for Jewelle. 'No talking while acting. Not even whispering. No foreign languages—'

'Not even French,' Jewelle says. Lionel is annoying in English; he is obnoxious in French.

'Not even French. No props. No mouthing. Kids, look.' He shows them the signs for book and television and movie and musical, for little words, for 'sounds like.'

Jordan says, 'Where's Ari?'

They all look around the room. Jewelle sighs. 'Jordy, go get him. He's probably still in Uncle Lionel's room. When did you see him last, Lionel?' she says.

Jordan runs up the stairs.

'I didn't lose him, Jewelle. He's probably just resting. It was a long trip.'

Ari comes down in crumpled khakis and a brown sweater. Terrible colors for him, Jewelle and Julia think.

In French, Lionel says, 'Good boy. You look ready for dinner. Come sit by me and I'll show you how to play this game.'

Ari sits on the floor in front of his stepfather. He doesn't expect that the game will be explained to him; it will be in very fast English, it will make them all laugh with one another, and his stepfather, who is already winking at stupid baby Corinne, will go on laughing and joking, in English.

The children perform their charades, and the adults are almost embarrassed to be so pleased. As Julia stands up to do *Love's Labour's Lost*, Jewelle says, 'Let me just run into the kitchen.'

Lionel says, 'Go ahead, Ma. You're no worse off with Corinne,' and Buster laughs and looks at the floor. He loves Jewelle, but there is something about this particular disability that seems so harmlessly funny; if she were fat, or a bad dancer, or not very bright, he would not laugh, ever.

As Julia is very slowly helping Corinne guess that it's three words, Jewelle walks into the living room, struggling with the large turkey still sizzling on the wide silver platter.

'It's that time,' she says.

Buster says, 'I'll carve,' and Jewelle, who heard him laugh, says, 'No, Lionel's neater – let him do it.'

They never finish the charades game. Corinne and Jordan and Ari collapse on the floor after dinner, socks and shoes scattered, one of Corinne's bronze roses askew, the other in Ari's sneaker. Ari and Jordan have dismantled the couch. Jewelle and Buster gather the three of them, wash their faces, drop them into pajamas, and put them to bed. They kiss their beautiful, damp children, who smell of soap and corn bread and lemon meringue, and they kiss Ari, who smells just like his cousins.

Buster says, 'Do we have to go back down?'

'Are you okay?' Jewelle rubs his neck.

'Just stuffed. And I'm ready to be with just you.' Buster looks at his watch. 'Lionel's long knives ought to be coming out around now.'

'Do you think we ought to hang around for your mother?'

'To protect her? I know you must be kidding.'

It's all right with Jewelle if Buster thinks they've cleaned up enough; the plates are all in the kitchen, the leftover turkey has been wrapped and refrigerated, the candles have been blown out. It's not her house, after all.

Lionel washes, Julia dries. They've been doing it this way since he was ten, and just as he cannot imagine sleeping on the left side of a bed or wearing shoes without socks, he cannot imagine drying rather than washing. Julia looks more than tired; she looks maimed.

'If your hand's hurting, just leave the dishes. They'll dry in the rack.'

Julia doesn't even answer. She keeps at it until clean, dry plates and silver cover the kitchen table.

'If you leave it until tomorrow, I'll put it all away,' Lionel says.

Julia thinks that unless he really has become someone she does not know, everyone will have breakfast in the dining room, and afterward, sometime in the late afternoon, when Buster and his family have gone and it's just Lionel and Ari, when it would be nice to sit down with a glass of wine and watch the sun set, she will be putting away her mother's silver platter and her mother-in-law's pink-and-gold crystal bowls, which go with nothing but please the boys.

Lionel and Julia talk about Buster and Jewelle's marriage, which is better but less interesting than it was, and Buster's weight problem, and Jewelle's languishing career as a painter, and Odean Pope's Saxophone Choir, and Lionel's becoming counsel for a Greek shipping line.

Lionel sighs over the sink, and Julia puts her hand on his back. 'Are you all right? Basically?'

'I'm fine. You don't have to worry about me. I'm not a kid.' He was about to say that he's not really a son, any more than he's really a father, that these step-ties are like long-distance relationships, workable only with people whose commitment and loyalty are much greater than the average. 'And you don't have to keep worrying about . . . what was. It didn't ruin me. It's not like we would ever be lovers now.'

Julia thinks that all that French polish is not worth much if he can't figure out a nicer way to say that he no longer desires her, that sex between them is unthinkable not because she raised him, taught him to dance, hemmed his pants, and put pimple cream on his back, but because she is too old now for him to see her that way.

'We were never lovers. We had sex,' she says, but this is not what she believes. They were lovers that night as surely as ugly babies are still babies; they were lovers like any other mismatched and blundering pair. 'We were heartbroken and we mistook each other for things we were not. Do you really want to have this conversation?'

Lionel wipes down the kitchen counters. 'Nope. I have never wanted to have this conversation. I don't want anything except a little peace and quiet – and a Lexus. I'm easy, Ma.'

Julia looks at him so long he smiles. He is such a handsome man. 'You're easy. And I'm tired. You want to leave it at that?'

Lionel tosses the sponge into the sink. 'Absolutely. Take care of your finger. Good night.'

If it would turn him back into the boy he was, she would kiss him good night, even if she cut her lips on that fine, sharp face.

'Okay. See you in the morning. Sleep tight.'

Julia takes a shower. Lionel drinks on in the kitchen, the Scotch back under the sink in case someone walks in on him. Buster and Jewelle sleep spoons-style. Corinne has crawled between them, her wet thumb on her father's bare hip, her small mouth open against her mother's shoulder. Jordan sleeps as he always does, wrestling in his dreams whatever he has failed to soothe and calm all day. His pillow is on the floor, and the sheets twist around his waist.

Julia reads until three A.M. Most nights she falls asleep with her arms around her pillow, remembering Peaches's creamy breasts cupped in her hands or feeling Peaches's soft stomach pressed against her, but tonight, spread out in her pajama top and panties, she can hardly remember that she ever shared a bed.

Ari is snuffling in the doorway.

'Come here, honey. *Viens ici, chéri.*' It is easier to be kind to him in French, somehow. Ari wears one of Buster's old terry-cloth robes, the hem trailing a good foot behind him. He has folded the sleeves back so many times they form huge baroque cuffs around his wrists.

'I do not sleep.'

'That's understandable. *Je comprends.*' Julia pats the empty side of the bed, and Ari sits down. His doleful, cross face is handsome in profile, the bedside light limning his Roman nose and straight black brows.

'Jordan hate me. You all hate me.'

'We don't hate you, honey. *Non, ce n'est pas vrai. Nous t'ai-mons.*' Julia hopes that she is saying what she means. 'It's just hard. We all have to get used to each other. *Il faut que nous . . .*' If she ever had the French vocabulary to discuss the vicissitudes of divorce and future happiness and loving new people, she doesn't anymore. She puts her hand on Ari's flat curls. *'Il faut que nous fassions ta connaissance.'*

She hears him laugh for the first time. 'That is "how do you do." Not what we say *en famille.*'

Laughing is an improvement, and Julia keeps on with her French – perhaps feeling superior will do him more good than obvious kindness – and tries to tell Ari about the day she has planned for them tomorrow, with a trip to the playground and a trip to the hardware store so Lionel can fix the kitchen steps.

Ari laughs again and yawns. 'I am tired,' he says, and lies down,

putting his head on one of Julia's lace pillows. *'Dors bien,'* the little
boy says.

'All right. You, too. You *dors bien.*'

Julia pulls the blankets up over Ari.

'At night my mother sing,' he says.

The only French song Julia knows is 'La Marseillaise.' She sings
the folk songs and hymns she sang to the boys, and by the time
she has failed to hit that impossible note in 'Amazing Grace,' Ari's
breathing is already moist and deep. Julia gets under the covers
as Ari rolls over, his damp forehead and elbows and knees pressing into her side. She counts the books on her shelves, then
sheep, then turns out the bedside lamp and counts every lover
she ever had and everything she can remember about them, from
the raven-shaped birthmark on the Harvard boy's shoulder to the
unexpected dark brown of Peter's eyes, leaving out Peaches and
Lionel senior, who are on their own, quite different list. She
remembers the birthday parties she gave for Lionel and Buster,
including the famous Cookie Monster cake that turned her
hands blue for three days, and the eighth-grade soccer party that
ended with Lionel and another boy needing stitches. Already six
feet tall, he sat in her lap, arms and legs flowing over her, while
his father held his head for the doctor.

Ari sighs and shifts, holding tight to Julia's pajama top, her
lapel twisted in his hands like rope. She feels the wide shape of
his five knuckles on her chest, bone pressing flesh against bone,
and she is not sorry at all to be old and awake so late at night.

Fort Useless and Fort Ridiculous

Lionel Sampson reads to his brother from the flight magazine. "'The Seeing Eye dog was invented by a blind American.'"

Buster laughs. 'Really. *Invented*. Man must have gone through a hell of a lot of dogs.'

Julia's sons, Buster and Lionel, are flying from Paris to Boston, to be picked up and driven to their mother's house for Thanksgiving. Their driver will be an old Russian guy they've had before, big belly, a few missing teeth, with cold bottled water and *The New York Times* in the backseat. The two men are as happy as clams not to be driving in Buster's wife's minivan with all the kids and their laptops and iPods and duffel bags and Jewelle's gallon containers of creamed spinach and mashed sweet potatoes, which Jewelle now brings rather than making them at her mother-in-law's, because now that Julia's getting on, although the house is clean and Jewelle is not saying it's *not* clean, you do have to tidy up a little before you get to work in Julia's kitchen, and Jewelle would just rather not.

Lionel closes the magazine and the homely flight attendant brings them water. (Remember when they were pretty? Lionel says. Remember when Pop took us to Denmark, Buster says, and they all wore white stockings and white miniskirts?) The flight attendant lays linen napkins in their laps. Lionel likes first class so much that even when a client doesn't pay for it, he pays for the upgrade himself, and he's paid for Buster's upgrade, too. Lionel spends more on travel than he does on rent. His wife thinks he's crazy. Patsine grew up riding the bumper of dusty Martinique buses and as far as she's concerned, even now, your own seat and no chickens is all that anyone needs.

Buster opens another magazine. 'Looky here, little girl in northern India is born with two faces. Only one set of ears, but two full faces. She's worshipped in her village. Durga, goddess of valor.'

'Jesus,' Lionel says. 'What's wrong with people?' He looks at the picture of the little girl. 'Patsine's pregnant.'

'Oh, great. Good for you. Patsine's great.' Buster has disliked all of Lionel's other girlfriends and wives. The mean ones scared him and the nice, hopeful ones depressed him and Jewelle would say to him, after each meet-and-greet, 'All I'm saying is, just once, let him bring someone who isn't a psycho, a slut, or a Martian. Just once.' Buster pats his big brother on the knee and says, Well, aren't you the proud papa, and the homely flight attendant smiles at them both. *Mes félicitations, monsieur.* She brings them pâté and crackers and two flutes of Champagne. Lionel gives his Champagne to Buster and asks for sparkling water.

Buster keeps reading. 'It says the village chief wants the government to build a temple to the two-faced baby.'

'Who wouldn't,' Lionel says.

They're over the north Atlantic, only ten hours until home and eating a pretty good lunch, as Buster is not one to say no to a good meal. Buster sips his Champagne and Lionel drinks his Perrier and stifles his envy and longing by reviewing all the terrible things that happened to him when he was drinking. He nearly killed an old lady on a Sunday drive; he fell down a flight of stairs and ripped open his scalp, so that when he sat in court the next day, the judge finally said, M. Sampson, the blood is distracting me, and Lionel left to tighten his bandage and came back to a trail of red drops at his side of the table. He lost the case and the goodwill of his partners. If you want to look at the big picture, as Lionel tries to these days – his drinking has led to failed relationships with women who had nothing in common except bad judgment and despair.

As her husband and brother-in-law are over the north Atlantic, Jewelle piles all of her children's things into the van and Jordan and her nephew Ari play basketball and Patsine makes several slow, steady trips to the van, each time carrying something small and not too heavy. Corinne doesn't help even that much, because she's taken off to her best friend's house, so she and the other girl can weep and embrace as if the Thanksgiving weekend apart is a life sentence. Jewelle can't say a thing to her daughter about her drama-queen behavior or her aggrieved and enormous uselessness because they have just gotten over a huge blowup about people of color, a category in which Jewelle Enright Sampson (English, Irish, and Belgian) does not figure, but her daughter, Corinne Elizabeth Sampson, does. (I joined the NMS Students of Color group, Corinne told her family, after her first day of middle school. I'm secretary. No one said, What color is that? And no one pointed out that Corinne was a few shades lighter than even the all-white people in the family. Her brother, Jordan, who is more coffee-with-a-lot-of-cream, snickered, and her father, who is a brown-skinned man, shook his head fondly. Jewelle called her mother-in-law, the only other white mother of tan children whom she knew, and complained. Julia told her that white mothers of black children were screwed

whichever way they went: white trash or in denial or so sup-
portive, they're punch lines for black *and* white people, filling
their shopping carts with Rastafarian lip balm and Jheri curl
products and both kinds of Barbie dolls. Someone's got to be the
mammy, she said to Jewelle; unfortunately, it's our turn. Think
Halle Berry, she said; she seems to like her mother.)

When everyone is safely in the van, Jewelle wants to discuss
the visit to Julia's. I'm not *criticizing,* she says. I didn't say the
kitchen *isn't* clean, she says to Patsine. Patsine has visited their
mother-in-law only once before and the kitchen was neither
dirty nor clean; it was unexceptional and she doesn't care. Patsine
says to Jewelle, You must forgive me, I am completely exhausted,
and she closes her eyes. Corinne sits between her brother and her
cousin and she is very aware of her cousin Ari's long thigh pressing against hers, of his fidgeting from time to time, of his bare
arm across her shoulders. All the children are listening to their
music and Patsine is sleeping, or pretending to sleep, and Jewelle
just drives to the Cape.

As the Russian guy is waiting for Buster and Lionel, as Jewelle
is driving everyone to the Cape, Julia and her dog, Sophie
Tucker, and her friend Robert lie in bed.

'Everyone is coming home later,' Julia says.

'So you've said. I won't leave a trace.'

Robert gets out of bed and stands in front of the window,
looking out at the ocean. The soft light falls over him, over his
big shoulders and thick torso and thick legs, everything just
faintly webbed by age except his impossibly bright gold hair.

'I don't suppose you'd like to come to dinner,' Julia says. 'You
could bring Arthur.'

Robert shakes his head and gets back into bed. Julia tucks two
pillows under his knees to protect his back.

'Oh, darling, could you . . .' he says.

'Oh, darling yourself,' Julia says and gets him another glass of cold water.

'You're too good to me. Let's get facials Saturday. On me.'

'I could use one,' Julia says, and she thinks that she could more than use one, that when she stopped coloring her hair, she just let the whole edifice collapse, from roof to rail, except for long walks with the dog.

Robert put his hands at his temples and pulls. He says 'Honey, who couldn't use one? I myself am going to start taping my eyebrows to my hairline like Lucille Ball.'

'Okay,' Julia says. 'Me, too.' She rests her head on his shoulder and Robert strokes her hair, tucking a few strands behind her ear. 'You won't come?'

'No,' Robert says. 'We can't. You have nice ears.'

'They've held up.'

'They have held up *wonderfully*,' he says, and he pulls the quilt up over Julia's bare shoulder and begins snoring.

A few hours later, Robert goes home to his lover, Arthur, who looks at Robert over his newspaper and sighs. Julia puts on her raincoat and takes Sophie Tucker for a walk.

Robert is sitting at the kitchen table, waiting for Julia's family to come. He's been there all morning. He hears the car coming up the drive and goes to the porch. Jordan sees him first.

'It's the old man,' he says, and Jewelle peers forward.

Robert taps on the van window and helps Patsine out of the van. He's very strong for an old man. Jewelle moves too quickly for him to open the door for her and she feels a little slighted that he doesn't, and as she is thinking that her mother-in-law must have fallen asleep on the couch, Robert pulls the two women toward the side of the porch, toward the browning hydrangeas. He tells them that Julia is dead.

He tells them everything he knows about the accident, which is only what the police told him when he had come back to the house for tea and found no Julia, and there was blood on the road and Sophie Tucker whimpering on the porch. Robert carried Sophie Tucker inside and the two policemen said it was a terrible accident, they said no alcohol was involved, they said the boy told them the dog ran across the street and Julia ran after it, and in the wet weather, the boy lost control of the car. The boy was in the hospital, the police said, and Julia was dead.

Robert hugs each of the women and Corinne runs over, like a little girl in a bad thunderstorm, to push her way under her mother's arm. Patsine wishes her husband were here now to tell Ari, this boy she hardly knows, that his grandmother, whom she hardly knows, is dead. She tells Ari, in French, what has happened and he looks at her, stone-faced, and goes to his room in the attic. Jordan presses himself to Jewelle's other side and he finds Corinne's hand. Jewelle kisses both of them, frantically, and says, Oh, I'm sorry, honey, your nana is just so sorry not to be here.

Jewelle and her children go into the house and upstairs like one person. Robert offers Patsine his arm and the two of them stand in the front hall, until Robert says that perhaps he ought to go home and Patsine agrees.

When Buster and Lionel arrive, pulling their bags out of the trunk, Jewelle and Patsine run out to meet them on the driveway and the two men back away, a little, before their wives even speak. Lionel drops to his knees on the lawn and Buster kneels beside him and the two women sit down beside them, all of them on the damp, crisp grass as the driver pulls away. The four of them unload Jewelle's van and Lionel and Buster go from room to room, kissing the children good night. In the morning, they find Ari in his grandmother's bed.

'Is anyone going to the store?' Lionel yells up the stairs, and no one answers. Jewelle is walking on the beach. Patsine is napping. Jordan lies on one of the twin beds in the attic room, looking at a few old copies of *Playboy* his father or his uncle must have left behind. Corinne has taken over the living room, her dirty sneakers and sweaters trailing over the sofa and a gold-framed photograph of her latest hero, Damien de Veuster, dead leper priest, on the coffee table. It's Jordan who has the right disposition for yoga, Lionel thinks; the boy's a limpid pool of goodness in a family of undertow, and Lionel doesn't know where he gets it. (Julia would have said that Jordan was very like Lionel's father's father, Alfred Sampson, who even as a black man in Worcester, Massachusetts, in 1963, and even among white people hoping the world would never change, was revered throughout the town, and when he died, Irish cops sent flowers.) But Jordan is in the attic with his door locked and here instead is Corinne, a big-busted, wild-haired girl, her bodhichitta tank top rising over her round, tan belly, her green stretch pants dipping very close to her ass crack, racing toward enlightenment and altruism like the Cannonball Express.

'You wanna take the bike to the grocery, Corinne?' Lionel asks.

Corinne puts a finger to her lips, as if her uncle Lionel is disturbing not her, *which wouldn't matter in the least*, but the tranquillity of her spiritual guides. She exhales deeply and squeezes her eyes closed.

'Christ almighty.' Lionel yells upstairs. 'Is anyone going to the goddamned store before it closes?'

Lionel can't go; he doesn't have a license. France – his home for some thirty years and a nation exceptionally tolerant of drinking and driving – lowered the blood-alcohol level to something like a glass of water with a splash of Pernod and now he can't drive anywhere, not legally. He doesn't try. Not driving is his penance, like not drinking, which is itself so preoccupying and gives him such a novel and peculiar and fraught perspective on every activity, he could almost say he doesn't mind, although he has thought a lot about Balvenie Scotch in a heavy crystal glass for the last two days. Ari jumps down the stairs in two huge steps, punches his stepfather in the arm, and hangs in the doorway to watch Corinne breathe. He breathes with her for a moment. Late last summer, Corinne put her hand on his cock by accident when he spilled his juice and she went to help him mop it up and then she felt him and she dropped the roll of paper towels in his lap and went back to her seat, but that moment is what Ari has come back for.

Late last summer, when everyone had come to Julia's for Labor Day, Julia took them all into town for Italian ices. The eight of them sat on the wrought-iron benches in front of Vincenzo's, sucking on paper cups of lemon and tangerine. Julia stood up. She threw her paper cup to the ground and cupped her hands around her mouth. She yelled, 'Robert. Robert Nash.' And at the far end of the street, two men turned around and came toward her. Julia began to hurry toward the taller man, and he put his arms around her and all they could see was his crisp white shirtsleeves and gold watch, and when Julia stepped back and put her hand to his face, they saw his pressed jeans, his bare feet in Italian loafers. *'Très chic,'* Jewelle whispered. Julia and the old man hugged again and finally

Julia introduced everyone. ('Oh, Robert, my son Lionel, my grandson Ari, my granddaughter, Corinne, my grandson Jordan, my son Buster – I'm so sorry, honey, I should say my son Judge Gabriel Sampson and his wife, Jewelle. How's that?') And the old man looked Lionel up and down in an unmistakable way. ('I'd know you anywhere,' he said. 'Your father's son.') He shook hands with everyone. He said, 'It's a pleasure to meet you all. This is my companion, Arthur.' The other man looked like a middle-aged hamster and he cradled a big bouquet from the florist, wrapped in lavender tissue and cellophane.

Jordan poked Ari and Ari rolled his eyes.

Robert said, 'And what are you two young men doing for amusement?'

He didn't sound like an elegant old fruit; he sounded like a distinguished and rather demanding English professor, and Julia hid her smile when the boys dropped their eyes. Robert used to reduce college boys of all kinds, potheads, lacrosse players, and clean-cut Christians, to tears with that tone.

Ari shrugged. Conversation with American strangers was Jordan's department.

Jordan said, 'We might do a little fishing.'

'Fly-fishing?'

'No. Just, you know, regular,' Jordan said.

Lionel nodded. 'Just reel and rods and worms. Nothing fancy.'

Robert smiled again. 'Well, if you can handle a little motor-boat, I have one just rusting in the driveway. You're welcome to it.'

Everyone except Arthur smiled and Lionel could see the man calculating the cost of the lawsuit when one of the boys lost a hand in the propeller or came home crying after an afternoon skinny-dipping at Robert's.

Lionel put a protective arm around each boy and began to shift them away.

Robert said, 'Well, come look at the boat if you want. And there's a basketball court across the street. My neighbor's in Greece and it just sits there. It's a waste.'

'We could ride over tomorrow,' Jordan said

'*C'est de la balle.*' Ari glanced toward the old man. 'Cool.'

'Just as you say. Arthur, do show them where we are,' Robert said, and Arthur handed each of the boys a business card with Robert's name and phone number and a little pen-and-ink map on the back, marking their house with a silver star.

Robert said to Julia, 'And you must have these,' and he took the huge bunch of pink and yellow alstroemeria from Arthur, flowers they'd gotten for their front hall, and handed them to Julia. She kissed him again and ducked her head into the flowers, sniffing, although there was no real scent, and she exclaimed, like a girl, all the way home.

Lionel and Julia walked behind the others.

'You think the boys should go over there?'

Julia turned on him. 'He's an old friend of mine, Lionel. He was a friend of your father's and he was extending himself, out of kindness, to my *grandchildren*.' And Lionel was glad he didn't say what he was thinking.

Finally, someone does go to the grocery store and people sit, in knots of two or three, on the deck, or walk on the beach or walk in and out of Julia's room. Lionel and Buster smoke on the front porch. Someone orders in bad pizza and they eat it off paper plates and even Jewelle does nothing more in the kitchen than dump the cold slices in a pile and refrigerate them. By ten o'clock, Buster and Jewelle are listening to Lionel and Patsine in the next room. Lionel is talking angrily and Patsine makes a soft, soothing sound. Then Lionel gets up and goes down the hall for a glass of water and they can hear everything, even the click of the bedroom door as Lionel closes it. Patsine asks a question and Lionel gets back into bed and then there is more whispering and a little uncertain laughter and then Buster is glad he can't see Jewelle's face while his brother gets a blow job.

When Buster was fifteen and Lionel was twenty-five, Julia sent Buster to spend the summer with his brother in Paris. Buster spent his days riding the Métro, listening to music from home, and trying to pick up girls. At night, Lionel made dinner for them both.

'How's it goin'? With the ladies?'

Buster shrugged. Lionel poured them both a glass of wine.

'Listen to me,' Lionel said, 'and not to those assholes back home. You do not want to get advice from sixteen-year-old boys. You don't want to be the kind of guy who just grabs some tit or a handful of pussy and then goes and tells his friends so they can say, "You da man."'

'No,' Buster said.

'That's right, no, you don't. You want to be the kind of man women beg for sex. You want women saying, "Oh, yes, baby, yes, baby, yes"' and on the last 'yes,' he got up, took a peach from a bowl on the counter, and sliced it in half. He threw the pit into the wastebasket and he put the fruit, shiny side up, in Buster's hand.

'Here you go. See that little pink point. You got to lick that little point, rub your tongue over and around it.' He smacked

Buster on the back of the head. 'Don't slobber. You're not a washcloth. You. Are. A. Lover.'

Buster breathed in peach smell and he flicked his tongue at the tiny point.

'That's it, that's what I'm talking about. Lick it. It won't bite you, boy. Lick it again. Now, you get in there with your nose and your chin.'

'My nose,' Buster said, and Lionel pressed the tip of Buster's nose into the peach.

'Your nose, your chin. Your forehead, if that's what it takes.'

Buster gave himself to the peach until there was nothing but exhausted peach skin and bits of yellow fruit clinging to his face. Lionel handed him a dish towel.

'How long do you do it for?' Buster asked.

'How long? Until her legs are so tight around your head you can't actually hear the words but you know she's saying, Don't stop, don't stop, oh, my God in heaven, don't you stop.'

'And then what?' Buster picked up another peach, just in case.

'And you keep on. And then she comes. Unless. Unless, you're slurping away down there for ten minutes and nothing's happening, you know, and all of a sudden she arches her back like this' – and Lionel arched his back, until his head was almost to the floor – 'and she yells, Oh, Jesus, I'm coming.' Lionel screamed. And then said, 'If that happens, she's faking.'

Buster almost choked on this, the thought that he would practice all summer, become as good a lover as his brother, and then the girl would only be pretending to like it?

'Oh, why would she do that?'

Lionel shrugged. 'Because she doesn't want to embarrass your sorry ass and she also doesn't want to lie there all night, waiting for nothing.'

'That happens?'

Lionel poured them both another glass. 'Oh, yes. Sometimes you do your best, and it's not good enough. So you man up, limp dick, shattered spirit. You pick yourself up and you say to her, Tell me what you really want. You say to her, Put your little hand where you want mine to be.' Lionel drains his glass. 'And you do like she shows you. Don't worry – the ladies are going to love you, Buster.'

And Buster wraps his arm around his wife's soft waist, beneath her nightgown, and she pulls it up and places his hand on her breast. Their dance is Buster's palm settling over her nipple, his fingertips sliding up the side of her breast, Jewelle rolling over to put her face next to Buster's, Jewelle licking at the creases in Buster's neck. Jewelle runs her hand along the smooth underside of his belly and he sighs.

'Oh, you feel so good,' she says. 'You always do.'

'My Jewelle,' he says.

'Oh, yes,' she says. 'No one else's.'

They love this old dance.

'I think we should do it right away. We're all here.' Jewelle has waited for Lionel to speak but he's been lying on the couch for ten minutes, not saying a word.

'What is the "it"?' Patsine asks.

Jewelle looks at Patsine. Patsine has something pointed and sensible to say about everything, all the time.

'I think the "it" is a memorial service.'

Lionel lifts his head a bit, so he can see everyone.

'I hope that little sonofabitch dies,' he says, and he sits up, changing his tone. 'You know, her wishes were very clear.

Cremation and lunch. No clergy, no house of worship, and no big deal. Obit in the *Cranberry Bog Times* or whatever and that's it.'

'Cremation?' Patsine asks, and shrugs when everyone looks at her. Julia was not her mother and it's not her business but she liked Julia very much and she would not slide a beloved into the mouth of a furnace by way of farewell.

'Why not? It's not like she was Jewish,' Corinne says. It really isn't Patsine's place to ask all of these questions when she's been married to Uncle Lionel for about five minutes.

'Her father was Jewish,' Lionel says, and everyone looks at him.

'Her father was Jewish? Julia was half Jewish?' Jewelle says.

'Well, not the side that counts,' Lionel says.

'I'm part Jewish?' Corinne says.

'Yes,' Lionel says. 'You are not only a quadroon, you are also, fractionally, a Jewess. You can be blackballed by *everyone*.'

Buster puts his hand on Corinne's shoulder and shakes his head at his brother.

'Nice.'

Lionel lies back down. He recites.

'Ma's mother was Italian. Her father was Jewish. We never met either of them. The old man ran off and left them when Ma was a girl and her mother raised her nothing, which is why we are the faithless heathen we are. Long after the divorce, the old man dies in a car accident – I think.' He looks at Buster, in case he's gotten it wrong – it's thirty-five years since he heard the story – but Buster shrugs. He was even younger when Julia told them the story and it doesn't seem to him that he ever heard it again. Buster shrugs again, to show that he's already forgiven his brother for teasing Corinne. She needs it; his daughter has become like fucking Goebbels on the subject of race and he can't stand it. 'He never remarried and he left all his money to Ma's mother. She went on a round-the-world cruise after Ma graduated college and then ... she dies. That's all, folks.' Lionel spreads his arms wide, like Al Jolson.

Patsine says flatly, 'Jewish men do not abandon their wives.'

Is that so, Jewelle thinks. She guesses some French Jewish married man sometime must have not left his wife for Miss Patsine Belfond, and Jewelle arches an eyebrow at Corinne. Lionel kisses Patsine's puffy ankle. He loves her politically incorrect and sensible assertions. Fat people do eat too much. Some people should be sterilized. The darker people's skins, the noisier they are, until you get to certain kinds of Africans who are as silent as sand.

'Well, apparently one did,' Lionel says cheerfully. 'Although Grandpa Whoever, Morris, Murray, Yitzhak, made up for it by leaving Grandma Whoever a lot of money, which was great until she died of food poisoning in Shanghai or—'

'Bangkok.' Buster says. 'Bhutan?'

'Burma?'

'She died of food poisoning?' Corinne says.

'Bad shrimp,' Lionel says, closing his eyes.

He hears his brother say, 'Or crab,' and he smiles.

'People don't *die* from food poisoning,' Corinne says.

Jewelle has had enough. 'Your aunt Helen almost died from food poisoning when we were girls. We were at the state fair and she got so sick from the fried clams she was hospitalized for it. She vomited for three days and she was skinny as a stick anyway. She really almost died.' Corinne and Jordan stare at their mother. Their aunt Helen is big and imperturbable, a tax lawyer who brings her own fancy wine and her own pillow when she visits, and it's impossible to imagine her young and skinny, barfing day and night until she almost died.

Lionel presses his feet against his wife's strong thigh and keeps his eyes shut. If he keeps them closed long enough, everyone but Patsine and Buster will disappear, his mother will reappear, and the worst headache he has ever had will go away.

'I guess there are always things people don't know about each other. I didn't know that about Helen and the clams.' Buster takes out a pencil. 'I think we should do a little planning, for the service, the lunch, for Ma.'

'Fuck you,' Lionel says.

'I know.'

Robert has been standing in the doorway for about half a minute, listening to his friend's children. He wants to write it all down and tell Julia after. You wouldn't *believe* it, he'd say. They are all just like you said. Lionel is completely the master of the universe – you must have loved him a lot, darling, to give him that self-confidence – and Buster is Ted E. Bear on the outside but very strong on the inside; you'd sleep with Lionel but you'd marry Buster, is what I'm saying. Well, not you, of course, but me – back in the day. And poor Jewelle, doomed to be runner-up, isn't she, even with those absolutely fantastic tits and still workin' it, but my God, Patsine, what a piece of work. Don't ask her if that dress makes you look fat because she *will* tell you. But I can see why you were thrilled she married Lionel. She has bent that man to her will and he is so glad, I can tell you that. Jordan's a love; he's like Buster, although maybe without the brains. Julia would pretend to smack him and he would apologize and she would say, Go on, go on eviscerating my loved ones, you terrible man. And he'd say, Corinne, my God, that child is why convents were *invented*. And Ari is very sexy in that broody, miserable way but it's hard to see what exactly one would *do* with him. And Julia would look at him and he would say, I'm just sharing my observations, and she would say, You should be locked up, and he would say, And then you'd miss me, and she would say, Yes, I would, and I'd visit you in jail once a month and bring you porn.

Corinne sees Robert first and she pokes her uncle Lionel. They all look over at Robert and they all say hello, more or less.

'Would you like a cup of coffee?' Jewelle says.

'No, thank you. I'm sorry to disturb you. I just thought I would ... come by.'

'We're planning a service, just a lunch,' Lionel says, and Robert can see how hard the man is trying to be civil. 'Maybe you want to say a few words.'

'Yes,' Robert says to the roomful of people who don't want him there. He is an impediment; he is an awful, faggy roadblock to their mother's memory, and the sooner he picks up his odds and ends and goes back to Old Fagland, the better. Robert is not a brave man; he has stood up for himself a couple of times, in a polite way, over the course of seventy years, but he isn't the kind of person who stays where he isn't wanted. Julia was. Julia was just that kind of person, going where she wasn't wanted, telling people to go fuck themselves, and Julia had loved him. He had braided her long gray hair and they had discussed whether or not she should cut it after all this time, and he had rubbed moisturizer into the dry skin between her shoulder blades and trailed his fingers down her spine and toward the small folds of skin above her waist. Julia said, No playing with my love handles. Robert had leaned forward to kiss them and said, Lovely, lovely handles. Robert pulls up a chair and he pats Jewelle on the knee.

'If I may change my mind, coffee would be lovely.'

Lionel says, 'Maybe some Marion Williams in the background?'

Robert says, 'Absolutely. Julia was playing "Remember Me" just the other day.'

The day after the luncheon, they are still cleaning up. Buster washes and Lionel dries and Jewelle, who knows where everything goes, directs the putting away. Patsine sits at the kitchen table, with her feet up on a chair. Buster sings, 'Some of these days, you're gonna miss me, honey,' and Lionel growls, 'Some of these days, you're gonna miss me, babe,' and Patsine and Jewelle look at each other, eyes welling up, for their grieving husbands.

'Be useful,' Jewelle says to the boys, and she gives them both platters to put into the sideboard. There's no point in giving them the wineglasses. Corinne pokes her head into the kitchen and disappears.

'Corinne,' her mother says. 'I could use a hand here.'

Corinne walks into the middle of the kitchen in her grandmother's black T-shirt, her own yoga pants, her mother's black patent-leather pumps, and a green-and-black silk scarf tied around her neck, Apache-style. ('A-patch,' her grandmother said. 'It's a dance, not a rodeo.') Her eyes are bright red.

'Nana loved this song,' Corinne says. 'So, okay.'

Buster dries his hands and Lionel and his brother stand with their arms around each other.

'Pretty legs, great big knockers, that's what sells them tickets at the door. Honey, these are real show stoppers, it's what keeps 'em comin' back for more.'

Corinne sang this song with her grandmother when no one was home. They shimmied and shook their behinds and one time they both slid down the banister onto pillows. They did the Electric Slide and Nana taught her The Stroll, too, and they danced around the living room like crazy women until they fell onto the couch, laughing and breathless.

'Pretty legs, great big knockers, that's what put the two in two by four. Oooh, baby' – Corinne pauses for her big finish. She struts across the floor like a showgirl and flings open her arms – 'Oooh, it ain't the ballads, it ain't the rockers, it's pretty legs and . . . these great . . . big knockers!'

Her father and her uncle whistle and stamp their feet. Ari stares at her, and it's not that sly, slitty look that makes her feel like hiding in the bathroom; his eyes are wide open. Her mother sits down next to Patsine and Patsine is holding Jewelle's hand tightly but they are definitely smiling and Jordan shakes his head in admiration because there is no one like his baby sister. Corinne runs to her mother's lap and buries her head in Jewelle's shoulder. Jewelle puts her arms around her girl and showers her with kisses. Corinne can feel the bump of Patsine's belly pressing behind her and Patsine's hand on her hair.

Robert is standing on the other side of the kitchen, clapping. 'Oh, my dear, what a gift,' he says. 'What a send-off.'

Lionel looks at the empty kitchen table and he looks at the clock.

'It's dinner time.' He hands food to each person and soon the table is covered with three cartons of Chinese food, from Julia's favorite restaurant, and a deep dish of oyster stuffing and a Tupperware of sweet potatoes with maple syrup and two kinds of chocolate-pecan pie, one for the people who like bourbon and one for people who like it and have to avoid it, and a casserole of creamed spinach with half a nutmeg taped to the top, for the last minute. Jewelle sticks one of the good silver spoons into the bowl of cranberry sauce she brought from home and Buster sets bottles of pear and apple cider and red wine on the table and hands out the crystal wineglasses to everyone. Patsine rests her hands on the baby.

Lionel stands up and lifts his glass and looks at his brother. 'Remember this one? A Jewish grandmother and her grandson are playing on the beach, building sandcastles. A wave comes along and drags the poor kid out to sea. The grandmother falls to her knees, screaming and crying. "Oh, God, oh, God, please save my only grandson. Please, he is the light of my life. Please, God, just save him, that's all I ask of you."'

'Oh, yeah,' Buster says and he stands up. 'And another wave comes and drops the little boy back on the beach, good as new. The grandmother hugs and kisses him. Then she looks up at the heavens and says, "Excuse me? He had a hat."'

Stars at Elbow and Foot

I feel my baby's arms around my neck. Hidden wrists, flesh the color and feel of white tea roses, the rising scent of warm cornbread. I wake up and find the pillow twisted beneath my chin, a few strands of my hair caught in the pillowcase zipper. Marc hears me or feels me beginning to cry and wards it off as best he can.

'Gotta piss,' he says, and he smooths the covers down as if to soothe his side of the bed.

I rock the pillow and reach for a Prozac and the glass of water on the nightstand. My whole house is decorated by an invalid: boxes of tissues, half-drawn curtains, sweaty nightgowns, aspirin, marjoram shower gel (guaranteed by Marc's New Age secretary to 'lift your spirits'), fading plants. I do not understand why death inspires people to give greenery.

Marc comes back to bed, and I am kind enough to pretend that I'm asleep. If I were awake, he would have to comfort me. The circles under his eyes darken and crease the skin down to his cheekbones. Why should either of us have to endure his comforting me? He puts his hand on my hip, as if to balance himself, but I know he's checking. Am I twitching, am I sweating, are my shoulders heaving? He's a good man; he will avoid me only once. Having got off the hook earlier, he is compelled to be attentive. I sound like I hate him, which I don't.

I do fantasize about his death, however. I strangle him with the umbilical cord, the blue-pink twist they took off Saul's little no-neck. The doctor, my own obstetrician – a perfectly pleasant, competent woman, a Democrat who sits with me on the boards of two good causes – is perforated by the smallest, sharpest scalpels, as in an old-fashioned knife-throwing show, until she is pinned to the wall of the operating room in pieces, her lips still moving, apologizing, but not so profusely that I might think she was *at fault* and sue her for malpractice or wrongful death or whatever it is that my brother-in-law told us we could sue for. My wrongful life, my dying marriage, how about the house plants and the students I don't give a damn about? For the nurses and the intern who assisted Mary Lou, I use dull scalpels, and I stick them with horse-size epidural needles when they try to escape.

I made an attempt to go back to my office three weeks ago. I picked up my mail and was doing fine, ignoring the silences and the sotto voce inquiries, which practically screamed 'Better you than me.' Martha, our department secretary – old, frightened, useless since we all got computers – handed me my messages and a stack of departmental memos. Her ancient poodle was wheezing on his little bed beneath her desk.

'Your shirt . . .' she said, and I looked down at the wet blue circles and left.

I sat in the ladies' room, pressing my breasts, kneading my shirt and my bra until tiny white tears dripped onto my fingers. I left my mail on the floor, and someone sent it to me anonymously, with kind intentions, two days later.

I go back again, braced with a Percodan-Prozac cocktail, which you will not find in the *Physician's Desk Reference*. Information about an MLA conference I seem to have organized in Edinburgh is coming through on the department fax. The man faxing me is very excited, and his words leap about on the cheap, oily paper. He is expecting a draft of my presentation in two weeks and me in four. I don't think so. I tell Martha to fax him back that I will not attend and that I will not send the notes for my talk.

She is concerned. I treat Martha the way my mother taught me to treat our domestic servants. I am gracious and reasonable and accommodating. She adores me (and appreciates her annual Westminster dog show tickets), and the faculty Marxists (former Marxists – I don't know what they do with themselves now) gnash their teeth over us. Martha hesitates. It cannot be good for me professionally to cancel at this late date. Perhaps I will not be asked to chair a panel again soon. Perhaps my reputation at the university will diminish and Martha's office status will go from endangered to extinct. I fax the message myself: 'Cannot come. Baby dead. Maybe next year. Onora O'Connor.'

A girl is waiting for me in the hall. I don't mind girls too much, and I can even feel sorry for them, since I know what's in store for them and they don't. When I was her age, I'd look at women like me with just that same disgusted disbelief. Their stomachs billowed out, their asses dragged, their hair hung in limp strands or was sprayed up into alien shapes. Why did they do that to themselves? They must all have been ugly girls and never recovered. But I was not an ugly girl, I put this young thing in the shade when I was her age. I did art modeling for tuition money – servants were a phase, not a lifestyle – and loved it. My body defied gravity, defined lush perfection. Peach juice would run out if I was bitten. I was fucking perfect for three years of my life, and not too shabby until the recent past.

I signed her forms, promised her she could be in my Auden seminar come fall, and escaped, feeling like a check bouncer in a mom-and-pop grocery. Sure, here's my address, watch me record the amount, like it matters. There's nothing in the bank. I am no more going to teach in the fall than play third base for the Yankees.

I leave the building, passing clusters of women. I hate them all, I don't even see the men. When I hear or smell babies coming, I leave the room. These women, all these women, are pregnant, or will be, or have been, or don't want to be, or have suffered some made-for-TV disaster like mine. It doesn't matter; whether they are like me or lucky, I hate them, and I seem to make it pretty clear, because they turn just a little, feet unmoving while their hips shift, and I cannot join them without barging in.

I find a woman sitting in my kitchen, not obviously pregnant but she might be — she could let it drop in the middle of our conversation or else make a *huge* effort and say nothing at all so Marc can struggle with telling me privately. I wonder if he's sleeping with her, but I can't imagine it. He looks as bad as I do. Every time he shaves he nicks another spot; his whole face is lightly gouged, as if he'd been rather listlessly assaulted. There are four deep-green rows of wine bottles on our kitchen counter. Marc has been steadily working through cases of California Merlot and Zinfandel.

'I'm Jessica? From the Neonate Program at the hospital? Memorial Unit Three?' She goes on talking, but I'm stuck. Doesn't she know who she is? Is she asking *me*? Does she think I've forgotten the floor name? Does she think I remember her? Marc is nodding, with tears in his eyes. She must be talking about Saul.

'. . . that you might be interested in . . .'

'What?'

She sighs, just a little bit – I should appreciate how patient and understanding she's being. Do I look like I give a fuck? You, do you think I can even smell you without wanting to puke? I may start puking if she doesn't leave soon. Hormones, medication, lots of obvious explanations for my sudden vomiting. I measure the distance to the kitchen sink and figure whether I could hit her shoes on the way. She's still talking, and Marc has put his hand on my shoulder. Saul is definitely the subject.

'. . . your loss. I worked with one woman who went through this experience, and I think she found it very helpful. So I mentioned it to your husband.'

'What?'

'The Pediatric Volunteer Program. After orientation, you spend time with children on the unit until they go home.'

'Or die.'

Jessica looks at Marc, who is no longer touching my shoulder in a display of emotional support. He cradles his face in his left hand, rolling a wet cork across the table with his right index finger.

'Oh no, you don't spend time with terminally ill children. Our volunteers visit with the children recovering from surgery, getting fitted for prostheses, things like that. Not terminal cases.'

I can see her thoughts through a suddenly opened window in her forehead. Jesus, she's thinking, this woman is clearly not suitable for any kind of program, how do I leave without upsetting her? The transparent patch in Jessica's forehead is a product of sleep deprivation, as Mary Lou has already explained to Marc and me. The moments when Saul, at various ages, comes to me and weeps in my arms, the tendency to see people's words as they say them and sometimes when they don't, the sensation that objects are only two-dimensional – these are typical symptoms of sleep deprivation. Not to worry.

'I'll think about it. Why don't you leave your card. Thanks for coming. Good-bye.' I think this comes out pretty well, but I can see from her face that I have left out something key, like inflection. Too bad. If she wants affect, she can talk to Marc. I go upstairs and lie down with my shoes on (but my soles don't touch the bedspread – I'm not that far gone) until I hear the front door close.

Another agonizing evening with the O'Connor-Schwartzes begins. Marc is solicitous, then hurt, then apologetic, then furious, then guilty, then back to the beginning, then exhausted. He usually falls asleep between guilt and the third bottle of wine.

I cannot kill myself – we do not commit that sin, it is *such* bad form – but I find myself teetering at the stair landings, walking quickly on the narrow, slick marble steps of the library, seeing how long I can keep my hands off the steering wheel. Come and get me.

This is not a hospital ward, it is the Hieronymus Bosch Pediatric Purgatory. I have been told to wait with the other child lovers shuffling along in pastel sweatsuits and massive sneakers or two-hundred-dollar cardigans thrown over jeans and posy-covered turtlenecks. Apparently, only women are in need of this kind of entertainment. As we go through the halls of gasping infants, and toddlers with metal shunts sticking out of their heads, and older children playing tag with their IVs, I notice that my little group is more varied than I thought. Two of the six look late-middle-aged, and their expressions are of pleasant concern and universal affection. Two others are quite young, very Junior League, and if they have lost babies they've been spending quite a bit of time in the gym ever since. The woman right next to me is black, meaning the color of strong coffee, and *her* expression, at least, is familiar to me. She looks enraged and terrified, and when she sees a nurse her lips curl up and back, revealing wonderfully pointed incisors. When we are seated for orientation, in a windowless room with firmly cushioned chairs and love seats, I perch on the edge of a table, and the little nurse leading the group knows enough not to encourage me to join the circle. She asks what each of us hopes to get out of this program, and the others say whatever they say, and the black woman and I snarl and look away. Even I, with my impaired judgment, cannot believe that they're going to let people like us have contact with helpless children. Then she asks if we have preferences about the kids we spend time with. The others say prettily that it really doesn't matter. The she-wolf says, 'Not a black child,' and I say nothing at all.

I ask for a little time to get acclimated, and the nurse lets me trespass quietly, unsupervised. All the children I see are engaged. They are being fed and held, or being sung to as their dressings are changed. They cry out briefly as their scarlet stumpy parts are washed and rewrapped. When the nurses and aides see me watching, they scowl or smile quickly; visitors are not much help. Some of the rooms are overflowing with Mylar balloons, photo-filled bulletin boards, parents, toys, comic books. I am looking for a room with nothing but a kid and a cot.

He is there, at the end of the hall. He comes out of his room to greet me in a state-of-the-art wheelchair, its front built up like a combination keyboard and portable desk. He holds a silver stick in his mouth and presses the keys on the console with it. We watch each other. He is ugly, not at all what Saul would have been. Sallow, greasy little rat face, buzz-cut black hair, stick-out ears. As he bends over the console, I see the back of his thin, hairy neck.

'Hey,' he says, letting go of the stick. I thought he couldn't be more than three, but no toddler could speak like that – as if he'd been living on the streets for fifteen years and this hospital was just one more dead-end job.

'Hey, yourself.' I'm blushing.

'Could you move?'

I flatten myself against the wall and he rolls past, stick pressed hard to the flat orange disk in a row of concave blue buttons. The wheelchair has tires fit for a pickup truck, and the sides go up to his neck like a black box. I look down as the whole thing lumbers past. Under his little T-shirt he has no arms.

'Bye,' I say.

'Yeah.'

I cannot befriend the nurse at the front desk, but I do persuade her to tell me about him. Jorge. His story is horror upon unending horror – proof, not that I needed it, that the thought of a God is even more frightening than a world without one. Nobody is coming to take him home. He is not considered lovable, and the occasional saints – the foster parents who take in the AIDS babies and the cancer-ridden children – don't want him. What does he like? I ask the nurse. Nothing, she says. Whatever he likes, he's been keeping it to himself.

I wait by his room. He will not show his pleasure, but he will be reluctantly, helplessly pleased. Who has ever come back for a second, nonclinical look?

'Gum?'

'What kind?'

'Bubble Yum. Mint or grape.' It *is* what I chew.

'Grape.' He opens his mouth, and I unwrap the gum and place it on his white-coated tongue. He chews away, and then purses his lips around his joystick and moves off. At the end of the hall, he sits up and looks over his shoulder at me. He tongues the stick aside, keeping the blue gum in.

I wave. 'See you tomorrow, Jorge.'

At home, I prepare for diplomacy and war. I shower, even using the marjoram gel. My spirits *are* lifted. I make Julia Child brisket and arrange a pretty salad. I open a bottle of Stag's Leap and use the big-bowled wineglasses, the ones I have to wash by hand.

I tell Marc about him, lying. I make him sound sweet, responsive, appreciative. I don't tell the story the nurse told me: how he spat in the face of an aide, saving up a mouthful of penicillin to do so. I don't mention his all-over ugliness, the gooey squint in his right eye, the slight fecal odor surrounding him. I might as well have told Marc the truth. No, he says, we cannot take a disabled child right now.

We? I have to laugh. That old joke: What do you mean 'we,' white man? I pick over the words in my mind, to get him to say yes, and then I don't care.

'I'm bringing him home if they let me. He doesn't have to be in the hospital, but his family can't care for him, and his needs are too much for a residential place.' Of course they'll let me. It must cost a fortune to keep him. And he's so ugly.

'If you bring him home, I don't know . . . I don't think I can stay. Please don't do this to us.'

*

An aide brings Jorge off the elevator, and they both stare at me in surprise. I open my briefcase slowly, making a show of the tight buckles as Jorge approaches. I can hear the warm, sticky roll of the tires on the linoleum floor. We'll have to pull up the guest room carpeting.

'Gum?' he says.

I unwrap the gum and put it in his mouth, telling him my name so that the grape sugar on his tongue will become his thought of me.

He nods and chews. I sneak my hand to the vinyl headrest, almost skin temperature, and smoothed by his neck and hair.

'Let's go find the unit chief,' I say, and Jorge follows, the heavy movement of the chair shaking the floor beneath us.

I get into bed with the phone book and my list: medical equipment, pharmacy (delivery service?), furniture, foreign-language tapes (in case his Spanish is better than his English), carpenter (ramp). I underline 'carpenter' twice and call three names, leaving messages on their machines. It can't take more than a week to put a ramp where the kitchen steps are now. In my mind I move the living-room furniture around and get rid of the glass coffee table. When Marc falls asleep, dried red wine sitting in the corners of his mouth, I get up and move the actual pieces, shoving the coffee table into Marc's study for now. My body hums. I hang up my clothes, wipe Marc's damp mouth with my fingers, and pull the blanket up around him. I fall asleep easily, dreaming of Jorge, my little egg, rolling around on our queen-size bed, the silk spread smooth beneath his skin.

Hold Tight

My senior year in high school, I was in two car accidents, neither of them my fault, and I was arrested twice, also not my fault. I couldn't keep my hands on the wheel, and the guardrails flew right at me.

I found myself on emergency room examining tables, looking into slow-moving penlights, counting backward from forty to demonstrate consciousness, and calling my mother terrible names. I hate hospitals. The smell makes me sick, and the slick floors trip me up. When I visited my four dying grandparents, who dropped like dominoes the winter I was ten, I had to leave their rooms and go throw up. By February I had a favorite stall. With my mother, I could never get that far; before I even saw her I'd throw up from the thick green smell laid over the pain and stink and helplessness. When there was no reason to keep her, they let her come home.

My mother painted about forty pictures every year, and her hands smelled of turpentine, even when she just got out of the shower. This past year she started five or six paintings but only finished one. She couldn't do the big canvases anymore, couldn't hang off her stepladder to reach the upper corners, and that last one was small enough to sit on a little easel near her bed so she could work on it when she had the strength. After December she didn't leave the bed. My mother, who could stand for hours in her cool white studio, shifting her weight from foot to foot, moving in on the canvas and backing off again, like a smart boxer waiting for the perfect opening. And then, in two months, she shrank down to an ancient little girl, loose skin and bones so light they seemed hollow. A friend suggested scarves for her bald head, but they always slipped down, half covering her eyes and ears, making her look more like a bag lady than a soap opera star. For a while she wore a white fisherman's hat with a button that said 'Don't Get Me Mad,' and then she just gave up. I got used to the baldness and to the shadowy fuzz that grew back, but the puffiness in her face drove me crazy. Her true face, with cheekbones so high and sharp people didn't think she spoke English, was hidden from me, kidnapped.

When I got too angry at her, I'd leave the house and throw rocks against the neighbors' fences, hoping to hit someone's healthy mother not as smart or as beautiful or as talented as mine. My friends bickered with their mothers over clothes or the phone or Nathan Zigler's parties, and I wanted to stab them to death. I didn't return calls and they all stopped trying, except for Kay, who left a jar of hollyhocks or snapdragons on the front porch every few weeks. When I can talk again, I'll talk to her.

I could hardly see the painting my mother was still working on, since I went blind and deaf as soon as I touched the door-knob. I stared at the dust motes until my vision blurred and I could look toward the bed. My mother held my hand and sighed, and her weakness made me so angry and sick that I'd leave the room, pretending I had homework. And she knew everything, and I couldn't, and cannot, forgive myself for letting her know.

It was June, and everything outside was bright green and pale pink, and our house was dark and thick with dust. My mother used to say that we were messy but clean, and that used to be true. My father hid out in his study, emerging to entertain my mother and then lumbering back to his den. He'd come out, blink in the light, and feel his way to the kitchen, as if he'd never been in our front hall before. We avoided dinner conversation by investing heavily in frozen foods. He'd stay with my mother from five to six, reading to her from the *National Enquirer*, all the Liz Taylor stories, and then I'd take over the chitchat brigade while he drank bourbon and soda and nuked a Healthy Choice. The nurse's aide went home at five, and my father and I agreed we could save money by not getting another aide until the late shift. Six terrifying hours every night. While my mother rested a little, if the pain wasn't too bad, I'd go down to the empty kitchen and toast a couple of apple-cinnamon Pop-Tarts. Sometimes I'd smoke a joint and eat the whole box. If my father's door was open, I'd sit in the hall outside and wait until the sharp, woody smell brought him out shaking his head like a bloodied stag; we didn't have the energy to really fight. More often than not, we'd end up back in the brown fog of his study, me taking a few last puffs with my legs thrown over his big leather armchair, my father sipping his bourbon and staring out at the backyard. I ate Cheez Doodles most of the night, leaving oval orange prints all over the house. We took turns sitting with my mother until eleven. I watched the clock. One night I woke up on the floor of my mother's room, my feet tangled in the dust ruffle. I could see my father's black shoes sticking out on the other side of the bed, gleaming in the moonlight. He'd fallen asleep on the floor too, his arms wrapped around my mother's cross-stitch pillow, the one that said, 'If you can't say anything nice, come sit by me.' I don't know what happened to the aide that night. By morning I was under my father's old wool bathrobe and he was gone.

On her last good days, in March and April, I helped my mother paint a little. She always said I had a great eye but no hand. But my hands were all she had then, and she guided me for the bigger strokes. It was like being a kid again, sitting down at our dining-room table covered over with a dozen sheets of slippery tan drawing paper.

And I said, 'Mommy, I can't make a fish, not a really *fishy* one.' And she told me to see it, to think it, to feel its movements in my hand. In my mind it glistened and flipped its adorable lavender tail through bubbling rainbows (I saw *Fantasia* four times), but on paper all I had were two big purple marks and two small scribbles where I wanted fins. She laid her big, square hand over mine lightly, like a magic cloak, and the crayons glided over the paper and the fish flipped its tail and even blew me a kiss from its hot-pink Betty Boop lips. And I was so happy that her hand could do what my mind could see.

By the end of June, though, she stopped trying to have me do the same for her. We just sat, and I'd bring in paintings from the year before, or even five years before, to give her something new to look at. And we looked hard, for hours, at the last painting she'd done on her own, not a sketch or an exercise, a finished piece called *Lot's Wife*. The sky was grays and blues, beginning to storm, and in the foreground, in the barren landscape, was a shrouded figure. Or it could have been just the upright shroud itself, or a woman in a full-length muslin wrap. But the body was no longer alive; it had set into something dense and immobile. And far off to the right, bright and grim, were the little sticky flames of the destroyed city, nothing, not even rubble, around it.

'It's so sad,' I complained to my mother.

'Is it?' She hardly talked anymore; she didn't argue; she didn't command. She never said, 'Can I make a suggestion?' A few requests for nothing much, mostly silence. She took a deep breath. 'Look again. The sky is so full and there is so much happening.' She looked cross and disappointed in my perception until she closed her eyes and then she just looked tired.

My graduation was the next day, and it went about the way I expected. I overslept. My father overslept. The aide didn't wake us when she left. I didn't even open my eyes until Kay called me from the pay phone at school. I told her I didn't know if I could get there on time. I didn't know if I wanted to. I asked my father, who shrugged. He was still half asleep on his couch.

'I don't know if you want to go, Della. I suppose you should. I could come if you like.'

My father was, and is, a very quiet man, but he wasn't always like *that*. This past year she took the life right out of him. I have spent one whole year of my life with a dying woman and a ghost.

I went, in my boxer shorts and ratty T-shirt, and until I saw all the girls slipping their blue robes down over off-the-shoulder clouds of pink and white, I forgot that we were supposed to look nice. Kay flattened my hair with spit, stuck my mortarboard on my head, and elbowed me into our section (Barstow, Belfer). In our class picture there are five rows of dyed-to-match silk shoes and polished loafers and a few pairs of sneakers and my ten dirty toes. I didn't win any prizes either, which I might have if I hadn't been absent for fifty-seven days of my senior year.

Kay's parents, who are extremely normal, dropped me off on their way home to Kay's graduation party. Mrs Belfer showed me the napkins with Kay's name flowing across in deep blue script, and she reached into the bag on the front seat to show me the blue-and-white-striped plastic glasses and the white Chinet plates.

'Send our . . . Tell your father we're thinking of you all,' Mrs Belfer said. Kay and I had made sure our parents didn't know each other, and even when my mother was okay, she was not the kind of person to bond with other mothers.

My father made room for me on the porch swing. He ran one finger over the back of my hand, and then he folded his arms around his chest.

'How'd it go?'

'Okay. Mr Switzer says hi.' Mr Switzer was my ninth-grade algebra teacher. He used to play chess with my father, when we had people over.

'That's nice. You were a hell of a chess player a few years ago. Eight years ago.'

I didn't even remember playing chess; my father hadn't taken the set out for ages, and when he did, he didn't ask me to play, he just polished the marble pieces and rubbed a chamois cloth over the board. My mother got him that set in Greece, on their honeymoon.

'Eight years ago I was a chess player?'

My father shut his eyes. 'I taught you when you were five. Your mother thought I was crazy, but she was wrong. You were good, you got the structure immediately. We played for a few years, until you were in fourth grade.'

'What happened?' I saw him sitting across from me, thinner, with more brown hair. We were on the living-room floor, a little bowl of lemon drops between us. My mother was cooking chicken in the big red wok, and the chess pieces were gray-and-white soldiers. My queen was grey with one white stripe for her crown.

'Mommy got sick, the first time. You don't remember?'

I didn't say anything.

'You don't have to remember, Della. We don't even have to talk about this now. Your mother says, your mother used to say, that I don't say what needs to be said.'

He put his head back, and I did too. We looked up at the old hornet's nest in the corner of the porch.

'Car accidents or no, she's going to die. She is going to leave us to live this life. Even if I am blind drunk and you are dead in a ditch, she is still going.'

The swing creaked, and I watched our feet flip back and forth, long, skinny feet, like our hands.

'The aide's leaving. Let's go upstairs. It'll be a treat for your mother, two for the price of one.'

'I'll stay here.'

His fingers left five red marks on my arm, which bruises up at nothing.

'Please come.'

The swing rocked forward, free of us, and I followed him.

When she died that night, I wrapped the painting of Lot's wife in an old sheet and hid it in the closet, behind my winter boots. My father said it was mine. We sprinkled her ashes at the Devil's Hopyard.

My father began tucking me in, for the first time in years. He did it for weeks. We still hadn't really cleaned up, not ourselves, not the house. My father stepped over my CDs and cleared a space for himself on my bed. He said, 'It's a little late for bed-time stories, I guess.'

'Tell me about Mommy.'

'All right,' he said. 'Ask me something. Ask me anything.'

'Anything?' I didn't even know how many siblings my father had, and now I could ask him anything?

My father put the bottle of Jack Daniel's on the floor and rubbed my feet. 'Cast discretion to the winds, Della.'

'Why did Mommy get cancer?'

'I have no idea. I'm sorry. Next?'

'Did Mommy mind your drinking?'

'Not very much. I don't think I drank too much when she was well, do you?'

'I don't remember. Next. Were you and Mommy virgins when you got married?'

My father laughed so hard he stamped his feet up and down and wiped his eyes.

'Christ on a crutch, no. Your mother had had a dozen lovers before me – I think a dozen. She may have rounded down to the nearest bearable number. I was a callow youth, you know, I didn't really appreciate that being last was much, much better than being first. And I had slept with two very patient girls when I was at Swarthmore. Slept with. Lain down with for a few afternoons. Sorry. Too much?'

'Was it great, with Mommy?' I said this into my pillow.

My father pushed the pillow away from my ears. 'It was great. It was not always fireworks, but it was great, and when it was fireworks—'

'She rocked your world.'

My father patted my feet again. 'That's right. That's a great expression. She rocked my world.'

*

I still don't know where to hang the picture. My father says no room in our house is right for it. We don't want it to be in a museum. I unwrap it at night and prop it up next to my bed and fall asleep with my hand on the clean canvas edge, and I smell the oil and the wood frame, and I smell salt.

The Gates are Closing

Help me.

I slid my hands up the legs of Jack's shorts to stroke the top of his thigh, and he lost his grip on the paint roller. A hundred tiny drops flew through the air at me. Thoroughly speckled, squinting to keep the paint out of my eyes, I stroked higher under his boxers, right up the neat, furry juncture of his crotch.

'Jesus,' he said. 'It's not like I have any balance anyway.' Which is true. He has Parkinson's, and no sensible group of people would have him painting their synagogue if it weren't for the fact that he's been painting houses for twenty-five years and is the synagogue president's husband. I volunteered to help because I'm in love with Jack and because I like to paint. I lay down on the dropcloth and unbuttoned my shirt.

'Want to fool around?'

'Always,' he said. There has never been a sweeter, kinder man. 'But not right now. I'm pretty tired already.'

'You rest. I'll paint.'

I took off my shirt and bra and painted for Jack. I strolled up and down with the extra-long paint roller. When the cracks in the ceiling lost their brown, ropy menace, I took the regular roller and did the walls. I poured Jack tea from my thermos and I touched my nipples with the windowsill brush.

He sat up against the bima, sipping sweet milky tea and smiling. His face so often shows only a tender, masked expressiveness, I covet the tiny rips and leaks of affect in the corner of his mouth, in the middle of his forehead. His hand shook. He shakes. Mostly at rest. Mostly when he is making an effort to relax. And sometimes, after we've made love, which he does in a wonderfully unremarkable, athletic way, his whole right side trembles and his arm flutters wildly, as if we've set it free.

I told a friend about me and Jack painting the synagogue for Rosh Hashanah, and this woman, who uses riding crops for fun with strangers and tells me fondly about her husband's rubber fetish, got wide-eyed as a frightened child and said, 'In shul? You made love in shul? You must have really wanted to shock God.' I said, 'No, I didn't want to shock God' – what would have shocked God? two more naked people, trying to wrestle time to a halt? – 'it was just where we were.' And if someone had offered me the trade, I would have rolled myself in paint and done dripping off-white cartwheels through the entire congregation for more time with Jack.

Rosh Hashanah and Yom Kippur are my favorite holidays. You don't have to entertain anyone or feed anyone or buy things for anyone. You can combine skipping waves of kindly small talk with deep isolation, and no one is offended. I get a dozen invitations to eat roast chicken the night before, and a dozen more invitations to break the fast, including the one to Jack and Naomi's house. I think her name was Nancy until she went to Jerusalem in eleventh grade and came back the way they did, lean and tan and religious and Naomi. Jack thinks she's very smart. He went to Catholic school and dropped out of Fordham to run his father's construction business. Mouthy Jewish girls who can talk through their tears and argue straight through yours, myopic girls who read for pleasure – for Jack, this is real intelligence. And Naomi Sapirstein Malone totes him around, her big converted prize, the map of Ireland on his face and blue eyes like Donegal Bay, nothing like the brown eyes of the other men, however nice their brown eyes are, not even like our occasional blue-eyed men, Vilna blue, the-Cossack-came-by eyes, my mother says.

My mother still couldn't believe I'd even joined a synagogue. Two bar mitzvahs when I was thirteen set off an aversion to Jewish boys that I have only overcome in the last ten years. And if I must go, why not go someplace nice, with proper stained glass and a hundred brass plaques and floral arrangements the size and weight of totem poles? There, you might be safe. There, you might be mistaken for people of position, people whom it would be a bad idea to harm. When my brother Louis had his third nervous breakdown and they peeled him out of his apartment and put him in a ward with double sets of locking doors and two-way mirrors, the doctors tried to tell me and my mother that his paranoia and his anxious loneliness and his general relentless misery were not uncommon in children of Holocaust survivors. My mother was not impressed and closed her eyes when Lou's psychiatrist spoke.

We went out for tuna fish sandwiches and I tried to tell her again, as if it were only that she didn't understand their zippy American medical jargon. I counted Lou's symptoms on my fingers. I said that many young men and women whose families had survived the Holocaust had these very symptoms. I don't know what I thought. That she would feel better? Worse?

'Well, yes, of course, they suffer. Those poor wretches,' she said, in her most Schönbrunn tones.

'Like us, Meme. Like us. Daddy in Buchenwald. Grandpa Hoffmann in Ebensee. Everyone fleeing for their lives, with nothing. The doctor meant us.'

My mother waved her hand and ate her sandwich.

'Please. We're very lucky. We're fine. Louis has your Uncle Morti's nervous stomach, that's all.'

Louis recovered from his nervous stomach with enough Haldol to fell an ox, and when he got obese and shaved only on Sundays and paced my mother's halls day and night in backless bedroom slippers, this was Uncle Morti's legacy as well.

> Your might, O Lord, is boundless.
> Your lovingkindness sustains the living.
> Your great mercies give life to the dead.
> You support the falling, heal the ailing, free the fettered.

How can you say those prayers when your heart's not in them, Jack said. My heart is in them, I said. I don't think belief is required. I put my hand out to adjust his yarmulke, to feel him. I never saw anything so sweetly ridiculous as his long pink ears anchoring that blue satin kippah to his head.

You could wear a really dashing fedora, I said. You have that sexy Gary Cooper hat. Wear that. God won't mind. God, I said, would prefer it.

Naomi's break fast was just what it was supposed to be: platters of bagels, three different cream cheeses in nice crystal bowls, roasted vegetables, kugels, and interesting cold salads. There was enough food that one wouldn't be ashamed in front of Jews, not so much that one would have to worry about the laughter of spying goyim.

I helped Jack in the kitchen while Naomi circulated Sometimes I wanted to say to her, How can you stand this? You're not an idiot. Doesn't it make you feel just a little ridiculous to have gone to the trouble of leaping from Hadassah president to synagogue president in one generation and find yourself still in your mother's clothes and still in your mother's make-up, and still in your mother's psyche, for Christ's sake? I didn't say anything. It was not in my interest to alarm or annoy Naomi. I admired her publicly, I defended her from the men who thought she was too shrill and from the women who thought their husbands would have been better presidents and therefore better armatures for them as presidents' wives, seated next to the major donors, clearly above the *balabostas* at God's big dinner party. We'd had forty years of men presidents, blameless souls for the most part, only the occasional embezzler or playboy or sociopath. Naomi was no worse, and she conveyed to the world that we were a forward-looking, progressive congregation. I don't know how forward-looking Jews can actually be, wrestling with God's messenger, dissolving Lot's wife, wading through six hundred and thirteen rules for better living, our one-hundred-and-twenty-year-old mothers laughing at their sudden fertility, and our collective father, Abraham, willing to sacrifice his darling boy to appease a faceless bully's voice in his ear.

Jack and I were in charge of the linguine with tomato-cream sauce, and we kept it coming. He stuck his yarmulke in his back pocket and wrapped Naomi's 'Kiss Me, I'm Kosher!' apron around me. On the radio, an unctuous reporter from NPR announced that people with Parkinson's were having a convention, that there was an ACT-UP for Parkinson's sufferers ('I'd like to see that, wouldn't you?' Jack said). The reporter described the reasonably healthy people, the leaders, naturally enough, angry and trembling but still living as themselves, just with a little less dopamine, and he interviewed the damned, one worse than the next, a middle-aged classics professor, no longer teaching or writing, his limbs flying around him in mad tantric designs; a young woman of twenty-five, already stuck in a wheelchair, already sipping from the straw her mother held to her lips as they roamed the halls of the Hilton looking for the sympathetic ear that would lead to the money that would lead to the research and the cure before she curled up like an infant and drowned in the sea of her own lungs.

'Morris Udall, respected congressional leader for thirty years, lies in this room, immobile. His daughter visits him every day although he is unable to respond—'

This is endless heartbreak. I don't even feel sorry for Mo Udall, God rest his soul, he should just die already. There is no reason for us to listen to this misery. I want to plunge my tongue down Jack's throat, pull gently on his chest hairs and do everything he likes, knot my legs tight around his waist and open myself up to him so wide that he falls into me and leaves this world forever.

We look at each other while the radio man drones on about poor Mo Udall, his poor family, all his accomplishments mocked and made dust (which is not the reporter's point, presumably) by this pathetic and terrible disease. Jack looks away and smiles in embarrassment. He listens to this stuff all the time, it plays in his head when there is no radio on at all; he's only sorry that I have to listen too.

It's better to cook with him and say nothing, which is what I do. I want to hold him and protect him; I want to believe in the possibility of protection. Growing up in the Hoffmann family of miraculous escapes and staggering surprises (who knew Himmler had a soft spot for my grandfather's tapestries, who knew the Germans would suddenly want to do business and keep their promises), I understood that the family luck had been used up. I could do well in life, if not brilliantly, and if my reach did not exceed my grasp, I would be all right. My grasp included good grades, some success as a moderately good painter, and lovers of whom I need not be ashamed in public.

> We abuse, we betray, we are cruel.
> We destroy, we embitter, we falsify.
> We gossip, we hate, we insult.
> We jeer, we kill, we lie.

One can recite the *Ashamnu* for hours, beat one's breast in not unpleasant contemplation of all one's minor and major sins, wrapped in the willing embrace of a community which, if it does very little for you all the rest of the year, is required, as family is, to acknowledge that you belong to them, that your sins are not noticeably worse than theirs, that you are all, perverts, zealots, gossips, and thieves, in this together.

'A girl from one of the art galleries wished me Happy Yom Kippur,' I said to Jack.

'Hell, yes. A whole new Hallmark line: Happy Day of Atonement. Thinking of You on This Day of Awe. Wishing You the Best of Barkhu.'

We had all risen and sat endlessly through this second holiday, and my own silent prayers got shorter and shorter as a few *alter kockers* and two unbearably pious young men lengthened theirs, making it clear that their communications with God were so serious and so transporting they had hardly noticed that the other three hundred people had sat down and were waiting to get on with it. When the faintly jazzy notes of the shofar had been sounded the correct number of times, I had the pleasure of hearing last year's president say Jack's name. John Malone. Not Jack. In the shul 'Jack' sounded too sharply Christian, so clearly not part of us. Jack Jack Jack, I thought, and I would have shot my hand up to volunteer to rebuild the back steps with him, but I myself always questioned the motives of women volunteering to help on manual labor projects with good-looking men. I didn't think badly of them, I just couldn't believe they had so little to do at home, or at the office, that the sheer pleasure of working with cheap tools on a Sunday afternoon was what got them helping out my darling Jack or Henry Sternstein, the best-looking Jewish man with dimples and beagle eyes and, according to Naomi's good friend Stephanie Tabnick, a chocolate-brown beauty mark on his right buttock, shaped very much like a Volkswagen.

> Open for us the gates, even as they are closing.
> The day is waning, the sun is low.
> The hour is late, a year has slipped away.
> Let us enter the gates at last.

Jennifer, their daughter, came into the kitchen to nibble. I smiled and put a dozen hot kugel tarts, dense rounds of potato and salt and oil, to drain on a paper towel near her. Jack was fond, and blind, with Jennifer. She was tall and would be lovely, smart and soft-hearted, and I think that he could not stand to know her any other way, to have her suffer not only his life but hers. When Jennifer succeeded in the boy venues, Naomi admired her extravagantly and put humiliating tidbits in the synagogue newsletter about Jennifer's near miss with the Westinghouse Prize or her stratospheric PSATs; when Jennifer failed as a girl, Naomi narrowed her eyes venomously. Fiddling with her bra strap, eating too many cookies, Jennifer tormented Naomi, without meaning to. Jennifer sweated through her skimpy, badly chosen rayon jumpers, built to show off lithe, tennis-playing fourteen-year-olds, not to flatter a solid young woman who looked as if in a previous world she would have been married by spring and pregnant by summer. And Naomi watched her and pinched her and hissed at her, fear and shame across her heavy, worried face.

I love Jennifer's affection for me; that it is fueled by her sensible dislike of her mother makes it better, but that isn't the heart of it. The person Jennifer and Jack love is the best person I have ever been. My mother's daughter is caustic and cautious and furiously polite; my lover's lover is adaptable, imaginative, and impenetrably cheerful. Jennifer, I said to her at her bar mitzvah, surrounded by Sapirstein cousins, all with prime-time haircuts, wearing thin-strapped slip dresses that fluttered prettily around their narrow thighs while Jennifer's clung damply to her full back and puckered around the waistband of her pantyhose, Jennifer, your Hebrew was gorgeous, your speech was witty, and you are a really, really interesting young woman. She watched her second cousin toss long, shiny red hair and sighed. Jennifer, I said, and when I pressed my hand to her arm, she shivered and I thought, Does no one touch you?, Jennifer, I know I don't know you very well, but believe me, they will have peaked in three years and you will be sexy and good-looking and a pleasure to talk to forever.

She blushed, that deep, mottled raspberry stain fair-skinned girls show, and I left her alone.

Now, when I dropped by as a helpful friend of the family, she brought me small gifts of herself and her attention, and I even passed up some deep kisses with Jack in the garage, 'getting firewood' to give enough, and get enough, with Jennifer.

Jack put one hand on Jennifer's brown curls and reached for a piece of kugel. I looked at him, and Jennifer laughed.

'Oh my God, that's just like my mother. Daddy, wasn't that just like Ima? I swear, just like her.'

Jack and I smiled.

'You know, about what Daddy eats. She read that he should eat a lot of raw vegetables and not a lot of fat. Like no more quesadillas. Like no more of these amazing cookies. You are now in Fat-Free Country, folks, leave your taste buds at the door.' She grabbed four chocolate lace cookies and went out to the backyard.

I had read the same article about alternative treatments, in *Newsweek*, and I dropped ginkgo powder into Jack's coffee when I couldn't steer him completely away from caffeine, and sometimes, instead of making love, I would say, I would chirp, 'Let's go for a swim! Let's do some yoga!' and Jack would look at me and shake his head.

'I already have a wife, sweetheart. Andrea, light of my life. Darling Mistress. I don't need another one.'

'You should listen to Naomi.'

'All mankind, all humankind, should listen to Naomi. I do listen, and I take good care of myself. It's not a cold, D.M.'

I wanted it to be a cold, or even something worse, something for which you might have to have unpleasant treatments with disturbing, disfiguring side effects before you got better, or something that would leave scars like train tracks or leave you with one leg shorter than the other or even leave you in a wheelchair. Treatments that would leave you you, just the worse for wear.

Jack had come back to my house after we painted the synagogue. There are a million wonderful things about living alone, but the only one that mattered then was Jack in my bed, Jack in my shower, Jack in my kitchen. His eyes were closing.

'D.M., I have to rest before I drive home.'

'Do you want to clean up?'

'No, I'm supposed to be painty. I've been working. I'm not supposed to go home smelling of banana-honey soap and looking . . .'

His head snapped forward, and I put a pillow under it, on top of my kitchen table. He slept for about twenty minutes, and I watched him. Once, early on, I washed his hair. His right side was tired, and I offered to give him a shampoo and a shave. I leaned his head back over my kitchen sink and grazed his cheeks with my breasts and massaged his scalp until his face took on that wonderful, stupid look we all have in the midst of deep pleasure. I dried his gray curly hair and I buffed up his little bald spot and then I shaved him with my father's thick badger brush and old-fashioned shaving soap. My father was a dim, whining memory for me, but I put my fingers through the handle of the porcelain cup and I thought, Good, Papa, this is why you lived, so that I could grow up and love this man.

People came in and out of Naomi's kitchen, and Jack and I passed trays and bowls and washed some more dairy silver and put bundles of it into cloth napkins. I set them out on the dining-room table.

Naomi put her hand on my shoulder. 'He looks tired.'

'I think so,' I said.

'Will he lie down?'

I shrugged.

'Everyone's got enough food. My God, you'd think they hadn't eaten for days. Half of them don't even fast, the *trombeniks*.'

I started picking up dirty plates and silverware, and Naomi patted me again.

'Tell him we're done with the pasta. I'm serving the coffee now. He could lie down.'

'He'll lie down when they go home.'

Naomi looked like she wanted to punch me in the face. 'Fine. Then we'll just send them all home. Good *yontif*, see you Friday night, they can just go home.'

I dragged Naomi into the kitchen.

'Jack, Naomi's dying here. They're eating the houseplants, for God's sake. The bookshelves. Can't we send these people home? She's beat. You look a little pooped yourself.'

Jack smiled at Naomi, and she put her head on his shoulder.

'You're full of shit. Naomi, are you tired?'

'I am, actually. I didn't sleep last night.'

I am grateful for sunny days, and for good libraries and camel's-hair brushes and Hirschel's burnt umber, and I was very grateful to stand in their kitchen and bear the sight of Jack's hand around Naomi's fat waist and hear that Jack didn't know how his wife slept.

We threw six plates of rugelach around and sent everyone home. I left in the middle of the last wave, after they promised they wouldn't even try to clean up until the next day.

There was a message from my mother on my machine.

'Darling, are you home? No? All right. It's me. Are you there? All right. Well, I lit a candle for Daddy and Grandpa. Your brother was very nice, he helped. It's pouring here. I hope you're not driving around unnecessarily. Are you there? Call me. I'll be up until maybe eleven. Call me.'

My mother never, ever, fell asleep before two A.M., and then only in her living-room armchair. She considered this behavior vulgar and neurotic, and so she pretended she went to sleep at a moderately late hour, in her own pretty, pillowed, queen-size bed, with a cup of tea and a gingersnap, like a normal seventy-eight-year-old woman.

'Hi, Meme. I wasn't driving around looking for an accident. I came right home from Jack and Naomi's.' My mother had met them at an opening.

'Aren't you funny. It happens to be terrible weather here. That Jack. Such a nice man. Is he feeling better?'

'He's fine. He's not really going to get better.'

'I know. You told me. Then I guess his wife will nurse him when he can't manage?'

'I don't know. That's a long way off.'

'I'm sure it is. But when he can't get about, I'm saying when he's no longer independent, you'll go and visit him. And Naomi. You know what I mean, darling. You'll be a comfort to both of them then.'

I sometimes think that my mother's true purpose in life, the thing that gives her days meaning and her heart ease, is her ability to torture me in a manner as ancient and genteelly elaborate as lace making.

'Let's jump off that bridge when we come to it. So, you're fine? Louis is fine? He's okay?' I don't know what fine would be

for my brother. He's not violent, he's not drooling, he's not walking into town buck naked, I guess he's fine.

'We're both in good health. We watched a program on
Mozart. It was very well done.'

'That's great.' I opened my mail and sorted it into junk, bills,
and real letters. 'Well, I'm pretty tired. I'm going to crawl into
bed, I think.'

'Oh, me too. Good night, darling. Sleep well.'

'Good night, Meme. Happy Day of Atonement.'

I didn't hear from Jack for five days. I called his house and got
Jennifer.

'My dad's taking it easy,' she said.

'Could you tell him – could you just bring the phone to him?'

I heard Jack say, 'Thanks, Jellybean.' And then, 'D.M.? I'm glad
you called. It's been a lousy couple of days. My legs are just Jell-
O. And my brain's turning to mush. Good-bye, substantia nigra.'

'I could bring over some soup. I could bring some rosemary
balm. I could make some ginkgo tea.'

'I don't think so. Naomi's nursing up a storm. Anyway, you
minister to me and cry your eyes out and Naomi will what?
Make dinner for us both? I don't think so.'

'Are you going to the auction on Sunday?' The synagogue was
auctioning off the usual – tennis lessons, romantic getaways,
kosher chocolates, and a small painting of mine.

'I'm not going anywhere soon. I'm not walking. Being the
object of all that pity is not what I have in mind. I don't want you
to see me like this.'

'Jack, if I don't see you like this and you're down for a while,
I won't see you, period.'

'That's right. That's what I meant.'

I cry easily. Tears were all over the phone.

'You're supposed to brave,' he said.

'Fuck you. You be brave.'

'I have to go. Call me tomorrow to see how I'm doing.

I called every few days and got Jennifer or Naomi, and they would hand the phone to Jack and we would have short, obvious conversations, and then he'd hand the phone back to his wife or his daughter and they'd hang up for him.

After two weeks Naomi called and invited me to visit.

'You're so thin,' she said when she opened the door.

My thinness and the ugly little ghost face I saw in the mirror were the same as Naomi's damp, puffy eyes and the faded dress pulling at her hips.

'I thought Jack would enjoy a visit, just to lift his spirits.' She didn't look at me. 'I didn't say you were coming. Just go up and surprise him.'

I stood at the bottom of the stairs. 'Jack? It's me, Andrea. I'm coming up.'

He looked like himself, more or less. His face seemed a little loose, his mouth hanging heavier, his lips hardly moving as he spoke. The skin on his right hand was shiny and full, swollen with whatever flowed through him and pooled in each reddened fingertip.

'I can't believe she called you.'

'Jack, she thought it would be nice for you. She thinks I am your most entertaining friend.'

'You are my only entertaining friend.'

I sat on the bed, stroking his hand, storing it up. This is my fingertip on the gold hairs on the back of his wrist. This is my fingertip on the protruding blue vein that runs from his ring finger to his wrist and up his beautiful forearm.

'If you cry, you gotta go.'

'I'm not.'

'D.M., I may want something from you.'

I put my hand under the sheet and laid it on his stomach. This is my palm on the line of brown curling hairs that grow like a spreading tree from his navel to his collarbone. This is the tip of my pinkie resting in the thick, springy hair above his cock, in which we discovered two silver strands last summer. His cock twitched against my fingertip. Jack smiled.

'You're the last woman I will ever fuck. I think you are the last woman I will have fucked. You're the end of the line.'

I was ready to step out of my jeans, lock the door, and straddle him.

'I had a very good time. D.M., I had a wonderful time with you. My last fun.'

Naomi stuck her head in. 'Everything all right? More tea, Mr Malone?'

'No, dear girl. We're just having a wee chat.'

I never heard him sound so Irish. Naomi disappeared.

'Well, Erin go bragh.'

'You've got an ugly side to you,' he said, and he put one stiff hand to my face.

'I do. I am ugly sides all over lately.'

'When it gets bad,' he said, 'I'll need your help. I seem to have taken a sharp turn for the worse this time.'

I put my face on his stomach, which seemed just the same beautiful stomach, hard at the ribs and softer below, thick and sweet as always, no wasting, no bloating.

'And when I'm worse yet, I'll want to go.'

I saw Jack's face smeared against the inside of a plastic bag.

'That's a long way away. We all want you with us. Jennifer needs you, Naomi needs you, for as long as you're still, you know, still able to be with them.'

Jack grabbed my hair and pulled my face to his.

'I didn't ask you what they want. I didn't ask you what you want. I can't ask my wife. I know she needs me, I know she wants me until I can't blink once for yes and twice for no. She wants me until I don't know the difference. You have to do this for me.'

I put my hands over my ears, without even realizing it until Jack pulled them away.

'Darling Mistress, this is what I need you for. I can't fuck you, I can't have fun with you.' He smiled. 'Not much fun, anyway. I can't do the things with you that a man does with his mistress. There is just this one thing that only you can do for me.'

'Does Naomi know?'

'She'll know what she needs to know. No one's going to prosecute you or blame you. I've given it a lot of thought. You'll help me and then you'll go, and it will have been my will, my hand, my choice.'

I walked around the room. With a teenager and a sick man and no cleaning lady, Naomi's house was tidier than mine on its best day.

'All right? Andrea? Yes?'

'What if I say no?'

'Then don't come back at all. Why should I have you see me this way, see me worse than this, sweet merciful Jesus, see me dumb and dying, if you won't save me? Otherwise you're just another woman whose heart I'm breaking, whose life I'm destroying. I told you when I met you, baby, I already have a wife.'

  Avinu Malkenu, inscribe us in the Book of Happiness.
  Avinu Malkenu, inscribe us in the Book of Deliverance.
  Avinu Malkenu, inscribe us in the Book of Merit.
  Avinu Malkenu, inscribe us in the Book of Forgiveness.
  Avinu Malkenu, answer us though we have no deeds to
    plead our cause; save us with mercy and
    lovingkindness.

 'You're a hard man,' I said.
 'I certainly hope so.'

I am waiting. I have cleaned my house. I paint. I listen.

The Story

You wouldn't have known me a year ago.

A year ago I had a husband and my best friend was Margeann at the post office. In no time at all my husband had a final heart attack, I got a new best friend, and house prices tumbled in our part of Connecticut. Realtors' signs came and went in front of the house down the road: from the elegant forest-green-and-white 'For Sale by Owner,' nicely handmade to show that they were in no hurry and in no need, to the 'Martha Brae Lewis and Company,' whose agents sold only very expensive houses and rode their horses in the middle of the day when there was nothing worthwhile on the market, and then down, down to the big national relocator company's blue-and-white fiberboard sign practically shouting 'Fire Sale, You Can Have This House for Less Than They Paid for it.' I have thought that I might have bought that house, rented out my small white farmhouse, and become a senous capitalist. My place was nothing special compared to the architect's delight next door, but it did have Ethan's big stained-glass windows, so beautiful sightseers drove right up our private road, parked by the birches, and begged to come in, just to stand there in the rays of purple and green light, to be charmed by twin redheaded mermaids flanking the front door, to run their fingers over the cobalt blue drops sprayed across the hall, bezel set into the plaster. They stood between the cantering cinnabar legs of the centaur in the middle of the kitchen wall and sighed. I always said, 'Come in,' and after coffee and cookies they would order two windows or six, or one time, wild with real estate money, people from Gramercy Park ordered a dozen botanical panels for their new house in Madison, and Ethan always said, 'Why do you do that?' I did it for company and for money, since I needed both and he didn't care. If I didn't make noise or talk to myself or comment aloud on the vagaries of life, our house rang with absolute silence, and when Ethan asked for the mail, or even when he made the effort to ask about my bad knee, not noticing that we last spoke two days before, it was worse than the quiet, and if I didn't ask the New Yorkers for money, he'd just shuffle around in his moccasins, picking at his nails, until they made an insulting offer or got back in their cars.

Six months after Ethan died, I went just once to the Unitarian Widows Group, in which all the late husbands were much nicer than mine had been and even the angriest woman only said, 'Goddamn his smoking,' and I thought, His smoking? Almost all that I liked about Ethan was his stained glass and his small, wide hands and the fact that he was willing to marry little Plain Jane when I thought no one would, and willing to stay by me during my miscarriage-depression. That was such a bad time that I didn't leave the house for two months and Ethan invited the New Yorkers in just to get me out of bed. All in all it seemed that if you didn't hate your silent, moody husband after twenty years and he didn't seem to hate you and your big blob of despair, you could call it a good marriage, no worse than others.

I have dead parents — the best kind, I think, at this stage of life — two sisters, whom I do love at a little distance, a garden that is as close to God as I need it to be, and a book group I've been in for fourteen years, which also serves as mastectomy hotline, menopause watch, and PFLAG. I don't mind being alone, having been raised by hard-drinking, elderly parents, a German and a Swede, with whom I never had a fight or a moment's pleasure, and so I took off for college at sixteen, with no idea of what to say to these girls with outerwear for every season and underwear that was nicer than my church clothes. Having made my own plain, dark way, and having been with plain, dark, but talented Ethan all that time, I've been pleasantly surprised by middle age, with yoga and gardening for my soul and system, and book-keeping to pay the bills. Clearly, my whole life was excellent training for money managing of all kinds, and now I do the books for twenty people like Ethan, gifted and without a clear thought in their heads about how to organize their finances or feed their families, if they are lucky enough to have more than a modest profit to show for what they do.

I didn't call my new neighbors the Golddust Twins. Margeann, our postmaster, called them that. She nicknamed all the New Yorkers and pre-read their magazines and kept the cat-alogues that most appealed to her. Tallblondgorgeous, she said. And gobs of money, she said. Such gobs of money, and he had a little sense but she had none, and they had a pretty little blond baby who would grow up to be hell on wheels if the mother didn't stop giving her Coca-Cola at nine in the morning and everything else she asked for. And they surely needed a book-keeper, Margeann said, because Dr Mrs Golddust was a psychiatrist and Mr Golddust did something mysterious in the import and export of art. I could tell, just from that, that they did need me, the kind of bookkeeper and accountant and paid liar who could call black white and look you straight in the eye. I put my business card in their mailbox, which they (I assumed she) had covered in bits of fluorescent tile, making a rowdy little work of art, and they called me that night. She invited themselves over for coffee on Sunday morning.

'Oh my God, this house is gorgeous. Completely charming. And that stained glass. You are a genius, Mrs Baker. Mrs Baker? Not Ms? May I call you Janet? This is unbelievable. Oh my God. And your garden. Unbelievable. Miranda, don't touch the art. Let Mommy hold you up to the purple light. Like a fairy story.'

Sam smiled and put out his hand, which was my favorite kind of male hand, what I would call shapely peasant, reddish-brown hairs on the first joint of each finger and just a little ginger patch on the back. His hands must have been left over from early Irish farmers; the rest of him looked right out of a magazine.

'I know I'm carrying on, but I can't help it. Sam darling, please take Miranda so Janet and I can just explore for two minutes.'

We stood in the centaurea, and she brushed her long fingers against their drooping blue fringe.

'Can I touch? I'm not much of a gardener. That card of yours was just a gift from God. Not just because of the bookkeeping, but because I wanted to meet you after I saw you in town. I don't think you saw me. At the Dairy Mart.'

I had seen her, of course.

'Sam, Janet has forgiven me for being such a ditz. Let's see if she'll come help us out of our financial morass.'

Sam smiled, scooped Miranda up just before she smacked into the coffee-table corner, and said that he would leave the two of us to it and that he didn't use his old accountant anymore, so any help at all would be better than what he had currently. He pressed my hands together in his and put two files between them, hard red plastic with 'MoBay Exports, Incorporated' embossed across the front, and a green paper folder with Dr Sandra Saunders' stationery sticking out of it. I sent them away with blueberry jam and a few begonia cuttings. Coming from New York, any simple thing you could do in a garden was wonderful to her.

Sandra said, 'Could you possibly watch Miranda tomorrow? Around five? Just for a half hour? Sam has to go to the city. Miranda's just fallen in love with you.'

After two tantrums, juice instead of Coke, stories instead of videos, and no to her organdy dress for playing in the sandbox, it was seven o'clock, then eight. I gave Miranda dinner and a bath, and I thought that she was, in fact, a very sweet child and that her mother, like mine, might mean well but seemed not to have what was called for. When Sandra came home, Miranda ran to her but looked out between her legs and blew me a kiss.

'Say "We love you, Janet,"' Sandra said.

'We love you, Jah-net.'

'Say "please come tomorrow for drinks, Janet."'

Miranda sighed. 'Drinks, Jah-net,' she said indulgently.

I planted a small, square garden for Miranda near Sam's studio, sweet william and campanula and Violet Queen asters and a little rosemary bonsai that she could put her tiny pink plastic babies around. Sandra was gone more than Sam was. He worked in the converted barn with computers and screens and two faxes and four phone lines, and every time I visited he brought me a cup of tea and admired our latest accomplishments.

He said, 'It's very good of you to do this.'

'I don't mind,' I said.

'We could always get a sitter,' he said, but he knew I knew that wasn't true, because I had done their books.

Can I say that the husband was not any kind of imposter? Can I say that he was what he really was, a modestly well-known cartoonist? That they lived right behind me, in a house I still find too big and too showy, even now that I am in it?

I haven't even introduced the boyfriend, the one Sandra went off to canoodle with while I baby-sat. Should I describe him as tall and blond when in fact he was dark and muscular, like the husband? It will be too confusing for the reader if both men are dark and fit, with long ponytails, but they both were. And they drove the same kind of truck, which will make for more confusion.

I've given them wholesome, blandly modern names, while wishing for the days of Aunt Ada Starkadder and Martin Chuzzlewit and Pompeo Lagunima. Sam's real name conveys more of his rather charming shy stiffness and rectitude, but I will keep 'Sam,' which has the advantage of suggesting the unlikely, misleading blend of Jewish and New England, and we'll call the boyfriend Joe, suggesting a general good-natured lunkishness. Sandra, as I've named her, was actually a therapist but not a psychiatrist, and I disliked her so much I can't bear to make you think, even in this story, that she had the discipline and drive and intellectual persistence to become a physician. She had nothing but appetite and brass balls, and she was the worst mother I ever saw.

I wished her harm and acted on that wish, without regret. Even now I regard her destruction as a very good thing, and that undermines the necessary fictive texture of deep ambiguity, the roiling ambivalence that might give tension to the narrator's affection. Sandra pinched Miranda for not falling asleep quickly enough, she gave her potato chips for breakfast and Slurpees for lunch, she cut her daughter's hair with pinking shears and spent two hundred dollars she didn't have on her own monthly Madison Avenue cuts. She left that child in more stores than I can remember, cut cocaine on her changing table, and blamed the poor little thing for every disappointment and heartache in her own life, until Miranda's eyes welled up just at the sound of her mother calling her name. And if Sandra was not evil, she was worse than foolish, and sick, and more to the point, incurable. If Sandra was smooched inside a wrecked car, splattered against the inside of a tunnel, I wouldn't feel even so sad for her as I did for Princess Diana, for whom I felt very little indeed.

I think the opening works, and the story about the widows' group is true, although I left out the phone call a week later, when the nicest widow, who looked like an oversized Stockard Channing, invited me to dinner with unmistakable overtones and I didn't go. I wish I had gone; that dinner and its aftermath would make a better story than this one I've been fooling with.

Parts of the real story are too good, and I don't want to leave out the time Sandra got into a fistfight with Joe's previous girl-friend, who knocked Sandra right into her own potato salad at the Democrats' annual picnic, or the time Joe broke into the former marital home after Sandra moved out, and threw every-thing of Sam's into the fire, not realizing that he was also destroying Sandra's collection of first editions. And when he was done, drunk and sweating, as I sat in Sam's studio watching through the binoculars Sam had borrowed from my husband (Ethan was very much my late husband, a sculptor, not a glass-maker, but correct in the essentials of character; he wasn't dead before I met them, he died a year later, and Sam was very kind and Sandra was her usual charming, useless self), I saw Joe trip on little Miranda's Fisher-Price roller skate and slide down the ravine. I walked home, and when Sam called me the next day, laughing and angry, watching an ambulance finally come up his long gravel drive and the EMTs put splints all over Joe the Boyfriend, I laughed too and brought over corn chowder and my own rye bread for Sam and Miranda.

I don't have any salt-of-the-earth-type friends like Margeann. Margeanns are almost always crusty and often black and frequently given to pungent phrases and homespun wisdom. Sometimes they're someone's clever, sad-eyed maiden aunt. In men's stories they're either old and disreputable drinking buddies, someone's tobacco-chewing, trout-fishing grandpaw, or the inexplicably devoted sidekick-of-color, caustic and true.

My friends in real life are two other writers, the movie critic for our nearest daily newspaper and a retired home-and-garden freelancer I've been playing tennis with for twenty years. Estelle, my tennis buddy, has more the character of the narrator than I do, and I thought I could use her experiences with Sandra to make a story line. Sandra had sprinkled her psychobabble dust all over poor Estelle, got her coming three times a week, cash on the table, and almost persuaded her to leave Dev, a very nice husband, to 'explore her full potential.' Estelle's entire full potential is to be the superb and good-natured tennis partner she is, a gifted gardener (which is where I got all that horticultural detail), and a poor cook and worse housekeeper for an equally easygoing man who inherited two million dollars when he was fifty and about whom I can say nothing worse than at eighty-three Dev's not quite as sharp as he was, although he's nicer. I could not imagine how else Estelle's full potential, at seventy-seven, with cataracts in her left eye, bad hearing, and not the least interest in art, theater, movies, or politics, would express itself. I persuaded Dev to take her on a fancy cruise, two weeks through the canals of France, and when they came back, beaming pinkly, a little chubby and filled with lively remarks about French bread and French cheese, Estelle said nothing more about her underdeveloped potential and nothing more about meeting with Sandra.

I see that I make Sam sound more affably dodgy than he really is. He wouldn't have caught my eye in the first place if he were no more than the cardboard charmer I describe, and he was tougher than Joe in the end. Even if Sandra hadn't been a bad mother, I might have imagined a complex but rosy future with Sam and Miranda, if I were capable of imagining my future.

I don't know what made Sandra think I would be her accomplice. If you are thin and blondly pretty and used to admirers, maybe you see them wherever there are no rivals. But hell, I read the ladies' magazines, and I drove all the way to Westport for the new haircut and spent a lot of money at various quietly chic and designery stores, and although she didn't notice that I was coming over in silk knit T-shirts and black jeans, Sam did. When Sandra called me, whispering from Joe's bed, 'Ohmigod, make something up, I lost track of the time,' I didn't. I walked over and made dinner for Sam and Miranda, and while Miranda sat in front of her computer, I said, 'I'm a bad liar. Sandra called from Joe's. She asked me to make something up, but I can't.'

There is no such thing as a good writer and a bad liar.

After she moved out, she called me most mornings to report on the night before. She was in heaven. Joe was a sex god, but very jealous of Sam. Very silly, of course. Very flattering.

I called Joe in the late afternoons. I said, 'Oh, Sandra's not there? Oh, of course.' Joe was possibly the most easily led person

God ever made. I didn't even have to drop a line, I just dangled it loosely and flicked. I said, 'She's not at the office. She must be at home. I mean, at Sam's. It's great that they're getting along, for Miranda's sake. Honestly, I think they're better friends now that they're separated.'

I did that twice a week, alternating times and varying my reasons for calling. He hit her once. And she told me and I touched the greenish bruise along her jaw and begged her to press charges, for a number of reasons, but she didn't.

The part where Joe drove his car into the back of Sam's house is too good to leave out too, and tells funnier than it really was, although the rear end of his pickup sticking out through acres of grape arbor was pretty amusing, as was the squish-squish of the grapes as Joe tried to extricate himself and the smell of something like wine sweeping over us as he drove off, vines twirling around his tires.

I reported Sandra to the Ethics Committee of the Connecticut Society for Marriage and Family Counselors. Even though the best of them hardly have anything you could pass off as ethics, all the things she told me – her financial arrangements with her patients, and the stock tips they gave her, and her insistence on being paid in cash, and in advance – and the fact that I, who was no kind of therapist at all, knew all these things and all her clients' names, was enough to make them suspend her license for six months.

Sophisticated readers understand that writers work out their anger, their conflicts, their endless grief and rolling list of loss, through their stories. That however meanspirited or diabolical, it's only a story. That the darkness in the soul is shaped into type and lies there, brooding and inert, black on the page and active, dangerous, only in the reader's mind. Actually, harmless. I am not harmless.

The story I began to write would have skewered her, of course. Anyone who knew her would have read it and known it was she and thought badly of her while reading. She would have been embarrassed and angry. That really is not what I have in mind. I want her skin like a rug on my floor, warm throat slit, heart still beating behind the newly bricked-up wall. In stories, when someone behaves uncharacteristically, we take it as a meaningful, even pivotal moment. If we are surprised again and again, we have to keep changing our minds, or give up and disbelieve the writer. In real life, if people think they know you, know you well enough not only to say, 'It's Tuesday, Amy must be helping out at the library today,' but well enough to say to the librarian, after you've left the building, 'You know, Amy just loves reading to the four-year-olds, I think it's been such a comfort to her since her little boy died' – if they know you like that, you can do almost anything where they can't see you, and when they hear about it, they will, as we do, simply disbelieve the narrator.

I find that I have no sympathy with the women who have nannies on top of baby-sitters on top of beepers and pagers and party coordinators, or with the ones who want to give back their damaged, distressing adopted children, or with the losers who sue to get their children back from the adequate and loving parents they gave them to three years before. In my world none of them would be allowed to be mothers, and if they slipped through my licensing bureau, their children would be promptly removed and all traces of their maternal claims erased.

I can't say I didn't intend harm. I intended not only harm but death, or if not her death, which I think is a little beyond my psychological reach, then her disappearance, which is less satisfying because it's not permanent but better because there is no body.

As Sandra's dear friend and reliable baby-sitter, it was easy for me to hire Joe to do a little work on my front porch, easy to have him bump into my research assistant, the two of them as much alike as two pretty quarter horses, easy to fuel Sandra's anxious wish to move farther out of town. Easy to send the Ethics Committee the information they needed to remove her license permanently, easy to suggest she manage Joe's business, easy to suggest that children need quality time, not quantity, and that young, handsome lovers need both, easy to wave Sandra and Joe off in a new truck (easy to come up with ten thousand dollars when you are such a steady customer of the local bank and own your home outright).

And I am like a wife now to this lovely, talkative man who thinks me devoted and kind, who teases me for trembling at dead robins on the patio, for crying openly at AT&T commercials. And I am like a mother to this girl as rapacious and charming and roughly loving as a lion cub. The whole house creaks with their love, and I walk the floors at night, up and down the handsome distressed-pine stairs, in and out of the library and the handmade-in-England kitchen and through a family room big enough for anything but contact sports. In the daylight I make myself garden, fruit trees, flowers, and herbs, and it's no worse than doing the crossword puzzle, as I used to. I've taken a bookkeeping class, and we don't need an accountant anymore. I don't write so much as an essay for the library newsletter, although I still volunteer there, and at Miranda's school, of course, and I keep a nice house. I go to parties where people know not to ask writers how it's going, and I play quite a bit of tennis, in nice weather, as I always have. And although I feel like a fool and worry that the teacher will sense that I am not like the others, I go to tai chi twice a week, for whatever balance it will give me. I slip into the last row, and

I do not look at the pleasant, dully focused faces of the women on either side of me. Bear Catching Fish, the teacher says, and moves her long arms overhead and down, trailing through the imaginary river. Crane, and we rise up on one single, shaky leg. At the end of class we are all sweating lightly and lying on the floor in the dusty near-dark of the Gelman School gym. The floor smells of boys and rubber and rosin, and I leave before they rise and bow to each other, hands in front of sternum, ostentatiously relaxed and transcendent.

In the northwest corner of our property, on the far side of the last stand of skinny maples, I put up twin trellises and covered them with Markham's pink clematis and perle d'azur, and Dutchman's-pipe, for its giant heart-shaped leaves. I carried the pieces of a large cedar bench down there one night and assembled it by flashlight. I don't go there when Sam or Miranda are home; it would be unkind, and it would be deceitful. There is no one in this world now who knew my little boy or me when I was twenty-eight and married four years and living in graduate housing at the University of California at Berkeley. When Eddie was a baby we lived underneath a pale, hunched engineer from New Jersey, next to an anguished physicist from Chad and his gap-toothed Texan wife who baked cornbread for the whole complex, and across from a pair of brilliant Indian brothers, both mathematicians, both with gold-earringed little girls and wives so quick with numbers that when Berkeley's power went out, as it often did during bad weather, the cash registers were replaced by two thin, dark women in fuchsia and turquoise saris rustling over raw silk cholis, adding up the figures without even a pencil. Our babies and toddlers played in the courtyard, and the fathers watched them and played chess and drank beer, and we all watched and brushed sand out of the children's hair and smoked

Marlboros and were friends in a very particular young and hopeful way.

When Eddie died, trapped inside that giant ventilator, four times his size without being of any use to him or his little lungs, they all came to the funeral at the university chapel, and filled our apartment with biscuits and samosas and brisket and with their kindness and their own sickening relief, and we left the next day like thieves. I did not finish my Ph.D. in English literature, my husband did not secure a teaching position at the University of San Francisco, and when I meet people who remember Mario Savio's speeches on the steps of Sproul Hall and their own cinder-block apartments on Dwight Way, I leave the room. My own self is buried in Altabates Hospital, between the sheet and the mattress of his peach plastic isolette, twisted around the tubes that wove in and out of him like translucent vines.

I have made the best and happiest ending that I can in this world, made it out of the flax and netting and leftover trim of someone else's life, I know, but made it to keep the innocent safe and the guilty punished, and I have made it as the world should be and not as I have found it.

William and Clare

Your Borders, Your Rivers,
Your Tiny Villages

I Love to See You Coming,
I Hate to See You Go

The Old Impossible

Compassion and Mercy

Your Borders, Your Rivers,
Your Tiny Villages

At two o'clock in the morning, no one is to blame.

We'd been watching CNN, one scene of disaster leading to the next, the reporter in front of what might have been a new anthrax outbreak giving way to the military analyst in the studio with new developments in Kabul, when William put his hand on my breast. My husband was asleep upstairs, dreaming of making the deal that would put us on high ground when the entire economy collapsed, and William's wife was asleep in the guest room, getting her restorative eight hours. I think of Isabel as forcefully regular and elegant in all of her habits, and I'm sure she thinks of me as a little askew in all of mine.

William's hand trembled slightly. Our two plain gold wedding bands twinkled in the light of the TV screen. He touched my breast through my bathrobe and my pajamas – I had dressed for watching TV with William as if for bundling – for a very long time. His touch, left forefinger on left nipple, through wool and flannel, should have been numbing in its dreamy repetition, but it was not; it captured my whole body's attention. We kept our eyes on the TV. Finally, he fumbled under my robe and opened two buttons of my pajama top. His hand moved across my breast, and I sighed. I heard him breathing, hard and damp, and I put my hand on his big belly. It does not seem possible that we are people with three children, two marriages, and a hundred and ten years between us.

The first time I made out in a car, it was with Roger Saleta from Far Rockaway. We were trying to end the war in Vietnam by flooding the local draft board with mail and marching in front of it whenever our class schedules allowed. I had spoken at a big rally, wearing an electric-blue nylon halter top and my tight bell-bottoms with a crucified Jesus painted on the right leg. (I pretended not to know, and it may have been that I actually did not know then, why some people found this offensive. 'I'm not mocking Jesus,' I told my mother. 'I'm just representing him, on my jeans.') Roger circled around the parking lot after the rally and offered me a ride in his gold Camaro. We drove to Jones Beach, miles from the protest, miles from social studies and home ec, and we stayed in the car while the waves crashed and we worked at each other. Hands and mouths. Necks and elbows. He licked me through my jeans until they were wet and dark blue from inseam to belt buckle. I wanted to bang my head against the back of the seat from pleasure, and dug my hands into his black curls instead. This boy, not my idea of a lover, not even my idea of a date, had my body humming, dancing its tiny, fierce dance in the backseat. His hands under me and his mouth shamelessly pressed against me, as if the rest of the world could sink into the ocean out there and we would not even blink, or maybe, yes, blink dully, just once, before we returned to the real world of my pussy and his mouth. Later, we went to his prom, and I saw that he couldn't dance, which I hadn't known, and that his eyes were much too close together, which I had known and ignored, and I was a big disappointment to him that night.

*

William whispered something to me, but they were showing night bombing in the north and I couldn't hear him over the shouting correspondent. 'May I?' he said again, and put his mouth over my nipple. William is English, and he has beautiful manners. He has never failed to open the door, to pull out the chair, to slip off the coat, to bring flowers and send thank-you notes. It is not an affectation. Charles, my husband, is the same way, and it's not an affectation in him, either. They are both sons of determined English mothers and quiet American fathers who let their wives have their way. Charles and William are friends, Isabel and I are friends. It is all just as bad as it sounds. The close friendship has always been between me and William, from the moment we stood snickering together at that first faculty meeting until now. Everybody knows that William and I are, inexplicably but truly, best friends. I think his size and my shyness, and, of course, Isabel's beauty and Charles's good looks, gave us permission to love each other and hold hands in public, looking, I'm sure, like a woolly mammoth and a stiff-tailed duck, just that odd and just that ridiculous.

Even when they moved back to Boston after their one year in New Haven, back to his university and her real estate, we stayed friends. Isabel and I have had pedicures together, we've dissected our husbands and considered the possibility that a little collagen around the mouth might not be a bad idea. All four of us have sat at our kitchen tables, talking through their daughter's suicidally bad time in Prague and our son Danny's near-engagement to an awful girl from Bryn Mawr. I like that William is such a good storyteller; she likes that Charles is so clever with his hands. When we visit, she gives him a 'Honey Do' list and he pops around their house with his toolbox all afternoon and Isabel follows behind, handing him nails and a caulk gun, while William and I play Scrabble. She used to ask me for advice on getting William to watch his weight, which I gave, which was useless, and I felt terrible for her. After his first heart attack, she called me in tears, and I thought, Well, of course he has got to exercise and drink less and stop smoking and cut out the bacon and if I were his wife I would have him on egg whites and a thimbleful of sherry, but I'm not. William called me from the hospital and said, 'Please eat some butter for me.' We continued to meet at every intriguing restaurant he'd hear about, Abbott's Lobster in the Rough, Ma Glockner's for the chicken dinner, and we spent half a day finding a little place in Kent that had outstanding macaroni and cheese.

We've come to our quartet already grown up, with our long-standing convictions and habits and odd ways in place, and none of us has changed very much since we met. Isabel is much fitter and William is a little fatter and Charles dropped tennis for golf, coming home flushed and handsome, cursing cheerfully about his handicap and his stroke. Charles and William and Isabel e-mail one another news every day, and when we're together, Charles and William watch CNN for hours, drinking their Guinness. They talk like they've just come from a meeting with the Joint Chiefs of Staff, and Isabel joins in, perching on the end of the sofa near William, clucking her tongue when the scroll at the bottom of the screen says: AIR STRIKES HIT ALL AL QAEDA TRAINING CAMPS IN AFGHANISTAN . . . DURING THE RAID ON BEIT JALA, ISRAELI FORCES ARRESTED 10 PALESTINIANS AND KILLED 6. I don't know if she is clucking because six isn't enough or because it is way too much. Isabel reads *The Wall Street Journal* and *The New York Times* every day and I don't. It's not as if I waltz around the homestead with a big bow in my blond curls, picking daisies and waiting for the grown-ups to sit down to the nice dinner I've made. I teach, I go to the movies, I talk to my grown sons frequently (Adam is a news-watcher, Danny is a news-avoider, and all that matters to me is that they both live in small, safe towns in the Midwest and neither has children). I don't watch the news with my friends' avidity; I have not constructed a mental map of Afghanistan so that I can track troops, bombs, and food drops, and I will not even discuss whether or not we should call Bobby Bernstein, Charles's new golfing partner, and ask him for doxycycline.

William and I had a date to watch *Mrs Dalloway*. Charles and Isabel had kissed good night, the way we often kiss one another, something more than lips on cheek, nicely suggestive of restrained passion, as if, under the right circumstances, Charles and Isabel and William and I would just fall upon each other.

'Let's watch a bit of the news first,' William said. I made popcorn for later. We would sit with my feet in his lap, and he would ask for another beer and more salt, and I would get it. Then William would sigh with pleasure at having everything he wanted, and so would I.

The Appalachian Trail through New Jersey is like the road to hell. My boyfriend Danny and I slogged through swamp and low water, past dozens of orange blazes, which indicated not trail but possible paths through purgatory, until in the dark we found a flat, meadowy place. As soon as we stopped moving, mosquitoes descended upon us, attacking every moist, warm spot. They flew into our eyes, our mouths, our ears, burrowing through our wet, salty hair to our scalps. Trying to be quick in their buzzing black fog, we threw down our tarps and our sleeping bags and dove into them, clothes and boots still on. It was eighty degrees outside and perhaps ninety-five in our sleeping bags, but the choice was to be bitten all night or lie in pools of sweat until dawn. Danny zipped our bags together, and we rolled back to back, rank and itching and, as I recall, furious with each other – me because he had picked the trail into Rattlesnake Swamp, him because I laughed unkindly every time he unfolded our Sierra Club map that afternoon and said, 'This looks right.' Just before dawn, the bugs disappeared to digest and rest up to prepare for the second wave. Danny, the gentlest of boys, willowy and devoted, slid on top of me, rolled my underpants down to my ankles with one hand, pushed my legs apart, and came into me like a stranger. We lay there, stuck together from hip to collarbone, faces turned away, until it was light enough to leave.

William said, 'Come here, on top of me. Come sit on my lap, darling.' In six years, he has never called me anything but my name. Just one time, when we were chatting on the phone and his other line rang, he said, 'Hold on a tick, dear.' I climbed up on him, just as he asked, and draped myself over his stomach, resting my face against his shoulder, kissing it through his shirt. I unbuttoned his collar and ran my fingers around his thick neck, into his hair and down through the gray hairs beneath his undershirt.

'Oh, yes,' he said. I turned around and lay back against him, and he cupped my breasts under my pajama top, and we watched Jeff Greenfield and then the young woman who dyed her hair brown to go to Afghanistan. 'At least it's not Fox,' William said. 'Fox News, bloody Bill O'Reilly. Pandering little hairball.' He put his hands around my waist and pressed me close to him, and I could feel his stomach, his shirt buttons, his belt buckle against my spine, and his very hard erection underneath me.

I said I could feel him, and I put my head back so he would kiss my neck. He slid his lips up and down, and then his teeth and then his tongue. He pressed me closer. 'You should have known me twenty years ago,' he said. 'Thirty years ago. Back in my flowering youth.' I said that I was just as glad not to have known him in his flowering youth and that it had never occurred to me that I would know him this way, even in his autumnal splendor.

'What now?' he said, and we both looked to the right and the left, to Isabel on one side and Charles on the other and the television in front of us. I shrugged and I felt William shrug, too. 'Face me,' he said. 'I miss seeing you, otherwise.'

I swung around and unbuttoned another button. 'This is so terrible,' I said, and I think he wasn't sure if I meant what we were watching or what we were doing.

'We are not terrible people,' he said.

He was so big, there was so much to him; it was a great comfort, to find warm flesh everywhere I turned, his big thighs beneath me, like ground. At the beach last summer, he'd kept to his linen pants and guayabera ('Fat men may not appear in bathing suits,' he said), but he showed his broad white feet, in the sand. I thought every part of him must be a pink-tinged white, wide and thick and immaculately kept. His heart was beating like a drum.

'This could be it,' he said. 'The big bang. That would take some explaining.'

'It won't be your problem,' I said, and he laughed, bouncing me in his lap a little.

'Touch me,' he said.

I unzipped his pants and reached into his big blue-striped shorts and held his penis in my hand. I touched him as best I could, moving my fingers in the small space beneath his belly, in the little cave of his pants and boxers. He put his head back and closed his eyes, and he looked just the way he did at our lunches, greedy and delighted and deeply attentive. His whole body shuddered when he came, and even before his eyes were open, he'd pulled out a beautiful white handkerchief and cleaned up.

'Messy,' he said. 'Marvelous.' He cleared his throat and put the handkerchief away. 'Darling. Something for you?' He picked me up and laid me back on the couch. I shook my head. I still had my socks and slippers and everything else on. William took my slippers off.

'What a little chatterbox you are,' he said, and while I was laughing, he knelt down on the floor in front of me, muttering about his knees and the state of our carpeting, and pulled my pajama bottoms down and put his face between my legs. I put his glasses next to mine on the coffee table. When he got back up on the couch, breathing like a freight train and smoothing out my pajamas, Greta Van Susteren was still answering questions on her show, which William said was an excellent forum for the slightly informed. He handed me the remote.

'Turn it off, please,' he said. 'Put your head here.'

I laid my head on his shoulder again and put my slippers back on.

'It's almost three,' I said.

'I know,' he said. 'Not yet.'

We held hands, and then he hoisted himself up, bringing me with him.

'People,' he said. I nodded.

'No harm done, I hope? You're not going to look at me tomorrow with barely disguised horror?'

'No,' I said. 'Nothing like that.'

I put away the popcorn and rinsed the bowl while William finished his beer.

'How about a cigar?' he said.

William has moved to cigars from cigarettes, not exactly the dramatic change his doctors hoped for, and moved from cream in his coffee to fat-free half-and-half, which he now talks about the way other men talk about working out. When he smokes, I take a few puffs, to be companionable.

We sat on the back porch, the wood cold under my ass. 'Do you need a coat?' he asked.

'I'm fine. How about you? You don't have a jacket on.'

'I keep me warm,' he said. 'My thermostat is set rather high.' The moon shone through the clouds.

'The leaves are going,' he said.

I puffed on his cigar.

'William,' I said.

He stood up slowly, using the banister for leverage.

'It's still a beautiful night,' he said. He lay down on the ground. 'Climb on,' he said. 'Let's go for a ride.'

The moon lit up the whole yard and William, white beneath me. I folded my robe and tucked it under his head. Tiny leaves shook loose, bronze snow floating down upon us, sticking gently in my hair and his, until we were almost covered.

I Love to See You Coming,
I Hate to See You Go

William has gout.

It is the worst and most embarrassing pain of his life. His true nature, his desires and hidden history are revealed. By his foot.

Before he can get to the phone, the machine picks up.

'It's me. I heard the gout's back. Call me.'

Clare's messages are always like this, concerned and crabby, as if having to make the call will cause her – probably has caused her; the plane is pulling away even as she speaks – to miss her flight.

'I'm here,' William says.

'Okay, do you want to just get Thai in Springfield?'

Springfield is almost halfway between Clare's house and his. William doesn't have the energy even for Thai in Springfield.

'Christ. Why don't you just drive up here and bring lunch?' He would like to patch things up with Clare, but just putting down the phone drives two long, thick needles of uric acid deep into his ankle. He should have flowers in the house. He should shave. It won't be romantic.

Clare gets her car washed and drives up. She has to make sure that her visit takes place when her husband won't want to come, and there are things she cannot cancel and things she doesn't want to cancel, and in the end she sticks a note on her door, changing her office hours, and loads up the car. Usually she brings William corned beef on rye, or pâté and pumpernickel, and a big can of Guinness, and once, when they were right in the thick of things, she brought a box of Krispy Kremes and a bottle of Sancerre, but none of that is right for someone with gout. She packs two cooked, skinless chicken breasts, blanched broccoli, a basket of Maine blueberries (she read up after the first attack, and every website said blueberries), a box of chocolate soy shake, and a little tub of tofu. It's not romantic.

Clare knocks twice and comes in. If Isabel were there, they'd hug and kiss before she was ushered into the Presence. And if Isabel were upstairs and not too close by, William would kiss Clare hard on the lips and then he'd ask her to do things that he wouldn't ask of Isabel. If Isabel were there, she'd make Clare stay over when it got late, and lend her her own ivory linen pajamas. Clare would lie awake listening for William and imagining him listening for her, under the faded pink comforter, in his daughter's old room. Neither one of them would slip down the hall at two A.M., they wouldn't expect it of each other, but at breakfast, while Isabel showered, Clare would look at William with a sort of friendly disdain, and he would look at her as if she were selling drugs to schoolchildren.

William calls her name from the living room. He would get up, but it hurts too much. He usually shaves twice a day. He usually wears custom-made shirts and mossy, old-fashioned cologne, and he would prefer not to have Clare see him in backless bedroom slippers and green baggy pants, dragging his foot from room to room like road kill, but when he says so, she laughs.

'I've seen you worse,' she says, and there is no arguing with that. It seems to William that Clare last saw him looking good, well dressed and in control of himself a year and a half ago, before they were lovers. Now she's seen him riddled with tubes, hung left and right with plastic pouches, sweating like a pig through a thin hospital gown that covered about a third of him.

Clare puts her groceries away in Isabel's kitchen. Isabel has been telling William to change his ways for twenty years, and now he has to. Clare puts the chicken breasts in the refrigerator and thinks that that must be nice for Isabel.

William sits back in his armchair, moving his right foot out of harm's way. If Clare gently presses his foot or lets the cuff of her pants just brush against his ankle, it will hurt worse than either of his heart attacks. He sees Clare angling toward him and moves his leg back a little more.

'Don't bump me,' he says.

'I wasn't *going* to bump you.'

Clare sits on the arm of the chair and glances at his foot. It's her job not to take any notice of it. She can notice the slippers and green gardening pants, and she can say something clever about it all, if she can think of something clever, which she can't. Isabel says clever, kind things to William when he's under the weather. Clare's seen it. Isabel arranges him beautifully, she flatters him into good behavior, she buys chairs that fit him and finds huge, handsome abstracts to balance the chairs; she drapes herself around him like wisteria and she carries his hypertension pills, his indomethacin, his cholesterol pills, and his prednisone in an engraved silver case, as if it's a pleasure. The last time William and Clare had sex, William rested above Clare, just for a minute, catching his breath. He slipped off his elbows, and his full weight fell onto her. 'Jesus Christ,' she'd said. 'You could kill someone.' William did laugh but it's not something she likes to remember.

'God, it's like a giant turnip,' Clare says, putting her hand over her mouth.

It is exactly like a giant turnip and William is happy to hear her say so. His heart rises on a small, breaking wave of love just because Clare, who says the precisely wrong and tactless thing as naturally as breathing, is with him, and will be right here for almost twenty-four hours.

'Really, cooked turnip.'

'Well, the skin begins peeling in a couple of days, the doctor says, so it'll be even more disgusting. Hot, peeling, naked turnip.' He leans forward and kisses the shoulder closer to him.

'Did Isabel leave food for you?'

'Hardly any. The three things I can eat. When she comes back the two of you can have a big party, tossing back shots of vodka, licking caviar out of the jar.'

'Isabel wouldn't do that to you.'

'You would.'

'Probably,' Clare says, and bends to kiss him. Everything she thought about while driving up, how much trouble he is and how selfish and where all that shameless piggery has gotten him (gout and her), is nothing when he kisses her, although even when their lips touch, even as the soft, salty tip of his tongue connects to hers, they are not the best kisses she's ever had.

When they stop kissing, William says, 'Take off that ugly brown coat and stay a while, won't you?'

A month before the gout attack, Clare made William come with her to visit her uncle David. William clutched the staircase with both hands and made her carry his hat, his jacket, and the bottle of wine.

'You didn't say it was a walk-up.'

'It's two flights, William, that's all. Just rest for a minute.'

It was a bad idea. William said it, panting up the stairs, and he said it again when Uncle David went into his kitchen to get William a glass of water. Uncle David said it when William went to use the bathroom.

William washed his face with cold water and took his hypertension pills. He looked at the Viagra pills he'd been carrying around, in a tiny square of plastic wrap twisted like the wax-paper salt shakers his mother made for picnics. He'd been hoping for several weeks that he and Clare would go for a very elegant autumnal picnic in the Berkshires and that afterward they would stop into one of the seedy motels on Route 183. (When they did finally have the picnic and they did find the Glen Aire motel, the Viagra mixed badly with William's hypertension pills, and right after getting the kind of erection the online pharmacy had promised, he passed out. Clare drove them home in her aggressive, absentminded way, blasting the horn and sprinkling the remaining six blue pills out the window, as William rested, his face against the glass.)

'What do I want to meet him for?' Uncle David said. 'He seems like a nice man but I like Charles.'

'He's my best friend. That's all. I wanted my best friend to meet my favorite relative.'

'Only relative.' David shrugged.

It was so clearly a bad idea, and so clearly understood by all parties to be a bad idea, that Clare thought she should just take William back downstairs and send her uncle a box of chocolates and a note of apology.

William came out of the bathroom, mopping his face, and shook Clare's uncle's hand again.

'Nice place. I'm sorry Clare made me come.'

'Me, too. She's hard to argue with.'

The two men smiled, and William picked up his coat.

'Those stairs'll kill you,' David said. 'Why don't you have a beer, and then go.'

They had their beers as if Clare wasn't there. They talked about baseball, as the season was under way, and they talked about electric cars, which was even more boring than baseball. Clare sat on the windowsill and swung her feet.

William used the bathroom again before they left. David and Clare looked at each other.

David said, 'You can't hide someone that big. Where would you put him, sweetheart? He'd stick out of the closet and you can't put a man like that under the bed.'

Clare knew Charles was never going to walk in on her and William. It was probably not a great idea to sleep with William; she knew it wasn't a great idea almost immediately after it happened. She had managed to upend something that had sat neatly and foursquare beneath them, and even if William shouldered the blame, even if Charles was good enough to blame William, Clare never thought you could fault a man for taking sex when it was offered, any more than you'd blame the dog for flinging himself on a scrap that missed the plate. She knew she'd done more than just tilt the friendship between the four of them, but she was not ruining their lives with brilliantined paramours, sidecars, and cuckolds, the way her uncle made it sound. She was not ruining their lives at all, and you might think that the man known in her family as the Lord Byron of Greater Nyack would understand that.

'What can I say?'

'He makes you feel so young?' David sang. 'He makes you feel like spring has sprung, songs must be sung? Like that?'

'No. You don't have to be ugly about it. I think ... I make him feel alive.'

David shook his head. 'I'm sure you do. That's what these things are for.'

Clare looked out the living room window and counted three women pushing strollers, four boys smoking cigarettes, seven bags of garbage.

'Don't bring him again.'

'I get it,' Clare said. 'I'm sorry.'

'You're not listening to me. Don't do this.'

'All *right*.'

William walked in to see Uncle David whispering in Clare's ear and Clare pulling on her coat. William would rather have danced naked in a Greyhound bus station, he would rather have danced naked wearing a big pink party hat and matching pink boots, than stay another minute in Clare's uncle's apartment.

The men shook hands again and Clare kissed her uncle on the cheek, and he patted her face. They didn't like to fight.

In the car William said, 'What was that for?'

'I thought you'd like each other.'

'You embarrassed him,' William said, and he thought it was just like her to make that perfectly decent old man meet her lover and force him – not that she ever thought she forced anything upon anyone – to betray Charles by saying nothing or to betray Clare, which of course he would never do. It was just exactly like Clare to act as if it'd been a pleasant visit under normal circumstances.

William dropped Clare off at the university parking lot and drove back to Boston. She watched him pull away, the gray roof silver from the halogen street lamps, the inside brightened for just a second by the green face of his phone and the deep yellow flare of his lighter.

*

At four o'clock, William takes the round of pills Isabel left in a shot glass by the kitchen sink. At five, he falls asleep, and Clare reads their newspaper and then William's old *Economist*s. At six, while William snores in his recliner, she calls Charles to say that William is under the weather, Isabel is still on duty with her mother, and she, Clare, will stay overnight with William. As she talks, Clare gets her sweater out of the dining room and kicks her shoes into the rattan basket in the front hall.

'Don't kill him,' Charles says. Clare is not famous for her bed-side manner.

'He's a pain in the ass,' Clare says, and it's not just her faint reflexive wish to throw Charles, and everyone, off the track. Isabel and Charles and all of their combined children could walk through the house right now, looking for trouble, and there'd be no sign, no scent, no stray, mysterious thread, of anything except an old, buckling friendship.

William snorts and wakes up, his hair wild and waving like silver palm fronds. He looks like he might have had a bad dream, and Clare smiles to comfort him. He looks at her as if he's never seen her, or never seen her like this, which isn't so; he's seen her a hundred times just like this, seated across from him deep in thought, flinging her legs over the arm of the chair to get com-fortable.

'Oh, here you are,' he says.

Clare drops the magazine on the floor. William looks encour-agingly at the handsome bamboo magazine rack on the other side of the chair, and Clare stands up.

'Do you want some dinner?'

'How can you?' William asks. 'What kind of dinner?'

'Aren't you the most pathetic thing.' Clare walks over to smooth his dream-blown hair. They stay like this so long, her hands on his head, his head against her chest, that neither one of them can think of what the next natural thing to do is.

'We could go to bed,' William says.

Clare goes into the kitchen, gathers up everything that wasn't eaten at lunch and every promising plastic container, including a little olive tapenade and a lot of pineapple cottage cheese, and lays it all on the coffee table in front of William with a couple of forks and two napkins.

'You do go all out,' he says.

'I don't know how Isabel caters to you the way she does. If Charles were as much of a baby as you, I'd get a nurse and check into a hotel.'

'I'm sure you would.'

He doesn't say again that they could go to bed; she heard him the first time. That lousy picnic might have been the last time. This might not be the farewell dinner (and you could hardly call it dinner – it's not even a snack, it's what a desperately hungry person with no taste buds might grab while running through a burning house), but it has that feeling. She's brought him sensible food, and no wine; she hasn't made fun of his slippers or the gardening pants; she's worn her ugly brown coat and not the pretty blue one they bought together in Boston. An intelligent, disinterested observer would have to say it doesn't look good for the fat man.

'Let's go to bed,' Clare says. Husbands and wives can skip sex, without fuss, without it even being a cause for fuss, but Clare can't imagine how you say to the person whom you have come to see for the express purpose of having sex, Let's just read the paper.

'You look like a Balthus,' William says later. '*Nude with Blue Socks.*'

'Really? I must be thirty years too old. Anyway, Balthus. Ugh.' She pulls the socks off and throws them on William's nightstand. They're his socks. He must have a dozen pair of navy cashmere socks and he's never asked to have these back. And Charles has never said, Whose are these? They cover Clare almost to the knee, the empty heel swelling gently above her ankle. She wears them all the time.

William lies under the sheets and the comforter, leaving his foot uncovered and resting, like the royal turnip, on a round velvet pillow taken from Isabel's side of the bed.

'Is it better?' Clare asks.

'It is better. I hate for you to have to see it.'

Clare shrugs, and William doesn't know if that means that seeing his foot grotesquely swollen and purple cannot diminish her ardor or that her ardor, such as it is, could hardly be diminished.

'I don't mind,' she says. She doesn't mind. She didn't mind when her kids were little and projectile vomiting followed weeping chicken pox, which followed thrush and diarrhea; she didn't mind the sharp, dark, powdery smell of her mother's dying or the endless rounds of bedpan and sponge bath. She would have been a great nurse, Clare thought, if the patients never spoke.

'You looked very cute in those socks, I have to tell you.' William puts a hand on Clare's stomach.

'I don't know,' Clare says. 'I think . . . maybe we have to stop this. I think . . .'

William laughs before he sees her face. This is exactly what he has hoped not to hear, and he thought that if she was naked beside him, bare even of his socks and her reading glasses, they would get through the night without having this conversation.

Clare turns on her side to look at him. 'You don't think I might have a guilty conscience?'

William sits up and puts on his glasses. He doesn't think Clare has a guilty conscience; he doesn't think she has any kind of conscience at all. She loves Charles, she loves her sons, and she's very fond of William. She'd found herself having sex with William when they were bombing Afghanistan and it seemed the world would end and now they are bombing Iraq and the evening news is horrifying, rather than completely terrifying, and whatever was between them is old hat; it's an anthrax scare, it's Homeland Security; it's something that mattered a great deal for a little while and then not much.

'You might have a guilty conscience. Sometimes people confuse that with a fear of getting caught.'

Clare does not say that she would cut William's throat and toss his body in the dump before she would let Charles find them and that there is clearly something wrong with William that he would even mention it.

'I don't want to get a guilty conscience. Let's just say that.'

William pushes the socks off the nightstand. There is nothing to be gained by arguing. What they have is nothing to their marriages. Clare to Isabel, he to Charles: two cups of water to the ocean. There's no reason to say: Remember the time you wore my shirt around the motel room like a trench coat and belted it with my tie to go get ice? How about when you sat on top of me in East Rock Park and you pulled off your T-shirt and the summer light fell through the leaves onto your white shoulders and you bent down close to me, your hair brushing my face, and said, 'Those Sherpas ain't got nothin' on me, boy.' I have never known another woman who can bear, let alone sing, all of *The Pirates of Penzance,* and who else will ever love me in this deep, narrow, greedy way?

'We'll do whatever you want,' he says.

Now Clare laughs. 'I don't think so. I think what I want, in this regard, is not possible.'

'Probably not.'

Oh, put up a fuss, Clare thinks. Throw something. Rise up. Tell me that whatever this costs, however pointless this is, the pleasure of it is so great, your need for me is so tremendous that however this will end – and we are too old not to know that it'll end either this way, with common sense and muted loss and a sad cup of coffee or with something worse in a parking lot somewhere a few months from now, and it's not likely to cover either one of us with glory – it is somehow worth it.

William closes his eyes. I would like it if seeing you would always make me happy, Clare thinks. I would like to have lost nothing along the way.

'What do you think?' she says.

William doesn't open his eyes and Clare thinks, Now I have lost him, as if she has not been trying to lose him without hurting him, for the last hour. She crosses her arms on her chest, in the classic position of going to bed angry (which William may not even recognize – for all Clare knows, he and Isabel talk it out every time, no matter how late), and she thinks, Maybe I just want to hurt him a little, just to watch him take the hit and move on, because he is the kind of man who does. Except in matters of illness, when he sounds like every Jewish man Clare knows, William's Presbyterian stoicism makes for a beautiful, distinctly masculine suffering that Charles can't be bothered with. She uncrosses her arms and puts a hand on William's wide, smooth chest. He looks at her hand and breathes deeply, careful not to shift the comforter toward his foot.

'I don't know,' he says. 'Farewell, happy fields?'

'You're not helping.'

'I'm not trying to help.'

'Oh,' Clare says.

'It's late,' William says.

'I know.' Clare rolls toward him.

'Watch out for the turnip.'

'I *am.*'

Her head is on his chest, her chin above his heart. His hand is deep in her hair. They sleep like this, a tiny tribe, a sliver of marriage, and in their dreams, Clare is married to Charles and they are at Coney Island before it burned down, riding double on number seven in the steeplechase, and they are winning and they keep riding and the stars are as thick as snow. And in their dreams, William is married to Isabel and she brings their daughter home from the hospital, and when William sets her down in the crib, which is much larger and prettier than the one they really had on Elm Street, he sees their baby has small sky-blue wings and little clawed feet.

William kisses the baby's pearly forehead and says, to his wife in the dream and to Clare beside him, It's not the end of the world, darling.

The Old Impossible

Clare can't walk.

.She has sprained her ankle so badly, it's no better than broken. Marble step, wet leaf, a moment of distraction, and she was pulled up, several feet above the landing and dropped like a bag of laundry, her fingers sliding down the wet iron banister, her feet bending and flopping like fish. Three of her anterior ligaments snapped off as she landed, two small pieces of bone clinging to their ends, and the white rubbery fibers and the tiny triangles of bone continue to float where they should not be, above her ankle's hinge.

Her husband props the crutches up against the coffee table, tilting the handles in Clare's direction, and after he's laid a pillow under her mottled pink-and-blue ankle and a towel over the pillow and a bag of ice over everything, he brings in tea for Clare and her uncle David. He leaves to run errands. Neither of them asks Charles what kind of errands or when he'll be back; he carried and fetched and did for them all morning, and if he had said that he was going off to bet on greyhounds, or try a little Ecstasy, or worse, Clare and David would understand. Clare and David share a strong dislike of being, and caring for, the disabled. David is in Clare and Charles's house to recover from triple-bypass surgery and to entertain his niece during her period of limited mobility. Mostly, they read together in the living room.

'He *is* sweet,' Clare says aloud. It's not what she usually says about her husband. She thinks good things; she thinks interesting, she thinks handsome (the first thousand times he stepped out of the shower, water still flowing down the runnel of his spine, she thought, Jesus, Mary, and Joseph, how can anyone be so beautiful), she thinks he is much nicer than William ever was. William would have shaken his head over her ugly ankle, made his own coffee, and waddled upstairs, leaving her lying on the couch like in *What Ever Happened to Baby Jane?* Clare doesn't think about William every day anymore; she thinks about him mostly when she is falling asleep or when she's about to see him, which will be in the next few minutes. William and Isabel are pulling up to Clare and Charles's front door right now. William struggles with his cane and himself and a bag of nectarines. Isabel gathers up the groceries and a canvas tote of mysteries. She looks away as William rocks himself up and out of the passenger seat.

Uncle David reaches for his tea, which will not be the way he likes it, but he has made up his mind not to complain. The man went to the trouble of making tea. David didn't quite catch what Clare said about Charley. He hopes she isn't complaining. She's no day at the beach, his niece; the sprained ankle has not made her a happier, nicer person. If he were Charley, he would make up pressing business in Baltimore, never mind a few errands downtown.

'This is okay,' Uncle David says. 'This is fine. He makes a better cup of tea than you do.'

'Well, good. Half English. The Magna Carta. Men's shoes. Tea.'

'And roast beef,' David says, and he is about to add 'and

sodomy' just to keep the conversational ball rolling, when Isabel he can't remember her last name walks into the room, with bags of things. No one bothered to tell him she was coming. He would have put on a fresh shirt. He might have shaved. She's a good-looking woman, and well read for a real estate agent, and she has that quality, that way of making it clear that she wants him to get what he wants, that makes even plain women – and Isabel is not plain – very attractive. Clare is the more interesting person; as a human being, he'd pick Clare over Isabel, but he can't see how you'd be married to Isabel and chase Clare. It would make no sense, except David does remember chasing, and catching, a big, bushy-haired girl with thighs like Smithfield hams, and after her, chasing an Egyptian ballerina whose kohl ran onto his linen sports coat, so he had to just leave it, streaked and stuffed into a wastebasket, in Grand Central Terminal – all while married to the most beautiful woman in the world, a woman who turned heads until the day she died. He can see his wife and those girls, and a few other women, all rotating delicately in the same shadowy, treacherous light.

'We brought nice things,' Isabel says, and kisses them both.

'You smell good,' Clare says. Clare doesn't smell good. She smells like rancid butter and wet wool. She smells just like a yak, and her one skimpy shower didn't change that or keep her hair from hanging in limp coils, so that she now has yak ears as well. Uncle David, for whom the word *natty* was invented, who loved to tell people that his late wife always got ready for bed behind a closed door and that as far as he knew, she woke up every morning with brushed hair and a hint of lipstick, should not have to see his niece like this. She's not fit for company, even if it is only Isabel and William, and it never is only Isabel and William. What comes through the door is William as only Clare knows him, naked on a motel bed, sweating like a man with a fever, or cupping her chin in a restaurant and leaning forward with great, premeditated grace to kiss her. And right behind those stolen pictures come Clare's old friends Isabel and William, the four of them playing Monopoly at Cape Cod, and right behind them, her husband, Charles, slicing limes, and behind Charles, their sons, not as they are now, but pink and adorable in their footy pajamas, Danny holding his father's hand, Adam carrying his briefcase. Some of you will simply have to go, Clare wants to say. She smoothes out her ice pack, watches her uncle leer at Isabel, and longs for the thick, amiable hours of Percocet.

William comes in, leaning heavily on a cane, and Clare can't even say hello; the sight of the cane just snaps her mouth shut.

David stands up to shake William's hand and tries to take the bag of nectarines from him. He stands to demonstrate to Isabel – and it's all right for William and Clare to see this, too; he has no objection to either of them noticing – that David and Isabel are the only two people in the room able to get up and down from the furniture whenever they please. William hugs the nectarines.

'What happened to you?' David says.

William is sorry to see David, as he always is. David is the living embodiment of William's bad conscience about sleeping with Clare, and he is not a rueful, forgiving conscience. He is Conscience as a caustic, sensual, dyspeptic old man.

'Nothing much,' William says. 'How's the heart?'

Isabel says, 'Where's Charles?'

'He's running errands,' Clare says, and Isabel picks up the tea tray. Privately, Charles and Clare call Isabel The Governess. Isabel purses her lips just a tiny bit as she gathers the cups, and Clare can see her thinking that Charles is out gallivanting – and that would be Isabel's word for it, *gallivanting* – when he should be home supervising Clare, who might try to get herself a glass of water, or worse. It's very pleasant, it is just very warming, to have poor, good Charles on the receiving end of Isabel's disapproval for a change, and Clare throws her shoulders back and down to lengthen her neck and smiles up at William, who smiles back with relief, thinking, She's all right, she's just sick of being Charles's little cripple, as who wouldn't be.

William stands in front of Clare.

'Sit,' Clare says, and he sits in the armchair across from David, miles away from Clare, close enough to David to pat him on the knee or, alternatively, smash him in the throat and kill him.

'Sitting,' William says. 'Shall I roll over, too?'

'What's with the cane?'

'It helps me walk more comfortably.' The thought of discussing his rheumatoid arthritis with Clare is disheartening. It is unbearable.

'Oh,' Clare says. She looks down at the bag of books Isabel has brought and pulls one out. 'God bless Isabel. I like this series.'

William smiles politely.

'I never read them,' he says. 'You know, Isabel goes through hundreds.'

'Are you in pain?' Clare says accusingly.

'Yes,' he says, and Clare thinks, Oh, God, he's dying.

'I'm just in pain,' he says. 'I'm not dying.'

He shouldn't have come. He should have let Isabel come down by herself, and the women could have had some girl talk and clucked their tongues over the stupidity or cupidity of men, about which he would never argue, and have a few measured glasses of white wine (which is completely untrue to his memory of Clare, who pulled a bottle of Balvenie out of her suitcase when they were still twenty miles from their motel). He's not going to tell Clare, least of all when she's lying there like the little match girl, and certainly least of all while her uncle David sits before them like a cross between Cerberus and Mel Brooks, that he feels like he's been dying for some time. He has not been happy to see daylight any morning that he can remember, and he falls into sleep as if he's been wrapped in chains and tossed overboard.

'I'm not dying,' he says again.

'I hope not,' Clare says, and shifts her weight to look at him more closely.

'For the love of Jesus,' David says. 'He's limping, he's not dying. Who are you, Dr Kevorkian?'

Clare looks at William and smiles. David sees. He could sit here all night, is how David feels, keeping an eye on this big fat smoothie who's just as crazy about Clare as he ever was. Clare's feelings he can't read. She looks old and tired, and in David's experience old and tired is not a breeding ground for illicit love. Not in women. In men, sometimes it makes them try a little harder, to get the woman to chase the old and tired away.

'So, what a pair,' David says. 'Pair of lame ducks.' They shrug, like a pair.

'Since my ankle,' Clare says, 'I'm only reading about the ambulatory. Cowgirls, lady mountain climbers. Strong-minded women paddling down the Amazon, with their bare hands. Shrunken heads in their lace reticules. Banana leaves on their feet.'

'Really,' William says.

'Your mother was a great walker,' David says. Evoking Clare's mother seems like a good idea. His sister was hell on hankypanky, and everybody knew it. She threw David out of her house on four different occasions because of hanky-panky. He was sitting on the curb after one Thanksgiving, up to his ass in dead leaves, in front of that house they had in, where, Lake Success, and it was little Clare who came out with his coat, his hat on her head, carrying a beer and a handful of pigs-in-blankets. Life is short, David thinks, and walks out.

'Why don't you just sit by me?' Clare says. 'You can provide the elevation.' She would ask for more ice, she could actually use some more ice, but if William goes to get it, Isabel will intercept him and want it done properly and bring it herself, knowing that William will bring back three ice cubes in a dripping dish towel. If ice were what Clare wanted most, she would ask Isabel.

William hoists himself up, which he would rather Clare didn't see, and limps over to the couch. She's already seen him limping so there's no help for that, and he holds her feet up and puts himself under them and sinks back onto the sofa, pain gnawing at his hip.

'A lot of activity here,' Clare says.

'Oh, yes, quite a ruckus,' William says. 'I am not going back to that chair anytime soon. David can come back in with Hera and her peacocks, I'm staying on this couch, under these bumpy black-and-blue little feet.'

'And the peacocks are for?'

'Peacocks pulled her royal wagon. I have no idea why. She drove everybody crazy. A vigilante about adultery. Most of the myths are about her driving someone insane with her suspicions.'

'Gosh, I wonder who wrote those stories. She wasn't wrong, right? Zeus fucked everything. Ship to shore. Ox to goose. Whatever.'

'Oh, yes.'

Isabel comes into the room and looks at them. There are things she could say, there are plenty of things she could say about her husband, who doesn't like her coat to brush against him when he's driving, who so prefers some space between him and everyone else that he makes reservations for four even when it's the two of them, and who is now making himself into a footrest for their friend Clare. But Clare looks terrible, crumpled and waxy, and her hair, and the two of them are not likely to run off for some brisk lovemaking – how could they and what has it ever been between them but the rubbing up of two broken wings? And Isabel believes that life is what you make it. She adjusts Clare's pillow.

'Do you need anything? David wants to take a little walk, and it's just so gorgeous today—'

Clare and William look out the living room's bay window at the beautiful autumn day, and sigh, as if they have given up all hope of ever walking unaided on beautiful days.

'It's really beautiful,' Clare says. I am the worst person in the world, she thinks.

'It is,' William says. Go, in Christ's name, he thinks, and take that awful little man with you.

'We've got an hour to ourselves,' William says. 'Where should we start?'

'How's Emily?'

'Oh. Fine. She's liking law school – what can I say? You want to talk about our kids?'

'No. What's the matter with your leg?'

'Oh, for fuck's sake. I'd rather talk about the kids. I have bad arthritis, that's all. It acts up. I'm doing what I'm supposed to. Glucosamine chondroitin. Physical therapy. Whole grains. What do you want from me?'

'That's good,' Clare says. 'I'm glad.' She doesn't look glad. She looks chastened and sulky, and she pulls at the corner of her quilt until a wisp of cotton batting appears.

'What's wrong? Comparing yourself to Isabel? Thinking how I'd be curled into a fetal position by now if I were in your hands?'

It is a terrible thing to think and a terrible thing to be seen thinking – Isabel is a better wife than I am – and still Clare's glad that William knows her.

'Jesus, be nice. Nicer.'

'I don't have to be nice. Leave the quilt alone. I miss you every day, and we're not even friends anymore.'

'We are.'

'We are not, and do not dishonor the memory of that beautiful thing by saying otherwise. You know we're not.'

Clare wipes her eyes with a corner of the quilt. 'Fine. Jesus.'

'Less than an hour. If your uncle doesn't come scuttling back to check on us.' William picks up Clare's hand and kisses it. He takes a nectarine out of the bag and wraps her hands around it.

'Look at the size of this,' Clare says.

Clare twists the nectarine sharply, and it falls into halves, each one a brilliant, glazed yellow with a prickled hot-pink center. The pit falls onto her lap. They eat their halves and watch each other eat, and they drip, just a little, on the quilt. Clare wipes her chin with her wet hands, and then she wipes her face again, on the quilt.

'Napkins would have been good,' Clare says.

William shrugs. 'I like this,' he says. He lifts up the quilt and wipes his hands on Clare's jeans.

'Oh, what is *this*,' she says. If they're going to start acting like the senior-citizen version of *Tom Jones,* smearing their faces with nectarine juice and carrying on, the next thing you know, they'll be hobbling off to motels and looking up positions for the disabled in the sex books. William does not look at all embarrassed; he looks as he always looks: imperturbable, and mildly intrigued, inclined to be benevolent, if no discomfort is involved. Privately, Isabel and Clare call William The Last Emperor and there have been times when Isabel has called Clare to say, 'L.E. is driving me mad. Why don't you and Charles come up before I put glass in his cereal?'

'I love a nice nectarine,' William says. 'My mother made a nectarine tart, I remember. Sliced nectarines and a little brown sugar on top of a brick, just a giant slab of really good pie crust.'

William kisses Clare's right hand, then her left, lightly, absentmindedly, as if in passing.

'What's this?'

'Nothing,' William says. 'Tell me something else. Tell me a secret.'

'Oh, a secret. What a baby. You mean something Charles doesn't know?'

William bites his tongue. He doesn't think Charles knows much, but he could be wrong. He thinks that Charles has been so lucky and so handsome for so long that he's come to think that the world is actually filled with honest men making fair deals and bad people being thwarted by good ones. This is what William prefers to think. Before he slept with her, William thought that Clare had gotten the better half of the bargain. He even said so to Isabel, a few times. Clare is good, spiky company, and she is the very best companion to have in a bad situation. Trouble brings out the cheer beneath her darkness, unlike everyday life, which tends to have the opposite effect, and she holds her liquor like an old Swede, but Charles has to put up with that squinty, unyielding nature, and he does it with real grace,

William thinks. In private conversation, the men call Clare The Cactus.

A small boy sticks his head around the doorway and stares at William, rather coolly, from under his long lashes. It is the same look David gives him, now pasted onto a round brown face. William knows he knows the boy, who he is and his place in the world (third grade, grandson of the cleaning lady; Clare likes him; Charles wouldn't know him if he fell over him), but nothing else, like his name or why he is wandering around Clare's house, comes to mind.

'You have company,' he says. Small boys are not his department. Small girls are delightful; he would entertain a roomful of little girls, if it were necessary.

'Hey, Nelson.' Clare waves to the boy. The boy doesn't say anything.

'Nelson Slater, come on. You've met Mr Langford before. Last summer.'

Nelson nods. Clare sighs. It's not the short, vicious hiss that signals her annoyance. It's not the mild, watery sound she makes when her children call while she's working. It's the sigh of someone settling in for a short, satisfying tussle. If she were upright, Clare would roll up her sleeves.

The boy sits down across from them on the floor. Clare and William smile helplessly. He slides to the floor so easily, he glides right down, and later, he will spring right up. It is a lovely thing to watch, the way gravity barely holds him.

Nelson has come to play checkers. Clare taught him when he was a little kid, and since the accident, Nelson makes a point of coming by every few days, eating the cookies that are always on the coffee table, and fitting in a quick game. His grandmother is collecting old clothes for church, from the garage, and he has

364 *Amy Bloom*

fifteen minutes, she says. He might be able to beat Clare in fifteen minutes. It would be better if the fat man went outside, but
it's okay – Nelson can just keep his eyes on the board and on
Clare's skinny hands, looking closely at the tree of veins on the
back of each one, blue branches pointing toward the fingers.

'All right,' Clare says, like she's giving in, like she isn't completely ready to kick his ass. 'Set it up.'

Nelson plays as he always does, death in a bow tie, moving his
front line cautiously but already dreaming of the queens slaugh-
tered in their castles, gazing down at his men in terror and
admiration, flames leaping orange and blue across their wooden
walls.

'Game of Pharaohs,' William says. The kid must study Egypt.
Mummies and Cleopatra's negritude and the pyramids are what
pass for history now. Half an hour left, and they're going to spend
it with Clare's little friend.

Nelson pauses in front of one of Clare's pieces. It's not an
advantageous jump.

'If you can jump, you must,' William says.

'Shut up. He knows.'

Clare rolls her eyes so Nelson can see: Ignore him. Nelson
nods. He has met some very nice white people, but none of
them have been men. He jumps Clare's piece, and she jumps his.

'Watch yourself, young man,' Clare says.

'You watch yourself,' Nelson says, and laughs.

'Tough guy,' William says, and Nelson smiles tightly and looks
away.

William sees Nelson's opportunity, an unguarded square that
will open up the board for him. You have it, William thinks, you
may as well take it. He looks closely at Nelson, as he used to look
at his daughter when they played Scrabble. See it, he thinks, see

it. Do it. Nelson looks at William as if he's spoken and scans the board. Nelson thinks hard. The man's face is all lit up with wanting Nelson to win. Nelson and the fat man are going to beat Clare, is what Nelson sees. Nelson jumps like crazy, bouncing his man two, then three times and pounding his fists on the floor.

Clare claps.

'Good God. Well. Let's see what I can do with this . . . ruination.' It is short work after that. Nelson's men saunter around the board picking off Clare's pieces and when she has trouble reaching to discard them, he scoops them up for her, tossing them in his palm once or twice and laying them on the side of the board in a neat line. They look good, one big red dot after another.

Mrs Slater honks the horn, which is not what she usually does, but she still has to set up the Jumble Sale and the Baked Goods Table today, and this stop for winter clothes is out of her way. There's no help for it, poor Clare, and it's worth it for the six coats and the many pairs of shoes and the men's suits that will go fast, but this is not something she has time for today.

Sorry to leave the scene of his triumph, Nelson leaps up, to show off for them one more time, graceful and determined as a knight on horseback, and he trips over his untied laces. He puts his hands out toward the floor, but the edge of the coffee table, a sheet of granite, catches him fiercely on the face, and he is down on the rug, screaming in pain and fear and because blood is flowing right into his eye. William very gently puts Clare's feet aside, picks up the boy, and carries him into the kitchen.

'It's okay,' he says. 'It's okay. It's just blood, it's okay.' It may not be okay, but William can see both eyes whole and no bone showing, and if the boy's not blind or crippled, it should be more or less okay.

Clare comes in on her crutches, white around the mouth. She

runs cold water and hands an icy dish towel to William, who lays it on the small curvy wound, a little red mouth exhaling blood. Nelson stops screaming. Blood soaks the dish towel.

William says, 'A couple of Band-Aids, Clare?' and he pulls the edges of the gash together tightly, so tightly Nelson squirms under him, but William pins him gently and puts the bandages on, butterfly-style.

'Clare, you want to tell his mother, his grandmother, so the poor woman doesn't have a stroke when she sees him?'

Clare wants to stay, but Nelson is nestled on the kitchen counter, resting so comfortably against William, she has to go tell his grandmother the bad news and let William be the hero. (Isabel told her that when baby Emily cried in her crib, Isabel and William would stand, locked hip to hip, in the doorway, each trying to get to her first, each trying to persuade the other that it didn't *matter*, that they just didn't want to *trouble* the other. Clare could not imagine Charles fighting her for the privilege of changing Danny's diaper.) She turns around for a last look, and Nelson is laughing into William's chest; Zeus holding Ganymede beneath his dark wing.

Nelson's grandmother raised three boys and one girl, and an accident that does not involve a broken limb or serious impairment is, as far as she's concerned, the best one can hope for in this treacherous world.

'He's fine,' Clare says. 'He cut his forehead on that granite coffee table. You know.' They have both banged their knees, badly, on that coffee table, and they both watch Nelson walk out the door, followed by William, and they both think that if Clare and Nelson had not been playing checkers, if Nelson had been helping his grandmother in the garage, like the good boy he is, he would not be marching toward them, a wounded boy soldier, with two pale-pink Band-Aids, already darkly bloodstained in their centers, laid above his beautiful eyes. His shirt is ruined.

'I have some plain white T-shirts,' Clare says. 'I know you're pressed for time.' She holds the door for Nelson, and he slides into the backseat to stretch out. His head hurts and there were no cookies and it seems like years ago that he was jumping Clare's pieces and killing her queens where they stood. He puts his head on the pile of coats.

'Don't bleed on those coats, little man. Are you okay? Do you want me to drop you at Auntie's?'

'No.' His friends will be at the church. It will look like he has been in a big fight, which he sort of has, and that will be pretty cool. Clare turns the topcoat inside out so the silky lining is against his cheek. No one but Clare would do that for him. 'I'm okay. We can go.'

'I'll go back and get a T-shirt,' Clare says.

Nelson looks at his grandmother in the rearview mirror. He is not going to, and he doesn't think his grandmother will expect him to, or let him, wear one of Clare's own white T-shirts to the church Fall Festival, and a T-shirt that belonged to her husband would fit him like a dress. His grandmother smiles at him in the mirror and shakes her head at Clare.

'Don't you worry – probably some fine shirts in the backseat. Nelson can have his pick. Bye, now.' She steps on the gas, like that, and they are off, down the driveway.

Nelson sits up to see Clare waving to him and the fat man giving him a salute. He lies back down on the black silk and replays the last few minutes of the game until they get to church.

'My ankle is killing me,' Clare says. 'How's your hip?'

'He's a big boy.'

'Yes, he is.'

'He'll play basketball, I guess.'

'Oh, for Christ's sake. Is that what you'd have said about Adam?'

Her son Adam is six-three, and although William is fond of him, the kid is such a sport of nature, he always hoped his Emily, tall and broad-shouldered, would never take a shine to him because their children would have been freaks, some kind of advanced-race humans, who would have lost all control of their huge, flailing limbs.

'Adam? That boy could beat Adam at one-on-one now. I love you.'

So it is not a discussion of the limited options for nonwhite children, and it is not a discussion of the hideous fate of young black men, and there's no reason to talk about Adam right now. Clare cannot stop staring at her watch. The second hand is hammering around the dial.

'Oh, I know,' she says. 'How about a little Percocet? Just a quarter, take the edge off.'

'Is that a good idea?' William says. If she had offered him a bottle of almost anything, William would have taken it, but prescription drugs that make you feel better scare the shit out of him.

Clare takes a white pill out of her pocket and bites it in half. She spits half of it back into her hand and swallows.

'Here. Half. You don't have to take it.'

William takes it. It seems like an extremely reckless and adolescent thing to do, but he isn't operating any heavy machinery, he isn't driving or running for office, he is just sitting on the couch with his old friend, waiting for his wife to come back.

It dissolves in Clare's throat, leaving a sandy, salty trail. She pulls herself up to William and hugs him.

'You were very good with Nelson. After a while.'

'He's a good kid. He was lucky.'

'You can't beat lucky,' she says.

'We've been lucky. So far,' William says.

'We really have.' Clare lies down again, her head in William's lap, her feet up on the sofa's arm. William looks down into her eyes, unsmiling, and she looks away.

Maybe, Clare thinks, when Isabel and David return, William will have migrated back to the armchair, reading something high-toned, and I will be resting, attractively, or reading, attractively. And when Charles comes back, he'll find the four of us talking over drinks and eating the goat cheese and crackers that Isabel brought. He'll join us. He'll put his hand on my horrible hair, as if it is nice hair, and he'll sit where William is sitting now.

It is such a golden picture, the five of them. The six of them – Clare pictures Nelson, too, sitting on the other side of her, in a clean shirt, holding a couple of the cookies she'd forgotten to put out for him before. The light shines on Charles's lovely Nordic hair, a mix of blond and gray, as if the boy and the man will coexist forever, and Isabel is bringing out the best in everyone in her kindest, most encouraging way, as if all she has ever wanted is to help Clare make a nice party, and David tells his stories of Second Avenue, and there is nothing in them, not Great-Aunt Frieda, not the death of little cousin Renee, to make Clare cry, and William tells her that he will love her forever, that nothing has been lost, after all, and he mouths the words so that no one can hear him, but her, of course, and it is so beautiful, so drenched in the lush, streaming light of what is not, she closes her eyes to see it better and falls asleep.

William relaxes. There really is nothing more to do. He can just close his eyes, too. Clare's hair fans out across his lap. Her hands press his to her chest. The objects in the room darken, until it is a black reef from couch to table to chair, and no one turns on the light. William and Clare sleep, as if it is a quiet night in their own home, as if they are lying naked and familiar in their own bed.

Compassion and Mercy

For JOB

No power.

The roads were thick with pine branches and whole birch trees, the heavy boughs breaking off and landing on top of houses and cars and in front of driveways. The low, looping power lines coiled onto the road, and even from their bedroom window, Clare could see silver branches dangling in the icy wires. Highways were closed. Classes were canceled. The phone didn't work. The front steps were slippery as hell.

William kept a fire going in the living room and Clare toasted rye bread on the end of fondue forks for breakfast, and in the early afternoon, they wrapped cheese sandwiches in tin foil and threw them into the embers for fifteen minutes. William was in charge of dinner and making hot water for Thai ginger soup-in-a-bowl. They used the snow bank at the kitchen door to chill the Chardonnay.

They read and played Scrabble and at four o'clock, when daylight dropped to a deep indigo, Clare lit two dozen candles and they got into their pile of quilts and pillows.

'All right,' William said. 'Let's have it. You're shipwrecked on a desert island. Who do you want to be with – me or Nelson Slater?'

'Oh my God,' Clare says. 'Nelson. Of course.'

'Good choice. He did a great job with the firewood.'

William kept the fire going all night. Every hour, he had to roll sideways and crouch and then steady himself and then pull himself up with his cane and then balance himself, and because Clare was watching and worried, he had to do it all with the appearance of ease. Clare lay in the dark and tried to move the blankets far to one side so they wouldn't tangle William's feet.

'You're not actually helping,' he said. 'I know where the blankets are, so I can easily step over them. And then, of course, you move them.'

'I feel bad,' Clare said.

'I'm going to break something if you keep this up.'

'Let me help,' Clare said.

When the cold woke them, Clare handed William the logs. They talked about whether or not it was worth it to use the turkey carcass for soup and if they could really make a decent soup in the fireplace. William said that people had cooked primarily in hearths until the late eighteenth century. William told Clare about his visit to his cardiologist and the possible levels of fitness William could achieve. ('A lot of men your age walk five miles a day,' the doctor said. 'My father-in-law got himself a personal trainer, and he's eighty.') Clare said maybe they could walk to the diner on weekends. They talked about Clare's sons, Adam and Danny, and their wives and the two grandchildren and they talked about William's daughter, Emily, and her pregnancy and the awful man she'd married ('I'd rather she'd taken the veil,' William said. 'Little Sisters of Gehenna'). When the subject came up, William and Clare said nice things about the people they used to be married to.

*

It had taken William and Clare five years to end their marriages. William's divorce lawyer was the sister of one of William's old friends. She was William's age, in a sharp black suit and improbably black hair and bloodred nails. Her only concession to age was black patent flats, and William was sure that most of her life, this woman had been stalking and killing wild game in stiletto heels.

'So,' she said. 'You've been married thirty-five years. Well, look, Dr Langford—'

'"Mister" is fine,' William said. '"William" is fine.'

'"Bill"?' the woman said and William shook his head no and she smiled and made a note.

'Just kidding. It's like this. Unless your wife is doing crack cocaine or having sex with young girls and barnyard animals, what little you have will be split fifty-fifty.'

'That's fine, Mrs Merrill,' William said.

'Not really,' the woman said. 'Call me Louise. Your wife obviously got a lawyer long before you did. I got a fax today, a list of personal property your wife believes she's entitled to. Oil paintings, a little jewelry, silverware.'

'That's fine. Whatever it is.'

'It's not fine. But let's say you have no personal attachment to any of these items. And let's say it's all worth about twenty thousand dollars. Let's have her give you twenty thousand dollars, and you give her the stuff. There's no reason for us to just roll over and put our paws up in the air.'

'Whatever she wants,' William said. 'You should know, I'm not having sex with a graduate student. Or with porn stars.'

'I believe you,' Mrs Merrill said. 'You may as well tell me – it'll all come out in the wash. Who are you having sex with?'

'Her name is Clare Wexler. She teaches. She's a very fine

teacher. She makes me laugh. She can be a difficult person,' he said, beaming, as if he were detailing her beauty. 'You'd like her.' William wiped his eyes.

'All right,' said Louise Merrill. 'Let's get you hitched before we're all too old to enjoy it.'

When they could finally marry, Clare called her sons.

Danny said, 'You might want a prenup. I'm just saying.'

Adam said, 'Jeez, I thought Isabel was your friend.'

William called Emily and she said, 'How can you do this to me? I'm trying to get pregnant,' and her husband, Kurt, had to take the phone because she was crying so hard. He said, 'We're trying not to take sides, you know.'

Three days after the storm had passed, classes resumed, grimy cars filled slushy roads, and Clare called both of her sons to say they were essentially unharmed.

'What do you mean, "essentially"?' Danny said, and Clare said, 'I mean my hair's a mess and I lost at Scrabble seventeen times and William's back hurts from sleeping near the fireplace. I mean, I'm absolutely and completely fine. I shouldn't have said "essentially."'

William laughed and shook his head when she hung up.

'They must know me by now,' Clare said.

'I'm sure they do,' William said, 'but knowing and understanding are two different things. *Verstehen und erklären.*'

'Fancy talk,' Clare said, and she kissed his neck and the bald top of his head and the little red dents behind his ears, which came from sixty-five years of wearing glasses. 'I have to go to Baltimore tomorrow. Remember?'

'Of course,' William said.

Clare knew he'd call her the next day to ask about dinner, about Thai food or Cuban or would she prefer scrambled eggs and salami and then when she said she was on her way to Baltimore, William would be, for just a quick minute, crushed and then crisp and English.

They spoke while Clare was on the train. William had unpacked his low-salt, low-fat lunch. ('Disgusting,' he'd said. 'Punitive.') Clare had gone over her notes for her talk on *Jane Eyre* ('In which I will reveal my awful, retrograde underpinnings') and they made their nighttime phone date for ten P.M., when William would be still at his desk at home and Clare would be in her bed at the University Club.

Clare called William every half hour from ten until midnight and then she told herself that he must have fallen asleep early. She called him at his university office, on his cell phone, and at home. She called him every fifteen minutes from seven A.M. until her talk and she began calling him again, at eleven, as soon as her talk was over. She begged off the faculty lunch and said that her husband wasn't well and that she was needed at home; her voice shook and no one doubted her.

On the train, Clare wondered who to call. She couldn't ask Emily, even though she lived six blocks away; she couldn't ask a pregnant woman to go see if her father was all right. By the time she'd gotten Emily to understand what was required, and where the house key was hidden, and that there was no real cause for alarm, Emily would be sobbing and Clare would be trying not to scream at Emily to calm the fuck down. Isabel was the person to call, and Clare couldn't call her. She could imagine Isabel saying, 'Of course, Clare, leave it to me,' and driving down from Boston to sort things out; she'd make the beds, she'd straighten the pictures, she'd gather all the overdue library books into a pile and stack them near the front door. She'd scold William for making them all worry and then she would call Clare back, to say that all broken things had been put right.

Clare couldn't picture what might have happened to William. His face floated before her, his large, lovely face, his face when he was reading the paper, his face when he'd said to her, 'I *am* sorry,' and she'd thought, Oh, Christ, we're breaking up again; I thought we'd go until April at least, and he'd said, 'You are everything to me – I'm afraid we have to marry,' and they cried so hard, they had to sit down on the bench outside the diner and wipe each other's faces with napkins.

Clare saw that the man in the seat across from her was smiling uncertainly; she'd been saying William's name. Clare walked to the little juncture between cars and called Margaret Slater, her former cleaning lady. There was no answer. Margaret's grandson Nelson didn't get home until three so Margaret might be running errands for another two hours. They pulled into Penn Station. If Margaret had a cell phone, Clare didn't know the number. Clare called every half hour, home and then Margaret's number, leaving messages and timing herself, reading a few pages of the paper between calls. Goddammit, Margaret, she thought. You're retired. Pick up the fucking phone.

Clare pulled into their driveway just as the sun was setting and Margaret pulled in right after her. Water still dripped from the gutters and the corners of the house and it would all freeze again at night.

'Oh, Clare,' Margaret said, 'I just got your messages. I was out of the house all day. I'm so sorry.'

'It's all right,' Clare said, and they both looked up at the light in William's window. 'He probably unplugged the phone.'

'They live to drive us crazy,' Margaret said.

Clare scrabbled in the bottom of her bag for the house key, furiously tossing tissues and pens and Chap Sticks and quarters onto the walk, and thinking with every toss, What's your hurry? This is your last moment of not knowing, stupid, slow down. But her hands moved fast, tearing the silk lining of the bag until she saw, out of the corner of her eye, a brass house key sitting in Margaret's flat, lined palm. Clare wanted to sit down on the porch and wait for someone else to come. She opened the door and she wanted to turn around and close it behind her.

They should call his name, she thought. It's what you do when you come into your house and you haven't been able to reach your husband, you go, *William, William, darling, I'm home,* and then he pulls himself out of his green leather desk chair and comes to the top of the stairs, his hair standing straight up and his glasses on the end of his nose. He says, relief and annoyance clearly mixed together, *Oh, darling, you didn't call, I waited for your call.* And then you say, *I did call, I called all night, but the phone was off the hook, you had the phone off,* and he says that he certainly did not and Margaret watches, bemused. She disapproved of the divorce (she all but said, I always thought Charles would leave you, not the other way around) but gave herself over on the wedding day, when she brought platters of deviled eggs and put Nelson in a navy-blue suit, and cried, shyly.

'Fulgent,' William said after the ceremony, and he said it several times, a little drunk on Champagne. 'Absolutely *fulgent.*' It wouldn't have mattered if no one had been there, but everyone except William's sister had been, and they got in one elegant foxtrot before William's ankle acted up. William will call down, 'I'm so sorry we inconvenienced you, Mrs Slater,' and Margaret will

shake her head fondly and go, and you drop your coat and bag
in the hall and he comes down the stairs, slowly, careful with his
ankle, and he makes tea to apologize for having scared the shit
out of you.

Margaret waited. As much as she wanted to help, it wasn't her
house or her husband and Clare had been in charge of their relationship for the last twenty years; this was not the moment to
take the lead. Clare walked up the stairs and right into their bedroom, as if William had phoned ahead and told her what to
expect. He was lying on the bed, shoes off and fully dressed, his
hand on *Jane Eyre,* his eyes closed, and his reading glasses on his
chest. ("'He is not to them what he is to me,'" Jane thought.
"'While I breathe and think I must love him.'") Clare lay down
next to him, murmuring, until Margaret put her hand on Clare's
shoulder and asked if she should call the hospital or someone.

  'I have no idea,' Clare said, lying on the bed beside William,
staring at the ceiling. These things get done, Clare thought,
whether you know what you're doing or not. The hospital is
called, the funeral home is contacted, the body is removed, with
some difficulty, because he was a big man and the stairs are old
and narrow. Your sons and daughters-in-law call everyone who
needs to be called, including the terrible sister in England who
sent them a note and a chipped vase, explaining that she could
not bring herself to attend a wedding that so clearly should not
be taking place.

  Margaret comes back the next day and makes up one of the
boys' bedrooms for you, just in case, but when your best friend
flies in from Cleveland, you are lying in your own room,
wrapped in William's bathrobe, and you wear his robe and his

undershirt while she sits across from you, her sensible shoes right beside William's wing tips, and she helps you decide chapel or funeral home, lunch or brunch, booze or wine, and who will speak. Your sons and their wives and the babies come and it's no more or less terrible to have them in the house. You move slowly and carefully, swimming through a deep but traversable river of shit. You must not inhale, you must not stop, you must not stop for anything at all. Destroyed, untouchable, you can lie down on the other side when they've all gone home.

Clare was careful during the funeral. She didn't listen to anything that was said. She saw Isabel sitting with Emily and Kurt, a little cluster of Langfords; Isabel wore a gray suit and held Emily's hand and she left as soon as the service ended. At the house, Clare imagined Isabel beside her; she imagined herself encased in Isabel. Even in pajamas, suffering a bad cold, Isabel moved like a woman in beautiful silk. Clare made an effort to move that way. She thanked people in Isabel's pleasant, governessy voice. Clare straightened Danny's tie with Isabel's hand and then wiped chocolate fingerprints off the back of a chair. Clare used Isabel to answer every question and to make plans to get together with people she had no intention of seeing. She hugged Emily the way Isabel would have, with a perfect degree of appreciation for Emily's pregnant and furious state. Clare went upstairs and lay down on the big bed and cried into the big, tailored pillows William used for reading in bed. Clare held his reading glasses like a rosary. Clare walked over to the dresser and took out one of William's big Irish linen handkerchiefs and blotted her face with it. (Clare and Isabel did their dressers the same way, William said: odds and ends in the top drawer, then underwear, then sweaters, then jeans and T-shirts and white socks. Clare put William's almost empty bottle of Tabac in her underwear drawer.) She rearranged their two unlikely stuffed animals.

'Oh, rhino and pecker bird,' William had said. That's how he saw them, and two years ago Clare had found herself in front of a fancy toy store in Guilford on a spring afternoon and found herself buying a very expensive plush gray rhino and a velvety little brown-and-white bird and putting the pair on their bed that night.

'You're not so tough,' William had said.

'I was,' Clare said. 'You've ruined me.'

Clare wanted to talk with Isabel about Emily; they used to talk about her all the time. Once, after William's second heart attack, when William was still Isabel's husband, Isabel and Clare were playing cards in William's hospital room and Emily and Kurt had just gone off to get sandwiches and Clare had stumbled over something nice to say about Kurt, and Isabel slapped down her cards and said, 'Say what you want. He's dumb in that awful preppy way and a Republican and if he says, "No disrespect intended," one more time, I'm going to set him on fire.' William said, '*De gustibus non est disputandum*,' which he said about many things, and Isabel said, 'That doesn't help, darling.'

Clare looked at William's lapis cuff links and at the watch she'd given him when they were in the third act of their affair. 'You can't give me a watch,' he'd said. 'I already have a perfectly good one.' Clare took his watch off his wrist, laid it on the asphalt, and drove over it, twice. 'There,' she'd said. 'Terrible accident, you

were so careless. You had to replace it.' William took that beautiful watch she'd bought him out of the box and kissed her in the
parking lot of a Marriott halfway between his home and hers.
He'd worn it every day until last Thursday. Clare walked downstairs holding William's jewelry, and when she passed her sons
pouring wine for people, she dropped the watch into Danny's
pocket. Adam turned to her and said, 'Mom, do you want a few
minutes alone?' and Clare realized the time upstairs had done her
no good at all. She laid the lapis cuff links in Adam's free hand.
'William particularly wanted you to have these,' she said, and
Adam looked surprised – as well he might, Clare thought.

Clare took the semester off. She spent weeks in the public library,
crying and wandering up and down the mystery section, looking for something she hadn't read. A woman she didn't know
popped out from behind the stacks and handed her a little ivory
pamphlet, the pages held together with a dark-blue silk ribbon.
On the front it said, GOD NEVER GIVES US MORE THAN WE CAN
BEAR. The woman ran off and Clare caught the eye of the librarian, who mouthed the words 'ovarian cancer.' Clare carried it
with her to the parking lot and looked over her shoulder to make
sure the woman was gone and then she tossed it in the trash.

After the library, Clare went to the coffeehouse or to the
Turkish restaurant, where they knew how to treat widows. Every
evening at six, men would spill out of the church across the street
from the coffeehouse. A few would smoke in the vestibule and
a few more would come in and order coffee and a couple of
cookies and sit down to play chess. They were not like the chess
players Clare had known.

One evening, one of the older men, with a tidy silver crew cut and pants yanked up a little too high, approached Clare. (William had dressed beautifully. Clare and Isabel used to talk about how beautifully he dressed; Clare said he dressed the way the Duke of Windsor would have if he'd been a hundred pounds heavier and not such a weenie and Isabel said, 'That's wonderful. May I tell him?')

The man said gently, 'Are you waiting for the meeting?'

Clare said, in her Isabel voice, that it was very kind of him to ask, but there was no meeting she was waiting for.

He said, 'Well, I see you here a lot. I thought maybe you were trying to decide whether or not to go to the next meeting.'

Clare said that she hadn't made up her mind, which could have been true. She could just as soon have gone to an AA meeting as to a No Rest for the Weary meeting or a People Sick of Life meeting. And Clare did know something about drinking, she thought. Sometime after she and William had decided, for the thousandth time, that their affair was a terrible thing, that their love for their spouses was much greater than their love for each other, that William and Isabel were *suited,* just like Charles and Clare were suited, and that the William and Clare thing was nothing more than some odd summer lightning that would pass as soon as the season changed, Clare found herself having three glasses of wine every night. Her goal, every night, was to climb into bed early, exhausted and tipsy, and fall deeply asleep before she could say anything to Charles about William. It was her version of One Day at a Time, and it worked for two years, until she woke up one night, crying and saying William's name into her pillow over and over again. Clare didn't think that that was the kind of reckless behavior that interested the people across the street.

The man put 'AA for the Older Alcoholic' in front of Clare and said, 'You're not alone.'

Clare said, 'That is *so* not true.'

She kept the orange-and-gray pamphlet on her kitchen table for a few weeks, in case anyone dropped in, because it made her laugh, the whole idea. Her favorite part (she had several, especially the stoic recitation of ruined marriages, dead children, estranged children, alcoholic children, multiple car accidents – pedestrian and vehicular – forced resignations, outright firings, embezzlements, failed suicides, diabetic comas), her absolute favorite in the category of the telling detail, was an old woman carrying a fifth of vodka hidden in a skein of yarn. Clare finally put the pamphlet away so it wouldn't worry Nelson when he came for Friday night dinner. Margaret Slater dropped him off at six and picked him up at eight-thirty, which gave her time for bingo and Nelson and Clare time to eat and play checkers or cribbage or Risk.

Nelson Slater didn't know that William's Sulka pajamas were still under Clare's pillow, that the bedroom still smelled like his cologne (and that Clare had bought two large bottles of it and sprayed the room with it, every Sunday), that his wing tips and his homely black sneakers were in the bottom of the bedroom closet. He knew that William's canes were still in the umbrella stand next to the front door and that the refrigerator was filled with William's favorite foods (chicken-liver pâté, cornichons, pickled beets, orange marmalade, and Zingerman's bacon bread) and there were always two or three large Tupperware containers of William's favorite dinners, which Clare made on Friday, when Nelson came over, and then divided in halves or quarters for the rest of the week. Nelson didn't mind. He had known and loved Clare most of his young life, and he understood old-people craziness. His great-aunt believed that every event in the Bible actually happened and left behind physical evidence you could buy, like the splinter from Noah's Ark she kept by her bed. His Cousin Chick sat on the back porch, shooting the heads off squirrels and chipmunks and reciting poetry. Nelson had known William Langford since he was five, and Nelson had gotten used to him. Mr Langford was a big man with a big laugh and a big frown. He gave Nelson credit for who he was and what he did around the house and he paid Nelson, which Clare never remembered to do. (A man has to make a living, Mr Langford had said one time, and Nelson did like that.) Nelson liked the Friday night dinners, and unless Clare started doing something really weird, like setting three places at the table, he'd keep coming over.

'Roast pork with apples and onions and a red wine sauce. And braised red cabbage. And Austrian apple cake. How's that?'

Nelson shrugged. Clare was always a good cook, but almost no one knew it. When he was six years old and eating ginger-bread in the Wexler kitchen one afternoon, Mr Wexler came home early. He reached for a piece of the warm gingerbread and Nelson told him that Clare had just baked it and Wexler looked at him in surprise. 'Mrs Wexler doesn't really cook,' he said, and Nelson had gone on eating and thought, She does for me, Mister.

Clare put the pork and apples on Nelson's plate and poured them both apple cider. When Nelson lifted the fork to his mouth and chewed and then sighed and smiled, happy to be loved and fed, Clare had to leave the kitchen for a minute.

After a year, everything was much the same. Clare fed Nelson on Friday nights, she taught half-time, she wept in the shower, and at the end of every day, she put on one of William's button-down shirts and a pair of his socks and settled down with a big book of William's or an English mystery. When the phone rang, Clare jumped.

'Clare, how are you?'

'Good, Lauren. How are you? How's Adam?'

Her daughter-in-law would not be deflected. She tried to get her husband to call his mother every Sunday night but when he didn't (and Clare could just hear him, her sweet boy, passive as granite: 'She's okay, Lauren. What do you want me to do about it?'), Lauren, who was properly brought up, made the call.

'We'd love for you to visit us, Clare.'

I bet, Clare thought. 'Oh, not until the semester ends, I can't. But you all could come out here. Anytime.'

'It really wouldn't be suitable.'

Clare said nothing.

'I mean, it just wouldn't,' Lauren said, polite and stubborn.

Clare felt sorry for her. Clare wouldn't want herself for a mother-in-law, under the best of circumstances.

'I'd love to have you visit,' Clare said. This wasn't exactly true but she would certainly rather have them in her house than be someplace that had no William in it. 'The boys' room is all set, with the bunk beds and your room, of course, for you and Adam. There's plenty of room and I hear Cirque du Soleil will be here in a few weeks.' Clare and Margaret will take Nelson, before he's too old to be seen in public with two old ladies.

Lauren's voice dropped. Clare knew she was walking from the living room, where she was watching TV and folding laundry, into a part of the house where Adam couldn't hear her.

'It doesn't matter how much room there is. Your house is like a mausoleum. How am I supposed to explain that to the boys, Clare? Am I supposed to say Grandma loved Grandpa William so much she keeps every single thing he ever owned or read or *ate* all around her?'

'I don't mind if that's what you want to tell them.'

In fact, I'll tell them myself, Little Miss Let's-Call-a-Spade-a-Gardening-Implement, Clare thought, and she could hear William saying, 'Darling, you are as clear and bright as vinegar but not everyone wants their pipes cleaned.'

'I don't want to tell them that. I want – really, we all want – for you just to begin to, oh, you know, just to get on with your life a little bit.'

Clare said, and she thought she never sounded more like Isabel, master of the even, elegant tone, 'I completely understand, Lauren, and it is very good of you to call.'

Lauren put the boys on and they said exactly what they should: Hi, Grandma, thanks for the Legos. (Clare put Post-its next to the kitchen calendar, and at the beginning of every month, she sent an educational toy to each grandchild, so no one could accuse her of neglecting them.) Lauren walked back into the living room and forced Adam to take the phone. Clare said to him, before he could speak, 'I'm all right, Adam. Not to worry,' and he said, 'I know, Mom,' and Clare asked about his work and Lauren's classes and she asked about Jason's karate and the baby's teeth, and when she could do nothing more, she said, 'Oh, I'll let you go now, honey,' and she sat on the floor, with the phone still in her hand.

One Sunday, Danny called and said, 'Have you heard about Dad?' And Clare's heart clutched, just as people describe, and when she didn't say anything, Danny cleared his throat and said, 'I thought you might have heard. Dad's getting married.' Clare was so relieved she was practically giddy. 'Oh, wonderful,' she said. 'That nice, tall woman who golfs?' Danny laughed. Almost everything you could say about his future stepmother pointed directly to the ways she was not his mother – particularly nice, tall, and golfs. Clare got off the phone and sent Charles and his bride – she didn't remember her name, so she sent it to Mr and Mrs Charles Wexler, which had a nice old-fashioned ring to it – a big pretty Tiffany vase of the kind she'd wanted when she married Charles.

The only calls Clare made were to Isabel. She called in the early evening, before Isabel turned in. (There was nothing she didn't know about Isabel's habits. They'd shared a beach house three summers in a row and she'd slept in their guest room in Boston a dozen times. She knew Isabel's taste in linens, in kitchens, in moisturizer and make-up and movies. There was not a single place on earth that you could put Clare that she couldn't point out to you what would suit Isabel and what would not.) She dialed her number, William's old number, and when Isabel answered, she hung up, of course.

Clare called Isabel about once a week, after watching *Widow's Walk,* the most repulsive and irresistible show she'd ever seen. Three, sometimes four women sat around and said things like, 'It's not an ending; it's a beginning.' What made it bearable to Clare was that the women were all ardent Catholics and not like her, except the discussion leader, who was so obviously Jewish and from the Bronx that Clare had to Google her and discover that she had a Ph.D. in philosophical something and converted to Catholicism after a personal tragedy. Clare got to hear a woman who sounded a lot like her great-aunt Frieda say, 'I pray for all widows, and we must all keep on with our faith and never forget that Jesus meets every need.' Clare waited for the punch line, for the woman to yank her cross off her neck and say, 'And if you believe that, *bubbeleh,* I've got a bridge I'd like to sell you,' but she never did. She did sometimes say, in the testing, poking tone of a good rabbi, 'Isn't it interesting that so many women saints came to their sainthood through being widows? They were poor and desperate, alone in the world with no protection, but the sisters took them in and even educated their children. Isn't it *interesting* that widowhood led them to become saints and extraordinary women, to know themselves and Jesus better?' The other widows, the real Catholics, didn't look interested at all. The good-looking one, in a red suit and red high heels, kept reminding everyone that she was very recently widowed (and young, and pretty) and the other two, a garden gnome in baggy pants and black sneakers that didn't touch the floor and a tall woman in a frilly blouse with her glasses taped together at the bridge, talked, in genuinely heartbroken tones, about their lives now that they were alone. They rarely mentioned their husbands, although the gnome did say, more than once, that if she could forgive her late husband, anyone could forgive anyone.

Clare dials, as soon as the organ music dies down, and Isabel picks up after one ring. Clare doesn't speak.

'Clare?'

Clare sighs. Hanging up was bad enough.

'Isabel.'

Isabel sighs as well.

'I saw Emily a few weeks ago. I dropped off a birthday present for baby Charlotte. She's beautiful. Emily seems very happy. I mean, not to see me, but in general.'

'Yes, she told me.'

'I shouldn't have gone.'

'Well. If you want to offer a relationship and generous gifts, it's up to Emily. Kurt's mother's dead. I guess it depends on how many grandmothers Emily wants Charlotte to have, regardless of who they are.' There was no one like Isabel.

'I guess it does. I mean, I'm not going to presume. I'm not going to drop in all the time with a box of rugelach and a hand-knit sweater.'

'I wouldn't think so. Clare—'

'Oh, Isabel, I miss you.'

'Good night, Clare.'

When Clare gets off the phone, there's a raccoon in her kitchen, on the counter. It, although Clare immediately thinks He, is eating a slice of bacon bread. He's holding it in his small, nimble, and very human black hands. He looks at her over the edge of the bread, like a man peering over his glasses. A fat, bold, imperturbable man with a twinkle in his dark eyes.

Even though she knows better, even though William would have been very annoyed at her for doing so, Clare says, softly, 'William.'

The raccoon doesn't answer and Clare smiles. She wouldn't have wanted the raccoon to say, 'Clare.' Because then she would have had to call her boys and have herself committed, and although this is not the life she hoped to have, it's certainly better than being in a psychiatric hospital. The raccoon has started on his second slice of bacon bread. Clare would like to put out the orange marmalade and a little plate of honey. William never ate peanut butter, but Clare wants to open a jar for the raccoon. She's read that they love peanut butter, and she doesn't want him to leave.

In an ideal world, the raccoon would give Clare advice. He

would speak to her like Quan Yin, the Buddhist goddess of compassion and mercy. Or he would speak to her like Saint Paula, the patron saint of widows, about whom Clare has heard so much lately.

Clare says, without moving, 'And why is Saint Paula a saint? She dumps her four kids at a convent, after the youngest dies. She runs off to *hajira* with Saint Jerome. How is that a saint? You've got shitty mothers all over America who would love to dump their kids and travel.'

The raccoon nibbles at the crust.

'Oh, it's very hard,' Clare says, sitting down slowly and not too close. 'Oh, I miss him so much. I didn't know. I didn't know that I would be like this, that this is what happens when you love someone like that. I had no idea. No one says, There's no happy ending at all. No one says, If you could look ahead, you might want to stop now. I know, I know, I know I was lucky. I was luckier than anyone to have had what I had. I know now. I do, really.'

The raccoon picks up two large crumbs and tosses them into his mouth. He scans the counter and the canisters and looks closely at Clare. He hops down from the counter to the kitchen stool and onto the floor and strolls out the kitchen door.

Clare told Nelson about the raccoon and they encouraged him with heels of bread and plastic containers of peanut butter leading up the kitchen steps, but he didn't come back. She told Margaret Slater, who said she was lucky not to have gotten rabies, and she told Adam and Danny, who said the same thing. She bought a stuffed-animal raccoon with round black velvet paws much nicer than the actual raccoon's, and she put him on her bed with the rhino and the little bird and William's big pillows. She told little Charlotte raccoon stories when she came to babysit (how could Emily say no to a babysitter six blocks away and free and generous with her time?). She even told Emily, who paused and said, with a little concern, that raccoons could be very dangerous.

'I don't know if you heard,' Emily said. 'My mother's getting married. A wonderful man.'

Clare bounced Charlotte on her knee. 'Oh, good. Then everyone is happy.'

Opening the Hands Between Here and Here

On the dark road, only the weight of the rope.
Yet the horse is there.

JANE HIRSHFIELD

Between Here and Here

For ESBL

I had always planned to kill my father. When I was ten, I drew a picture of a grave with ALVIN LOWALD written on the tombstone, on the wall behind my dresser. From time to time, I would add a spray of weeds or a creeping vine. By the time I was in junior high, there were trees hung with kudzu, cracks in the granite, and a few dark daisies springing up. Once, when my mother wouldn't let me ride my bike into town, I wrote, *Peggy Lowald is a fat stupid cow* behind the dresser but I went back the same day and scribbled over it with black Magic Marker because most of the time I did love my mother and I knew she loved me. The whole family knew that my mother's feelings were Sensitive and Easily Hurt. My father said so, all the time. My father's feelings were also sensitive, but not in a way that I understood the word, at ten; it might be more accurate to say that he was extremely responsive. My brother, Andy, drew cartoon weather maps of my father's feelings: dark clouds of I Hate You, giving way to the sleet of Who Are You, pierced by bolts of Black Rage.

Most of the mothers in our neighborhood were housewives, like my mother. But my mother was really a very good cook and a very accomplished hostess, even if the things she made and the way she entertained is not how I would have done it (red, white, and blue frilled toothpicks in lamb sausage pigs-in-blankets on the Fourth of July, trays of deviled eggs and *oeufs en gelée* – with tiny tulips of chive and egg yolk decorating each *oeuf* – to celebrate spring). My mother worked hard at what she considered her job, with no thanks from us and no pay, aside from the right to stay home.

Five minutes before the start of a cocktail party or bridge night, my father would make himself comfortable on the living-room couch, dropping cigar ash on the navy-blue velvet cushions, or he'd stand in the kitchen in his underwear, reading the newspaper while my mother and I put out platters and laid hors d'oeuvres around him. Sometimes, he'd sit down at the kitchen table and open the newspaper wide, lowering it almost to the tabletop, so we'd have to move the serving dishes to the counter. One July Fourth, when I was about twelve and Andy was ten, my father picked up an angel on horseback as my mother was carrying the tray past him. 'What is this, shit on a stick,' he said, and knocked the whole plate out of her hands, and then there we were, my mother and Andy and me, scrabbling to grab the hot, damp, oily little things from under the sideboard and out of the ficus plants. My father picked up a couple and put them in my mother's apron pocket, saying, 'You kids crack me up.' He was still chuckling when the doorbell rang and my mother went back into the kitchen and Andy and I went to our rooms, and he was still smiling when he opened the door for Mr and Mrs Rachlin, who were always the first.

When I got to college, other people's stories were much worse. A girl down the hall told her parents she was pregnant her senior year of high school and they drove her to a home for unwed mothers on Christmas Eve and moved out of town. A boy I liked had a long, ropy scar on his back from a belt; my roommate had cigarette burns on her instep. Gross cruelty with canapés and bad temper hardly seemed worth mentioning. (Amazingly, my brother chose to come out to both my parents his sophomore year. He said my mother wiped away a quick tear and hugged him and thanked him for telling her, and just as I was about to say, Good for Mom, Andy told me that Dad had lowered his newspaper, poked him in the stomach, and said, 'A fat fag? Not much fun in that,' and gone back to his paper.) In law school, at night, over drinks, everyone told funnier family stories and no one pulled up their shirt or rolled down their socks to show their scars. When it got really late, a few guys told my kind of stories and then they would say, frankly or sadly or fondly, that these things happened only when the old man had been drinking.

My father didn't drink. He had a glass of white wine at the cocktail parties, and in the summertime, when he was grilling hamburgers, he'd have a beer. One glass of wine. One beer. I didn't have to watch to see if this was the drink that turned Good Daddy into Bad Daddy; there was no slow, nightly disintegration of the self. I never had to tiptoe around Daddy Sleeping It Off, because my father took a four-mile walk every day, and if it rained, he spent an hour on the rowing machine in the basement. Andy and I always caught the late bus home, and after dinner we did our homework in our rooms, and when I got a stereo for my fifteenth birthday, Andy and I would lie on my floor and listen to loud rock and roll, very, very quietly.

'Am I talking to myself, goddammit?' my father said one night at dinner, and in the silence Andy said, 'I guess so, Dad,' and I laughed, which I knew was a mistake even as my lips parted, and my father stood up, hands wandering from head to head, unable to choose which one of us to kill first. I pushed Andy under the table and pulled him down the hall to my bedroom and pressed the lousy little push-button lock on the door. My father threw our dinners on the floor. My mother was still sitting at the table, trying to be calm, which did sometimes work, and sometimes not, as when he took her two favorite silk scarves and used them to stake his tomato plants, or another time, famous in our family, when he drove her car to a used-car lot, sold it, and took a cab home with a bag of cash in one hand and a box of pizza in the other.

'You could kill yourself on these creamed onions,' he said, stepping over them, and I could hear my mother murmuring agreement and I heard him say, pleasantly, that sometimes the kids were too smart for their own damned good. I heard my mother agree with that, too, and my father said he would catch the tail end of the news. About an hour later, my mother knocked on my door and handed us two plates of plastic-wrapped dinner, the meat-loaf slices reconstructed and carrot-raisin salad instead of the creamed onions.

I dated a few boys of the kind you'd expect from a girl like me with a father like that, with no real harm done, and in the middle of law school, I met Jay Johnson. I won him the way poor people occasionally win the lottery: Shameless perseverance and embarrassingly dumb luck, and every time I see one of those sly, toothless, beaten-down souls on TV holding a winning ticket, I think, Go, team. When we went to his family in Wisconsin to announce our engagement (on our side, my mother took us both to lunch at her favorite restaurant on Northern Boulevard and my father met Jay the night before the wedding), I found a second family; the Johnson women were good, tireless cooks and all the men, including mine, could build you a willow rocking chair or a pair of handsome nightstands in just a few afternoons. And, as it happened, almost all of them were recovering alcoholics. I fell in love with them all. The Johnsons drank coffee and Diet Coke all day (even the toddlers had highballs of fresh milk with a splash of black coffee at breakfast) and at cocktail hour my mother-in-law served Ritz crackers with cheddar cheese and a giant pitcher of Virgin Marys with Tabasco and celery sticks for garnish. You could smoke a pack of cigarettes or eat an entire sheet of crumb cake if you wanted and no one said a word. Most of the Johnsons are obese chain-smokers, and if, like me, you are not, and on top of that, never drank to excess, you are admired almost every day, from every angle. I am the Jackie Kennedy of the Johnson family and it's been a wonderful thing. We still go to Racine for the major holidays.

My brother went a different way, as casting directors like to say in Hollywood, which is where he settled and what he became. After twenty years of smoking pot every day, for his health, as he put it, Andy found himself at a dinner party in West Hollywood, seated next to a handsome tree surgeon in good, but not coke-fueled, spirits, with compatible politics, no diseases, and absolutely no interest in celebrities. According to Andy, who was calling me with updates from restaurant vestibules, men's clothing stores, and his own bathroom, they had amazing sex fourteen days in a row, without pot or liquor, at the end of which Andy said, Please, marry me, and Michael said, You bet, and they bought a house in Silver Lake the day it went on the market. Andy said that if Michael and affordable housing weren't signs of a Higher Power, he didn't know what were and he quit every-thing cold turkey the day they moved in, dropping off a four-hundred-dollar Moroccan hookah and a bunch of hand-blown glass bongs at the men's homeless shelter on the way. For the last eight years, he's been doing an hour of yoga every morn-ing, much the way the Johnsons drink coffee, bake, and whittle. Aside from being in much better shape than he used to be, Andy is the same good and dear person he always was, although Michael says, when I'm visiting, as I'm sure Jay says about me, it's not all sweetness and light. You will have noticed that neither of us has children.

I'd been waiting for the call about my father since he turned sev-enty. I thought that would be a nice gift from the universe – ten or fifteen healthy years of widowhood for my mother, traveling with friends, taking courses at the Elderhostel, and winding up in her eighties on a hotel veranda sipping a tall, fruity drink with someone who looked like Mr Rachlin. I hoped Mr Rachlin was still alive and I hoped that my father wouldn't dawdle in shuffling off this mortal coil. He'd had a fairly serious car accident when he was sixty-eight, which left him limping a little, and he was a heavy cigar smoker, which seemed promising. I sent him crys-tal ashtrays and silver cigar cutters for his birthdays, expensive humidors and a subscription to that stupid cigar magazine for Christmas, and when friends went to Cuba, I'd ask them to bring back a box for my father. I was, roughly speaking, watching the clock.

Their next-door neighbor found my name on the tiny phone list my mother kept taped to the kitchen wall. Your father's too upset, Mrs Cannon said, so I'm calling. Andy and I met at the airport and rented a car and drove to our house. Mrs Rachlin greeted us very warmly and Mr Rachlin waited in the living room, sitting next to my father, who was reading the paper. Mr Rachlin jumped up to hug us. He jerked his head toward my father. 'It hasn't really sunk in,' he said, and Andy and I nodded. My father said, 'Hey, kids.' Mrs Cannon left a lasagna on the kitchen table. Broadway Delicatessen delivered platters twice, fried chicken from the hospital where my mother volunteered, and right before dinnertime, six pounds of corned beef and pastrami, with a pound each of cole slaw and kosher dills, from my father's law firm. We let the Rachlins go home and I gave Mr Rachlin a little kiss for my mother's sake. My father unwrapped the corned beef and made himself a sandwich.

'You kids want some?'

We said we weren't hungry. My father ate his sandwich over the sink.

'You slimmed down,' he said to Andy. 'The trick is keeping it off. Discipline. Without that, the avoirdupois just piles back on.'

I put all the food in the fridge and, for the same reason that I still recut the flowers in a bouquet before I put them in a vase with an aspirin and always put scented soaps in with my underwear and cedar chips in with my sweaters in May, that is, because I am my mother's daughter, I made us all sit down in the living room, To Talk.

'Go ahead,' my father said, flirting with a corner of the front page.

'Daddy,' is how I started, and I couldn't say another word. On the phone I always called him Alvin, as if it were a joke.

Andy picked up the ball and ran with it. Nope, my father said. No sitting shiva; your mother and I didn't believe in that. And no memorial service; your mother wouldn't have wanted that. I couldn't imagine why she wouldn't have wanted it but my father was adamant about everything. Cremation, he said; your mother felt very strongly about that – you know she hated cemeteries. And I'll take care of it.

'We'd like to participate,' I said.

'The fact is,' my father said, 'I already had it taken care of.'

'Where's the urn,' I said.

My father laughed. 'What, you don't believe me?' He pointed to the sideboard, and we saw a black box about the size of a lunch thermos and sealed with gold tape, sitting next to a bottle of Tia Maria, two bottles of sherry, and a bottle of Scotch someone gave my father fourteen years ago. Andy and I got up to look at it.

'And the will,' my brother said. 'I'm just asking because—

'She left everything to me,' my father said, 'but if you kids want something from her jewelry box, go ahead and take it.'

My father picked up the paper in both hands, and we went into their bedroom, which was as neat as it always had been, except for my father's underwear on my mother's bargello bench. Her jewelry box was on their dresser, centered beneath their big Venetian mirror.

'I wish she had something you'd want,' I said.

'She kept Poppa's watch in the bottom,' he said. 'I'll take that. I don't think the Erwin Pearl clip-ons are going to work for me.'

Our grandfather's handsome old Hamilton watch was not in the bottom of her jewelry box. And her good pearls were gone and her diamond watch and the sapphire earrings and matching bracelet she'd bought for herself on her sixtieth birthday, cashing in the bonds her father left her.

'Daddy,' I said. 'Mom's good stuff is missing.'

'Nothing's missing,' he said coldly, and I thought, Christ, I'm going to have to show him, but he cleared his throat and said, 'I put all of her valuables in a safety-deposit box. With people in and out of the house, it seemed smart.'

There was no answer to that. 'Oh, good thinking,' I said. I went back to their bedroom with a handful of plastic bags.

'Just take half of it,' I told Andy. 'In case you have a daughter or you have a friend with a daughter or you start dressing up. Just take half of every fucking thing that's in there.'

He picked up a turquoise bracelet and a handful of cheap Indian bangles and I nodded. I put the beautiful Italian shoes she stopped wearing when she got bunions into a garbage bag and I put the beautiful heavy silk French scarves that she wore until she died in my suitcase. When Andy and I had cleaned out her closet and her jewelry box, leaving her track suits and sneakers and her sensible poly-silk blouses for my father to deal with, we went into my room. I pressed the push lock on the door.

'Please sleep in here,' I said.

Andy patted my hand. 'We didn't say good night.'

'Good night,' we both yelled through the closed door.

'Good night, kids,' he yelled back. 'I'll be back for lunch.'

We took a walk in the morning and threw some bad costume jewelry (Boca Bohemian, Oaxaca Farm Girl) into Long Island Sound and cried and talked while the gulls circled and we waited until my father came back. I made three corned-beef-pastrami-and-cole-slaw sandwiches and we each took an A&P diet soda from the case on the kitchen counter.

'So,' Andy said. 'No service, no interment, no obit, and no visiting. Is that it?'

'That's it,' my father said.

'Do you need anything?' I said.

'Like what?' my father said.

'We'll head to the airport this afternoon, then,' Andy said.

'Sure,' my father said. 'You've got jobs, don't you?'

I didn't stop speaking to my father. I did what my mother would have wanted me to do. (I like to think that her wish was for my father to have slipped painlessly and just hours after Andy was born into a deep crack in the world and never return, but I could never get her to say so. What I wanted was to have come out of her womb armed to my little baby lips and killed him with my superpowers before the cord was cut.) My weekly phone calls had none of my mother's social flourishes. (It doesn't hurt to be nice, she said, but that wasn't true in this case.) I did make sure my father wasn't dead and that he was not, with his driving, a danger to others or, with some old-man slippage in hygiene or nutrition, a danger to himself. I hired Delphine Jones to keep the house tidy and to look in on him three times a week, and when she couldn't stand him anymore ('Your father is a very exacting man,' she said, her island lilt just about knocked flat after days and weeks with Alvin Lowald), she would pass him on to a colleague for a week of R & R.

Delphine called me on a Wednesday afternoon in January.

'I see the pipes have burst,' she said. 'Your father isn't sure who to call.'

I called Andy, and he called a plumber, who, for only fourteen hundred dollars up front, would make things right, and I found the Cutler Brothers Catastrophe Company, whose receptionist said, very kindly, that they specialized in 'this kind of thing,' and I canceled my appointments and got back on a plane to make sure that things were okay. ('I'll give you a million dollars if I don't have to go this time' Andy said. 'Seriously. I will give you

a weekend at the spa of your choice. I will buy you diamond earrings.')

I rang the doorbell and my father let me in. Aside from needing
a haircut, he looked good. The house did not. And it smelled the
way it had forty years ago, when our whole family sat on the
kitchen porch and watched Long Island Sound rise past the pear
tree and onto the driveway and then into the TV room, which
had never really recovered.

'Better late than never,' he said. 'The girl left a note for
you.'

The note said, as I knew it would, that Delphine found herself too busy to clean for my father, and it was her distinct
impression that he actually needed more than a cleaning person
since, as she wrote in her neat, curvy handwriting, there was an
exceptional amount of filth and personal uncleanliness accumu-
lating from week to week (she itemized the most offensive
occurrences at the bottom of the page). She was happy to rec-
ommend Beate Jaszulski, a Polish person who had been a nurse
in Poland and whom she had met at adult education. She left me
Beate's number. My father and I ate the only things in the refrigerator, hard-boiled eggs and American cheese, and he asked why
Andy hadn't come. I said Andy was very busy, and my father
snorted.

'Busy sucking some guy's cock,' my father said.

'You know,' I said conversationally, 'we try to be nice to you.
We try to be nice, which isn't easy because you are an emotional
black hole and the coldest, most self-centered sonofabitch I have
ever known, we try to be nice in honor of our mother's memory.
So, if you can't be civil, why don't you just shut the fuck up?'

My father took his slice of cheese into the living room and read until he heard me go to bed.

In the morning, I showered with my mother's Arpège bath soap and used her antique hair dryer and got dressed and started again. I suggested that it might be wise to sell the house and move into assisted living. Near me, I even said.

'The only way I'm leaving this house is feet first,' he said.

I have to say, I did laugh and I did say, 'That's not a problem.' Oh, we should have smothered him the night after my mother died, we should have just snuck into their bedroom, pulled back that Venetian damask duvet cover she was so proud of, put the matching pillows over his face, and leaned in until he stopped moving.

'Look,' I said, 'You can sell the house and move into assisted living or you can keep the house and hire someone to care for you – a housekeeper-type person – and you do that for as long as you can afford it, and then your backup plan is you die before you run out of money.'

'Fine,' my father said. 'Hire someone. A nice pair of tits wouldn't hurt.'

Beate Jaszulski moved into my old room. My father handed her the car keys. (What do I need the hassle for? People drive like goddamn idiots around here anyway.) And every Friday, she dropped him off at the five o'clock movie, while she did the grocery shopping. She kept the house clean, he said (You can eat off the goddamn floor) and cooked the meals he preferred (Just plain food, he said, no French song and dance). Two boiled eggs and dry rye toast every morning, a grilled cheese sandwich every day for lunch, and two broiled lamb chops and rice for dinner, or sometimes, caution to the winds, she cooked a small rib eye with a side of mashed potatoes. I know this because I spoke to Beate every Sunday and she would recite the meals cooked, the walks taken, the minor household repairs her cousin Janek performed and she billed us for. She never complained about my father and she never criticized me for not visiting. At the end of every conversation, I'd ask to speak with my father, and she'd say, 'Sure. Sure, you want to talk to Dad,' sympathetically, as if she understood that I was so eager to talk to him, I just couldn't stand another moment of chitchat.

'Alvin,' I said.

'Alison.'

'How's it going?'

'Can't complain.'

'Okay. Good. Everything good with Beate?' What did I think? She would rob him and he would know and report it to me, in due time? She would, at not quite five feet tall and as big around, and sixty-five if she was a day, hurt him or seduce him?

'It's okay.' Sometimes he would tell me that Beate listened to the radio too loud or used too much ammonia on the kitchen floor or he'd found the lamb a little tough, and I would mention these things to her very delicately and she'd say, 'I take care of it.' No complaint was ever repeated. Andy referred to her as Mother Beate and he made a lot of jokes about the number of old men she had buried and their grateful children. ('That's how she got that Porsche and that house in Cap-Ferrat,' he said. 'God bless her.')

*

After about a year with Beate:

'Alvin,' I said.

'Alison. Alibaloo.'

'Dad? Are you all right?'

'Never better. Bea – how am I?'

I heard Beate talking in the background and my father chuckled and he said, 'There you go. I'm – how old am I, Bea? – there you go, I'm eighty-eight and holding my own. No pun intended.'

Beate got on the phone and told me that her own mother was dying in Poland and she had to fly home.

'Just for a week. I be back for Mr Lovald. I go on a Saturday, I be back on a Sunday.'

I asked if Beate had any thoughts about who would keep my father company, make his meals, drive him on his errands, do his laundry. 'Forget the laundry,' I said. 'It can pile up for a week. Who will do the other things,' I asked Beate, and there was a long, flat Polish silence.

'Fine,' I said. 'I'll be there Saturday and we can do the . . . handoff.'

Beate understood well enough what I meant and her voice brightened as we went back to her plans, which included drycleaning her raincoat, buying a pair of good boots, laying in a supply of frozen lamb chops and clean boxers for my father for a week, and bringing peanut butter to Ruda Slaska.

'Janek will take me to airport,' she said. 'Newark.'

My cab pulled up in front of the house at four o'clock. Beate showed me the eggs, the sliced American cheese, the rye bread, and the fourteen frozen lamb chops. She handed me the keys. She gestured toward my parents' bedroom.

'He naps,' she said. 'I see him Sunday. Seven days.' She held up seven fingers and then she picked up her suitcase and waved good-bye. As she stepped onto the porch, a car appeared, and my guess was that her cousin had parked up the street and was just waiting for my cab to leave.

Beate was out the door, and it would be just me and Alvin for the next seven days, unless I killed him, in which case I would spend at least half the week in jail. The house looked, somehow, more like my childhood home than it had for the last twenty years. Beate had found my mother's old spring slipcovers and covered the cigar-burned navy couch with pink and yellow chintz and she'd even found the yellow chintz pillows and the yellow-and-white-striped slipcover that went on my father's arm-chair. It was all aggressively and hopelessly cheerful, and I expected my mother to walk out of the kitchen, wiping her hands on a clean apron, and saying either, 'Who wants quiche?' which was a good day or, 'There's no reason to upset him,' which was not.

'Bea? Bea?' My father was yelling, pretty loudly.

I opened the door a crack. I had no wish to be in my parents' bedroom with my father, where he still slept on his side of the bed and where there was still, on my mother's nightstand, a box of tissues and a paperback.

'It's me, Dad. It's Alison. Beate'll be back in a week. I'm here in the meantime.'

'What?' he said and he sat up, patting his nightstand all over for his glasses, which were lying on the floor. I handed him his glasses.

'Thank you. You're a good kid,' he said.

His hair was going in four different directions and there were little scabs on his chest and the backs of his hands. He scratched a scab until it bled and he pressed his bleeding wrist against the sheet.

'Where's Bea?'

'She's gone to see her mother. In Poland. Her mother's not well,' I said, and I was trying not to yell because I knew that yelling did not help people understand you better.

'That's a shame,' he said. 'My mother died when I was nineteen and my father, I don't think he got over it. He became an old man overnight. You know what I mean?' I did know what he meant, of course, but since I had never heard my father mention his mother or his father or the emotional state of any living being, I was speechless.

'An old man overnight, Alison,' he said.

'I know what you mean,' I said. 'You want some lunch?'

I made two grilled cheese sandwiches and I wondered whether I should offer my father a beer, since on one hand, I had no idea who he was and in his altered state, alcohol might be bad for him, and on the other hand, what the hell. My father and I had our sandwiches. ('Burn it,' he said. 'That's what they used to say in the diner. Put a farmer on the raft and burn it.' 'What diner?' I said, and my father said, not unkindly, 'Well, you're no Julia Child.') And we drank our beers.

'*Salud, amor, y dinero*,' he said and clinked my bottle. 'Is everybody okay?'

'Sure,' I said. I didn't know who everybody was. He called Andy Fatso, he called Michael The Faigele, he called Jay Babe, the Blue Ox, and my mother had been dead for two years.

'I'll take a grilled cheese sandwich,' he said.

'Another? Okay.' Was this good? It could be good, an appetite for life or something like that, or it could be that he didn't know if he'd eaten or not.

'Can't I get some lunch?' he said, and I made the sandwich, which he nibbled and then he said, 'I'm gonna take a little nap.' He stood up and waited for me to stand up.

I walked him to the bedroom and to his bed and he used my arm to swing himself into bed.

'Good kid,' he said, patting my face.

I called Jay and he said, 'You are too Julia Child,' and we exchanged I love yous and he said, 'Hurry home,' and I said I would.

I called my brother and told him that he might not want to miss the Second Coming of Alvin Lowald, in which our father had been snatched by pod people who'd sent us a nice old man who thanked me and called me a good kid.

'Is this permanent?' Andy asked.

'I don't know. Maybe he'll be back to normal tomorrow.'

'Great. Back to the crypt. Does it *seem* like he's dying – is this pre-death niceness?'

I swore to him that our father did not seem to be dying, that he had done a good job on one and a half grilled cheese sandwiches and all of a Heineken and was now snoring loudly in his bed. Andy swore back that he would get on the redeye Thursday night, as soon as they were done casting a police drama in which none of the criminals or women could be more than five feet five, which was the height of this particular TV detective.

'Does he know you?' Andy said.

'I don't know. He looks glad to see me, so no. But he called me Alison, so yes.'

'See you Friday, unless he completely recovers, in which case you won't see me at all.'

'You better get me those earrings,' I said, and we hung up. I read my father's magazines until I fell asleep.

*

In my dream, it is pouring rain and I am driving our old Dodge Dart. My father's standing patiently on the steps of the old library, without a coat or an umbrella. He gets into the car and I have to help him with his seat belt. He clasps his wet hands in his lap. I want to drive him to his new apartment in the assisted living place, but he doesn't know the address and neither do I.

I'll just pop out here for directions, Daddy, I say, hoping that the two women I see standing under the green awning of a pretty restaurant will be knowledgeable and helpful and guide us to the assisted living place. They're not and they don't. One of the women says, Is that your father in the car? And I say, yes, that's why we're looking for his apartment, and she says she certainly never drove her father all over kingdom come in a goddamned monsoon without even an address, and the other one says, What a harebrained scheme, and they sound, together, exactly like my father, as I've known him. I get back into the car and my father looks at me with hope and just a little anxiety.

Is everybody okay? he says.

Yes, we are, I say, and I just start driving in the pouring rain, hoping that one of us will see something familiar.

My father yelled, 'Bea, Bea,' and I woke up and ran down the hall. I turned on the overhead light and handed my father his glasses as I sat down on the edge of the bed.

'Oh,' he said, and he clutched my hand. Any fool could see that he knew it was me. 'You're here.'

'I'm here. You probably had a bad dream,' I said.

'Could be.' He'd already lost interest. 'That's a pretty necklace,' he said. 'Was it your mother's?'

'No. I don't have any of Mom's jewelry.'

'That's a shame,' he said. 'I would think you'd have kept a few of her things, to remind you.'

I nodded.

'Well, we were a lucky family,' he said. 'All around us those years, kids were doing drugs, getting in trouble. People were divorcing, right and left. I always used to say, you know, at parties or things, "This is my original wife." We were lucky.'

I nodded again and took such a deep breath I felt my ribs separating from my sternum.

My father lay back down and I patted his hand. I smoothed the sheet.

'I'm going to turn out the light. I'll see you in the morning.'

I got to the door and turned off the light.

My father said, 'Is everybody okay?'

Permafrost

Terrible is terrible, Frances thought. There's no comparing one
bad thing to another. Whatever it is – hands blown off in Angolan
minefields, children in Chernobyl with tumors like softballs, a car
accident right around the corner – there's no measuring suffering.
Mrs Shenker disagreed. At night, while her daughter, Beth, was
knocked out by morphine, Mrs Shenker sat in the solarium, the
waiting room for the adolescent-medicine unit. She sat back in a
recliner and read aloud from her stack of printouts about the flesh-
eating bacteria that had attacked Beth nine days ago.

'Listen to this one,' she said to Frances. 'And hold on to your
hat. "I was diagnosed with necrotizing fasciitis after a vacation in
the Bahamas. We still don't know what caused it. Even though
I've had approximately thirty-four operations and three skin
grafts on my legs and groin and continue to have some trouble
with my lungs and kidneys, I consider myself lucky. My wife and
I have run into some financial difficulties and I am unable to
drive but we count our blessings every day." Can you fucking
believe this? Well, you probably can – you're a social worker.'

Frances could believe it. Frances's father raised Frances and her
sister, Sherri, on stories of polar expeditions that began with terrible errors in judgment and ended with men weeping over
frozen corpses, with people suffering horribly and still thanking

God for not having killed them outright when they got on the ship. When Sherri was eighteen and Frances was eleven, Sherri said, 'I want to experience Jesus' love and I want to help other young people know that they are not doomed.' 'Doomed to what?' Mr Cairn had said, but he said it to the front hall because Sherri had already run out the door, and it was no different, really, than a girl going off to be a Deadhead or driving to Los Angeles with some badass to become a porn star. When people in the neighborhood asked where Sherri was, Mr Cairn said, 'We lost her,' and nobody pressed him and they certainly didn't know he meant she'd gone to join the Exodus Ministry in Indianapolis. Sherri sent a Christmas card every year, and other than that, it was just Frances and her father, the storyteller.

S.S. *Terra Nova*

'*This* one's a day brightener,' Mrs Shenker said. 'This guy's an amputee himself, and a world-class athlete ...' Mrs Shenker skimmed ahead a few lines. 'Well, not a world-class athlete, clearly. But athletic, and he's invented these special responsive feet that give energy back to the leg, so you don't just walk around, clump, clump, clump, and there's a special suction cup so the whole leg just goes on – ' She makes a sharp, sucking sound.

Mr Shenker stood up. 'I'm going to take a little walk,' he said. Mrs Shenker and Frances saw him through the glass block wall of the solarium, chatting with Theresa the charge nurse and, like magic, two more nurses showed up and they passed a box of doughnuts around and Theresa disappeared for a moment and then reappeared, carrying real coffee cups and giving one to Mr Shenker. Mrs Shenker had the solarium and the doctors and

Mr Shenker had the nurses. Frances had bumped into him a couple of times when he was walking out of an empty exam room, straightening his tie, and when she looked over her shoulder, she saw a nurse come out and lock the door behind her. The nurses looked transformed; they looked as if they had been handed something immensely valuable and fragile, whose care could not be entrusted to ordinary women. Mr Shenker looked as he always did, handsome and doomed.

Frances said to Mrs Shenker, 'I have a few patients to check on. Do you want to sit with Beth?'

'Isn't she napping?'

Frances admitted that Beth probably was napping. (Although napping was not the right word; Beth Shenker was on enough methadone to anesthetize a three-hundred-pound man and the only thing that woke her for the first eight days was a gnawing pain of the kind you get with pancreatic cancer. On the bright side, while almost no one survives pancreatic cancer, Frances thought that Beth Shenker, like most necrotizing-fasciitis victims, would survive into old age.)

Mrs Shenker said, 'All right, it's almost time for *Judge Judy.* I'll go watch that with Beth. Tell Mr Shenker where I am, when you see him.'

Beth was dreaming. She was five, jumping up and down on her new big-girl bed in the middle of the night, clean sheets under her soft, pretty feet, the cool air tickling her soles as she jumped higher and higher, and in the dream, her little feet lit up the dark room like fireflies.

Lorraine Shenker smoothed Beth's sheet over the metal hoop that protected her legs and straightened out Beth's IV line and kept her eyes on Judge Judy, who was looking over her bifocals to tell a fat nineteen-year-old African American mother of twins that she *deserved* to lose custody of her children. The way Judge Judy waved her hand dismissively and then slipped off the bifocals to award damages to the girl's attractive, well-dressed brother, whose car the young mother had totaled while he looked after those twins, was wonderful. It would be nice if there were a *Dr* Judy, handing down diagnoses and reversing the decisions of other, dumber doctors. Dr Judy would have taken one look at Beth and said, firmly, This young lady is not going to have a gross and permanent disability. Case dismissed.

Frances walked past Beth's room, reading over Beth's chart, and by the time she got to the nurses' desk, Nathan Silverman was taking the cruller she wanted. Nathan Silverman was Beth's surgeon, and he'd done a great job and he told everyone he'd done a great job, and Frances thought, Narcissistic grandiosity with excellent fine-motor skills, and thinking that made her smile warmly whenever she ran into him.

Dr Silverman smiled back, yellow pieces of cruller flying everywhere, and Frances said, 'Hey, Dr Silverman,' and put her hand on her second choice, a chocolate doughnut. Her fingers sank deep into the chocolate icing. Dr Silverman brushed the crumbs from his tie and stretched his arms over his head. Finally, he said, 'Is Maria Lopez around?'

Frances said, 'I'm not sure. Maybe it's her break,' and she picked up a napkin with her free hand.

She didn't say, If you get a move on, you can probably catch up with Maria Lopez when she comes out of Exam Room #2, right after Mr Shenker.

'I just thought Maria might be chatting with Beth,' Dr Silverman said. 'You know, cheering her up.'

'Could be,' Frances said.

Maria Lopez was the pinup girl of the adolescent-medicine unit. She liked to slip off her white clogs and massage her lovely calves at the end of her shift and give everyone a good look at her rhinestone-studded toe ring.

What kind of grown woman wears a toe ring? Frances thought.

Dr Silverman said only, 'Let's get Beth thinking about recovery. She's just a kid, Frances.'

Frances thought about Beth's recovery all the time. Beth was thirteen, and although she could wear long sleeves to hide the river of scars that would always run up her right forearm and she could wear turtlenecks to hide the thick red web spread across her collarbone, she would always have a stump at the end of her left leg, and if Frances Cairn had had to contemplate all that at thirteen, she's pretty sure she would have flipped open her laptop as soon as she was conscious and Googled the most effective form of suicide.

S.S. *Endurance*

Dear Beth,

I hope your recovery is continuing to progress. As I hope you know, everyone at the hospital was impressed with your fortitude.

Frances crossed out 'fortitude' and wrote 'strength of character' and went back to 'fortitude,' which sounded sort of magnificent, even if Beth was unlikely to know what *fortitude* meant. Frances had never seen Beth read anything. Frances was with her every day for almost a month, holding her hands while Beth screamed as her arms and legs were debrided and bringing endless cups of juice and endless bags of ice chips. Frances watched Beth come out of two comas, and each time, she was the person who comforted Beth after Mrs Shenker and Dr Silverman had to tell Beth what day it was and how long her coma had lasted and then finally told Beth that she had only one foot. Frances did everything she could to bond with Beth and the Shenker family; at Beth's discharge, she walked the Shenkers to the lobby, she gave Beth a care package from the staff (lip balm and Lifesavers, a photo of Beth and the floor staff, a pink T-shirt that said NO LIMITS!, and a little stuffed penguin with a red-and-white Red Cross scarf around its neck). Between the multiple surgeries and the painkillers and the life ahead, Beth was hardly speaking when she left, and when Frances promised to visit Beth at home, Beth nodded, with her eyes closed, and the Shenkers drove off.

Dear Beth,

    I've been meaning to visit for the past three weeks but things have been really hectic at the hospital. Remember your old room 13a, the nicest private room? A new patient is in there. T—— has two broken legs – nothing compared to you, I know – and sadly, his father is facing charges for having thrown him off the roof of their apartment building. T——'s mother doesn't speak English and we have not yet found an Eritrean interpreter but Dr Silverman – I know you remember <u>him</u> – seems to think that if I act out each of his phrases carefully, T——'s mother will understand what's going on . . .

Frances's handwriting hadn't changed since the sixth grade. It was the round, hopeful handwriting of girls who wrote things like: *So glad we sat together in Econ! You rock. Let's B BFF. You are so awesome. Don't ever stop being who U R!* over the pictures of CLASS CUTUPS and the YOUTH EFFECTIVENESS SEMINAR; things that she, Frances, had never actually written to anyone. Frances's friends were the disfigured and the disabled, one way or another, and Beth Shenker would have been one of the pretty, giggling girls who looked right through them as they limped and staggered down the hall.

Dear Beth,

I've spoken to your parents several times and told them
of my plan to visit you. They couldn't care less, so I am
coming this Saturday morning, with cider and doughnuts.
Just like old times . . .

Kentucky Fried Chicken. ('Terrible stuff,' Mr Cairn said. 'Awful,' Frances said, and she passed the cole slaw and the biscuits they loved, a triple order every time, and the creamed spinach. It was a relief to eat hot food that neither of them had to cook, and they had done this every Friday night since Frances moved out to go to social-work school.)

'I'm raking tomorrow,' Mr Cairn said. 'Want to help out your old man?'

'I can't. I'm following up with a patient. The girl who contracted necrotizing fasciitis.'

Mr Cairn loved to hear about the dreadful things that befell Frances's people and to hear about the things that she did to help them bear their various crosses. He might have gone into social work himself, instead of hardware, if anyone had encouraged him. Mr Cairn shook his head sympathetically. 'I can't imagine.' He finished his second biscuit. 'The one with one foot and the father who's a ladies' man?' and Frances nodded. One night, instead of going back to her apartment after work, she'd driven over to watch *Law & Order* with her father, and she told him all about flesh-eating bacteria and the Shenkers.

'Is this an all-day visit?' Mr Cairn said. 'Because I don't like the sound of this household.'

'I won't be there for more than an hour.'

Mr Cairn pushed his chicken around on his plate.

'I could drive you,' he said.

'Daddy, you have to get a life.' Frances smiled when she said it.

Mr Cairn put his fork and knife on his plate and he took Frances's hand.

'There's someone special I'd like you to meet,' he said.

When Frances's mother died, her father staggered from room to room, crying. Frances and Sherri would walk into the garage for their bikes and find their father sprawled on the hood of the car, face buried in his chamois cloths. One Sunday morning, Sherri dumped a basket of wet clothes in the middle of the living room. 'I can't do it,' she said. 'I mean, I actually cannot do laundry. Daddy's crying in front of the dryer.'

The first day of first grade, Frances had to walk next door and ask Mrs Cohen to fix her hair because her father was crying so hard, he couldn't do her braids. Mrs Cohen did them and did them again the next day, and on the third day Mr Cairn took Frances to the barber and said, Please give her a haircut. Something short. And pretty.

If he had married Mrs Cohen he would not now be sitting in front of her with a crumb of fried chicken on his face, telling her to get ready to meet someone special.

'Sure,' Frances said.

'Maybe she'll take me off your hands,' Mr Cairn said.

S.S. *Endeavor*

A short, wide woman with Mrs Shenker's sharp chin and thick eyebrows opened the door.

'I am—' Frances said, trying to hold on to her muffler and her purse and the bag of doughnuts and the jug of cider and the brochure about a camp for teenagers with physical limitations, and Mr Shenker came into the front hall and opened the door wider.

'Hey. This is Miss . . . Frances,' he said. 'Sylvia, this is Frances. Frances, my mother-in-law, Sylvia Winik. Frances spent time with Beth at the hospital. Jesus, Frances, you look like Shackleton on his way to the North Pole.'

'I doubt it,' Frances said. Frances was *raised* on Ernest Shackleton and brave Robert Edwin Peary and that moron Robert Scott and the tragedy of his ponies, eaten by the explorers, because Captain Scott was too stupid to use a dog team. ('Too much an admirer of dogs, the way Englishmen sometimes are,' her father had said, as if they both knew people like that, people who loved their dogs so much they would try to go to the South Pole with horses, to spare the dogs discomfort.) Frances knew the beginnings and ends of every polar expedition and nothing she ever did was going to be like Ernest Shackleton, who was a hero in her household, like Kennedy or King, and Mr Shenker could just keep his big, fat, condescending, adulterous mouth closed.

'You might be thinking of Lawrence Oates,' Frances said, and

Mr Shenker looked at his mother-in-law and smiled. Lawrence Oates was one of the youngest men to accompany Scott and also the smartest, and when he understood he was dying of starvation and frostbite, he stopped eating entirely, gave away his compass, and lifted the flap of his tent to walk into the snow. 'I am going outside now,' he said, 'and I may be some time.' In their game of Great Expedition, this had been Frances's favorite part, and she would say those lines and run onto the porch, in her pajamas, and her father would wait just the right amount of time and then carry her back in, as if there were icicles hanging all over her and she had just hours to live.

'Lorraine,' Mr Shenker called out. 'Frances is here. From the hospital.'

Mrs Shenker came down the hall in sweatpants and a T-shirt, her hair in a ponytail.

'Frances, aren't you sweet,' she said. 'I didn't know you were ... Well, how nice. I was just doing some laundry. I thought it was going to rain, so we gave up on golf.' She put her hand on Mr Shenker's chest and he put an arm around her waist. 'You were right, I was wrong,' she said.

'We'll golf tomorrow,' he said. 'Sylvia can spoil Beth and we'll steal away.' The Shenkers and Mrs Shenker's mother all smiled at one another and finally Mrs Shenker said, 'Well, thank you for bringing a treat for Beth. Although, my God, we all ate enough doughnuts at that hospital ...'

Mr Shenker said, 'Always room for a few more.'

Mrs Shenker said, 'Let's just take a peek at Miss Beth and see how she's doing.'

'Hey, Frances,' Beth said. Beth was smiling and she wore a silky green T-shirt over her bandages and a green headband. There was a pull-up bar above her head and her bedroom was decorated like a tropical paradise. She sat in the middle of her big green-and-blue bed, surrounded by her laptop, her iPhone, and her remote control. A flat-screen TV was mounted on the opposite wall, with white-capped waves painted to unfurl around it. The doorway was as wide as a hospital room's. Pale-green mermaids raised their arms on either side of it, and there was an old-fashioned map of the world's oceans painted on the wood floor, and a wheelchair was folded up in one corner.

Mrs Shenker saw Frances looking. 'I know – we went all out. We had an architect in here and Beth drove him crazy until everything was just the way she wanted.'

Beth grinned and looked down to text someone.

'Pretty cool, right? I might become an architect. The disabled Americans thing, plus I love design. Did you see my dresser?' Her dresser was painted to look like a treasure chest, with gold coins and jewels glued all the way down the front, as if the treasure were spilling out. 'That was my idea.'

Frances sat in the small, comfortable armchair and Beth chatted a little, and answered e-mails. (Oh, my God, she said. No way. *No* way.) She texted friends and smiled at Frances to show that she didn't mean to be rude and went back to her laptop. Mrs Shenker's mother came in with a plate of peanut-butter-and-fluff sandwiches, each half topped with a strawberry slice and two glasses of milk.

'Nana, thank you,' Beth said, and her grandmother kissed her and said, 'Physical therapy in an hour, young lady,' and Beth struck a strongman pose and then offered Frances a sandwich and a napkin. Beth played some music on her computer and Frances and Beth ate their sandwiches, as if they were two girls in seventh grade, taking a homework break.

Frances ate her sandwich halves and thanked Mrs Shenker's

mother, who handed her a couple of warm cookies for the road. The Shenkers emerged arm in arm to thank Frances for coming. They told her that Beth was starting school in three weeks, and Mr Shenker said, She's nervous about it, but you know Beth — she always gets back on the horse.

Frances got in her car and drove around the corner and pulled over, to just sit for a while.

S.S. *Discovery*

Dear Beth,

I saw your picture today. Everyone in America must have seen it, plastered on the cover of People magazine. You look wonderful. Everything that was just on the cusp in you, when I knew you ten years ago, has absolutely flowered. I was sorry to read that your grandmother had passed but your parents look very well and, of course, very proud. I'm sure you are an inspiration to everyone around you, just as they said in the magazine. To have done what you've done — the Paralympics and now the triathlon and your work with teenagers — is very impressive.

Things have been quieter, here. I'm actually still at the hospital. I'm the Assistant Director of Social Work, which sounds like more than it is. I handle the scheduling and the outpatient programs but I don't do any hiring or firing.

My father — I think you met him the time my car broke down at your house — passed away about five years ago. I miss him. It's weird, at least it's weird to me, but I now spend most Friday nights with his widow, Carol Skolnick. I don't know if I ever mentioned it (probably not — we didn't

really talk about me, which was appropriate, since my home
visits were for you and to help with your post-traumatic
recovery), but my father remarried during the time you and
I were in contact. Anyway, Carol and I weren't exactly close
when my father was alive but since he died, she's reached
out to me, and now on Friday nights she lights a Yarsight
candle (I don't know if I've spelled this correctly) for my
father and for all of the other people we know who have
died (I don't include patients; we just mourn the people
we've known in our personal lives) and then we have
dinner, which is usually Kentucky Fried Chicken. It's sort
of a tradition.

The other big change is that I am in touch with my
sister, Sherri, who was not part of my life when you and I
knew each other. Sherri lives in Indianapolis and she and
her husband run a cleaning service. They clean up after
storms and other natural disasters in people's offices and
homes and also just regular cleaning. They have two girls,
who are almost as old as you were when I met you, and
they are wonderful girls. I only wish I had known them
sooner. Sherri called me after our father died and she said
to me, Your only family is me, and I remember saying that
it didn't seem like she wanted me in her life and she said
that that wasn't true, that our father had just abandoned her
after her religious experience (my sister is, I guess, a born-
again Christian and my father and I were the kind of
Congregationalists who didn't bother anyone, and I guess
that was an insurmountable difference between them, plus
my father and I thought Sherri was gay, which bothered her
more than us but she stopped being gay, apparently, when
she became born again and married Paul and had the girls).

It's a little odd being in their house sometimes, with Jesus
on every wall and pillow and Sherri censors the girls'
reading, like no Harry Potter because of the magic. (I have
to say this doesn't make any sense to me. What makes
magic particularly anti-Christian? I understand that calling
up Satan is definitely not good but I can't see how
Tinkerbell or flying carpets threaten anyone.) But it is their
house and their rules, and my nieces are happy and loving
girls, and Paul has been very welcoming in his quiet way,
and I am really grateful to spend their birthdays and
Christmas with Sherri and her family.

I've continued my interest in polar exploration and the
great expeditions, although I think it's safe to say this is not
a subject of general interest. They were just so
phenomenally brave. They lived on dog meat and willow
tea. They boiled old boots and ate them. They ate the
deerskin ties off their tents and then they cut up their tents
to make footgear, so they could go out and look for the
rescue ships. Lieutenant George DeLong of the U.S. Navy
spent two winters frozen in place 750 miles from the North
Pole, which is not that far – others had traveled farther –
and then his ship sank on June 12, 1881. There were
fourteen of them left, and still he wrote in his journal, 'All
hands weak and feeble, but cheerful.'

All my life, those men were my heroes. I think I would
have been better off with the astronauts or even the
Argonauts or with the saints, if we had been that kind of
family, or with the people who marched on Selma for their
rights. But my father loved these men and he didn't seem to
notice that they were all, really, pretty crazy and most of
them failures (Roald Amundsen was often the villain of

these stories and I think now it was because he knew what he was doing; he accomplished his goal and he went on to other successes, and all of that was despicable to my father). These people made terrible mistakes and the best and worst of them just shrugged and said that it was no one's fault at all, just the nature of life, just the inevitable outcome of what they had undertaken, but it wasn't true. They had something missing. They left things behind that other, more reasonable men would have known to bring. They brought the wrong food, and the wrong transportation. They held the fucking maps upside down half the time and one boat fell to pieces in the Arctic Ocean because, when the ship had sailed in sunnier climes, the crew had pulled nails out of it to trade for sex with the Polynesian women, since iron was so valuable. They could have been saved by vitamins, which were easy to buy and carry. They could have been saved by a wireless transmitter, which was not uncommon.

On one of Peary's expeditions, their boat was struck by moving ice, pressed between two icebergs by the current, and as the ship was sinking, water coming in through the port side, the crew and the scientists gathered a few things and scrambled onto the icy bluff. Finn Hamilton went below three times, because he couldn't decide what to take. He brought a compass and threw it to a crewmate already on land. He went down for his pipe, and halfway up the stairs, he went back down again for his Bible and he slipped and drowned, tangled up with a footstool.

Some of us are Finn Hamilton and some of us are Beth Shenker, I guess. I have somehow not had the right things for this journey and I have packed and repacked a hundred times as if somehow the right thing will be found in some small pocket, put in by someone with more sense or gift than me, but I'm always scrambling for the last-minute thing and I am always, always watching the boat pull away without me.

Your family was one of my early boats and you were the bright and amazing sail, and I am, as I said at the beginning, very, very proud of you.

By-and-by

Every death is violent.

The iris, the rainbow of the eye, closes down. The pupil spreads out like black water. It seems natural, if you are there, to push the lid down, to ease the pleated shade over the ball, down to the lower lashes. The light is out, close the door.

Mrs Warburg called me at midnight. I heard the click of her lighter and the tiny crackle of burning tobacco. Her ring bumped against the receiver.

'Are you comfortable, darling?'

I was pretty comfortable. I was lying on her daughter's bed, with my feet on Anne's yellow quilt, wearing Anne's bathrobe.

'Do you feel like talking tonight?'

Mrs Warburg was the only person I felt like talking to. My boyfriend was away. My mother was away. My father was dead. I worked in a felafel joint on Charles Street where only my boss spoke English.

I heard Mrs Warburg swallow. 'You have a drink, too. This'll be our little party.'

Mrs Warburg and I had an interstate, telephonic rum-and-Coke party twice a week the summer Anne was missing. Mrs Warburg told me about their problems with the house; they had some roof mold and a crack in the foundation, and Mr Warburg was not handy.

'Roof mold,' she said. 'When you get married, you move into a nice pre-war six in the city and you let some other girl worry about roof mold. You go out dancing.'

I know people say, and you see it in movies, cascades of hair tumble out of the coffin, long, curved nails growing over the clasped hands. It's not true. When you're dead, you're dead, and although some cells take longer to die than others, after a few hours everything is gone. The brain cells die fast, and blood pools in the soft, pressed places: the scapula, the lower back, the calves. If the body is not covered up, it produces a smell called cadaverine, and flies pick up the scent from a mile away. First, just one fly, then the rest. They lay fly eggs, and ants come, drawn to the eggs, and sometimes wasps, and always maggots. Beetles and moths, the household kind that eat your sweaters, finish the body; they undress the flesh from the bone. They are the cleanup crew.

Mrs Warburg and I only talked about Anne in passing and only about Anne in the past. Anne's tenth birthday had had a Hawaiian theme. They made a hot-dog luau in the backyard and served raspberry punch; they played pin-the-lei-on-the-donkey and had grass skirts for all the girls. 'Anne might have been a little old for that, even then. She was a sophisticate from birth,' Mrs Warburg said. I was not a sophisticate from birth. I was an idiot from birth, and that is why when the police first came to look for Anne, I said a lot of things that sounded like lies.

Mrs Warburg loved to entertain; she said Anne was her mother's daughter. We did like to have parties, and Mrs Warburg made me tell her what kind of hors d'oeuvres we served. She said she was glad we had pigs-in-blankets because that's what she'd served when she was just starting out, although she'd actually made hers. And did one of us actually make the marinara sauce, at least, and was Anne actually eating pork sausage, and she knew it must be me who made pineapple upside-down cake because that was not in her daughter's repertoire, and she hoped we used wineglasses but she had the strong suspicion we poured wine out of the box into paper cups, which was true. I told her Anne had spray-painted some of our thirdhand furniture bright gold and when we lit the candles and turned out the lights, our apartment looked extremely glamorous.

'Oh, we love glamorous,' Mrs Warburg said.

In the Adirondacks, the Glens Falls trail and the old mining roads sometimes overlap. Miles of trail around Speculator and Johnsburg are as smooth and neatly edged as garden paths. These are the old Fish Hill Mining Company roads, and they will take you firmly and smoothly from the center of Hamilton County to the center of the woods and up the mountainside. Eugene Trask took Anne and her boyfriend, Teddy Ross, when they were loading up Teddy's van in the Glens Falls parking lot. He stabbed Teddy twice in the chest with his hunting knife, and tied him to a tree and stabbed him again, and left him and his backpack right there, next to the wooden sign about NO DRINKING, NO HUNTING. He took Anne with him, in Teddy's car. They found Teddy's body three days later and his parents buried him two days after that, back in Virginia.

Eugene Trask killed another boy just a few days before he killed Teddy. Some kids from Schenectady were celebrating their high school graduation with an overnight camping trip, and when Eugene Trask came upon them, he tied them all to different trees, far enough apart so they couldn't see one another, and then he killed the boy who'd made him mad. While he was stabbing him, the same way he stabbed Teddy, two sharp holes in his heart and then a slash across his chest, for emphasis, for something, the other kids slipped out of their ropes and ran. By the time they came back with people from town, Eugene Trask had circled around the woods and was running through streams, where the dogs could not catch his scent.

The heart is really two hearts and four parts: the right and the left, and the up and the down. The right heart pumps blood through the lungs, the left through the body. Even when there is nothing more for it to do, even when you have already lost ten ounces of blood, which is all an average-size person needs to lose to bring on heart failure, the left heart keeps pumping, bringing old news to nowhere. The right heart sits still as a cave, a thin scrim of blood barely covering its floor. The less air you have, the faster the whole heart beats. Still less and the bronchioles, hollow, spongy flutes of the lungs, whistle and squeeze dry until they lie flat and hard like plates on the table, and when there is no more air and no more blood to bring help from the farthest reaches of the body, the lungs crack and chip like old china.

Mrs Warburg and I both went to psychics.

She said, 'A psychic in East Cleveland. What's that tell you?' which is why I kept talking to her even after Mr Warburg said he didn't think it was helping. Mrs Warburg's psychic lived in a run-down split-level ranch house with lime-green shag carpeting. Her psychic wore a white smock and white shoes like a nurse, and she got Mrs Warburg confused with her three o'clock, who was coming for a reading on her pancreatic cancer. Mrs Warburg's psychic didn't know where Anne was.

My psychic was on West Cedar Street, in a tiny apartment two blocks away from us on Beacon Hill. My boss's wife had lost a diamond earring and this psychic found it, my boss said. He looked like a graduate student. He was barefoot. He saw me looking down, and flexed his feet.

'Helps me concentrate,' he said.

We sat down at a dinette table and he held my hands between his. He inhaled and closed his eyes. I couldn't remember if I had the twenty dollars with me or not.

'Don't worry about it,' he said.

We sat for three minutes, and I watched the hands on the grandfather clock behind him. My aunt had the same clock, with cherrywood flowers climbing up the maple box.

'It's very dark,' he said. 'I'm sorry. It's very dark where she is.'

I found the money and he pushed it back at me, and not just out of kindness, I didn't think.

I told Mrs Warburg my psychic didn't know anything, either.

The police came on Saturday and again on Monday, but not the same ones. On Monday it was detectives from New York, and they did not treat me like the worried roommate. They reminded me that I told the Boston police I'd last seen Anne at two o'clock on Thursday, before she went to Teddy's. They said someone else had told them Anne came back to our apartment at four o'clock, to get her sleeping bag. I said yes, I remembered – I was napping and she woke me up, because it was really my sleeping bag; I lent it to her for the trip. Yes, I did see her at four, not just at two.

Were you upset she was going on this trip with Ted? they said.

Teddy, I said. Why would I be upset?

They looked around our apartment, where I had to walk through Anne's little bedroom to use the bathroom and she had to walk through my little bedroom to get to the front door, as if it were obvious why I'd be upset.

Maybe you didn't like him, they said.

I liked him, I said.

Maybe he was cutting into your time with Annie.

Anne, I said, and they looked at each other as if it was significant that I had corrected them.

Anne, they said. So maybe Teddy got in the way of your friendship with Anne?

I rolled my eyes. No, I said. We double-dated sometimes. It was cool. They looked at their notes.

You have a boyfriend? they said. We'd like to talk to him, too.

Sure, I said. He's in Maine with his family, but you can talk to him.

They shrugged a little. Maine, with parents, was not a promising lead.

They pressed me a little more about my latent lesbian feelings for Anne and my unexpressed and unrequited love for Teddy, and I said that I thought maybe I had forgotten to tell the Boston police that I had worked double shifts every day last week and that I didn't own a car. They smiled and shrugged again.

If you think of anything, they said.

It's very dark where she is, is what I thought.

The police talked to me and they talked to Rose Trask, Eugene's sister, too. She said Eugene was a worthless piece of shit. She said he owed her money and if they found him she'd like it back, please. She hid Eugene's hunting knife at the bottom of her root cellar, under the onions, and she hid Eugene in her big old-fashioned chimney until they left. Later, they made her go up in the helicopter to help them find him, and they made her call out his name over their loudspeaker: 'Eugene, I love you.

Eugene, it will be okay.' While they circled the park, which is three times the size of Yellowstone, she told the police that Eugene had worked on their uncle's farm from the time he was seven, because he was big for his age, and that he knew his way around the woods because their father threw him out of the house naked, in the middle of the night, whenever he wet his bed, which he did all his life.

Mrs Warburg said she had wanted to be a dancer and she made Anne take jazz and tap and modern all through school but what Anne really loved was talking. Debate Club, Rhetoric, Student Court, Model U.N., anything that gave you plenty of opportunity for arguing and persuading, she liked. I said I knew that because I had had to live with Anne for four years and she had argued and persuaded me out of cheap shoes and generic toilet paper and my mother's winter coat. She'd bought us matching kimonos in Chinatown. I told Mrs Warburg that it was entirely due to Anne that I was able to walk through the world like a normal person.

Mrs Warburg said, 'Let me get another drink.'

I lay back on Anne's bed and sipped my beer. Mrs Warburg and I had agreed that since I didn't always remember to get rum for our get-togethers, I would make do with beer. Anne actually liked beer, Mrs Warburg said. Mr Warburg liked Scotch. Mrs Warburg went right down the middle, she felt, with the rum and Coke.

'Should we have gone to Teddy's funeral?' she said.

I didn't think so. Mrs Warburg had never met Teddy, and I certainly didn't want to go. I didn't want to sit with his family, or sit far behind them, hoping that since Teddy was dead, Anne was alive, or that if Anne had to be dead, she'd be lying in a white casket, with bushels of white carnations around her, and

Teddy would be lying someplace dark and terrible and unseen.

'I think Anne might have escaped,' Mrs Warburg said. 'I really do. I think she might have gotten out of those awful mountains and she might have found a rowboat or something – she's wonderful on water, you should see her on Lake Erie, but it could be because of the trauma she doesn't—'

Mr Warburg got on the line.

'It's three o'clock in the morning,' he said. 'Mrs Warburg needs to sleep. So do you, I'm sure.'

Eugene Trask and Anne traveled for four days. He said, at his trial, that she was a wonderful conversationalist. He said that talking to her was a pleasure and that they had had some very lively discussions, which he felt she had enjoyed. At the end of the fourth day, he unbuckled his belt so he could rape her again, in a quiet pine grove near Lake Pleasant, and while he was distracted with his shirttail and zipper, she made a grab for his hunting knife. He hit her on the head with the butt of his rifle, and when she got up, he hit her again. Then he stabbed her twice, just like Teddy, two to the heart. He didn't want to shoot her, he said. He put her bleeding body in the back of an orange Buick he'd stolen in Speculator, and he drove to an abandoned mine. He threw her down the thirty-foot shaft, dumped the Buick in Mineville, and walked through the woods to his sister's place. They had hamburgers and mashed potatoes and sat on Rose's back step and watched a pair of red-tailed hawks circling the spruce. Rose washed out his shirt and pants and ironed them dry, and he left early the next morning, with two meat-loaf sandwiches in his jacket pocket.

They caught Eugene Trask when one of his stolen cars broke

down. They shot him in the leg. He said he didn't remember anything since he'd skipped his last arraignment two months ago. He said he was subject to fits of amnesia. He had fancy criminal lawyers who took his case because the hunt for Eugene Trask had turned out to be the biggest manhunt in the tristate area since the Lindbergh baby. There were reporters everywhere, Mrs Warburg said. Eugene's lawyers, Mr Feldman and Mr Barone, told Eugene that if he lied to them they would not be able to defend him adequately, so he drew them maps of where they could find Anne's body, and also two other girls who had been missing for six months. Mr Feldman and Mr Barone felt that they could not reveal this information to the police or to the Warburgs or to the other families because it would violate lawyer–client privilege. After the trial, after Eugene was transferred to the Fishkill correctional facility, two kids were playing in an old mine near Speculator, looking for garnets and gold and arrowheads, and they found Anne's body.

The dead body makes its own way. It stiffens and then it relaxes and then it softens. The flesh turns to a black thick cream. If I had put my arms around her to carry her up the gravel path and home, if I had reached out to steady her, my hand would have slid through her skin like a spoon through custard, and she would have fallen away from me, held in only by her clothes. If I had hidden in the timbered walls of the mine, waiting until Eugene Trask heard the reassuring one–two thump of the almost emptied body on the mine-car tracks, I might have seen her as I see her now. Her eyes open and blue, her cheeks pink underneath the streaks of clay and dust, and she is breathing, her chest is rising and falling, too fast and too shallow, like a bird in distress, but rising and falling.

We are all in the cave. Mrs Warburg went back to her life,

without me, after Anne's funeral that winter (did those children find her covered with the first November snow?), and Mr Warburg resurfaced eight years later, remarried to a woman who became friends with my aunt Rita in Beechwood. Aunt Rita said the new Mrs Warburg was lovely. She said the first Mrs Warburg had made herself into a complete invalid, round-the-clock help, but even so she died alone, Rita said, in their old house. She didn't know from what. Eugene Trask was shot and killed trying to escape from Fishkill. Two bullets to the heart, one to the lungs. Mrs Warburg sent me the clipping. Rose Trask married and had two children, Cheryl and Eugene. Rose and Cheryl and little Eugene drowned in 1986, boating on Lake Champlain. Mrs Warburg sent me the clipping. My young father, still slim and handsome and a good dancer, collapsed on our roof trying to straighten our ancient TV antenna, and it must have been Eugene Trask pulling his feet out from under him, over the gutters and thirty feet down. Don't let the sun catch you crying, my father used to say. Maybe your nervous system doesn't get the message to swallow the morning toast and Eugene Trask strangles you and throws you to the floor while your wife and children watch. Maybe clusters of secret tumors bloom from skull to spine, opening their petals so Eugene Trask can beat you unconscious on the way to work. Everyone dies of heart failure, Eugene Trask said at his trial.

I don't miss the dead less, I miss them more. I miss the tall pines around Lake Pleasant, I miss the brown-and-gray cobblestones on West Cedar Street, I miss the red-tailed hawks that fly so often in pairs. I miss the cheap red wine in a box and I miss the rum and Coke. I miss Anne's wet gold hair drying as we sat on the fire escape. I miss the hot-dog luau and driving to dance lessons after breakfast at Bruegger's Bagels. I miss the cold mornings on the farm, when the handle of the bucket bit into my small hands and my feet slid over the frozen dew. I miss the hot grease spattering around the felafel balls and the urgent clicking of Hebrew. I miss the new green leaves shaking in the June rain. I miss standing on my father's shiny shoes as we danced to 'The Tennessee Waltz' and my mother made me a paper fan so I could flirt like a Southern belle, tapping my nose with the fan. I miss every piece of my dead. Every piece is stacked high like cordwood within me, and my heart, both sides, and all four parts, is their reliquary.

When Your Life Looks Back

When your life looks back—
As it will, at itself, at you – what will it say?

Inch of colored ribbon cut from the spool.
Flame curl, blue-consuming the log it flares from.
Bay leaf. Oak leaf. Cricket. One among many.

Your life will carry you as it did always,
With ten fingers and both palms,
With horizontal ribs and upright spine,
With its filling and emptying heart,
That wanted only your own heart, emptying, filled, in
    return.
You gave it. What else could do?

Immersed in air or in water.
Immersed in hunger or anger.
Curious even when bored.
Longing even when running away.

'What will happen next?' –
the question hinged in your knees, your ankles,
in the in-breaths even of weeping.
Strongest of magnets, the future impartial drew you in.

Whatever direction you turned toward was face to face.
No back of the world existed,
No unseen corner, no test. No other earth to prepare
for.

This, your life had said, its only pronoun.
Here, your life had said, its only house.
Let, your life had said, its only order.

And did you have a choice in this? You did—

Sleeping and waking,
the horses around you, the mountains around you,
The buildings with their tall, hydraulic shafts.
Those of your own kind around you—

A few times, you stood on your head.
A few times, you chose not to be frightened.
A few times, you held another beyond any measure.
A few times, you found yourself held beyond any
measure.

Mortal, your life will say,
As if tasting something delicious, as if in envy.
Your immortal life will say this, as it is leaving.

JANE HIRSHFIELD

Where the God of Love Hangs Out

Farnham is a small town. It has a handful of buildings for the public good and two gas stations and several small businesses, which puzzle everyone (who buys the expensive Italian ceramics, the copper jewelry, the badly made wooden toys?). It has a pizza place and a coffee shop called The Cup.

Ray Watrous looked in The Cup's big window as he walked past. He saw the woman he'd represented in a malpractice suit ten years ago because laminated veneers kept falling out of her mouth. He saw the girl who used to babysit for them when Neil and Jennifer were small, now a fat, homely young woman holding a fat, homely little kid on her lap. He saw his daughter-in-law, Macy, at a table by herself, her gold hair practically falling into her cup, tears running down her face. Ray turned around and went inside. He liked Macy. He was also curious and he was semiretired and he was in no hurry to go to Town Hall and argue with Farnham's first selectman, a decent man suddenly inclined to get in bed with Stop & Shop and put a supermarket in the north end of town, where wild turkeys still gathered.

Ray liked having his son and Macy nearby. Sometimes Ray went down to New Haven for lunch and sometimes Neil drove up to Farnham, on his way to the county courthouse. They talked about sports, and local politics and the collapse of Western civilization. The week before, Neil mentioned that a girl he'd dated in high school was going to run for governor and Ray told Neil that Abe Callender, who shot out the windshield of his own car when he'd found his girlfriend and *her* girlfriend in it, a few years back, was now a state trooper in Farnham.

'Can I join you?' Ray said.

Macy twisted away from him, as if that would keep him from seeing her tears and then she twisted back and took her bag off the other chair.

'Of course,' she said.

Randeane, the owner and only waitress of The Cup, brought Ray a black coffee and put down two ginger scones with a dollop of whipped honey on the side.

Ray said, 'These scones have Dunkin' Donuts beat all to hell.'

Randeane thanked him. 'Cream and sugar?'

Ray, who was normally a polite man, said, 'The coffee could stand a little fixing up, I guess.'

Randeane put her pencil in her pocket and said, 'People love our coffee. It's fair trade. Everyone loves our Viennese Roast and our French Roast and I believe people come here *for* our coffee.'

Ray said, 'I hate to disagree, but they come for the pastries or the atmosphere or because of you but they don't come for the coffee.'

'I beg your pardon,' Randeane said.

Macy laughed and said, 'Wow, Ray.'

'I'm just saying, people don't come for the coffee.'

'I'll make you a fresh cup.'

Randeane brought him another coffee and Ray drank it. It

wasn't great. Macy ate a little bit of her scone and she sighed. Two high school girls sat down at the table next to them.

'I'm not *retarded,*' the skinny girl with pierced eyebrows said.

'I *know.* But, duh, you can't go for a job interview looking like that.' The other girl was chubby and cheerful and in a pink uniform.

'Fine,' the skinny girl said. 'Fix me.'

Macy and Ray watched the two girls walk hand in hand into the ladies' room.

'Girls are good at friendship,' Ray said.

Macy shrugged. 'I guess. I was thinking about my mother when you came in and saw me crying,' she said.

'My father was a no-good fall-down drunk,' Ray offered. 'My mother was as useless as a rubber crutch. But sometimes I miss her. That's the way the dead are, I guess. They come back better than they were.'

'We weren't close,' Macy said.

She'd been sitting in the kitchen just two days ago, thinking about gumbo and looking for filé powder, when the phone rang. Her mother said hello, she was just passing through and wanted to see Macy. She didn't say *hope to,* or *love to,* she said, 'I want to see you, kid. I'm in New Britain. There's a place just off Route 9. It's called the Crab Cake. Meet me there.' Her mother wore skinny black jeans and a yellow blouse and high-heeled yellow boots. She had a scarf pulled over her black hair and she sat in a booth, smoking, and when Macy came in, her mother didn't get up.

'Don't you look fat and happy,' her mother said.

Macy sat down.

'Surprised?'

'I'm surprised,' Macy said. It had been her plan that no one in her real life, meaning Neil and Neil's family, would ever meet her mother.

'I bet. Well, I thought it was time you and your old mother had a chat.'

It didn't take very long. Macy called her mother 'Betty,' which was her given name, and Betty called Macy 'Joanie,' which was hers. Macy's mother accused Macy of running away and Macy said that if she hadn't run away she'd be a fucked-up coke addict like her mother or worse. Betty said she had done her best and Macy stood up at that point. She said, Don't tell me that. Macy's mother said that they should let bygones be bygones, that she'd dumped Brad's mean, sorry ass anyway, years ago, and see how Joanie had turned out fine. She said she was on her way to Miami and if Joanie could spare her some traveling money, she'd get right into her car. Macy had four hundred dollars she'd put aside from housekeeping money and three hundred she'd gotten as a bonus from her company, another hundred she got for a winter coat she'd returned, and twenty bucks that she'd found in Neil's pants when she took them to the laundry. She'd put it all in an envelope before she got in her car to drive to the Crab Cake and she handed the envelope to her mother, who counted it.

'That's all I have,' Macy said. 'We're not millionaires.'

Her mother was cheerful, the way she always was when things were not as good as she hoped, but not as bad as they could be.

'You weren't hard to find,' her mother said.

'I wasn't hiding,' Macy said, and her mother smiled and put out her cigarette.

'Well, good. Then you won't mind if I come around again, when I'm passing through.'

'You come to my house and I'll shoot you myself. I'll say you snuck in and I shot you in self-defense, thinking you were a burglar. And I will cry my heart out to have killed my own poor, crazy mother, who should have been locked up in the first place.'

Macy's mother stood up.

'Aren't you a kidder. It's okay, you lie dormy, and so will I. Good luck,' her mother said, and Macy watched her drive off in a dusty blue station wagon.

A handsome black woman walked past The Cup's big front window.

'Looks like Nellie,' Ray said.

'Nellie of the coconut cake,' Macy said.

Ray shook his head. 'My wife can be a bitch.'

Macy said, 'I can't argue with you.'

Macy and Neil had met at his parents' house. It felt like a houseful of people to Macy, who had lived with one person or none, most of her life. Neil's sister, Jennifer, had brought Macy home with her after they ran into each other their senior year, at the Philadelphia Flower Show. (Just come home with me for the weekend, Jennifer had said. My parents will love you.) Neil was older than Jennifer and Macy by a couple of years and finishing law school; their cousin Howard, who lived in the maid's room because he couldn't face the real world after his time in Afghanistan, was making drinks for everyone.

Jennifer said, 'This is Macy. You'll love her.'

Neil squeezed Macy's hand and looked her right in the eye and she could feel herself blushing. Eleanor Watrous served chicken fricassee with dumplings and glazed carrots and a separate plate of bitter green salad with a disk of goat cheese in the middle. For dessert, Jennifer carried in a gigantic and snowy and objectively beautiful coconut cake.

Macy said, 'My goodness, that's gorgeous.'

Mrs Watrous waved her hand toward the kitchen and said that Nellie was gifted. (That's the housekeeper, Neil said quietly. She cooks when my mother wants to impress people.) 'I'll have Nellie wrap some up for you,' Mrs Watrous said, so that everyone could just picture Macy in her windowless room, sitting on her twin bed, unwrapping the slice of cake for a snack or for breakfast. Macy let her napkin slide to the floor so she could get a grip on herself. Neil's hand came crab-walking across the rug, toward Macy's napkin. He stroked her ankle and then he picked up the napkin and put it in her lap.

After coffee, Mr Watrous had said, Let's adjourn and Neil and Cousin Howard followed him into the study. The door to the study was not closed, and Macy sat in the chair nearest the door.

'Cute girl, Jennifer's little friend,' Neil's father said.

'She's hot,' Cousin Howard said, and then he picked up a magazine and started fanning himself.

'Christ, Howard,' Mr Watrous said. 'How's law school, Neil?'

'Okay,' Neil said.

'Getting any offers?'

'A few.'

'Stay out of the pigpen,' Mr Watrous said.

Cousin Howard said, 'Soo-eee. Here, piggy, piggy, piggy,' and Mr Watrous said, 'For the love of Jesus,' and the men came back into the living room. Neil sat down on the arm of Macy's chair and patted her hair.

Sunday afternoon, he drove Macy and Jennifer to the train station. He told his sister to go get the tickets and behind her, he kissed Macy, his narrow lips opening like a flower. He smelled of cinnamon and smoke.

The next time Macy and Neil visited the Watrouses, they were a couple.

Mrs Watrous asked Macy to help set the table, just to see if she knew where the glasses went and in what order. Macy laid glasses down over knives, water, white, and red, exactly as Emily Post recommended, and Neil's mother glanced over and said, as if it wasn't a test at all, Oh, who cares, really? These days, you could put a jug and four bowls on the table, couldn't you? Let's move to the patio. Macy drank three glasses of water, she was so nervous, and after Neil's father had asked about her parents and Macy had said that they were dead and that her only relatives were an aunt and uncle in Des Moines, they moved on to Macy's favorite classes. Everything went pretty well until Macy took a green olive out of the bowl next to her. It stuck to the roof of her mouth, its tip digging into the soft part at the back. She choked until she spat out the jalapeño pepper the olive was stuffed with, crying and swearing, Goddammit, oh, mother*fucker,* and Neil jumped up to get her water. Mr Watrous said those olives were going to kill someone and Mrs Watrous said that he'd eaten about fifteen of them so far. Finally, Macy took the glass of water from Neil and, in her relief, relaxed her arm and pushed the olive bowl onto the stone floor. Mrs Watrous walked to the kitchen for a thick dishcloth and Nellie the cook came in behind her with a dustpan and the glass shards were disappeared. When Mrs Watrous came back, Macy said, My God, I am *so* sorry. And Mrs Watrous said, It's all right. If I were the Queen of England, I'd have to throw another Baccarat bowl on the floor, just to make you feel at ease.

Macy was silent for the rest of dinner.

That's what I get, she thought. You listen and you listen and you copy their ways and who fucking knew that that bat, that blond bat in a Lilly Pulitzer sheath with her fucking family retainers, who knew I'd break her fucking Baccarat. Macy lived in a boardinghouse a mile from campus and cleaned all the rooms in the house on Saturdays for a break on her rent. On weekends she went to parties and had people drop her off at a trolley stop. She didn't have people over. She didn't go on vacation with other people's families. The girls Macy hung around with, girls like Jennifer and her friends, thought Macy lived with rich, strict relatives. They'd never seen a boardinghouse or a carpet sweeper or a shared bathroom. They didn't make their meals on a hot plate in their room, unless they were doing it for fun, and they didn't read Emily Post and Miss Manners like the Old and the New Testament.

Macy brought her lunch to campus every day and she ate in the handicapped-access bathroom. Afterward, she sat in the Student Center to socialize, and when the other girls ate two slices of whole-wheat pizza or a big bowl of soba noodles or a roast-beef sandwich, Macy smiled like Pietsie Cortland, who also didn't eat, for more normal reasons. Pietsie was Macy's favorite. Macy loved everything about Pietsie, including her name, which was so fancy, Macy wanted to take her aside and say, Good for you. (When they did get into the question of background, Pietsie said, Isn't it awful – it's for Van Piet, my middle name. You know, old name, *no* money, not a pot to piss in, and Macy heard the *ping* of real crystal.) Macy avoided anyone who seemed remotely interested in her family. Interesting was not good.

'It's okay,' Neil had said on the way back to his apartment. 'My mother has a strong personality. It'll be okay.'

Macy looked down at her hands, twisting in her lap.

'It'll be okay,' Neil said, 'because I love you. Ha,' he said, when she stared at him. 'You didn't know that, did you?'

'No,' Macy said, and she put her head on his shoulder and cried a little, at the thought of being loved by Neil Watrous, who was apparently without serious fault.

Neil pulled over and they kissed and then they drove to his apartment. They ran up the stairs, and by the time Neil had unlocked the door, Macy had her shoes and her blouse off and she flung herself on top of him, kissing his floppy brown hair and his big ears and the nicks where he'd cut himself shaving. They landed on his sofa. He kissed her stomach and her armpits. He ran his tongue from her ankle to her ear and they bit each other at every round and yielding spot. At one point, they found themselves with their heads hanging off the bed, their bare feet making dark, damp prints all the way up his wall.

'I was made to love you,' Neil said. He sang the whole Stevie Wonder song, naked, with his head touching the floor.

'And I you,' Macy said.

The summer before she'd met Neil, even though she was pretty sure that what she was looking for was not creative expression but something more like the makeover to end all makeovers, Macy had spent a week on scholarship at a writers' conference. She looked at the men and women around her and thought, We're like the people at Lourdes or the ones who go to the mud baths of that disgusting town with the sulfurous pools that everyone dunks themselves in, except we've brought our poems and short stories and inexpressible wishes, instead of scrofula and dermatitis.

She smoked like a chimney and wrote about whatever came

into her head, but only for a few pages and then she ran out of steam. She wrote about the man who sat next to her in the workshop, a seventy-five-year-old engineer from Salt Lake City, trying desperately to come out of the closet after sixty years and a wife, two kids, and six grandchildren. The engineer invited Macy out for a drink after class and they found a small table at a bad restaurant. He put his hand on Macy's and said, Dear, I love men. I know, Macy said. Everyone in their workshop knew; the engineer wrote about thighs like steel girders and asses like ball bearings and biceps like pistons. It's fine, Macy said. I love them, too. The engineer said, Women, I mean their private parts, make me want to vomit. Present company excepted, of course. Well, then you're making the right choice, Macy said. She swallowed her vodka gimlet and went to another reading. She went to every reading and performance that was scheduled and she went late, in hopes of finding a seat next to a good-looking man, or even just a nice man, and she stood in line to have books signed by people she thought were complete idiots, just to improve the odds. She wrote down a few other things that happened at the writers' conference, in a lavender suede notebook, and then she threw the notebook into the dumpster.

The day after he and Macy had had their tête-à-tête in the coffee shop, Ray stopped in on his way home.

'I hope I'm not keeping you,' Ray said.

Randeane smiled and said he wasn't and she poured his coffee.

'Randeane,' Ray said. 'That's sort of a Southern name, isn't it?'

'Left-wing Jewish father, hence the Jewfro' – she ran her fingers through her curly hair – 'and white-trash Pentecostal mother, hence the Randeane and the inability to finish my thesis. Yourself?'

Ray said that his parents weren't that interesting. English peddlers on his father's side, Norwegian farmers on his mother's, and really not much to them.

'Well, take some scones home. I'll just have to toss them tomorrow and I will be goddamned fuck-fried if I'm going to stay up and make bread pudding all night.'

'Absolutely not. Someone must be waiting up for you,' Ray said, and he thought that although it was difficult to imagine dying of embarrassment at his age, it wasn't impossible.

'Not really,' Randeane said, and she handed him a shopping bag of scones.

Neil had come to Ray a few weeks after the coconut cake dinner and told his father that he planned to ask Macy to marry him. Ray meant to say, Congratulations, but he heard himself say that although people of his generation married for life, he, personally, thought it was one of the worst and stupidest ideas ever foisted on mankind, second only to Jesus died for our sins, which was just ridiculous. Neil looked at him, a little cow-eyed, and Ray meant to shut up but instead he said, Everyone who gets divorced feels betrayed, whichever side you're on. But what's worse – everyone who gets married feels betrayed. The other person will let you down, son – they can't help it. We are all basically selfish beasts, and also, your wife will love your children more than she will ever love you. You're just the hod carrier, kid. You know what your mother says: You promised to love me for better or worse, Ray Watrous.

Neil said, 'I understand, Dad. I mean, I do.' He put his hand on Ray's shoulder and Ray was sorry he'd opened his mouth. 'It's a little different for me and Macy. It's just different for us.'

'I'm sure it is,' Ray said. 'She's a lovely girl. Let's not keep our brides waiting.'

A lot of Ray's friends called their wives their brides. Ray referred to Ellie that way once, in The Cup, saying, 'I'll bring some of these bagels home to my bride,' and Randeane flinched.

'That's an awful expression,' she said. 'It's like you keep her in a closet with a white dress and veil. Your very own Miss Havisham.'

'Not at all,' Ray said. 'It shows I still think of her the way I did when we were first married. It's flattering.'

'In a pig's eye,' Randeane said, and she shoved the bagels in a bag and threw Ray's change on the counter.

Before winter started, Ray bought a dog. ('Do you even like dogs?' Eleanor said.) He walked it every night past Randeane's house. Often Randeane was reading on her front porch; sometimes she was around the back, where she had a hammock, an outdoor fireplace, and two white plastic lounge chairs.

'Hammock or chaise longue?' Randeane said.

Ray said that he was more a chair kind of person, that hammocks were unpredictable.

'Oh, life's a hammock,' Randeane said.

'Exactly my point. I'll take the chair.'

'Remember Oscar? You met him once. He's asked me to marry him,' Randeane said.

Ray sighed.

'Don't sigh,' she said.

'That's what Ellie says to me. She says, "Don't sigh, Ray, this is not the Gulag." You know what else she says – after a few drinks, she says, "Ray, I promised to love you for better or worse." No one should make such a promise. I don't think I even know what it means – for better or for worse. Why would you be married to someone for worse?'

'You don't think I should marry him?'

'I met him once,' Ray said. 'Firm handshake.'

'Come lie in the hammock.'

'I can't do that,' Ray said.

'I'm pretty sure you can,' Randeane said. She kicked off her green slippers and climbed into the hammock. Her pants pulled up to her calves. 'At least you can push me.' Ray gave her a push and sat down again.

'You could marry me,' Ray said. 'We both know I'd be a better choice.'

Randeane looked up at the sky. 'I guess so,' she said. 'You, younger, single, maybe not so deeply pissed off and inflexible.'

'I don't think we'll be seeing that,' Ray said, and he stumbled a little getting off the chaise and took the dog home. He drove to The Yankee Clipper for a beer.

The parking lot was barely half full and Ray knew most of the cars. Leo Ferrante's BMW, that would be Leo, celebrating having persuaded the people in charge of Farnham that neither a Stop & Shop nor a horse crematorium was anything to get upset about. Leo would be drinking with his clients and sitting near Anne Fishbach. Every Tuesday night, Anne left her senile husband with a nurse and drove over to the Clipper. ('Aren't I allowed?' she'd said to Ray. 'Does this make me a bad wife? After fifty-three years?') She sat in a back booth and drank Manhattans until someone drove her home.

Ray recognized his next-door neighbor's green pickup. He

saw two guys from the Exchange Club walk out of the bar and
recognize *his* car and Ray knew enough to go somewhere else.
He drove about ten miles and pulled into a town he'd been to
only once, twenty years ago, to pick up Jennifer from a Girl
Scout jamboree. There were two bars, on either side of the wide
main street. One awning said PADDY O'TOOLE'S BAR AND GRILLE
and had gold four-leaf clovers in the window and on the awning.
The other said BUCK'S SAFARI BAR and had a poster of Obama in
one window and in the other, a poster of a black girl, with an
enormous cloud of black curls, standing with her oiled legs apart,
falling out of a tiny leopard-skin bikini. Ray thought, When it's
your time, it's your time, and he went in.

No one minded him. Back in the day, some young man might
have felt compelled to defend his manhood or his blackness or
the virtue of a waitress and Ray might have found himself scuf-
fling on a wet wood floor or a hard sidewalk, but not now. A
young woman and her date slid off their barstools into a booth
and the man indicated that Ray was free to take the man's seat.
The barmaid was short and wide, wearing a gold leather skirt and
gold nail polish. Her hair was cut close to the scalp and dyed
blond. She put a napkin in front of Ray and looked at him the
way she looked at every other man at the bar.

'Just a beer, please. Whatever's on tap.'

He could stay in Buck's all night. He could probably move
into Buck's. They seemed like nice people. They were certainly
a lot more tolerant of an old white man in their midst than the
people at the Clipper would be if some strange black guy bellied
up to the bar. Ray ordered another beer and a burger and he
watched the Steelers crush the Colts.

'Christ,' Ray said, 'no defense at all.'

'I hear you,' the man next to him said, and someone tapped Ray on the shoulder.

Ray's elbow tipped his glass and the man to his left caught it and the barmaid said, Good catch, and Macy was standing beside him.

'What in Christ's name are you doing here?' Ray said. 'Where's Neil?' In the five years since the wedding, Ray had never seen Macy take a drink, let alone in a black bar at the ass end of Meriden.

Macy shrugged. 'I used to live around here,' she said. 'I took a drive and . . . You want to get a booth?'

'I would,' said the man on Ray's left. 'I would definitely get a booth.'

'She's my daughter-in-law,' Ray said.

'Let he who is without sin, cast the first stone,' the man said.

'I thought you were from Iowa. Kansas? Was I wrong?' Ray said, when they'd brought their beers to a table.

'No. I said my parents were dead and I had an aunt and uncle in Des Moines. Which I don't.'

Macy drummed her fingers on the table.

'I love Neil,' she said. 'I really do.'

'I'm sure you do. And he loves you. Christ, you have only to look at him – he thinks you hung the moon.'

'Really? He wants to have a baby.'

'Good,' Ray said. 'Have two.' Babies having babies, he thought.

'He thinks I hung the moon? He's the best man I know,' Macy said. 'I'm just not who he thinks I am.'

'That's not the worst thing in the world,' Ray said, and Macy put her hand, cool and wet from the beer, over his lips. Her hand smelled like grapefruit.

'I don't mean he doesn't know my essence on some meta-physical level. I mean I have lied to him on a million different occasions about a million things.'

Ray nodded.

'When I was ten, my mother fell down on the kitchen floor, and blood was pouring out of her nose. So, you know, I under-stood she was OD'ing on coke.'

Ray nodded again, like women OD'ing on coke in front of their children was as much part of his life as reading the paper.

'I had this amazing babysitter, Sammy. So – I don't want this to take forever – when I'm fourteen my mother moves in with this guy, we'll just call him The Asshole, and I moved in with Sammy. It turns out, Sammy's a transvestite.'

Ray nodded again; he had defended a dozen middle-aged guys in dresses who were caught speeding.

'So, I do Sammy's hair and nails. And I do his friends', too, and Sammy basically sets me up in the tranny business in our TV room. I do hair, nails, and make-up every day after school and most of Saturday. When I graduate from high school, I have three thousand dollars in my savings account. Plus, I got into Bryn Mawr on scholarship *and* I graduated second in my class.' Macy smiled shyly. 'My name's not Macy. I changed it – I mean I changed it legally, when I was sixteen. Sammy's mother's name was Macy. So when we get to Bryn Mawr, Sammy is just the *shit*. All the parents *love* him. He drives off and he goes, *Au revoir,* honeybun, and don't look back. He got a horrible staph infection, from the acrylic nails. Ten days in the ICU. It was terrible. He was a really, really nice man,' Macy said, wiping her face with a beer napkin.

'When I was in college,' Ray said, 'I let a guy give me a blow job. Let me be clear. This guy paid me fifty bucks, which was a lot of money at the time, and I let him do me once a week for three years. If not for him, I would have had to drop out of college. You already know my father was a bum.'

'Thank you,' Macy said, and she laughed. Ray smiled.

'Also, you might already know this – I'm in love with Randeane.'

'I really like her,' Macy said. 'Everything about her, she's just so great. She's read everything. *I'm* sort of in love with her.'

'Maybe,' Ray said. He sighed and spread his arms along the back of the booth. 'I'm pretty sure not like this.'

One morning, Ray told Macy, he'd gotten to Randeane's late, between the morning people and the lunchtime people, and there was a man sitting at Ray's usual table.

Oh, Ray, Randeane said. This is my friend, Garbly Garble. Ray couldn't make out the man's name. He was taller than Ray, in his late thirties or early forties; it was harder and harder for Ray to tell anything except that someone was more or less his age. People under fifty looked like young people and people under thirty looked like children. The man stood up politely and shook Ray's hand. He shook it twice, not the hard handshake that even men Ray's age gave one another just to show they were still in the game, but a very gentle, slow handshake as if he was mindful of Ray's osteoporosis or arthritis or some other damned thing that would make Ray's hand crumble in his like an Egyptian relic. The man was clearly not thinking, So, this is the competition; he was thinking, Poor old Uncle Ray, or even poor Grandpa Ray, Civil War veteran. Nurse, get this man a chair. Ray walked out and across town to the office of Ferrante and Ticknor, Attorneys-at-Law. He walked along the narrow, cluttered river that ran through the park.

In Leo Ferrante's office, Ray cleared his throat and Leo put his hand up.

'Don't,' he said.

'What, you're psychic?' Ray said.

Leo said he was sorry, that in the past three days he'd had two old friends come in to divorce their wives and marry hot chicks.

'I wouldn't call her a hot chick,' Ray'd said.

Macy leaned forward, her face in her hands, lit up with the thought of Ray's love for Randeane. She looked about twelve years old.

'You deserve happiness, Ray.'

'And Eleanor? What about her happiness?'

Macy did not say that Eleanor's happiness was of no account to her.

Ray said, 'Someone's got to speak up for Ellie,' and he looked around Buck's as if the gold-haired bartender or the young couple might say something on Ellie's behalf. Like: Goddammit, that woman has – in her own way – devoted herself to you. Or maybe the bartender would say, Leave Ellie and your children will turn their backs on you. They think you're a good man. Leave Ellie to shack up with a young lady from the coffee shop, half your age. No fool like an old fool. Ray turned back to Macy but he could still hear the bartender and Leo Ferrante talking to him. Your prostate alone's enough to scare her off; you gotta get a guest room just to keep it somewhere. And your suitcase of Viagra and Levitra and don't forget the Allopurinol and the Amlodipine and the Flomax, without which you'll never piss again. And why shouldn't she want children, young as she is? She could have them with that tall, good-looking man, Ray heard the bartender say, and he looked at her and she winked, gold powder sparkling on her eyelids and cheekbones, shining across her breasts. She brought them another pair of beers and a bowl of nuts.

'Do you have any food?' Macy said.

'What do you like?' the woman said.

Macy looked around and she sniffed the air.

'Catfish, maybe,' she said.

The woman shrugged pleasantly. 'For two? Sweet-potato fries? Butter beans?'

'I have died and gone to heaven,' Macy said, and she almost clapped her hands.

'I don't think I can eat all that,' Ray said.

'I love it. I'll bring some home for Neil. Like they say, so good, makes you want to slap yo' mama.' Macy took a sip of beer and smiled. 'Sammy was a great cook. Actually, I'm a great cook.'

Turned on a dime, Ray thought. Two hours ago, she was going to hang herself in the garage because Neil didn't know her essence; now she's bringing him a Southern fried feast and they'll eat in bed. Laughing. Ray thought of Randeane and his heart clenched so deeply, he put his hands on the table.

'You *should* bring some home for him. I really can't eat that stuff anymore,' he said. 'Call him. Tell him you're coming home. Don't be afraid to tell him about your mother and about Sammy. He'll admire you for that stuff. For getting past it.'

'Okay,' Macy said, biting her lip. 'You really think so?' She took out her phone and checked her text messages.

'He's still at work,' she said, grinning like a kid. 'He's not even worrying.' She texted Neil and showed Ray: *B home soon, w fab dinner. Love u so.*

A big man came out of the kitchen and laid their food in front of them. He nodded toward the game on TV.

'That game's over,' he said. 'You know what Archie Griffin said, "Ain't the size of the dog in the fight but the size of the fight in the dog." These guys got no fight.'

'Hell of a player, Griffin. Two Heismans.'

The man paused, like he might sit down, and Macy moved over to make room.

'Great tailback,' the man said.

'Well, they measure these things differently now,' Ray said. 'For my money, Bronko Nagurski was the greatest running back.'

'Ah,' the man said. 'Played both sides of the ball. You don't see that anymore.'

'No you don't,' Ray said.

The man slipped the bill under Ray's plate. 'Come back soon.'

'Ray,' Macy said. 'If you want to be with Randeane, if you need, I don't know, support, I'll be there for you. Neil, too.'

Ray picked at the fries, which were the best fries he could remember eating. If he did nothing else to improve his life, he could come to Buck's every few weeks, have a beer and a plate of sweet-potato fries, and talk football with the cook.

Macy tapped the back of his hand with her fork. 'Ray. You be the quarterback and I'll be, I'll be the guy who protects the quarterback. I'll be that guy.'

'Honey,' Ray said. 'There's really no one like that in football.'

Right after Jennifer was born, they found cyst after cyst inside of Ellie, and when Jennifer was two, Ellie had a hysterectomy. Ray brought her an armful of red stargazer lilies from the florist, not from the grocery store or the hospital gift shop, because

Ellie was particular about things like that, and when he walked in, she smiled, closed her compact, and set her lipstick on the bedside table. She'd brought her blue silk bathrobe from home and had brushed her hair back in a ponytail and tied it with a blue ribbon. She made room for Ray on the bed and they held hands.

'The kids are fine,' Ray said. 'Nellie's got Neil making the beds and Jennifer's running into the wall about ten times a day. Then she falls down and laughs like a lunatic.'

'Oh, good,' Ellie said, and she looked out the window and sighed.

'Hey, no sighing,' Ray said. 'Everything's all right.'

Ellie said, 'No, it's not. I wanted one more baby. I wanted to be like everyone else. I didn't want to go into menopause at thirty-three, thank you very much, and I am not looking forward to having Dr Perlmutter's hand up my you-know-what every six months for the rest of my life.'

Ray squeezed her hand. 'For better or for worse. Isn't that what we said? So, this is a little bit of worse.'

Ellie tossed his hand aside and squinted at him, like the sexy, fearless WACs he admired when he was a boy, girls who outran and outgunned the guys, even in skirts and heels.

'You think this is worse?' Ellie said. 'Oh, shame on me. Sweetie, if this is what worse looks like – we'll be just fine.'

She'd said the same thing when his blood pressure medication chased away his erections and Viagra brought them back, but not the same. They were unmistakably old-man erections; they were like old men themselves: frail and distracted and unsure. He'd lain in bed with his back to her, ashamed and sorry for himself. Ellie turned on the light to look at him. She had her pink silk night-gown on and her face was shiny with moisturizer. She pulled up on one elbow and leaned around him. He saw the creases at her neck and between her breasts, the tiny pleats at her underarms, the little pillow of flesh under her sharp chin, and he thought, She must be seeing the same thing. She snapped off the light and put her hand on his shoulder.

'So what, Ray? You think this is the worst? You think, finally, we've gotten to "for worse"?'

Maybe not for you, Ray thought.

'It's not. It's not better, but it's not the worse,' she said.

Eleanor slid her hand under the covers and wrapped her fingers around his cock. She gave a little squeeze, like a salute. She pushed the covers back and pressed him onto his back. She talked while she stroked him. She told him about the guy who had come to do the patio and brought his four giant dogs with him; she told him about seeing one of Neil's friends from high school who'd said, when she asked how his mother was, Great, she's out on parole; she told him that she'd heard that young men shaved their balls now. Ray lifted his head and asked her if she would like that. I guess I would, she said. Is it unpleasant otherwise? Ray said. Oh, I don't know, Ellie said. It's like a mouthful of wet mitten – what do *you* think? When he stopped laughing, early in the morning, with a faint light falling on Ellie's silver hair held back with a pink ribbon and her slim, manicured hands, he came.

Ray followed Macy home from Buck's. He could see her dark outline in the car when they drove under a streetlight, her right arm up the whole time, talking on her phone. She honked twice when she got to her driveway and pulled in. Their porch light snapped on and the moths gathered. Macy ran onto the porch and Ray could see Neil, in just his underwear, reaching out for her with both arms.

Ray turned left instead of right and parked in front of Randeane's. From the car, he saw the white edge of her chaise. He saw just the green tips of her slippered feet. He honked twice and drove home.

Acknowledgments

My editor, Kate Medina, continues to be one of the luckiest breaks of my life, writing and otherwise. My agent, Jennifer Rudolph Walsh, is, always, a generous and serious reader, a gifted, relentless advocate and excellent company. My dear friend, Phyllis Wender, has always given me great support and continues to do so.

I want to thank the MacDowell Colony and Yaddo, where I made any number of wrong turns, and a few right ones. I also thank Wesleyan University's Olin Library and its resourceful and exceptional librarians.

I also wish to thank my very dear friend, and twin, Jack O'Brien, and his Imaginary Farms, which have given me safe haven, comfort, and more joy than one can imagine, while sitting at a table, in a barn, facing a wall.

I am very lucky in my friends and family, all of whom know lots of things I don't: Dr. Sydney Spiesel helped me with all medical questions, and infallibly; Jane Stern, divine interpreter of road food and the tarot, was generous with her time and talent; my niece Karina Lubell and her husband, Romain Mareiul, are responsible for any good use I have made of idiomatic French and are in no way responsible for my gaffes.

My reading family, Kay Ariel, Bob Bledsoe, Alexander Moon,

Caitlin Moon Sorenson, Sarah Moon and the late Malcolm Keith, all read with care and kindness and well-crafted criticism. My mother, Sydelle Bloom, was my uncritical and unconditionally appreciative reader, and I miss her every day. Michael Cunningham has always given me a much-needed boost and, as he does, Richard McCann has helped me through many difficult hours.

I must thank my dear cousin Harold Bloom, whose brilliance shines a light on all writers, past and present, and who helped me, with tea and wit, to find a better way to put almost anything.

Jennifer Ferri is the best. Period.

Finally, I thank my husband, Brian Ameche, for giving me everything I have ever hoped for.

Credits

Some of the stories in this work originally appeared in the following: 'Night Vision', in slightly different form, in the *New Yorker*, February 16, 1998; 'Stars at Elbow and Foot', in slightly different form, in the *New Yorker*, July 26, 1993, under the title 'Bad Form'; 'Hold Tight', in different form, in the anthology *Writer's Harvest*, 1994; 'The Gates Are Closing', in slightly different form, in *Zoetrope*, spring 1998; 'The Story' in different form, in *Story*, September 1999; 'Love Is Not a Pie' in *Room of One's Own* (1990), *Image* (Ireland, 1991), and *Best American Short Stories*, 1991; 'Sleepwalking' in *River City* (Fall 1991); 'The Sight of You' in *Story* (Summer 1992); 'Silver Water' in *Story* (Fall 1991) and *Best American Short Stories*, 1992; 'Semper Fidelis' in *Antaeus* (April 1993); 'When the Year Grows Old' in *Story* (winter 1992); 'Compassion and Mercy' in *Granta*, Summer, 2009; 'By-And-By' in *Ms.*, Summer, 2004; 'Between Here and Here' in *Narrative*, December, 2009; 'Your Borders, Your Rivers, Your Tiny Villages' in *Ploughshares*, Fall, 2002; 'The Old Impossible' in *Ploughshares*, Fall, 2006; 'I Love to See You Coming, I Hate to See You Go' in *Tin House*, Spring, 2004; and 'Permafrost' in *Yale Review*, January, 2010.

Grateful acknowledgment is made to the following for permission to reprint previously published material:

AWAY

'A beautiful novel, with a vivid, bewitching heroine' *The Times*

Young Lillian Leyb has come to America alone, her family murdered in a Russian pogrom in which her three-year-old daughter Sophie vanished. Determined to make her way, she is taken under the wing of a famous theatrical impresario in 1920s New York. But then her cousin arrives with news of Sophie. Driven by wild hope, Lillian sets off on an odyssey across America . . .

'Exceptional . . . Lillian is a captivating, wonderfully realised creation, and, most of all, Bloom's prose is full of an energy that can make you gasp' *Telegraph*

'A gutsy tale of displacement and love . . . a mesmerising journey' *Daily Mail*

'At her dazzling best – and *Away*, Bloom's second novel, shows her at the height of her powers – she isn't just skilful, smart and compassionate; she is incandescent . . . a masterpiece of construction' *Scotsman*

'The writing is sparse and tender, with revelatory doses of irony . . . A novel this gorgeous doesn't need humour, but what's better than laughing off a good cry? *Away* is a story to sink your heart into' *Elle*

Also by Amy Bloom and available from Granta Books
www.grantabooks.com

LUCKY US

'What I enjoyed most about reading *Lucky Us* was that I never knew what was coming on the next page – and it was always brilliant' Roddy Doyle

When Eva's mother abandons her on Iris's front porch, the girls don't seem to have much in common – except, they soon discover, a father. Thrown together with no mothers and a feckless father, Iris and Eva become one another's family. Iris wants to be a movie star; Eva is her sidekick. Together, they journey across 1940s America, from scandal in Hollywood to the jazz clubs and golden mansions of Long Island, stumbling, cheating and loving their way through a landscape of war, betrayals and big dreams.

'This is a novel of enormous charm; deeply touching about the unspoken love between sisters, and often very funny. Bloom is bliss' *The Times*

'A remarkable accomplishment. One waits a long time for a novel of this scope and dimension ... Amy Bloom is a treasure' Michael Cunningham

'Electrifying and inventive ... [a] worldly and sardonically funny tale' *Sunday Telegraph*

'Lavish with detail, daringly told ... *Lucky Us* is rich and strange [and] often exhilarating on the page. Its powerful images stay with you' *Financial Times*